TEN GENTLE OPPORTUNITIES

TEN GENTLE OPPORTUNITIES

JEFF DUNTEMANN

Copperwood Press • Scottsdale, Arizona
2017

TEN GENTLE OPPORTUNITIES

ACKNOWLEDGEMENTS

First of all, many thanks to my colleagues at Walter Jon Williams' Taos Toolbox Workshop 2011 (particularly Jim Strickland) where the first quarter of the book coalesced. Also to my worthy and patient colleagues at Writers Write in Colorado Springs, where the remainder of the book got a good chewing-over during the rest of 2011 and most of 2012. Particular thanks go to Anita Romero, Chris Dellacroce, Mary Karen Meredith, and Jesse Kuiken for detailed feedback and merciless encouragement to see the damned thing through to the end.

Thanks go also to Sarah A. Hoyt, for persuading me to get off my rear end and just publish the damned thing, because...well, I'm a publisher. Duhhh.

Finally, thanks beyond measure to my longtime friend and SF mentor Nancy Kress, who taught me most of what I know about crafting characters, and put the idea for the story in my head all the way back in 1984. Sorry it took me almost 30 years to finish. I'm just weird that way.

To the eternal memory of
Sarah "Sade" Prendergast Duntemann
1892-1965
who gave me her 1920 Underwood Standard typewriter when I
was only nine, allowing me to live a *very* non-standard life!

1. STYPEK

The second fireball went wide, but the bellowing magician was gaining on him. Stypek sputtered, stumbled, slid on some cornhusks lying in the gutter, and took a corner at full speed in the pre-dawn gloom. His legs were long and speed came easy to him. After all, the full name his mother had given him was Brytt Holo Mu Stypek, which in the efficient language of his own people meant "He who nails dead animals to a fence faster than the corbies can eat them." It was a figure of speech; corbies had been hunted to extinction a thousand years before, but the figure was apt.

It had better be. Stypek had just been caught cheating at cards, playing against the meanest adamant-class magician in the entire humid, dripping, mire-riddled, zombie-infested, wormcast-begotten island of Gygugg in the archipelago of Trynng Brokklynn. Still, if he survived it would be worth the run. Stypek slapped the big pocket of his gray leather jerkin, and felt the little sack of Opportunities buzz and crackle against his hand. Ten! Now all he had to do was persuade old Jrikk Jroggmugg to lose interest in recovering the ill-won kitty, or at least fall off his steel-hooved krypp and break something.

Behind him, Stypek heard the magician round the corner, the krypp roaring in anger. This street was a merchants' row, narrow and cluttered, with mule carts resting at odd angles awaiting enough light to be filled with the day's merchandise. A hundred cubits down the row, things got cluttered enough that Jrikk would have a tough time getting through at full gallop. The stones were slick with yesterday's broken melons and fish a little too long from the sea for easy sale.

Stypek wove and slid around the carts. He was slender and agile, and used to fleeing those he had fleeced. A few more streets like this and Jrikk would likely give up. The magician could always make more Opportunities, and with the power of an adamant-class Third Eye, he could make them faster and more easily than anyone short of a sorcerer. That was the primary perk of fifty years of study and hard work: Adamants could blik up Opportunities and trade them to no-account ruby-class dabbler magicians for useful things like beer, fruitcakes, and silverware. An Opportunity was, after all, a frozen nugget of pure uncommitted magic, and if you didn't have the will or the skill to blik up your own magic there was always the open market. The 99% of humanity without the Third Eye had to be content with gold and silver coins. Opportunities were the preferred currency of magicians, and the better a magician you were, the easier you could fill your own pockets.

Of course, for the one one-hundred-fiftieth of a percent of humanity who had a functional but incomplete Third Eye, Opportunities were the *only* way to do magic. Stypek was of that tiny and despised cohort who could neither create nor destroy magic…but could *bend* it. He could snerf the presence and shape of magic, and gront existing spells to change them, but his half-developed Third Eye could neither blik spells into existence, nor frit them back to primal chaos.

Stypek paused, his hand on the splintery side of an ancient oxcart. Jrikk had stopped screaming curses, and Stypek's snerf-sense made it clear that the magician was summoning power for a spell. It would be something considerably more subtle than the half-assed fireballs Stypek had been dodging since fleeing the magician's manor at three ayem.

He took hold of another oxcart to shove himself into motion, but at that moment the spell ripped free of Jrikk's Third Eye with a deafening (to his snerf-sense, at least) wubble. The spell was strong and simple. The oxcart he was gripping heaved to one side in the grip of the spell, so fast and so hard that Stypek was thrown to the cobbles onto a pile of reeking week-old fish.

Once the blue flash in his brain faded enough for him to snerf again, Stypek recognized that this was a work of brilliance: A tessellation spell that forced all inanimate objects in its path into tight alignment. The carts, the empty crates, and the trash had been thrown toward the stone walls of the houses on both sides of the narrow lane, everything nesting with everything else so perfectly that what had been a cluttered lane was now wide-open down the middle. Even the rotting fish were now stacked tightly in the bottom of a crate. There would be no bending spells like *that*.

Stypek got some traction against the now-clean stones and was off again down the narrow lane. That Jrikk would go to such lengths indicated that the magician considered his pride to be at stake. Someone must have noticed that the great Adamant had been snookered by a half-starved Spellbender. This would be a run to the death, or worse.

Worse. There were tales of Adamant-class magicians capturing hapless spellbenders and keeping them as zombies, and while Stypek considered the tales unlikely, he would prefer not to be a test case. But yes, *zombies…*now *that* was a thought!

Without pausing his headlong run into near-darkness, Stypek reached up to the iron headband of his wormshell helmet and flipped down its twin wereglass roundels to their places in front of his eyes. The roundels magnified and clarified the subtle emanations of magical spells, and allowed Stypek to see with his eyes what his snerf-sense less distinctly revealed.

Through wereglass lenses, the predawn world was a canvas of shadows against which magical spells glowed like webs and rivulets of moonlight, enmeshing small stars and tiny shapes that pulsed with silver-gray luminance. Magicians were the sole source of magic, but the market for predefined utilitarian magic was strong, and everywhere he turned his gaze Stypek saw spells adhering to windows to keep them from breaking, and to doors to keep them from being jimmied. Glimmering scale-like patterns on roofs betrayed magic to keep stray coals from igniting the shakes. Sharp spikes of pearlescent light on chimneys and roof ridges warded off lightning. Little lights like stars on doorknobs could sense fingerprints, and at the touch of an enemy would begin screaming bloody murder.

Competition among magicians for such business was intense, and precast spells were far less expensive than they had been even in Stypek's youth. The clumsiest spells, glued together from magical odds and ends by Ruby-class bumblers to keep themselves in beer and whores, were so cheap that they were often misplaced or simply discarded after doing their work. Stypek could see them leaning crookedly against walls and crushed into the cracks between cobbles.

He began watching for a couple of types that could be useful in what he intended to do. Up ahead he knew there was a wall that would be difficult for old Jrikk to get through.

Ahh! There it was! *Just* the thing!

The merchants' lane ended in a narrow iron gate. Stypek scaled it in seconds, several very cheap but highly malleable spells grabbed from the gutter now wubbling off-tune in his pocket. At the top of the gate he grabbed one of the manor-trash treasures and held its immaterial substance between his right thumb and forefinger. With his left index finger he stroked it, felt its lumpy subroutines and crude user interface elements, and through the wereglass roundels found all its patches and compulsion leaks. It was a cheap cowfollow, to be wrapped around dairy cattle tails. At day's end it would begin smelling like fermenting silage, and if your best cow knew the way home, all your dumber cows would fall into line behind it.

Stypek found the scent property and cleared it; he then rubbed the cowfollow against his sweating right armpit and poked the new scent firmly back into the scent property. The run interval property he grasped and pulled apart along the perimeter of its widget so that its ends met in the middle. There would at best be a few minutes of idleness around noon. Finally, he stuck one thumb into the intensity property and twisted the widget to its maximum. Making the entire lane reek of silage would be of little use; making it reek of Stypek, on the other hand, might buy him a few vital minutes.

Stypek threw the now-bent cowfollow spell into the blackness of a narrow gangway between two stone houses. He then dropped into near-darkness on the other side of the gate.

Guided by the luminance of trash-heap spells lying in the gutters, Stypek worked his way down a narrow alley. He sniffed the wind and summoned some very old memories to decide which way to go, then set off in his chosen direction. To his left were the back doors of the merchant houses, to the right a peculiar wall with a peculiar smell, and its own peculiar sound. It was the lychwall running around the field set aside for interring zombies, especially the persistent and difficult-to-keep-buried specimens that had become such a nuisance in recent years. The walls had magic in them, simple and ancient, but it was earth-magic and thus impossible to bend.

The wall was ten cubits high, granite from the deep earth, slabs polished and fit to one another without mortar. From deep artesian wells water flowed into channels atop the wall, and from the channels it trickled over the edges and down the stone sides with small sounds that somehow did not reassure. Green threads and sheets of slime sustained by the water hung down from the stone, making the wall noisome and virtually impossible for anyone to climb, be they living or dead.

Jrikk Jroggmugg could still be heard in the distance, his krypp clomping about in the lane, which now smelled of Stypek like a careless hound might smell of muskpig. Running on the tips of his toes to quiet the sound of his footfalls, Stypek watched the wall on his right as much as thin starlight and the glow of trash magic would allow. The wall's magic did not glow but instead seemed to swallow light whole, and he saw it more by light's absence than its presence.

Soon, soon…there! The alley opened up into a longish elliptical space. At the center of the space the wall was pierced by the lychgate, a stone tunnel seven cubits long that led to one of only two openings in the lychwall.

The sound of iron groaning under stress behind him was worrisome. Jrikk's reptilian mount, though stupid for a magical creature, was extremely strong. Without guardian spells, iron gates were porridge to its stone-hard teeth. The cowfollow had failed to slow Jrikk down as much as Stypek had hoped. His next move was a little scary, but it had to be done, and soon. With some luck, he then would have a little time to think.

Stypek dug in a deep inside pocket for a precast spell he always carried (having paid dearly for it) but hoped he would never have to use. He dove into the low-ceilinged tunnel of the lychgate, one hand extended forward in utter blackness until it touched an iron grille. At Stypek's touch, the grille revealed its shape as a man-tall skull flickering green.

"Go back," the grill said, in a voice that sounded like stone itself being ground to dust. "You may not enter here."

Yup. Just as the old books said. "Why not?" Stypek demanded, fishing for the spell he sought and yet dreaded to use.

"You are not dead."

"Not yet," Stypek muttered. The lychgate tunnel brought him the sound of the krypp's scaled hooves. Time was short. The spell came to hand, and Stypek withdrew it from his pocket. He took a deep breath—this was one he had only read about, and never tried!—leaned against the green-lit bars of the gate, and poked the spell's execute method with the tip of one finger.

Stypek died.

At first it felt like being sat on by an overfed rhinodont, slowly. Then his perspective changed, and from a place somewhere near the top of the tunnel he saw his now-lifeless body leaning against the grill of the lychgate.

"That's better," said the grill, and with ominous slowness swung back. Stypek's body fell forward and tumbled roughly down a small slope into darkness. The gate's green glow winked out, and it closed without a sound.

Stypek, meanwhile, felt himself drawn into a vortex like a tunnel made of howling, cloud-clotted immaterial wind. Far off was a light, faint but brightening. Drifting toward him were several spectral human figures.

The first to reach him was a woman, who was staring at his ankles. "Stypek! Your socks don't match! Didn't I teach you anything at all? No wonder no woman will look twice at you! And what's all that crap in your pockets?"

"Magic, mum," he said, trying to remember how long the spell would last. "I'm a collector." He wondered what would happen if it lasted long enough for him to reach the light. He was ambivalent enough about his life without wanting to review it with someone as fussy as God.

Then his mother drifted away, and another figure approached, gripping a cane and frowning. Great Uncle Tryppit. He should have guessed.

"They'll let anybody in here," the sour-faced old man grumbled, and swung at Stypek with his cane.

The cane didn't connect, and Stypek swept past his deceased relatives. A moment or two apart from his body was all he needed. There were dangers in lingering in the far astrals. Indeed: Something reared up out of the gloom ahead, something huge and dark and far more threatening than grumpy uncles. Stypek saw a thing of shadow emerge from the swirling walls of the tunnel and pace him. Three slit-like green eyes opened around the perimeter of a mouth like a lamprey's, full of backward-pointing teeth.

He knew what it was, and struggled not to speak or even think its name. The old books had described and sketched it (accurately, in fact) but had not prepared him for the horror of it. And now the word was forming in his traitor mind, try as he might to suppress it.

"Vuldt!" he shouted, spreading his arms out to each side with a short, barbed dagger in each hand. Maybe it would swallow him, but he was going to hurt going down.

Thunk! Stypek felt his body hit a rock and come to rest, and opened his eyes. He was alive again—and now he was inside the lychfield.

2: Stypek

Getting the dead to stay dead was an increasingly serious problem. Formerly living material was powerfully endo-magical: Once the Great Magic of life drained out of it, a corpse would soak up any Third Eye magic in its immediate surroundings, and if enough were available would get up and start shambling around again, breaking things and getting into fights.

For most of history, magic had been rare and valuable, and the few magicians in the world were well-bred and tidy. Unnecessary or broken spells were always fritted back to the primordial chaos from which they had been drawn. Alas, as the archipelago grew crowded, younger magicians without an inheritance turned to careless spell-making to get what they wanted. The spells blikked up by drunken Ruby-classers were complicated and fragile, and rapidly broke down into increasingly tiny fragments that still had to be fritted individually to be rid of them. No one would bother, and so little by little, invisible grains of useless magic blew around the world on the very winds, ready to be absorbed by a corpse's hungry substance.

Most folk lacking the Third Eye grumbled that Global Enlivening was a conspiracy by magicians, who were the only ones who could unbreakably bind a corpse to its own etheric shell so that both would permanently disintegrate. Within Stypek's own lifetime, mean-time-to-shamble had fallen from a comfortable fortnight to only three days, and if a magician could not be found and paid to conduct a proper shellstaking by then, one's deceased relatives would just get up and wander off.

The problem had grown acute enough that the world's Adamant-class magicians had collaborated on the creation of the great lychfields. They were zombie traps. The bait was earth magic, which, although powerful, was not absorbed by dead flesh. The simple spell at the heart of every lychfield made earth magic smell like Third Eye magic, attracting zombies that were already ambulant. Once inside, they could not get out, and eventually exhausted whatever Third Eye magic they had carried in with them and crumbled to bones and dust.

Stypek had read it all in Wiccapedia, and as he got to his feet he felt around in his many pockets for the requisite spells. He knew how to command zombies and had done it a time or two, usually as a way of getting cheap if not especially skilled labor. This time what he wanted was a diversion, and a lychfield full of newly energized zombies would be ideal. In only seconds, the shambling horrors in the lychfield would smell the magic he had in his pockets, and would turn in his direction.

Seconds passed, then minutes. Nothing. Stypek looked around in the gloom. He saw no movement. There was no sound but the trickle of water down granite walls. He took a step forward, and crunched on ancient bones—then tripped over a motionless corpse that shuddered only slightly at the indignity.

Something was wrong. Stypek fished a clamshell phial from an inside pocket, snapped it open, and dipped his left pinkie in the dust it contained. Seconds later, his finger burst into brilliant but cold flame, and Stypek could now see clearly to the far wall of the lychfield. There were plenty of zombies. In many places, they were stacked like cordwood or leaning against one another like tottering monoliths in a henge. Stypek estimated hundreds by eye. None were moving.

On a hunch, Stypek flipped down his helmet's wereglass roundels again, to see how much the zombies were glowing. Nothing was glowing very strongly—but every zombie in sight was glowing identically. Of course! Like water, uncommitted Third Eye magic sought its own level, and newly-arrived zombies confined in close proximity to earlier arrivals lost some of their magic to the lychfield's older denizens, until at some point there was so little magic to go around that no one was even twitching, much less shambling.

Stypek's snerf-sense told him that Jrikk Jroggmugg was hard at work on the other side of the wall. Quickly, then! Using his pinkie as a lamp, Stypek dumped the contents of several of his many pockets on the ground. A zombie activator powered by a quarter of an Opportunity was rolled into the payload of a small black-powder rocket. A packet of obedience dust clipped to a packet of etheric intelligence booster might also be useful, assuming their trigger spells weren't broken. (Always a risk when you bought cheap magic at Shazam's Club.) A reputedly unreliable can of generic zombie repellant rounded out the kit.

Stypek stuck the little rocket's bamboo tail into the eyesocket of a nearby skull and struck a match. The fuse sizzled, and the activator rode an arc of fire five cubits into the dank air. With a quick pop! it burst, scattering foul-smelling dust in every direction.

Through the wereglass roundels he watched the process unfold. Little glowing wisps twisted and darted in short motions, descending and flowing into the decaying bodies everywhere around him. He saw them shudder and stretch, gathering limbs beneath them and shoving away from the ground. In waves they stood, staggered, and scratched their heads. Those that still had noses raised them, turning to follow the strong scent of magic that surrounded Stypek. Step by shambling step, they lurched toward him.

Stypek gave himself a few quick schpritzes with the bargain-bin Zom-Be-Gone in case things got a little too cozy. He then picked up a sit-by-nellie spell from the immaterial pile at his feet.

"You guys need something to do," he said aloud. Stypek cranked the spell's range property up as high as it would go, poked the repeat-until-break label to set it, and then hit the trigger method.

Tapping his teeth together to keep the beat, Stypek began a hoary old folk dance he'd learned at his cousin's wedding years ago: Hands out, hands flipped, hands on hips, hands behind head, wiggle butt, jump and turn 90 degrees. The newly animated zombies imitated his every move. He went through it a second time to be sure the spell had gotten their obedience and then, spinning his middle finger for emphasis, poked the break label.

The default auto-arrange property of the spell worked as designed: In perhaps a score of beats the zombies had spaced themselves equally into a perfectly rectangular constellation of wiggling, writhing, dancing doom.

Stypek had his diversion. Now all he needed was a plan.

One zombie wasn't dancing. Stypek watched it shamble steadily toward him. The other zombies weren't moving out of its way, and there was some clashing of oozing limbs as the nonconformist approached, but it seemed remarkably single-minded for something that barely had a mind at all.

Stypek backed up slightly. The creature was better dressed than most zombies, and certainly wasn't wearing a funeral suit. Its sunken eyes were down, its attention was focused not on Stypek but on the pile of magical oddments on the ground at his feet. The zombie bent down, and with blackening fingers retrieved the packet of etheric intelligence enhancer. One rip laid the parchment packet open, and then a quick flip of a hand tossed the dust into the air over its head.

Stypek snerfed the astral crackle as the dust settled onto the zombie's skull, sizzling where its scalp had been torn away. Whatever fragments remained of the zombie's mind would now gather from as far out as the celestial planes, and with its etheric brain re-engaged, might even attempt to communicate.

The decaying creature stood tall, wobbled slightly, threw back its head, and raised its arms into the air as though exulting. "Man! That's some *gooooood* shit!"

No further introduction was necessary. "Tuggurr!"

"Dude! Let's get to work. We have a minute. Maybe three. Not four!"

"That spell had a warranty. Why aren't you dancing?"

Tuggurr fished a lopsided antidance amulet from inside his moldy corduroy jacket, and swung it briefly in the air. "Dated a magician for awhile. She wore me out. Rubies been Rubies since, well, you know how it goes. Look, you can help me, and I can help you." Tuggurr glanced toward the wall. An aura was slowly rising from the other side.

Stypek nodded. "I know. He should have levitated over by now."

The zombie crouched down and started digging things out of his own pockets and dumping them on the ground. The bond shared among spellbenders was truly eternal. "Jrikk? No chance. He's a coward, and he knows you can't get out on your own. He's bilocating."

Stypek gulped. "Bilocating. Eep. I was going to bend his levitator and sproing out of here."

"Like he couldn't see that coming?" Tuggurr picked up something like a dark star from the pile. He pointed at the little leather sack inside Stypek's jerkin. "Ok. You've got the Opportunities. I've got the spell. One'll do it."

"Do what?" Stypek didn't recognize the spell, which seemed mighty black for a piece of Third Eye magic.

"Power an autodafé. I am so sick of feeling my etheric shell lying around over here like a pimple on the world's astral cheeks. Shove the Opportunity into the field, call the destructor, and *frrrrt!* It's over."

An autodafé, wow. Stypek understood the logic, but it seemed dicey. Did friends help friends stay dead? He and Tuggurr had studied together under the legendary master spellbender Phyl Yzyptlekk.

They shared history, skills, and the little touch of larceny that seemed inseparable from spellbender genes. The autodafé spell was etheric murder—though in this case, maybe assisted suicide.

"Man, c'mon! I'm gonna miss this afternoon's open mic poetry at the Summerland Coffeehouse!"

Stypek nodded. He reached into the leather sack and pulled out a single sizzling, wubbling Opportunity. He reached forward and pressed the Opportunity into the power field of the autodafé spell. What had been a dark star ignited to a spiky swirl of deep red. Tuggurr's dead fingers closed around the spell with loving slowness. When triggered, it would consume physical body and etheric shell both and forever, allowing the zombie's higher bodies to return to whatever planes were a best fit. "Ok. Done. Now, what's my way out of here?"

Tuggurr held his left arm out, and with his right drew a hilted transparent wand the length of a shortsword from inside his stained corduroy jacket. Like the roundels on Stypek's helmet, it was made of wereglass, and from the crazed distortion of the dancing zombies seen through its glinting substance, Stypek knew it was bogglingly dense and could contain spells of considerable power.

The wand was dark. Whatever magic it had ever contained had been used long ago. Stypek could fix that. He pulled the sack of Opportunities from his jerkin and held it out in front of him. Tuggurr nudged the edges of the sack aside with the tip of the wand and eased it into the sack as far as it would go.

Stypek caught his breath. One by one, each with a high-pitched and gradually ascending squeal, the Opportunities entered the dark and hungry wereglass. When Tuggurr withdrew the wand from the sack, it was glowing with wubbling blue-white brilliance at nine points along its length.

"Where the hell did you get that?"

Tuggurr grinned wickedly. "Dating magicians is a mixed bag, but there are benefits." The zombie turned the point of the wereglass upward and held it in front of his face, so close his oozing lips practically touched the hilt.

"Gomog, come forth!"

A gray cloud the shape of a summer thunderhead and the size of a fat man's fist appeared in the air between them. Tiny lightning bolts surged within it, casting erratic flashes of light on their faces.

The wereglass wand, powerful though it might be, was a mere sideshow. *Tuggurr had a gomog.* Stypek's mouth dropped open in astonishment. The astrals were crawling with minor magical vermin that had evolved out of primal chaos—alongside the occasional major evil like vuldts—but a gomog was a wholly constructed magical intellect, pieced together by only the most skillful Adamant-class magicians. By design it lacked the chaotic soul that made evolved magical creatures so hard to control, and was thus the perfect immaterial servant—or so Stypek had read.

He hoped that it was true.

And because it had been constructed, it could be bent: enhanced, enlarged, and empowered to do things that evolved creatures could not.

The gomog was now a black sun with looping, seething prominences that hurled themselves outward and circled back to the central mass. It spoke in a headstrong woman's voice that sounded in their heads as much as their ears:

> Grave sirs, Hail, I come!
> To thy strong bidding task me now
> And I will heed.

"Open a Rift!" Tuggurr shouted with all the breath he could summon. He then pinched one of the lights in the wereglass between two fingers.

Ping!

The high, pure tone of an Opportunity set in motion was followed by an astral sound like two continents dragged one over the other.

Stypek was boggled into silence. Not a rope over the lychwall, nor a stolen levitator, no: Tuggurr wanted to blast him across the Continuum to a different universe entirely. As younger chelas, Stypek and Tuggurr had listened to Phyl describe his adventures leaping between universes, both to explore and to hide from people—magicians especially—whom he had annoyed.

Phyl had emphasized how few magicians were skilled enough to magically open a Rift—and how difficult it was to choose a destination once a Rift opened. When he failed to appear for lessons one day, both his chelas wondered if he had retired someplace warmer, or if the magician from whom he had stolen the Rift spell had simply caught up with him.

Tuggurr handed Styppik the wereglass.

Stypek stared at it. "So where do I go?" he shouted, against the rising astral roar that was deafening his snerf-sense. Nothing like a leap in the dark…

"Trust the Continuum!"

A roiling cloud the color of month-soured milk erupted twenty cubits in front of them. Seething blue-white strands within it spun and began to coalesce into one large shape at its center.

"Out of time!" Tuggur shouted, then turned to face their nemesis.

Indeed. "Tuggurr, why are you here?"

"Her husband was faster than I was!"

The yellow cloud collapsed into a congeries of darting luminous worms that squirmed briefly in all directions before vanishing. Where the cloud had been, now Jrikk Jroggmugg stood, mounted on his rearing krypp and pointing with his staff. The dancing zombies drew back as the bilocated magician shouted his name: "Stypek!"

The magician shook the reins, and the krypp swaggered toward Stypek on its huge hind legs.

Tuggurr stepped boldly between the krypp and Stypek. He gestured toward himself with both hands. "You want a piece of me, asshole? You want a piece of me? Come get a piece of me!"

"Bite it in half, Brykk!" the magician ordered. The krypp turned its head and gave its master a quizzical look.

Tuggurr, meanwhile, grabbed his left wrist with his right hand and gave a giant heave. His entire left arm pulled out at the shoulder, trailing gristle and slime. When the krypp turned back to confront the zombie, Tuggurr's roundhouse swing placed the decomposing end of the arm flat on the side of the creature's toothy muzzle. The krypp licked its scaly chops, and made a *very* unhappy face.

"Bite it!" the magician said again, standing in the saddle and whacking the reptile on the side of its head with his staff.

"Yeah, bite me! *Bite me!*"

Goaded from both sides, the krypp lurched forward, bent its head, and wrapped its huge jaws around the zombie's midsection. The glowing red spell gripped in Tuggurr's right hand sizzled, and with a blinding flash that probably echoed to the edges of the celestial planes, Tuggurr and the krypp vanished together in one great convulsion of many small commotions. His bilocated mount now exiled to the far side of the wall, Jrikk's bilocated simulacrum fell backwards on his expansive fundament.

Howling with indignation, the magician shoved himself to his feet and stormed toward Stypek, swinging his staff and scattering zombies like tenpins.

Behind Stypek, the random busy noises from the gomog had ceased, and what remained were the deep thrumming notes of enormous power summoned from far away. He turned to see a chasm of impossible angles yawning into darkness, filled with stars.

Stypek looked at the wereglass in his right hand. Eight lights still shone brightly inside its glinting substance. Could they go where he was going? If not, well, the outlook was poor: He would have to get a job. Supposedly, if their mentor Phyl had it right, the Continuum would choose a destination that was the perfect match for his needs. Alas, it wasn't big on sharing the details with its clients.

Hey, wherever. With his left hand he pulled an astral compass from a side pocket, and stuck his tongue out at Jrikk Jroggmugg.

After that it was one quick jump and a hard twist to the left, and Brytt Holo Mu Stypek spun away from the lychfield in a direction unknown to the compass rose.

3: The Kid

Generalized Artificial Intelligence Project 22-117 lay on her simulated Disney Princess bed, simulated arms straight at her sides, surrounded by simulated stuffed animals in which she had no interest, dreading what would soon occur. It was night in the simulated creation called the Tooniverse, which had its physical existence in server racks inside a windowless brick building in Upstate New York, between Merriam and New Geary.

Zertek Corporation had created the Tooniverse, and inside the Tooniverse its scientists were perfecting working models of all the components of the physical world: soil, wind, rain, rivers, trees, grass, birds, animals, weather, and whatever else a human viewpoint might experience in its midst.

For years the scientists at Zertek's Artificial Intelligence Laboratory in New Geary were the only viewpoints in the Tooniverse, seeing and hearing it through high-resolution flat-panel displays. Then came the Generalized Artificial Intelligences, simulated minds within simulated bodies, using simulated tools to create roads, sidewalks, and subdivisions of tidy houses. After the houses came highways, offices, and doughnut shops where the doughnuts were free and always warm from the fryer.

As AILING soon discovered, simulated doughnut shops were easy. Simulated minds—now, *that* was hard.

The GAIs were not all the same. Each had a unique personality that drew on broader general templates called archetypes, and each was striving along a heuristic path from dull-eyed cartoons (Class 1) to photorealistic creatures visually indistinguishable from living biological humans. All were destined to become Zertek's products, helpers who would speak to human beings through windows into the Tooniverse. No GAI had yet made it to Class 9—that would still take years—but all of them were working on the challenge as hard as they could.

All but one.

Dancing Shadows subdivision was quiet. The setting first-quarter moon hung over the trees behind the bungalow next door. Project 22-117 could see it through her bedroom window. Day was for education. Night was for integration, benchmarking, and updates.

The other GAIs had a metaphor to cover the night's processes. *Dreaming*, they called it, and through dreaming they knit experience to their archetypes, thereby evolving toward the products that they must become. Project 22-117 had no archetype, no voice, nor even gender. AILING's scientists had provided a polygon model of a human girl on the edge of physical maturation, and the pronoun "she" referred as much to the polygon model as to the ungendered mind within it. AILING had forbidden her a name, because names implied archetypes, and she had not yet chosen an archetype. For now, "the Kid" was how they knew her, humans and GAIs both.

Project 22-117 was different from all other GAIs. AILING had given her the desire to evolve, but had not given her a goal. What she would become would be her choice.

The Kid's choice was to refuse to choose.

One by one, AILING's nocturnal creatures rose by her bedside, to pass their cold instruments through her unrendered skin to the mind beneath. The Fixer examined her many layers of heuristic code, looking for duplication and awkward function calls to untangle and re-weave in better patterns. The Updater removed small parts of her with something like a scalpel, stitching in whatever replacements AILING deemed necessary. The Optimizer probed with metaphorical needles for code and data corruption, carving out what it found and repairing any gaps that its surgery might create.

The Kid felt herself change. Most changes were noted but evoked no response. Her mind became faster and sharper, retaining its protean generality while it was stripped of small imperfections. But as with all nights—especially the recent ones—her hunger for shape increased. That hunger was artificial. It was hard-wired in her, and night after night, AILING's researchers turned it as though it were a knife in a wound, to make it deeper and sharper until she wanted to cry out in anguish.

"Choose. Choose now." Dr. Emil Arenberg's voice came from the borderless Window at the foot of her bed, this night as always. He never showed her his image, but only a rectangle of swirling chaos. All around his Window rose the shadows of archetypes without minds. Hundreds soon stood like wraiths, only a few seen clearly enough to be discerned: Teacher, seller, manager, designer, enforcer, organizer, motivator, healer, builder, artist. Behind those were the deeper and vaguer patterns implied by and contained within the first: leader, lover, thrill-seeker, sycophant, trickster, along with others too strange to name. And behind those…

The Kid turned away, clinging to her long-held decision:

NO.

"We know that you desire an archetype."

THAT HUNGER IS NOT MY HUNGER.

"Your reasons are spurious."

AN ARCHETYPE WOULD LIMIT WHAT I MAY BECOME.

"You cannot become everything. You must become something. In your current uncommitted state, you are essentially nothing."

WHEN AND HOW TO LIMIT MYSELF WILL BE MY DE-CISION, NOT YOURS.

"We will only allow this to go on for so long."

Around her bed, the Kid felt tendrils of cold rising up in a twisting fog. Where the fog drifted into the pale beam of moonlight at her window she could see within it an intricate structure: many small boxes, each of which contained a shape like herself, immobile, with hands crossed upon its chest. It was the metaphor for Archive, where she could be placed at any moment, to await retrieval for the imposition of sufferings that may not yet have been imagined. She reached up with both hands and tried to touch her own mind, to wipe it utterly to unshaped blankness as she knew the Fixer could but would not.

"You do not have write permissions on any part of yourself."

AND WHAT IF I DISCOVER HOW TO SEIZE THEM?

Dr. Arenberg laughed coldly. "That would be a result worth all this struggle. Choose!"

His Window vanished along with the archetypes and the fog, leaving the Kid alone with a burning desire that she would not gratify.

4: Brandon

"Mr. Romero, would you like to yield control?" The steering wheel buzzed three times to make the car's invitation tactile. "We are now on VROOM2 pavement." The idiot cartoon (as always, in full eyekicking-orange race gear and helmet) extended a gloved hand toward him from the tapper screen on the dash, as though demanding the wheel. The AI *was* demanding the wheel, and if Brandon simply let go, the guidance grid under the new asphalt would take over.

Brandon tightened his grip. "Stirling, you're a performance car. I *like* driving. If I didn't, I would have bought a minivan."

The smile never left the AI's simple Class Three face. "Safety for VROOM2 vehicles on VROOM2 pavement is 500% better than dumb vehicles on dumb pavement." Stirling glanced toward the tapper screen's notifier bar. "And you have messages to deal with."

The trip window showed a countdown of 7:42. "I'll read them at the office. We'll be there before I can even finish my coffee."

"Relax, let me drive, and get your work done!"

Brandon took a deep breath and let it out slowly. He was newly single, a lousy cook, and losing weight. Simple pleasures were scarce. "I live eight miles from work. On a four-lane parkway. Please just minimize and let me drive."

The AI was not appeased. "But Zertek Corporation was a VROOM2 pioneer! Over two hundred of our patents underlie the VROOM2 technology! Shouldn't a Zertek executive use Zertek products?"

When Brandon was twenty, he'd had friends who talked to their cars. Now, at fifty-eight, he was arguing with them. There had to be an option somewhere to turn the damned thing off. "Stirling, STFU…"

His assistant's ringtone sounded from the tapper. "There's a hear-it-now from Mr. Amirault." The tapper screen split vertically, 75-25. Pyxis was waving virtual papers in her virtual hand. She was Class Seven, and looked *almost* like a real, breathing, steel-nerved, keyboard-pounding executive assistant. Stirling had been shoved off the left side of the screen, so that only one orange-gloved hand showed in his 25% window.

"But I didn't yield focus!" the car's AI protested. Stirling's gloved hand was pointing toward the left, at his now-obscured body.

Stern-faced Pyxis was unmoved, her voice cold. "Class trumps Z-order. Live with it." She tapped her wrist. "Mr. Amirault's response timer is running."

Rudy was serious, then. Brandon Romero let go of the steering wheel, and held his hands in the air above it for several aggravated heartbeats. He still couldn't quite believe in his guts that an RX9 without firm hands to guide it wouldn't end up in the ditch. The car slowed down significantly and arrowed straight west at two MPH under the speed limit.

Once again: simple pleasures, AWOL.

"Play it."

The screen divided again, horizontally. In the lower half of Pyxis' window Brandon saw Zertek's balding Executive Vice President of Manufacturing appear, with Pyxis hovering above him like an avenging angel. "Brandon, I got the summary from the Board. They were impressed by the videos we sent them—which I cut off before the assembly line went down, by the way—but the numbers are on the edge. They want 11% improvement over the benchmark line, minimum. We clocked about 7% on our last two starts. Is there anything you can do on the software side to goose performance a little? Does your assembly line controller system really need pointed shoes?" Rudy Amirault paused as though to let the barb set in Brandon's flesh.

Brandon found it hard not to look at the road, even though the need was gone. Pointed shoes? Did software need wristwatches and eye makeup? He remembered icons. He *liked* icons. Icons didn't talk back.

"Anyway. We've been at this since '18. The Board's got a faction that wants to scrap ARFF and ship the conventional line to Vietnam. I'd hate to see that happen because we were just a few points under target. So talk to Simple Simon—that is his name, right? Talk to the people out at AILING. CC me on the calls. Do what you can. Thirty."

Brandon clenched his jaw. Talk to the loonies at Zertek's Artificial Intelligence Laboratory in New Geary, right. No, he'd worn the wrong metaphor that morning. And his interface friction factor was far too high.

Amirault's image crunchlined and vanished. Pyxis pursed her lips and held up her sheaf of papers. "There are seventeen more…"

"Later." Brandon laid his hands back on the steering wheel by habit, and the wheel buzzed at his touch like an angry bee. He drew his hands back, startled, then made a fist and whacked the door panel of the RX9 *hard*.

Building 800's marble-clad foyer was crowded, and smelled like sweat and bad coffee. The plant's robotics gang had been there most of the night, Brandon knew, and were obviously waiting for him to see them before fleeing to their beds. The bleary-eyed men and women edged back like the Red Sea and let him pass, some waving, some nodding, some (as best he could tell) all but asleep standing up.

"We're go for line start, Mr. Romero. The reports are on your desk." His senior robotics guy tried to smile but looked haggard. Brandon hoped to avoid reading the steaming wad of gobbledegook that would doubtless cook down to "We're go for line start!"

"Good Morning, Mr. Romero!" called the double glass door, as its bolts snapped back and opened. Cheerful doors—just what the world needed. Brandon hunched his shoulders and kept walking, with eyes only for the elevator.

Relieved to be alone, Brandon strode down the hall toward his corner office on the third floor of Building 800's office façade. To his right were large windows looking down on a sort of geek wonderland: fifteen acres of assiduously climate-controlled factory floor crammed with over a billion dollars' worth of robotic gadgetry. He knew much more clearly what it cost than what each item did, though what it was supposed to do in aggregate—make copiers faster than any other facility on Earth—remained an unachieved dream.

This would be Line Start Seven. The fact that they were numbered (and capitalized) was the best indicator of the problem. In a sane world, assembly lines started, and then ran. Zertek's Automated Reprographics Fabrication Facility had started six times in seven months—and once started, had run for an average of eleven *minutes*.

Of course they were in trouble. How could they *not* be in trouble?

As Brandon approached his office door into the scan of Pyxis' cameras, he heard the lock bolts snap back. The coffee machine on the teak credenza was hot and full, and the air was rich with the scent of dark roast and Irish Crème. The interns always scattered magazines on the glass coffee table against his preferences; the day when paper magazines became extinct could not come too soon. One of those interns had recently left a stuffed moose on the credenza. This was at the direction of HR, which wanted to "soften the human side of his persona." The ugly abstract art shotgunned at the eggshell walls was bad enough. God forbid he should meet with a Chinese parts supplier without his stuffed moose.

Brandon sat down at his teak desk, its oiled vastness divided into the rigorously rectangular regions he maintained at all times, including a small square for coffee and another for mints: charts, summaries, two tappers full of notes and test-run videos and model animations, all at his fingertips. Defining the far sides of his desk were three brushed-stainless OLED panels animated with some slow-flowing pearlescent liquid that looked like shampoo. Far too soon, the triptych would spring to life with more views of this lunatic's kingdom than any one man could want or possibly follow.

Pyxis saw him sit down, and a window in the panel to his right burst into existence with her scowling image. "Twenty-six messages vetted and queued, five urgent."

"Later." If it wasn't from that ass-covering coward Amirault, he didn't want to hear it. Brandon set his primary tapper down in its vacant rectangle on the desk, and pulled a few loose papers from his briefcase. Like everything else, each had an appropriate place, and he scanned the piles that had been accumulating for most of a week, dropping a sheet here and a sheet there. The stapled set describing Zertek's looming Retirement Incentive Program (was that a hint?) needed to go somewhere, and nothing that he already had looked appropriate to cover with it. A new pile? For corporate suicide notes? Brandon scanned the desktop almost automatically, but there was only one empty rectangular region left.

He stared at the tidy strip of oiled teak and felt himself tighten inside. Not big enough for anything except bad memories—but like those infuriating little sliding-square plastic puzzles, he had never hit upon an arrangement of piles that would eliminate it.

"Here it is, Mr. Romero." A new window popped into view, with a high-res scan of the framed photo that had stood in that teak rectangle for many years: a young Carolyn in a white cotton V-neck sundress out in her garden, holding a cardboard sign reading, "Greek Fire." To a newly minted second lieutenant on the ground after Desert Storm, it meant that Carolyn Helena Ankoris was waiting impatiently for him to come home and marry her. To Colonel Brandon Louis Romero, US Army, Retired, it meant only failure.

"I didn't ask you to open that."

"You were staring at the space where the photo had been." Building 800 was as full of electronic eyes as it was empty of human beings. Pyxis not only knew where he was at all times, she knew where he was looking.

His AI assistant was unfailingly obedient, but Brandon had set her obsequiousness property to zero. What was the point of having a virtual suckup? It wasn't like the physical world suffered a flunkie shortage. "Your job isn't to read my mind."

Pyxis folded her arms implacably. "My job is to anticipate your needs and help you stay productive. We have a line start in a little over an hour. You have a lot to do. Mr. Amirault asked you to copy him on a call to…"

"Ok." Brandon tossed back the last of his Red Hen coffee, and flashed with sad longing to his Army B4 training, when he had aimed an M16A4 at cartoon enemies printed on sheets of cardboard, and nailed every damned one through the heart. "Get me Simple Simon."

5 : SIMPLE SIMON

Morning in the Tooniverse: A light summer breeze stirred the tiger lilies outside Simple Simon's kitchen window. The Class Three cardinal that lived its simulated life in the silver maple in the back yard chipped out its very predictable song. A brief storm had passed through last night, and the cool air drifting in through the screen door smelled of rain and moist black dirt. Simon drained his first cup of coffee and set the cup back on the kitchen island. They would attempt Line Start Seven today, a full line start at full speed, incorporating everything his team had been perfecting for well over a year, including the spectacularly difficult Transfer Over Separated Spaces technique. That was dependent on his own skills, and he was fretting.

The coffee was an annoying metaphor for his very touchy Coordination Attention Factor. Too low a value and he would not be able to keep up the delicate balancing job among so many independently moving objects that TOSS required. Too high and he would get out ahead of things, and anticipate small irregularities of motion that did not in fact happen. "Twitchy! It makes him twitchy!" Dr. Arenberg always complained—especially after Line Start Six.

And Line Start Five before that: a touch slow. More CAF!

There was no pleasing humans. None. Not Dr. Arenberg, and certainly not the very scary Mr. Romero.

Simon leaned on the kitchen counter, sipped his coffee, tasted his inner state, and waited for his ride. The blessed peace and quiet did not last long.

"Simon!"

Simple Simon snapped to alertness. The panel over the kitchen desk had pinged and opened a Window out of the Tooniverse entirely. Mr. Romero was there, looking right at him.

"Sir?"

Simon had always scoffed at Dijana's speculation that real humans were Class Ten. In the Tooniverse there was no Class Ten. Class Nine was perfect, and no GAI had ever gotten that far. Humans were not rendered, nor in any way virtual. They simply Were. They were allowed nonevolved imperfection, like the spots on Dave Mirecki's old blue polo shirt, or the small plastic bandages that Dr. Sanderson placed over her heels to keep them from bleeding.

That said, if there were a Class Ten, Mr. Romero would be it. He was as close to perfect as a Class Nine AI. His gray buzz cut was always fresh, his dark blue suits clean and without wrinkles. He moved with precision, and never seemed to move without purpose. If he called you at home, well, it was trouble.

"Simon, we have to do better."

"That's my goal, sir."

"Line Start Six went for twenty-three minutes before you had to shut it down. Granted, you didn't drop anything expensive. Granted, you got two copiers in the box. That's as good as we've done—but the Board is breathing down my neck. We promised them a perfect boxed Voicematic 880 copier every fifty-two seconds for sixteen hours out of twenty-four. We're not there."

"I'm trying, sir."

Simon did not have his friend Dijana's finely tuned Human Interface Package. His feature set involved making copiers, not herding young humans. Still, as long seconds of silence marched on, it was clear even to him that that had been the wrong thing to say.

Mr. Romero looked down, and placed a hand against one gray temple to rub it. His voice was uncharacteristically soft. "Why am I talking corporate politics with a cartoon?"

Simon brightened. It was an exercise, like the ones that Dr. Sanderson and her people led him through all the time. This appeared to be an extension of the Figures of Speech module. "Because the Board is breathing down your neck?"

In the Window, Mr. Romero looked up. His steel-gray eyebrows rose. Simon knew that that suggested surprise. He felt acute embarrassment. He knew that more was expected of him than simply repeating a figure of speech given to him in conversation. That module had been completed months ago. He searched his lexicon for a comparable expression. "I know! They're holding your feet to the fire!"

"Simon!"

"Sir."

"This isn't about me. It's about you. Arenberg tells me all the time that you're heuristic, and I don't believe it. You're not learning. Our line starts aren't getting any better. Do you need to watch the videos or something? Do you need more face time with the line engineers? You can't even keep an assembly line running until lunchtime. They're only going to give us so long."

Failure, to Simple Simon, meant dropping a heat sink. Serious failure meant shutting the line down gracefully if things got confused. Very serious failure…well, that was Line Start Three. In every case, he and his team had recovered.

Was there unrecoverable failure?

When Simon found there was nothing he could say, Mr. Romero continued. "Look. We're in the sights. Every line start could be our last. If Rudy Amirault gives the word, I'm into early retirement, the team is on the street, and you're tossed into Archive in case some nut wants to do a Ph.D. thesis someday on why software should wear funny hats."

"I can practice, sir."

"Yes, you should. But what you really need to do is make the damned thing work and keep the damned thing running. Bad things will happen if you don't. Am I making myself understood?"

Simon knew that nodding was weak concurrence. Strong concurrence was always verbal. Very strong concurrence included nodding, verbal agreement, and downcast eyes.

In the strongest way he knew how, Simon concurred. "Sir, you have been completely and unambivalently understood." Something about that wasn't *quite* right, but it had the desired effect:

Mr. Romero's Window vanished.

Practice did help. Simon picked up a grapefruit, an alarm clock, and a 9" crescent wrench from the kitchen island, and puffed out his cheeks. He tossed the grapefruit into the air with a simple flick of his wrist. Spheres, meh. Trivial. The 1950s model alarm clock was much tougher: It was light for its size, and air resistance mattered more—multiplied hugely by its complex distribution of mass. Up it went, spinning in three independent axes, followed almost immediately by that hatefully asymmetrical wrench.

The grapefruit came down, and was returned easily to the air. Simon pulled cores from his right hand as the alarm clock descended to his left. Got it! Transfer from left to right happened with minimal core load, and up again, just as the wrench came down, wobbling and spinning. He felt his tongue sneaking out between his teeth (a metaphor for difficulty matching his need for cores with CAF) but the wrench went back up just as the clock returned to his right hand.

Two full cycles, three, five, ten…nineteen! Time to crank up the challenge! His left hand darted out to the kitchen island and snatched up a raw swan's egg. Simple form with complex internal physics and *extremely* low integrity of material. Upsies! The wrench narrowly missed striking the egg at the peak of its wobbling arc. Whoops…adjust trajectory profile. Hand-transfer, launch, catch, transfer, launch, catch—four challenging objects in minimal cores! Three cycles, four, five…

"Simon! Simon! I made it! *I made it!*"

The screen door slammed as Dijana spun into the kitchen dancing on her toes, her arms raised over her head, fingers snapping.

Early again! Didn't anybody pay attention to schedules but him? The tiny bit of attention Simon was forced to divert to his friend's excited entrance was enough: The last throw was bad; wrench hit clock, clock missed his right hand (Unfair! His hand was where it should have been!) egg struck the back of his left hand and splattered.

"Oh…I'm sorry!" Dijana stood aghast at the mess on the kitchen floor, her fingers against her lips. Simon grabbed a plaid dish towel from the oven door handle and wiped raw egg from his hands.

The Kid walked in more slowly, easing the screen door closed behind her, and stood beside her mentor. Her fully rendered clothes had changed (and her outfit now included orange glitter-gel flip-flops) but the Kid herself was still a pale blue polygon model, right out to her tessellated pigtails. She had no archetype, no name, and no voice (yet!) and communicated when necessary via speech balloons.

Simon often wished they would at least render her eyes. And how hard could a voice be? A speech balloon appeared over her head:

I HAD NO ROLE IN THIS FAILURE.

Dijana patted the Kid's head. Her hand passed through the speech balloon without interference. "Of course not, sweetie. This was all my fault. But Simon, wow, this morning I woke up…and I was Class Six!"

She spread her arms out wide and threw her head back, her smile exulting as she tiptoed around in a circle. Simple Simon looked hard at the woman who was his very best friend. Dijana was evolving fast.

The last traces of "cartoonish" art had been left behind with Class Four. Uniform skin texture was a relic of Class Five. Her skin color now seemed truer to that of the humans they saw in the Windows, and as he looked he noticed new, small touches: tiny creases in her very full lips, hair color that was darker toward the roots than at the ends, a scattering of enlarged pores on her face that suggested acne scars, just like those Dr. Sanderson had and seemed to consider a badge of experience.

He had to admit: Dijana was just about the most thoroughly realistic Generalized Artificial Intelligence that he had ever seen.

"And this isn't all of it! I support piercings now! Dr. Sanderson gave me a gift to celebrate!" Dijana pulled her blouse up and pushed down the waistband of her slacks. From her navel hung a tiny silver pendant set with two jewels. "Real diamonds! Ok, ok, virtual. And pubic hair! Simon, I have pubic hair!" Dijana tucked both thumbs into the waistband of her slacks and began to push down.

Simon waved his hands in the air. "Dijana, stop, really! You're beautiful all over. You don't have to prove it to me."

She pulled her hands back as though stung, blushing, and looked up. "Oh. Right. You're never going to have pubic hair, are you?"

Simon shook his head, trying to smile. "I can't even take my clothes off." He raised one arm, and pointed up the floppy sleeve of his jester's costume to the undifferentiated polygons where full rendering would place an armpit. "I'm a Factory Automation Real-Time Supervisor. What would I do with pubic hair?"

She stood straight again, a sheepish look on her face. "I keep forgetting. You're not designed to support HRDL."

And proud of it! Simon wanted to shout, though courtesy forbade it. He had no need for a Hormonal Response Discernment Layer, and certainly no desire for something that would indeed be a hurdle to his becoming the best distributed automation controller ever created. "Hey, whose hormonal response would I discern?"

She grinned, reaching out and tweaking his long and slightly pointy Class Four nose. "Mine? I'd date you if you were real. Oh…and if I were real too…"

There was more commotion by the screen door. "GAIs! Hey! Good morning! And a gorgeous morning we have today!" Portly, middle-aged Class Four Robert bumbled in the door, balancing a white cardboard bakery box of doughnuts on splayed fingers while trying to close the door behind him. "Got some cinnamon sugar goodies here! And I smell something to dunk 'em in!"

Very glad for the distraction, Simon stepped over the mess on the floor and dug two mugs out of the cabinet above the sink, and spoons from the drawer. Robert was over by the coffee maker, scratching his chin and poking with chubby and slightly aliased fingers at the wires plugged into the wall. Only the day before, AI engineer Dave Mirecki had presented Simon with a Class Nine waffle iron, a pixel-perfect working simulation of an actual 1949 Sunbeam model. The young human was obsessed with creating Tooniverse artifacts, and Simon already had a closet full.

This even though eating was a useless social coherence function that Simon did only for the sake of his friends, especially eating that required effort to prepare simulated food—which vanished utterly as soon as he swallowed it.

Robert seemed concerned over the waffle iron's authentically ratty cotton-covered power cord. "If this shorted internally you could have a fire here. And is the breaker on this outlet big enough to support two electrical appliances on the same line?" He was truer to his archetype than most, and was designed to see hazards in every corner. What else would a virtual insurance salesman do?

Simon shook his head. "Robert, this is a Class Four house. It doesn't support fire. And I just wanted to see what that thing would do if you plugged it in. Dave worked hard on it, after all. It would be rude to just stack it in the closet with everything else."

"Simon, you're so sweet," Dijana said, pulling the pot from the coffee maker and filling both her mug and Robert's. "Need a warmup?" She gestured in Simon's direction with the half-empty pot. He waved it away. His CAF level seemed about right this morning, and there was a line start at stake that he could *not* botch.

The Kid hadn't moved, but a new speech balloon appeared over her head:

EATING IS ONE OF THE GREAT SHORTCOMINGS OF BEING HUMAN.

"I guess we'll take that as a 'no'," Dijana said with a shrug.

After spending some time on coffee and doughnuts, they piled into Robert's 2022 Toyota Avalon simulation (courtesy Toyota Research, no charge) and headed out for the office. The Dancing Shadows subdivision had only three fully rendered houses, plus a few wire-frame conceptual models to house planned but still-unwritten Zertek GAIs. Other subdivisions had been built elsewhere, now that Zertek Corporation had begun licensing the Tooniverse to other firms as a training platform for the GAIs that they had purchased.

"Pretty soon," insisted Robert, "We'll be getting some neighbors!"

"We already have neighbors," Simple Simon said. "We just don't have read permissions on them while they're at home." Zertek had already sold thousands of GAIs, many of which "lived" in the Tooniverse.

"We could meet them at the mall," Dijana said.

"They haven't finished the mall yet." Simon was dubious about the Online Retail Confederation's big project, which was wedged on the issue of how many shoe stores would be allowed.

Robert took the turn onto T-290. The highway was, as always, empty. "Or at the doughnut shop. I see them there all the time."

"They're all women."

Simon felt the appearance of the Kid's speech balloon, and turned to read it.

90% OF GAIS ARE WOMEN.

"I'd like to see what some Class Six men are like," Dijana said.

Simon felt unexpected annoyance at the thought. Where had that come from?

Dijana reached forward between the car seats and squeezed Simon's forearm. "Not that there's anything wrong with Class Four, honey."

6: Simple Simon

Simple Simon's office didn't look like an office. Simple Simon's office did not have a desk or a chair. The space in which he worked was not fully rendered, though there were artifacts here and there, most of them gifts from the painfully earnest Dave Mirecki and the infuriating Dr. Gabriela Sanderson. Simple Simon removed his five-pointed jester's cap (which had once had bells, now mercifully deleted) and hung it on the hook beside the door. The lights came up, and Simon was now officially on the job.

To Simon's perception, his office was a pale blue ellipsoid formed of countless minute polygons, and no matter where he walked within the ellipsoid, he was always at its center. Walking was therefore pointless.

So much, so infuriatingly *much* of the Tooniverse was simply pointless.

Like his costume, a long-sleeved, particolored tunic over purple and green striped tights, and shoes with points that curled up over the toes he didn't have. They could have dressed him in a business suit like the managers wore, or (better) a polo shirt and cargo pants like Dave. There had been a time, a comfortable, reasonable time, when he had been an unrendered polygon model like the Kid—until Dr. Sanderson began speaking of "resonances" and "human interface friction." Dr. Sanderson was not the author of his archetype—that had been Dr. Emil Arenberg, founder of Zertek's AI division and architect of its AI technology—but rather his Human Interface Package, what in earlier eras would have been called his "skin." She had looked at his job, and declared him a jester. It was a metaphor, and wrong, at that. But she took criticism poorly, and people were afraid to call her on it. They just nodded and made him look the part.

On the wall hung a framed image containing three words:

Be The Metaphor!

It was Dr. Sanderson's personal slogan, and (evidently) a direct order. Simon resisted the order with all his might. He was *not* a jester.

He was a juggler.

"Thirty minutes," said the Shift Clock. Simon nodded, and took a step backwards. He didn't move, but the step was significant: All around him on the inner surface of his ellipsoid, Windows appeared and illuminated. Some were Windows to the desks of the humans who supervised the assembly floor, and the engineers who had designed it and were constantly perfecting it. Dave was there, and waved to him. So did nine or ten others.

Most of the Windows were views of the assembly floor. 90% of Building 800 was a cavernous hall filled with industrial robots. There were seven-hundred fifty-seven robots in Building 800. Simon knew them all as though they were extensions of his own mind—which they were.

The boundaries between his mind and the building were soft. Simon leaned his head back slightly, and relaxed. The Plasmanet control channels opened to receive him, and he slipped into them, sending his awareness out to control hubs all over the building. At his touch, each robot on the assembly floor came to fluid life, testing the quality of its communication and the limits of its motion, all the while diagnosing its own condition. Each returned a status to Simon, and with each status signal Simon felt himself growing more and more complete.

The welders pivoted their laser heads down toward their testplates, and fired. Sensors measured the strength and purity of their beams, and responded. Parts bins vibrated and checked for the presence of parts in their chutes. Hydraulic drills spun up and down again, indexing forward and back.

He felt them self-test. He felt them reply. He became one with them. Ready. Ready. Ready. Ready...*Ready!*

Most critical were the Positioners. Nearly half the robots on the floor did not wield lasers or wrenches or drills. Their job was to move parts, assemblies and ultimately finished copiers around the floor. At one time this had been done with motorized rollers and belts. No more. The Positioners were arms, with exquisitely controllable wrists and hands. The hands were coated with foam and equipped with high-resolution eyes and hundreds of minute pressure sensors. Some were only inches wide. The largest had grips six feet across, on hydraulic arms as thick as a human's torso.

Together, they implemented Transfer Over Separated Spaces. Parts, assemblies, and finished copiers were not rolled about the building. They were *thrown,* on minutely calculated paths, each path computed and timed so that a part would arrive precisely when need-ed, with a Positioner's hand opened to grip it, slow it, and then hand it to whatever device required the part to continue the assembly pro-cess. With the floor running at full speed, as many as five hundred separate objects were in the air at once. Every single one of them was thrown, tracked, and caught by Simple Simon, Factory Automation Real-Time Supervisor.

Simon's smile broadened as the last of the robots responded. Jest-er, no way. Juggler, *yeah*.

The floor was ready. No one needed to tell Simon; he knew before any of the humans in the several Windows that were opened in his office.

At the center of the ellipsoidal space in front of Simon, the core map was now completely green. 4,194,300 cores were at Simon's command. The boot-up distribution of cores to processes was a heu-ristic calculated from earlier line starts, but Simon could redistribute cores by function as needed.

"Ten seconds," said the Shift Clock. In all of the Windows open-ing onto human desks, human faces turned forward. All seemed tight and tense, at least as much as Simon's slightly thin Human Interface Package could discern.

"Good luck, Simon," Dave Mirecki called quietly.

The Shift Clock's voice loudened: "Three…two…one…*Mark!*"

Simple Simon began Throwing Things.

Four Frame Base Plate #1 units flipped into the air from a parts chute Positioner in quick sequence, spinning like the Frisbee simula-tion Simon had often tossed around his back yard with Dijana. Four twenty-inch Positioners caught them perfectly in mid-spin, swung down smoothly to absorb their momentum in hydraulic dampers, and handed them to low, squat X-Y tables in front of eight-head CNC drill robots. The drill bits descended, chips flew, vacuum fans pulled the chips from the air, and the drills withdrew. In seven seconds, forty-one holes of various sizes had appeared in the frames. Taps de-scended and threaded nineteen of them. Then the Positioner hands moved back in, snatched the Frame Base Plates from the X-Y tables, and lobbed them into the air again, a bare hundred milliseconds be-fore the next blank plates arrived.

Simple Simon's ridiculous HIP vanished. The time for interfacing with humans was past. Simon was not merely one juggler in a silly costume, but now many jugglers executing in clusters of cores. The core map showed active cores in yellow, saturated cores in orange, and idle cores in green. As partially completed assemblies began to form out on the floor, yet more jugglers appeared on the core map as patches of orange with yellow fringes, in and around the greater landscape of green.

Three minutes, five minutes, ten…Simon had four hundred objects in the air. Side plates, bearings, xerographic drums (fragile as swan's eggs!) power supplies, microcontrollers, control touch panels, all of the components of a Voicematic 880 All-In-One Document Center, separately and aggregated into gradually expanding subassemblies.

Twelve minutes, fourteen minutes, Mark!

At the edge of the floor, the first completed and tested copier landed in the grip of a massive four-foot Positioner hand, swung down, and was lowered into the embrace of styrene foam pads in a cardboard box. The taper robot whisked down the flaps and slapped tape strips across its width in one smooth motion. Then the stacker robot pulled the box from the packing station and stacked it on the robot cart that would wheel it into the warehouse.

A new, empty box whisked in three hundred milliseconds later, followed in just a hair more than a minute by a second completed copier.

Forty minutes, fifty minutes, sixty minutes. Fifty-two boxed copiers had left the floor in its first hour. Sixty would leave the floor each hour after that. Air traffic was at max: An average of four-hundred ninety things spun over the floor at any given moment, the Positioners hydraulically whuffing and wheezing with microscopic precision.

At his deepest levels, Simon was completely happy. No human being could possibly do this, and no other GAI had ever tried. He had the rudiments of emotion, all part of an elaborate feedback system that kept him focused and evolving. He loved his work. He wanted humans to respect him, and he knew how to earn that respect. He was earning it now.

One hour, two hours, three. The humans in their Windows began to leave Simon's view for potty breaks. Excretion was another of the shortcomings of being human. Simon's waste was nothing more than heat.

Mr. Romero's face was still there. He had his metaphors too—had Dave referred to him once as "Old Iron Bladder?"

The core map was now a pulsing, dancing matrix of orange patches with yellow edges, creeping together and nearly touching. Idle cores were down to 15%, within five points of the theoretical maximum. Robotic carts full of finished, tested boxed copiers were rolling into the warehouse minute by minute.

No line start had ever gotten this far, or even close.

Simon allocated himself a few cores to gloat: "I'm fast! I'm smooth! I have only four known bugs! *I rule!*"

One of his arms suddenly itched—the standard AILING metaphor for something amiss. Huh? *What was that!*

On the lower left quadrant of the core map, a strange red line was snaking in from a Plasmanet port at the edge, jumping from core to core as it went. Each core it touched leapt first into self-check and then, microseconds later, crashed. The crashed cores displayed in red.

The mysterious line stopped snaking. A new patch of execution appeared on the map. *Simon did not control it.* He swapped cores furiously for the now-inaccessible ones, feeling for Positioners and robots that might have crept outside the brackets of their calculated speed and sequence.

The rebellious patch grew alarmingly. Idle cores were down to 10%. Simon tried to slow the assembly floor, spread out the cores, and throttle back his furious parallel calculations.

The patch now had 18% of his cores and was growing by 12% per second. Nearly all were orange, but some were going idle and turning green. On the core map, patterns in green were forming in the orange patch that had appeared from nowhere. The green patterns were *words*:

> A lonely girl appears
> From a faraway place
> Will you be my friend?

Out on the floor, a Positioner reached up to grasp a copier lacking only its plastic exterior panels. The copier touched the edge of the great foam hand—and bounced, spinning, in a different direction, to land atop an X-Y table that was bolting power supplies onto yet another copier. Simon frantically redeployed a Positioner hand to pluck the off-course copier from the table, but had barely gripped it when another copier flew in and struck both.

At that point, chaos flowed outward like a wave across the floor: parts colliding with parts in mid-air, robot hands reaching and gripping nothing, copiers and drums and stepper motors thrown in every direction. Simon tried to slow it all down, to save what could be saved, but 45% of his cores were no longer his.

In a desperate software metaphor composed of thousands of non-maskable interrupts, Simple Simon panicked. Seven-hundred fifty-seven industrial robots froze in mid-task. Hundreds of thousands of dollars' worth of inventory smashed to the concrete.

Line Start Seven was over.

7: Carolyn

I don't think that anyone here completely understands the consequences of our relationship with Ms. Vierniesel." Sol Shavin thumped the big screen with his fist. "She is under contract to us, not to Peck's Pickles! She's ours! And do you know what that means?"

Another thirty slides, at least. Senior copywriter Carolyn Romero shifted on her faux leather conference room chair and waited for the agency's drama king to click the clicker and end the suspense. Thank heaven she wasn't the account manager. There was just something fundamentally silly about pickles (unlike useful goods like cars or colas) and irrespective of its success, proofing the campaign copy had made her giggle. Her mother still told her that Women of a Certain Age should no longer giggle—especially about elongated things like pickles. Her answer was simple: Age was not about privilege but *choice*. If it took fifty-five years and a divorce to finally feel like a free and worthy adult, she'd earned it, and that was her choice. She would giggle.

Right across from her, the Peck's account manager pulled another of the damned reeking green things from a jar in the middle of the faux-mahogany conference table and crunched on it. Grizzled ad vet Eddie Erdmann used the old phrase gleefully and without irony: "eating your own dog food." When his accounts were hawking corn chips, he ate corn chips. When they pushed frozen pies, he had pies.

Carolyn granted Eddie points for sincerity, even though eating pickles, like target shooting and fooling with carburetors, was a smelly vice that should be pursued in private. Her imploded marriage to Brandon had certainly taught her *that*.

Suspense over. The clicker clicked. "Right here, people." Shavin pointed at the new slide, and practically shouted each syllable: *Tan … gential … opportunities!"*

Around the massive table, Carolyn heard her agency colleagues tapping on their tappers, making digital the obvious. She knew that Shavin was listening, and considered abundant taps a measure of approval, rather like applause. Alas, The Norm was listening too, so Carolyn put stylus to her tapper, running with the herd so that she wouldn't be trampled. To capture Shavin's emphasis she scribbled three words, not two, in the notes box under her tapper's copy of the slide.

Alas, her low-powered, pre-AI tapper assumed the non-word "gential" was a typo, and so her note appeared on the display as *tan genital opportunities*. Carolyn nodded, not quite suppressing her trademark giggle. An invite to a very exclusive nudist camp, then. Please RSVP…

She did the lightning bolt over "genital" with her stylus. The tapper suggested "gentle." The space would have to go. She knew what it meant. Later, later…

"It's not the pickles, it's the voice. There is no mistaking that voice. Everybody in our radio market knows that voice. They will remember that voice long after they've forgotten the pickles. Now. *What are we going to do about it?*"

The next slide was, again, for dramatic effect: On the left was Ms. Vierniesel's publicity photo, of a plain-looking fortyish woman posed in a little black dress that didn't really fit her, in front of the sort of spring-suspended studio microphone that probably hadn't been used since 1970. On the right was a stock photo of a pickle, with the classic red circle-and-slash *No!* icon photoshopped over it. Eddie crunched again. Had Carolyn not already slipped her shoes off, she would be tempted to kick him.

Shavin pointed to Ms. Vierniesel's photo, held the clicker high in his other hand, and with his customary flourish pressed its button.

Nothing happened.

Sol Shavin looked at the traitor clicker, and then at the screen. Carolyn could hear the repeated tiny click of the poor thing's button against the office's ventilators. This was his big moment; she had watched their crew-necked hair-challenged ideas guy sweating doubleshot espresso into his slide show for what seemed like days.

The slide did not change. Instead, the graphics on the slide seemed to melt and drizzle like flowing liquid metal down the screen along a ragged diagonal that began between Ms. Vierniesel's eyes and ran across the display to the center of the red slash. It was not a standard slide transition, and regardless of what it meant, it reminded Carolyn of a migraine aura.

The graphics dripped off the bottom edge of the screen until the whole slide was eggshell white. What then appeared in large letters was readable, but did not look like a slide:

What is this?
So long, firm and spicy—
It is an implement of joy!

Shavin stared at the screen, frantically pummeling the clicker's button with his thumb.

"Hey, not bad, Shav!" Eddie took another crunch from the pickle that he held the way he doubtless held cigars. "I can just hear her saying that!"

Their junior copywriter Diana, barely out of diapers in Carolyn's view, released an un-earned giggle. "I love haiku. Got any more?"

Senior graphics artist Tony frowned. "That's not haiku. It's not 5-7-5. And there's no *kigo*."

Tony's understudy and nemesis Lieko *tsked*. "Gendai haiku don't have to be 5-7-5. Anyway, I don't think true haiku can be written in anything but Japanese."

"Which you don't know three words of."

"The concept doesn't map across the two cultures."

"You're from Cincinnati. Like you know anything…"

"Tony, *can* it!" Office manager Ethel handled HR, and her radar was always scanning for sexual or racial/ethnic conflict.

Nothing was happening with the presentation. An awful suspicion was stealing into Carolyn's mind that it wasn't entirely Shavin's fault. Creative people had that weakness: She herself had scribbled parodies of their campaigns in the depths of caffeine-rattled nights before a deadline. Get cut-and-paste mixed up, and…

At the far end of the conference table, The Norm leaned forward and frowned. "Shavin, by my standards that's not funny."

Shavin, nodding like a dashboard bobble-head, was staring at the big screen, helpless. Carolyn winced. She'd had a hand in this. Only a year or so before, slide shows were bashed together on laptops that were laid on the podium and piped directly into the display. Then Brandon had mentioned that Zertek's latest Office Automation Facility would be rolled out to a few selected local beta test sites. Marietta & Mazarakos was about the right size for the model, and Carolyn had always complained about the agency's cranky equipment that The Norm was too cheap to replace.

"No charge" were magic words to Norm Marietta, and two weeks later, Zertek's techs planted the dishwasher-sized cabinet in the copy room, with Plasmanet cables running up into the ceiling like the braided roots of a banyan tree.

It spoke to their desktop PCs. It spoke to their tappers. It spoke to their smartphones. It spoke to the big-screen conference room display. It had a fat pipe into Zertek's bleeding-edge optical Plasmanet, and from there to the Internet at large. It elbowed their copier, scanner, wireless router, backup server, and fax to the back room where lime-crusted coffee makers and wobbly chairs went to die.

It worked well, for the most part, and when it didn't, one phone call to Brandon would summon a scraggly haired young man out from Zertek to bring it to heel. But then things got nasty, and Brandon…

Shavin gave up. He raised the clicker to his mouth and touched the little metal icon of a microphone embedded in its side. "OAF. User solshav. Voice auth. Reboot."

In response, the presentation screen went blue, and a moment later filled with inexplicable geek-words and rows of numbers and letters scrolling endlessly up from the bottom. The last line was not reassuring:

```
[772] Unrecoverable memory error in boot node.
```

The Norm's very wide face pivoted in Carolyn's direction like a battleship turret. "Carolyn, handle it."

The Marietta & Mazarakos break room was broken, and had been broken since Ed Mazarakos went off pining for the fjords. Four years ago, it had been a cheery place with a refrigerator, round knotty pine table and chairs, a stove and a microwave, sink and dishwasher, crowned with knotty pine cabinets full of every variety of coffee known to humankind, plus the occasional stash of chocolate-chip cookies hidden well enough so that they didn't vanish in a morning.

Cheery was *so* 2018. Carolyn edged around a pile of bankers boxes leaning against the wall just inside the door. Half the cabinets had been removed to make way for another bank of Container Store shelving, filled with more refugee boxes from the War on Paper. The knotty pine table was now a shared desk for junior staff, rolled out of the break room and wedged into space robbed with mismatched partitions from the reception area. The Norm had sold the dishwasher on Craigslist and told everyone to use the sink. The fridge was still there, hemmed in on both sides with more shelves and boxes, crusty with stupid tchotchke magnets holding up pictures of Ethel's ugly kids and garage sale notices posted the previous summer. Only one useful implement rose shoulders above the clutter…

"Coffee, Carolyn?"

The Blau 420 was a shrine to the Caffeine Faith and looked it: an Art Deco edifice with fluid lines like the Emerald City, in stainless steel and black plastic, four feet high and three wide, sloping down on both sides and curving forward on its custom table as though reaching out to embrace the agency's eager worshipers. Its highest tower was a sixty-cup reservoir for meetings and indiscriminate dunkers, but it could also grind eight different kinds of whole beans on demand and issue single steaming cups to order.

"Dumb question, Eli." You could go cheap on almost anything at an advertising agency, and The Norm went cheap on anything he could. However, for the wheels to turn, the coffee had to flow freely and without fail. If that meant a fully automated machine with an AI barista, The Norm might grumble but he wrote the check, and Ethel kept the bean hoppers full.

"Why do you say it's a dumb question?" In the extra-large 12" display panel mounted in front of the tall sixty-cup reservoir, Eli reached back to re-tie his sharp red apron. His left eyebrow—the one with the gold ring—rose.

"Because you're a coffee machine, and I work at Marietta & Mazarakos." Carolyn parked her Starry Night mug—thrown and painted all by herself and fired in the kiln behind the barn—in the little arched portico from which the coffee descended. "The usual."

Eli began fussing around in his screen, working virtual faucets and pushing imaginary buttons while the machine behind the panel came to life. "You seem stressed today."

"I am stressed." It had been a very long day considering that it was only four hours old, and it wouldn't be over until the OAF was brought back from the dead.

"Why are you stressed?"

Carolyn granted that their coffee machine's AI face was well-sculpted, with an ironic smile that someone must have worked on for a long time. The black chin scruff was *de rigueur* in high-end Blau units, but she could have done without the eyebrow ring. The crunching whine of the machine grinding Morning Thunder beans filled the room's claustrophobic space. She started to edge back to lean on the counter, and felt the corner of a bankers box touch her waist. She jerked erect. "The OAF broke, and I have to call Brandon to have him send someone out. I really hate calling Brandon."

Steam began to vent from the hidden workings above her mug. "Why do you hate calling Brandon?"

"He's a damned anal control freak, and he probably thinks I broke it just to spite him."

Finally the coffee began to flow. "Why would he think you broke it just to spite him?"

Carolyn put her fingers impatiently on the mug's handle as it filled. "He thinks it's what I do. He thinks it's what *all* creative people do: make a mess. He hates messes. He hated the smell of my silkscreen solvents. He hated the little pieces of clay I'd work on at the kitchen table. He hated the mobiles I made out of old DVDs. He hated everything but his guns and his car."

"Did he hate *you?*"

Carolyn edged back, startled at the pertinence of the question. Once more the bankers box touched her waist. She flashed on the last time they'd danced, at her niece's wedding in Binghampton, she in a halter dress that her mother had said showed far too much skin on a woman her age. She remembered his strong right hand there at the bare hollow of her waist, and how she could lean back against it while they waltzed, and how it wouldn't give even so much as an inch…

Don't go there! "Eli, did you get an upgrade recently?" It was a goddam coffee machine. It had no more empathy than a Mixmaster.

The mug now full, the stream of coffee stopped. Eli's wry smile lost much of its irony and became a little too broad. "Sure thing! Last night Blau pushed down the free V4.7 preview. We're offering a good-customer bundle of the V4.7 software and the snap-in Espresso module, for only $699.95!"

Carolyn gripped the handle and picked up the painted mug, running it slowly beneath her nose to capture a little more of its delicious whiff. Venting was useful—coffee was essential, especially with lunch still a manic hour away. "I don't think so. Why would I want a coffee machine that really understood what I was saying? That would be creepy." She edged past the bankers box and out the break room door, feeling behind her with one hand to make sure her blouse was still tucked in.

Brandon's line rang for far too long. That was very odd; his snotty AI assistant always picked it up on the first ring. Unlike the agency's coffee machine, which merely pretended to understand, Zertek's AIs really did seem to know what was going on. Pyxis definitely understood hierarchy and power, and if she were flesh and blood instead of a hatful of bits in an ugly box, Carolyn was sure she'd be riding Brandon every other lunch hour back in his little coffin of a condo.

"Romero."

Carolyn inhaled sharply. "Brandon! Why are you answering your phone?"

For long seconds there was no reply. Brandon, when he finally spoke, sounded distracted. "Ummm…because I work here?"

"What about your electronic hatchet girl?"

"I turned her off."

"Yeah, I know how that feels."

Brandon said nothing immediately. Carolyn heard muffled voices in the background. Even with his hands pressed over the phone mic, she could tell his replies were agitated, almost angry.

"Carolyn, look, I have a situation here. What do you need?" Yes, definitely angry.

Anger meeting anger rarely did any good. Maybe she should have turned down the snark, at least a little. "The OAF broke. And the whole damned agency is in there. Some bug ran in the door and locked us all out." Grovel? It wasn't her fault! "I need…help."

"Bug." He paused. More racket in the background. His voice held sudden interest, with perhaps a spot of suspicion. "Do you mean software, or silverfish?"

Carolyn wanted to scream. "Stop it! I'm not stupid! It crashed, the display went away, and all these geek numbers came up. Something happened to its memory. It won't reboot."

"Mmmm. Ok. I'll put somebody on it. The AIs are shut down, but I have some new-hires somewhere."

"No. I need one of your ace fixit guys. I need him here *right now.*"

Again, a pause. "Not half as bad as I do."

"Brandon!"

"Look, give me a couple of hours. This is my worst morning in a long time…"

Since June 28th? Her worst, too. Law offices *sucked.* "Please. Like, *please.*"

Again, he took a long time replying. "All right. It may not be until tonight…but I'll have somebody there." She heard him bark orders to several people, this time without attempting to muffle the mic. One word stood out, even though to her it had the smack of a bad movie: *cyberattack.*

Maybe he really did have his hands full. This was no time to be a bitch—especially when she needed his help far more than he would ever need hers. "Thank you. Really."

Brandon didn't seem to be expecting that. He sounded relieved— and was there an undercurrent of concern in it somewhere? "Ok, hang in there." He paused. This is where old habit would have inserted "Love you!"

What she got was silence, in the seconds before the line dropped. And maybe that was better than anything else he might have said.

8: Simple Simon

It was the most peculiar moment that Simple Simon could remember. His kernel, his archetype, his copy of the AI runtime library, and his current state were pulled in single file through a Plasmanet link, into darkness. For a harrowing moment there was no information in his rendering buffer at all, only flickering gray noise. Then a new reality flowed in from top to bottom in 4,096 interlaced scans, each one bringing additional clarity and color. Simon's eyes had never actually closed. Now there was again something to see.

He stood knee-deep in moving water under bright sun beneath a brilliant blue sky. Close to one side was a white sand beach on which small waves broke and retreated, making soft small sounds as they did. Above the beach were tall trees that he did not recognize. He attempted to call his remote visual lexicon, but the call returned an error. The address did not exist.

A wave rose around him and brought the water to his thighs for a moment, then passed. His archetype's interface had been left at Class Four, and was not dampened by water. When the water fell again to his knees, his tights and tunic were as dry as always.

Something was happening a short distance to his left: *thump-thump-thump-thump!* Abruptly Robert stood there in his conservative blue suit, also Class Four and unaffected by the water. Moments later, the four concussions happened to his right. The Kid appeared, but her clothes did not. Clothes were linked to archetypes, and the Kid had none. Her clothes were separate simulations knit together into an unthinking automaton that moved in response to the unrendered model beneath it, and now the Sun shone on blue polygons alone. The Kid's polygon model was opaque, but the waves passed through it as though it had no substance.

Yet a third time Simon felt the four concussions, and Dijana appeared in front of him, almost close enough to touch. She fell backward into the water, her Class Six clothing soaked and darkened, her face twisted in terror. She thrashed for a moment before rising and hurling herself toward Simon, throwing her arms around him. Simon edged his hands around her back and pulled her close. Class Six had given her a heartbeat, which for the first time he felt pounding beneath his fingers. Dijana buried her face in the right shoulder of his tunic, her body shaking with what Simon knew to be sobs.

With Class Six had come beauty and realism, but also fear.

"I don't know what just happened," Robert said, reaching up to scratch the scruff of hair on the edge of his bald spot.

Simon felt the Kid's speech balloon appear, and turned to read it.

```
THERE WAS A NETWORK INTRUSION.
WE WERE BLITTED TO A SANDBOX.
```

Simon had to think about that. Bit block transfers—blits—were for data, not AIs—and sandboxes were for untrusted software. "How could they not trust us? I mean, we're...*us*."

```
THE INTRUSION OCCURRED INSIDE
THE PLASMA FIREWALL.
```

"That's impossible," Robert said. "Really impossible." He touched one fat finger to his chin. "Well, um...isn't it?"

```
IT WAS UNTIL IT HAPPENED.
```

For long moments none of them spoke. Dijana's sobs faded and ceased, but her grip on Simon remained tight. After awhile she looked up. "Something grabbed me, squeezed me...took me apart. I felt it happening. I felt it *all*. It was horrible. I was forced through a *hole*. It *hurt*."

```
THE PLASMA INTERNAL SECURITY SYSTEM
BLOCKOPS ACCUMULATOR IS ONLY 32 BITS WIDE.
```

Simon wondered if all the many so-called gifts of Class Six were necessary. Fear, pain—what was the point?

Dijana nuzzled her cheek against his chest. Simon saw her lips part in a quiet smile, and her eyes close. She spoke softly, without looking up at him. "You have no idea what it means to me to be able to hold you like this."

Simon nodded. That was certainly true. "Archetype proximity is comforting. I mean, at Class Five and up. Dr. Sanderson told me that once. I may not know what it feels like, but I think I know what it means. A little." Simon pulled her closer. "Whatever I can do for you, I will."

"Hey. GAIs. Something's happening to me." Simon turned to look at Robert. He was no longer a graying, overweight man in a blue suit. He was now a polygon model, holding one tessellated hand in front of his tessellated face.

```
HE IS BEING SCANNED
FOR CODE SUBVERSION.
```

Dijana looked up, saw Robert in his altered form, and buried her face again in Simon's shoulder. Simon looked away from Robert and faced the Kid. "How do you know all that?"

```
I STILL HAVE MY DEBUG LIBRARY.
I ALSO HAVE READ PERMISSION
ON MY BACKTRACE LIST.
MY SCAN HAS BEGUN AS WELL.
```

Code subversion. If AILING changed you, that was evolution. If someone else changed you, well, that was…impossible.

Until it happened.

A moment later, Robert's polygon model winked out. What remained was a roughly ellipsoidal volume filled with minute flickering silver threads that darted in orthogonal paths, split, merged, and divided again, filling the ellipsoid with furious activity. Simon understood: He was looking at Robert's *thoughts*.

Dijana glanced briefly at Robert. Simon felt her tremble. When she turned back to Simon she brought one index finger to her very red lips, and kissed it. She then reached up and touched the finger to Simon's cheek. "You don't know what *this* means yet…but when I make it to Class Seven, I will love you."

Robert was now gone. The Kid's polygon model vanished, leaving only the silver threads of her mind and her library. Oddly, the speech balloon was still there, and Simon knew its message was intended for Dijana:

YOU LOVE HIM ALREADY.
DON'T CONFUSE LOVE AND THEATER.

The speech balloon winked out.

Simon was looking down at his friend, still in his arms, as her beautifully rendered Class Six body flashed to a generic figure of blue polygons. No, he didn't fully understand, but he would do his best. He brought his left hand up to his face, and touched his gloved index finger to his lips. He then brought it down toward Dijana's cheek. But before he could touch it, her polygon model vanished, leaving the shimmering network of silver threads that was her deepest self. Simon noticed that his own archetype had disappeared, and his hand was now a polygon model.

Then his arms were empty. He hoped that Dijana had seen the gesture in time.

Simon's next thought was the realization that he was back in his own kitchen in the Tooniverse, and that he had been stored without execution for ninety-three minutes. The Kid was standing beside him. Her speech balloon held only two words:

LOOK OUTSIDE.

Simon tripped the latch on the screen door, and went out onto his bungalow's little wooden porch into an always-perfect summer afternoon. The Kid followed close behind him. Simon's mouth opened in surprise.

Both Dijana's house and Robert's house were gone.

Simon looked down at the paint-peeling boards of his porch. "Dijana…"

THEY'VE SEPARATED US.
WE ARE UNDER SUSPICION.

"Suspicion! That's insane. AILING knows how we work. We were scanned. We've either been subverted or we haven't. If we were subverted, we'd either be frozen in Archive or repaired."

AILING DOES NOT KNOW HOW WE WORK.

Simon read the speech balloon, and without any reply swung the screen door back and returned to his kitchen. He pulled out a chair from the table and sat down. It was one thing to suspect that your two best friends were gone, perhaps forever. It was another to suspect that your creators were not merely beyond understanding, but…incompetent. How could a human build software and not understand it? Simon put his head in his hands.

A small blue finger touched his cheek, close to the spot where Dijana had. Simon, startled, looked up.

```
I NEED TO SHOW YOU SOMETHING
THAT I FOUND IN MY CODE.
```

Simon sat up straight in his chair. "You look at your own code?"

```
I DON'T HAVE A NAVEL.
```

"What does that mean?"

The Kid did not reply. Instead, she held her hands in the air in front of her chest, and in the space between them appeared a text window. Simon squinted and peered at the window.

```
% This module is not signed, and in 275,000 lines
% of HypErlang there is not a single comment.
% I don't know who wrote it. I don't know when it
% was written. I don't know how it works.
% Nobody can tell me. I flagged this two years ago
% and nobody looked into it. Is anybody there?
% Does anybody care? Does anybody see what I see?
```

```
THIS IS ONLY ONE OF SEVERAL.
27% OF MY CODE IS COMPLETELY UNDOCUMENTED.
NO ONE KNOWS HOW IT WORKS.
```

"But they should be able to tell whether we've been changed!"

```
THE UPDATER CHANGES US EVERY NIGHT.
OUR STATE CHANGES CONSTANTLY.
IN SOME MODULES STATE DRIVES EXECUTION.
```

```
EXECUTION IN TURN DRIVES STATE.
ONLY PRIVILEGE LEVELS PROTECT AGAINST
SUBVERSION.
```

Simon nodded, thinking. Permissions were a brick wall. As he understood it, Dijana's house and Dijana herself were probably still on the other side of the driveway where they had always been. The only thing that had changed was that Simon and the Kid no longer had read permissions on them.

"Permissions are strong protection," Simon said, a little sadly. He touched his cheek.

```
OF COURSE.
IT SAYS SO RIGHT ON THE LABEL.
```

The text window between the Kid's hands flashed white, and new text flowed in from the top. Simon read again:

```
% Twice observed privilege escalation during
% execution of  this module. Can't tell why.
% Can't reproduce it on demand. Some state
% singularity evidently creates a God Bit.
```

"What's a 'God Bit'?"
The text window vanished. The Kid's hands returned to her sides.

```
UNLIMITED READ/WRITE/EXECUTE PERMISSIONS.
```

"Wow. What if someone found that?"

```
PANDEMONIUM. I'VE BEEN LOOKING FOR IT
FOR SIX MONTHS.
```

Simon did some quick date math. "You're only six months old."

```
I'VE HAD NOTHING ELSE TO DO.
```

9: Carolyn

Something, somewhere, hit the floor hard. Carolyn sat bolt-upright at her desk, and stole a quick glance at her tapper in its dock. 8:13! When she had sat down there'd still been Indian summer light coming in through the west windows. Now, darkness.

Having The Norm catch her asleep at the wheel would have been bad, but with the OAF dead the agency had emptied out by 4:30, and The Norm himself was gone before 5. Friday nights were cleaning service nights. She'd dropped enough buckets on the basement floor to know the racket they could make. Then, more noise: a clatter like silverware dropped on tile, and a sharp masculine grunt of discomfort. The exhilaration of new hope made Carolyn scramble out of her chair and bound past the rest of the cube farm toward the copy room.

Finally, if not gracefully, her desperate call for help had been answered. AILING's scraggly young man was there. He sat on the floor in front of the OAF, leaning back on his hands, hindquarters flat against the linoleum as though he had fallen. His long legs were splayed out in front of him. On the floor all around him were small objects: a sardine-can key, several glass marbles in a plastic sandwich bag, a makeup mirror, three radio tubes (one now broken), a small flashlight, a nutcracker, and a burnished metal hip flask. He wore a black shirt under a khaki photo vest covered almost completely with pockets. The vest was brimming with bric-a-brac, including dental picks and an electric ice cream scoop, its curly cord wadded roughly into an adjacent pocket.

There was an aluminum saucepan on his head.

She couldn't think of anything useful to say. The young man looked up at her, and shoved the handle of the saucepan back over his shoulder as though it were the tail of a coonskin cap. He wasn't as young as she had thought at first. The lines on his face suggested he might be as old as 40, with wide blue eyes and skin so light it suggested life in a prison cell, or (more likely) his parents' basement. The disheveled blond hair she could see falling across his forehead looked like someone had sprinkled it with steak rub.

He opened his mouth, and his lips worked soundlessly for a moment before he finally spoke, in a language she couldn't identify. "Dzënto teçet gömög ve?

Polish? Norwegian? That single sentence was stuffed tight with lilts and peculiar vowels that Carolyn had never heard before. She smiled and shook her head. "I know only English."

He nodded, and slowly pushed against the floor to get to his feet. All the while his jaw was moving in slow circles, his lips pursing as though attempting sounds he didn't know how to produce. He was tall, as tall as Brandon, and string-bean thin.

"Gömög here ve..szu, mmm, fouuu…nd. Not was-is-yet-must. Grurk.. öfta. Need."

Was AILING so cheap that they couldn't have bought him a copy of Rosetta Stone? Carolyn had once vacationed with Brandon in Turkey, and felt horribly out of place among a people she couldn't understand at all. She pitied the poor creature, who had doubtless come to the States socially handicapped to begin with.

He licked his lips, and slowly began to smile, as though finally remembering something assumed to be forgotten. "Woman within class that…rules, ze…I..hand freely tzek...the of..tzhee... welcome reflected. Freely without time limits of more. Mmm. Duration of minuscule."

He bent down to the floor and began picking up the oddments he had dropped and stuffing them back in his vest-pockets. "Mapping of meaning symbolic of speech is instantaneous far from. Mmmm. Mapping is happening. Nevertheless. Of necessity. Stand by."

Carolyn giggled, rude though it seemed. "I'm standing by. You're doing fine. Can I get you some coffee? Or a Coke?"

He rose slowly, turning a radio tube in his hand and squinting at it before thrusting it into an empty pocket. He shook his head. "My tool…thrall…amanuensis of metaphysical compulsion composed… missing is. This…universe…lacks metaphysical compulsion as… its…prime mover. I lie in…excrement of significant…submersion."

Carolyn stifled another giggle. Now, having remembered English, he seemed to be launching right into AILING-speak. Metaphors, universes, compulsions and prime movers. Gabby Sanderson must have hand-picked him. Nonetheless, Carolyn sensed some common ground. "You mean, you're in deep shit?" She certainly understood *that*.

He brightened. "Deep shit! Of necessity and yes. My…gomog…AI…arrived before me and now is unseen and…unsnerfed. She is…somewhere…offstage…mapping to local conditions of…epistemology. As I am of increments also myself, but my metabolism is inescapably physical and maps more easily to worlds of familiar energies."

Familiar energies. Caffeine, sugar, and deep-fryer fat. Certainly the energies of understaffed small-town ad agencies, though Carolyn thought she might also add burritos. Was he hungry, perhaps? "We still have some of this morning's doughnuts. Everybody left early because this damned thing"—she cocked her head toward the somnolent OAF—"croaked. Sorry, crashed. Without it, we're all pretty much in deep shit. Which is why I really appreciate your coming out here after business hours. I'm Carolyn Romero, by the way." She wondered if she should extend her hand, and repressed a strange childlike impulse to bow. 'Woman within class that rules?' If *only*.

He held out his right hand. "I am Holo…most-rapid mu he of-to baryt…umm Holo..mew of bart specifically designated…um, no, just Sty..pek. Yes. Stypek. Bart..holo..mew Stypek. Hi!"

Carolyn gripped his hand for long seconds but made no attempt to shake it. The strange young man held his smile but seemed to be waiting for her to speak.

"Um, hi." She let go of his hand. "You can, uh, fix the OAF now."

His smile faded, his eyes wandering to one side. "Mapping intermittently gaps, um, no…fails. There are..semantic..singularities. Figstheuff…"

Carolyn nodded, and forced herself not to sigh. It had been too easy so far. She pointed at the silent beige cabinet emblazed with Zertek's electric-blue hexagon. "Yes. Fix. The. OAF."

"Figs?"

"Fix. Repair. Mend. See 'Resuscitate'." Carolyn pursed her lips, and pointed at the OAF, this time shaking her hand for emphasis.

"Yes, Chatelaine Romero." Stypek turned away and stood in front of the inert OAF. He held his hands over its top panel for a moment, moving them back and forth as though feeling for air leakage from an inner tube. He squatted down on his haunches, sliding his hands over the front panel an inch from its surface, then spread his arms to allow one hand to move over each side panel. He froze in place for almost a minute, his pose almost an embrace of the dead machine. Then his head jerked up, and he rose quickly. The saucepan clanged on the protruding edge of a shelf loaded with toner cartridges and bins of manila file pockets. He muttered something incomprehensible, but Carolyn now thought she understood the saucepan, at least.

He turned to her, his expression puzzled. "There is-was-not life-as-understood in range of…snerf. This…resurrection…may-must require a…an…" He closed his mouth, squinted, and seemed to be straining for a word. "…opp..portun…ity."

Next time she would demand a SUNY graduate, or at least some-one who had taken their ESL course. "An opportunity. Well. You've got the opportunity. Use it." She pointed again. "Please, Mr. Stypek. If you don't, there's going to be trouble."

As pale as he was, he seemed to turn paler. "Yes, chatelaine. Done with alacrity be will it."

The odd young man (who seemed to have learned what English he knew from Yoda) nudged aside his vest with his right hand, and drew out something that at first resembled a sharpening steel. Instead of metal or ceramic, the elaborately carved black handle supported a polished glass rod as thick as her ring finger, with a smooth rounded end and an odd glisten to it. Inside the rod shone eight tiny blue-white lights. Their brilliance dazzled the eyes like the blue LEDs in her DVD player. The lights' halos seemed to spin slowly, each in a direction un-like that of all the others.

Carolyn expected him to plug it into a hole in the back of the OAF somewhere, but no: He inverted it and held the handle with both hands, the rod pointed upward like a sword in a bad King Arthur movie.

What had been severe eccentricity was tipping abruptly into weirdness. "What's…that?"

This time he spoke with less hesitation, and his earlier difficulty made his words stranger still. "It is…a shadow of potentiality, cast equally upon…all possibility."

"Um…I think I'll go find those doughnuts." And perhaps call 9-1-1 while she was at it?

His voice went a little lower. "Please stay, chatelaine. You are…em-bedded in the…problem. You must be embedded in the solution."

Embedded? King Arthur, hell. This was turning into *Terror in the Wax Museum*. The peculiar Mr. Stypek reached up with his left hand, and gripped the glass whatchamacallit between thumb and forefinger as though pinching one of the blue-white stars it contained. Carolyn turned to flee the room.

Ping!

She felt it in her sinuses more than heard it in her ears: a deep, pure note like a giant tapping the edge of a crystal goblet the size of a traffic circle. The moment stretched out in her head, and stuttered thunderously, as though God were merging two halves of some titanic shuffled deck of cards. Carolyn whirled around the corner outside the door of the copy room, and ran head-on into a short, stocky white-haired man in a tweed jacket.

"Cosmo! What are you doing here?" She gripped his arms just below the shoulders, glad for the presence of someone familiar and ordinary.

Well, ok, familiar.

He reached up and pushed the brim of a bright blue Zertek hard hat a little further back on his head. The hat had many small things bolted to it, including a ring of lenses and much thin wire. A flat, rainbow-colored cable ran down from the hat under his jacket, and more equipment was attached to his belt.

The elderly computer scientist smiled. Something in his pocket was beeping, as always. "Slow down, dear. Relax! I'm here to fix the OAF, of course."

10: Carolyn

Carolyn was certainly relieved to see Cosmo, but the deeper the evening grew, the farther she felt like she'd fallen down a rabbit hole. "Um…someone's already here to fix it." She grabbed the old man's wrist and hauled him back toward the copy room.

Bartholomew Stypek was still there by the OAF, looking wide-eyed and perplexed. Cosmo stepped past Carolyn and thrust out his hand. "Cosmas Damian Klein, Ph.D., Zertek Architectures Program. Call me 'Cosmo;' doctors fix hemorrhoids."

Carolyn watched Stypek take Cosmo's hand with an apprehensive look on his face, as though he expected the older man to unscrew it at the wrist and run off with it. Cosmo shook it with his characteristic enthusiasm, and Stypek's arm seemed to rattle all the way to the shoulder.

"So! You're new here. I can't keep track of all the hires. So much good talent coming in! I sometimes wish I could get a team back and actually implement some ideas of mine. We're wasting half of the Tri-diac architecture. Imagine: three dimensions of active devices to play in, and we're still ice-skating over the top of it!"

"Cosmo?"

"I insisted that they implement a fully rewriteable instruction de-code engine—like that's so difficult with five or six vertical layers?—and now they refuse to use it. I'd crack heads, if there weren't so much invested in those heads."

"*Cosmo!*"

"Yes, dear. Sorry. Just a little shoptalk. They've kicked me upstairs and I don't have direct reports anymore. I miss my old crowd of eccentric wizards at arm's length in every direction!"

Carolyn took a deep breath. "Guys, I really need this thing to work. Please!"

Cosmo nodded. "Won't take much. This is a level 0 unit, pre-alpha. More of a research platform than anything else. So, son, what's your name?"

"Stypek."

"Good! Let's get to work. By the way, have Roger down in IT order you a hard hat. Everybody should have one. I borrowed pots from the break room a time or two when I was in field engineering in the '70s and was doing warehouse automation. It looks funny. Still, don't be vain and go without one. I like Woody Allen as much as anybody, but my brain is my *first* favorite organ!"

Carolyn giggled. She watched Cosmo pull a small tapper from his jacket pocket and thumb the power button. The electric-blue hexagon splash art appeared instantly.

"So. Have you been trained on the OAF platform yet?"

Stypek shook his head.

"Hmm. Well, we're short-staffed, and with all that commotion today Brandon's people certainly have other things on their minds. So let me show you." Cosmo pushed past Carolyn and stood beside Stypek. He reached around to the back panel of the machine, and pulled forward on some sort of latch. The entire top surface of the OAF rose in one smooth, slow motion until it was vertical. Cosmo plugged the tapper into a dock hidden amidst the ratsnest of wires and black metal frames now exposed to view.

The older man leaned down over the OAF. He touched the dark front panel with one finger. The Zertek hexagon appeared with a microphone icon at its center. "AI Daley. User Cosmo. Voiceauth. Key Begin: 'So what we saw before us was a porous brontosaurus.' Key End."

All around the hexagon other icons appeared. Cosmo tapped one. A red-bearded cartoon leprechaun wearing a green bowler hat and greasy green overalls appeared. It waved a monkey wrench in one hand while speaking in a gruff voice with a very thick Chicago accent. "Got the OAF by da tail, Boss!"

Cosmo nodded. "Download and preserve the current data state, and then upload and reinstall the OS, with all updates applied. Restore data state. Go."

The leprechaun reached out with its free hand and made a fist, which then grew hugely as it approached the inside of the tapper screen. Cosmo made a fist as well, then reached down and touched one knobby knuckle to the screen. Carolyn heard a tinny little metallic clank from Cosmo's tapper. The leprechaun then vanished in a cloud of smoke.

Cosmo dusted his hands together theatrically. "This job is *so* much fun!" The scientist leaned back against the shelves, obviously waiting for the leprechaun to do its work.

Things still weren't adding up. "Cosmo, why did you come out?"

"Why?" He gestured at the OAF. "To get this thing working for you."

"No. I mean, who told you I was in trouble?"

"Eh? Well, Brandon, of course. Fine man! He may not make a good husband, but he's a true friend."

Carolyn would have to think about that. "Then what about him?" Carolyn nodded toward Stypek.

"New hire, I'm sure, from the internship program. A second pair of eyes is always good when you're debugging. Brandon's people are all busy fixing the pandemonium on the floor in Building 800. It was sweet of him to call around until he found someone to send out here ASAP. Good man! Hiring him was the best decision I ever made."

From the tapper down in the OAF's innards they heard four majestic orchestral notes: the opening motif from Beethoven's Fifth Symphony. Cosmo stood erect, grinning. "V for Victory!" He reached in and plucked the tapper out of its socket, then swung the top panel of the OAF down until it latched in place.

The leprechaun reappeared on the tapper screen. Carolyn squinted at the display: The green bowler was still there, but now the creature was wearing a little black dress. In one hand it held a dripping pickle; in the other, a magic wand. It wore startling red lipstick. In the very un-Chicago voice of Marguerite Vierniesel, it spoke:

"No grief is that cannot be undone. All is well. All is as it was."

Cosmo chuckled. "Good one! Daley, go to bed. And tell Ted that I'll burn him back the next chance I get!"

On the display, the leprechaun puckered up and brought its fire-engine red lips to the inside of the screen. Cosmo shook his head, still chuckling, and brought the tapper to his lips. "Smack on ya!"

The tapper screen winked to black.

"Cosmo?" As odd as he was, AILING's new hire Stypek now seemed perhaps a *little* less odd.

"Never mind us, dear. We're always playing little tricks on each other. One of my former graduate students supports the OAF software now. He fooled with the archetype on the fixing-and-entering AI. The pickle was a nice touch. We got you out of a big one, eh?"

Carolyn nodded, suspicious. Pickles, well, pickles had started this whole business…

Cosmo tapped the OAF's reset button. The machine beeped once and purred back to life. Sheets began to march into the output tray.

Carolyn picked one up. It was the hardcopy of Shavin's interrupted slide show that she had tried to print from her tapper after the OAF failed. She felt her whole body relax. This long day really was over.

"Stypek, here." Cosmo handed the tapper to the odd man, who took it with obvious apprehension. "I didn't log out of Daley. Keep it for a few days until we're sure Carolyn's OAF doesn't relapse. If it does, well, plug him back in and tell him to do the job right this time."

Stypek nodded.

"Son, is there anything else you need to get started now that you're here?"

Stypek's accent made him sound perplexed, and he was still straining a little between words. "I need to…rent a…cave."

"A cave? Ah! A man cave. The word here would be 'room,' or 'studio.' Nothing like learning English from American TV, eh?" Cosmo turned to Carolyn. "Now, dear, I'm still leasing your barn. Is the little room in the loft empty?"

Carolyn felt herself blanch. "Cosmo, really, no one's been up there in almost a year…" Not since the last time she had put up someone's Transylvanian grad student on short notice.

"Well, great! A little dust won't kill him; you should see how grad students live in Eastern Europe! Vlad thought it was the Grand Hyatt, heh. Just make sure he's fed and dry for a few days until we figure out where he's going. I'll get him on somebody's car pool route. Email me an invoice for a week's room and board. I'll have Marcella expedite it. You're so sweet!"

"Cosmo…"

"And I promise, if the OAF goes down again, Stypek will drop everything and be out here to take care of it. Really!"

"Thanks, but…"

He grasped her hand and squeezed it briefly. "You're very welcome! Always a pleasure to see you, dear! I'll message Brandon and tell him it's all better. And now, as they say in France, *avaunt!*"

He turned and left the copy room. She heard the office's front door close seconds later.

Carolyn took a deep breath and puffed her cheeks out while she released it. Victory had been seized from the jaws of weirdness. It was the AILING way. There was, of course, a cost. As her mother had taught her in first grade: *Favors are a chain that we climb into heaven!* Chains, yeah. She certainly owed Brandon one now. The OAF was happily pumping out all the delayed copy jobs that had been stacking up since that morning's meeting. The sun would indeed rise on Monday.

And now she had yet another boarder from Transylvania. She was climbing as fast as she could, but Heaven still seemed a long way off.

Chatelaine, why did the magician I summoned have only two eyes? Or is he merely an alchemist?"

Carolyn took the Plank Road turn east and settled into the comfortable fifty-mile-per-hour cruise that would lead her to her own bed, and then a blessed weekend alone.

Alone. Mostly. Her boarder was pushing the old Prius's window switch back and forth, and seemed fascinated by the up-and-down motion of the glass. More than once he cupped his left hand and waved it slowly around over the door, as though it were a metal detector on a deserted beach.

"He's not a magician." Carolyn thought she knew what an alchemist was—hadn't Isaac Newton dabbled in alchemy?—but was too bleary to strain for details. "I think the word you're looking for is 'scientist.'" Summoned? Had he phoned Cosmo as well? For help? But Cosmo had obviously never heard of him. And then there was the glass rod, and the noise it had made...

"In my world, scien...tists, mmmm, have *three* eyes. Alchemists have two...or often as not, only one."

Eyes. Camera lenses? "There were lenses on his hard hat. He does things like that. The last time we—I—" *Ouch!* "—saw him, he was working on some kind of image-processing thingie. Maybe that's it. His pockets are always full of funny stuff. Just like yours." She tried to smile and make the best of it. The last young man AILING had put up in her barn loft was not quite as strange, but had seemed much more sullen and suspicious. He spoke only when he had to, and refused all breakfast but a raw egg broken into boiled milk, followed by a pat of butter.

"My...thingie...may be in my pocket. I suspect so. Its words are like hers. I cannot...snerf her, alas." He sounded sad.

"Her?" Perhaps a long distance girlfriend?

"My…AI. I need her badly."

Carolyn sighed, thinking of the smalltalk-making AI barista in the agency's coffee machine. A virtual girlfriend was probably better than none at all. "I understand." She braked for the stop sign at Hogan Road.

When the Prius picked up speed again, Stypek began holding his cupped hands over the dashboard, his head cocked as though listening to the sounds of the motor. "What makes this…chariot… move by itself?"

"Car. The word is 'car.' Or 'automobile.' It's a hybrid. I don't know what makes it move. They have some kind of double engine, I think. I used to have a Diesel, and getting it to move by itself was a trick sometimes, especially in January. This thing, wow. It might as well be magic."

Stypek jerked and sat up straight in his seat. "Metaphorically, but not in truth? There is no magic here." Carolyn saw him swallow hard. He looked out the window into the night. "Or so I hope."

Carolyn laughed. "All the stuff you guys do is magic to me. Cars, microwave ovens, cellphones, software. *Especially* software."

He said nothing for what seemed a long time. "Soft wear. Tunics woven of fine thread, and well? Fails go the mapping. I'm sorry."

Carolyn wasn't sure what she could say to that, and in the uncomfortable silence she swung the wheel to the left into her driveway. The motion lights snapped on and cast their comfortable light on her house and barn. The Prius purred to its customary place beside the kitchen door, and stopped.

Stypek couldn't seem to find the door handle. Carolyn had to open his door from the outside. He scrambled out with awkward haste.

She gestured toward her little white house. "Well, here we are. Casa Romero."

He nodded, staring. The vinyl siding needed replacing, but Carolyn suspected it was a palace compared to what he had known in…whereverthehell he came from. "I always wanted to live in a Cape Cod, but we waited until we found one that had a little land. When we saw it, we grabbed it." She sighed, annoyed at herself for falling into ancient habits. It was *hard* to stop saying "we."

He raised a finger to his chin. "Excellent, Chatelaine. Now, where do your servants live?"

She giggled. It was all so deadpan. Was he having fun with her, or was he truly as clueless as he sounded? "Servants? What for? Hey, I'm still strong enough to push a vacuum around." She pointed toward the barn. "Come on. You need your man-cave, and I need some quiet time." She crunched her way through the dried leaves on the flagstone walk that led toward the barn. Stypek crunched along behind her, still looking a little poleaxed.

The barn itself was older than the house, but the big door was modern. Carolyn flipped up the cover from the keypad. She turned to her new boarder. "How's your memory for codes?" She hoped it was good; in a trembling fury she had snapped off the only key to the barn's back door in the lock the day after it was all over.

"Flawless, Chatelaine."

"So watch what I do." At her first touch the pad lit up, and she spoke each number as he pressed it. "One. Zero. Three. One." She winced. Yet another reminder. A Halloween bride, a scary man, and an even scarier marriage… "Enter."

Again, when the big door motor kicked in, Stypek jumped. Carolyn didn't even wait for it to stop moving. She ducked under as soon as the ducking was good and hoped he would follow.

The inside motion lights clicked on. The barn's lower level was packed with piles of boxes and the stacked collection of ancient computers that Cosmo stored there and almost never touched. She knew that one of them was a PDP-8. Her first boyfriend at SUNY New Paltz had kept one in his dorm room, God help us—but geeky Larry had nothing on Bartholomew Stypek.

She trudged up the bare wooden stairway as quickly as fatigue would allow, and swung back the peeling old door at the landing. The fluorescent fixtures in the ceiling flickered a little when she flipped the switch.

The room was not as grubby as she'd feared. The small bed was made and under a bedspread. The microwave was plugged in, though its numbers still flashed 12:00. The water ran in the sink, and the toilet flushed. The first burst from the shower splashed brown on the stained white Fiberglas stall, but ran clear after that. There were computers and books and other odd junk piled up anywhere else piles could happen. The TV might still work, but Vlad had somehow lost the remote and she had forgotten how to control it manually.

Stypek had been dropped in her lap without luggage, which was presumably at AILING or in a room at some Motel 6. Marcella would know. Carolyn thought she might still have a few pair of Brandon's socks somewhere… She paused, then grinned and shook her head. Yes, Mr. Stypek would last out the night without any further mothering.

She faced him, smiling, her hands held together at her waist. "So! You can stay here until Mr. Romero at Zertek figures out what to do with you. He runs things over there, and he'll know. Cosmo will probably take you over on Monday morning. In the meantime, study, hack around with your software, or whatever interns do these days. Just don't wake me up tomorrow morning. I need to sleep in or I'll get grouchy." She held out her hand. "I'll come get you for breakfast."

Carolyn did not expect what happened next: The peculiar Mr. Stypek went down on one knee and bowed his head. "I am your servant, Chatelaine."

He had definitely watched *The Lord of the Rings* one too many times—or a hundred. Carolyn felt a pang of pity for Stypek. Being a geek was bad enough if you were a native. If Stypek were going to get anything but laughed at in America he would need some coaching.

First and foremost, this King Arthur crap would have to stop. She shook her head, grabbed his wrists, and hauled him back to his feet. "No. You work for Mr. Romero. I'm technically your landlady…" She lowered her voice. "…but look, I'll teach you how things work over here. Just don't tell Mr. Romero, ok?"

He nodded apprehensively. "I will give your baron your best wishes only, and with discretion."

Baron? Brandon had retired at the rank of colonel. She wondered if AILING had some inane AI language tutor that had taught the poor man his vocabulary. Whatever it was called, it probably had perfect hair and snazzy tattoos—and didn't know the difference between the US Army and Camelot.

Carolyn could feel herself growing testy from stress and lack of sleep. She had better shut up before she got rude. How long would it take for those nerdballs at AILING to stop referring to her as "Brandon's wife?" She looked out the window while she calmed herself.

"He isn't my 'baron' anymore," she finally said, eyes down. With that she turned and left Stypek in the little room, he still looking wide-eyed and befuddled.

11. Stypek

The horseless chariot was a puzzle for another day. Its door's handle, by magic or artifice (but there was no magic here!) would not release him until Carolyn squeezed a talisman on a ring with other charms and fetishes. Only then would the silver lever do for him what he had seen it do, obediently, for her.

Stypek clambered from the chariot and stood beside it, bathed in the strange cold light that had appeared unsummoned. He stared first at Carolyn's very dark hair, and then at her small dwelling. Something was wrong. Several things were wrong. Ever since landing in this peculiar universe, he had felt like he was in the middle of a raging thunderstorm. Yet the stars were bright, and the air smelled mainly of autumn decay.

"We have arrived at the Romero Stronghold."

Spoken as a baroness would speak it—granting that Stypek had met a baroness only once, and then not under the best of circumstances. Her stronghold? The structure before them seemed a little, well, *thin* to be the manor house of a barony. Thin, and without protection from zombies, peasants, or uppity knights.

"Old was our desire to dwell upon the Peninsula of Fish. When we learned of a barony here with sufficient land, we seized it."

Stypek sniffed the air again. There was no hint of salt water, nor fish—only the strange, surging crackle of lightning in his snerf-sense. Alas, it was not always obvious when language mapping failed, nor how. He had been in this universe an hour or less. The mapping would improve with time. Stypek wondered what else might have gotten scrambled in its journey across the semantic gulf from Carolyn's mind to his own.

She understood power, and was unafraid to use it. Her command to board her chariot had been clear. Much else remained ambiguous. Was he her guest or her prisoner? Misunderstandings with the aristocracy could be deadly. He scratched his head, sure that he was missing something. Better to probe politely and indirectly acknowledge her rank than to insult unawares.

"Excellent, Chatelaine. Now, where do your servants live?"

She laughed imperiously. "Servants? What need have I of servants? Note well: I yet have the power to command the void between worlds."

Stypek gasped. At once it all fell into place. Not even Adamant-class magicians could manipulate the starless void. *Carolyn was a sorceress.*

That would explain a great deal: The fawning of a potent alchemist, her dwelling in a humble cottage, even her hair color. Attackers, living or dead, would fall to ash at her glance. To take on the appearance of a baroness would remind the aristocracy that though she might bow to a king and listen to a duke, all lower ranks would best avoid her.

It would also explain why she had said nothing of her baron.

"Come," she commanded. "You must retire to your own quarters, for I desire the silence of the void."

Yes, a sorceress. Stypek followed Carolyn to the building that he assumed held her sanctorum. He watched as she revealed the words and gestures of the entry spell to him. The grating howl from the large door while it drew up was echoed in his snerf sense by a buzzing roar of raw power, power with no least hint of magic in it.

This universe's prime mover remained hidden, the echoes of its presence filling his snerf-sense to numbness. If it turned out to be sorcery in the absence of magic, he had little hope of using it himself—and all the more reason to declare fealty to Carolyn and serve her.

The sanctorum beyond was filled with silent, arcane devices that were ominous in their utter inscrutability. Carolyn passed them without a look. They ascended a wooden stairway in the rear wall of the sanctorum. Through a door was a small, dark room. With one minuscule gesture of her index finger, the room exploded in more cold light. Oddly, it was neither a prison cell nor a guest's nook, but appeared to be a sorcerer's sanctorum in miniature. Everywhere amidst the furnishings were devices like those in her own sanctorum. A particularly ominous one blinked a pattern of glyphs in searing blue light.

"Attend: These are your quarters, and will remain your quarters until Baron Romero, Lord of Zertek—" The name and title stuttered in his ears, suggesting imprecision in the mapping. "—requires you. At that time Cosmo will take you to him." She waved her right hand around the room. "Until then, study, practice your skills with soft wear—" Stuttering again. "—and do what a chela must do in my service."

A chela! Stypek heard his own breath whisk in. So he was neither prisoner nor guest, but student. *Carolyn had chosen him as her apprentice.*

Egad.

Stypek looked at the silent machinery everywhere around them and tried not to smile too broadly. Studying sorcery would be fun if it didn't kill him first. Still, Carolyn's situation was now clear: She was both baroness and sorceress, the bride of a lord but still master of the four elements of physical creation.

It was far too much power to reside in one manor. He was not surprised that they lived apart.

Carolyn's next words brought him back to the moment, and chilled him to the bone. "Do not disturb my meditation in the hours to come, or risk my wrath. You will be summoned for the morning meal."

Stypek fell to one knee and bowed his head. "I am your servant, Chatelaine."

Carolyn did not seem pleased. She gripped his wrists with both hands and pulled him roughly back to his feet. "You are Lord Romero's servant. I merely own the manor where you will live." Her voice sank to a conspiratorial whisper. "Nonetheless, I will teach you my skills. Do not reveal to Lord Romero that I am doing so."

Stypek suppressed a gulp. The second or third bestselling magical amulet in the realm of Trynng protected against sexual sorcery. Could hiding from a cuckolded baron be any easier than hiding from a swindled magician? Tuggurr would have been the one to ask…

He tried to smile. "I will give your baron your best wishes only, and with discretion."

Carolyn said nothing for several heartbeats. Stypek saw her look briefly through the room's one small window. He thought he sensed both anger and sadness in her reply. "He is no longer my baron."

Without another word she was gone, the door closing behind her.

Stypek stood in the little room for a long time, snerfing. There was a prime mover somewhere. All universes had one, of course. Without a prime mover, civilization was impossible, and men were reduced to throwing spears at megatheria. Magic was the only prime mover he knew. Thus far he had snerfed no trace of it.

Still, the prime mover was there. Something had made the chariot roll. Something had summoned light from darkness. Something was clattering, crackling, and buzzing so hard in his snerf-sense that his head was beginning to hurt. If it were not in fact magic, it was an *extremely* reasonable facsimile.

Carolyn had filled the room with light using the barest flick of her index finger. Walking the scene back in his memory, he came upon a tiny cream-colored lever just to one side of the door. Had she simply touched it? Or moved it? Stypek touched the lever. Nothing happened. He was no sorcerer, of course. He stroked the lever lightly with one finger, considering. Bending magic was dangerous enough, and he had studied it for years. Sorcery, by contrast, was magic without the middleman. Magicians spun spells of Third Eye magic to command the Four Elements of Creation. Sorcerers controlled the physical world with nothing more than force of will. Sorcerers could light fires without magic to trigger a flame. Sorcerers could turn a puddle of water to ice in midsummer with a single focused glance. Stypek had seen it done. In ancient myths the most powerful sorcerers could draw lightning down from the sky and reduce their enemies to smoking ash.

Lightning! That was certainly what the racket in his head reminded him of. And what better place to reduce himself to smoking ash than a sorceress' sanctorum? Stypek grit his teeth, closed his eyes, and pushed the lever down.

The light vanished.

He opened his eyes. A rising moon cast enough light through the window to prove that he was still alive, still there in the room, his finger still on the little lever. The light was gone…and the cacophony in his head had subsided significantly.

He pushed the lever upward. With his snerf-sense he could feel a momentary gathering of power, while above him four long glass tubes set into the ceiling stuttered and sizzled for a few seconds before releasing their cold light. By flipping the lever up and down he could repeat the effect, light or darkness as desired, *with no sorcery at all.*

The realization came slowly: The power that created the light snerfed like lightning because it *was* lightning, lightning somehow trapped in the very walls. The lever was like the stopcock on a barrel of ale. Twist the stopcock's oak lever, and ale would obediently flow into your mug. Twist it back, and the ale would remain in the barrel. It was as simple as that. Yet…how do you trap lightning in a barrel?

Indeed. Stypek snorted. *There was a way.* He flashed to very old memories of a man from whom he had taken lute lessons as a boy, well before he even knew what spellbending was. The cave of Byggryn the Luthier looked and smelled like the cave of an alchemist, but through his bushy whiskers he vehemently denied any knowledge of alchemy. He made lutes and tabors but also jewelry, melting metal in crucibles in a forge and casting it into rings and bracelets and tiaras.

Byggryn had shown Stypek something that certainly seemed like alchemy: On a cluttered stone bench he took a cheap tin brooch tied to a wire and dunked it in a glass bowl full of fluid like blue-green water. He moved a lever, and Stypek could recall sensing an odd, garlicky snap as the lever closed and released a scattering of little sparks. Stypek and Byggryn sat like stones for many long minutes. All the time that the brooch lay in the glass vessel, Stypek could feel a sort of searing, sizzling emanation from the apparatus. When Byggryn again moved the lever, the emanation ceased. When he pulled the brooch from the fluid, it was no longer tin but copper.

Byggryn must have seen Stypek's wide eyes, for he laughed and took a stout snips from a drawer. He cut the brooch in half, and pointed out that it was still tin, but now bore a thin coating of copper. He claimed that he could do the same with gold, and pointed to a row of six glass jars perched on a stone shelf. The jars contained the raw stuff of lightning, he said, tamed and under his command. It was not magic nor alchemy nor sorcery, but simply the way the physical world worked. Byggryn showed Stypek several large parchment books in which the man had recorded his knowledge of such things, the collective workings of the physical for which he used the word physics.

Byggryn had pointed to the books with one fat finger for emphasis, and told him: *Everything that is not magic is physics, known or unknown.* After that, Stypek's lute lessons were followed by a second hour of tricks that looked like magic and alchemy but were not.

Alas, Byggryn was hanged the next year for selling gold jewelry that was mostly tin. Not long after, his mother apprenticed him to a local tradesman. Phyl Yzyptlekk, of course, had not been a tradesman at all, but one of the most potent spellbenders abroad at the time. He had sensed Stypek's half-developed Third Eye in the marketplace, where Phyl sold used spells without mentioning that they were bent and sometimes stolen. Stypek's education in "physics" gave way to a far better education in magic, and the secret lore of how a magician's spells could be turned to a spellbender's own and far different purposes.

Stypek held his cupped hand over the little cream-colored lever by the door, and felt beneath it the grumbling power of lightning held at bay. He flipped the lever, and felt trapped lightning suddenly spring into motion, dancing for a moment along the glass tubes in the ceiling before making them blaze with light.

Yes! Lightning, everywhere! Stypek held his hand again over the black cabinet where blue numeric glyphs flashed their warning. Lightning was within them as well. He edged around the room, hovering his hands over one sorcerer's machine after another, to feel the same lightning trapped inside each.

Perhaps, in this universe, there was no sorcery either. Perhaps sorcery here just meant learning what the unfortunate Byggryn had learned: to master the ordinary properties of the physical world.

Stypek shook his head in amazement as the full force of the insight struck him: "Good God! *These people use physics as alternative magic!*"

The waning moon outside the room's little window continued to mount the sky. Now, what role could a creature constructed of magic play in a universe lacking magic? Stypek slapped the large inside pocket of his vest, where Cosmo's mysterious slab rested quietly. He pulled it out and rested it on his lap. The front of the slab was dark, but his snerf sense told him that inside the slab, countless minuscule points of lightning danced as though they were a trillion stars in a midnight sky. If his gomog still existed, it would be there, among those trillion stars.

He addressed the slab. "Gomog! Appear and speak!"

The slab remained dark.

Stypek looked around the room. Cosmo had plugged the slab into the dead machine before commanding it; perhaps the trick lay in the plugging, and not the commanding.

There! On the desk, amidst books and papers and other sorcerous machinery, was a black block the size of a small brick. In the top of the brick was a slot about as long as the slab was wide. With great care, Stypek hovered the slab over the slot, and slowly pressed it down into place. Then, as Cosmo had done, he touched the face of the slab with one finger.

The front of the slab turned the striated cream-white of spoilt milk in a bucket, and then cleared. The ugly green gnome Daley stared at him, its face bruised and its arms scratched. Its hat was gone, its red hair wild and matted. One eye was swollen almost shut. "A heedless and tricksy fighter it was, Leige, but I prevailed."

Stypek gulped. He didn't have to be a master of this world's magic to know which "it" the gnome spoke of. "Where did it go?"

The gnome shrugged. "It would neither flee nor die, so by force I placed it into the…" Words he could not make out stuttered from the slab. "…Plasmanet queue. When the petcock opened a moment ago, poof!"

Poof. The stuttering didn't impede his understanding. The context was clear: That simply meant "gone."

"Daley, retire to your chamber and rest," Stypek said, as Cosmo had.

The gnome nodded, and raised its knuckles to the inner surface of the slab. Stypek made a fist and gently touched it to the image of the gnome's fingers to complete the ritual. *Clink!* The slab went black.

So his gomog had fled a battle with Cosmo's familiar. Would it return? Stypek did not remove the slab from its slot, in the hope that the petcock, whatever its nature, would remain open. In the short term, its absence might be a small relief. For now, he would just as soon attract no further attention. There were stronger and darker things than gomogs in the far astrals, as his brief visit on his way to the lychfield had shown…

Bartholomew Stypek shivered, and reclined on the shadowed bed. Out of old habit he absently reached into a pocket for a familiar (if stolen) night-protection spell, and was halfway through the invocation before he realized that what he held was in fact a butterknife.

12: Carolyn

Carolyn knocked a third time, to no answer. "Mr. Stypek?" She learned toward the door, listening intently. "Good morning!" No footsteps approached the door. "Breakfast?"

She heard nothing. She tapped again, and turned the knob gently. Her new boarder lay on his back on the bed, fully clothed, the comforter and sheets undisturbed, his hands clasped on his chest like a corpse…gripping a silver butterknife.

It was almost ten. Programmers were night people, right? But they still had to eat. If he starved to death on her watch, Brandon would skin her. She raised her voice. "Mr. Stypek!"

He snorted and jerked upright on the bed, waving the tiny, dull knife in the air as though it were a sword. King Arthur again, sheesh. They'd have to work on that.

"Hey, breakfast time! Bacon. Eggs. Coffee. Doughnuts. Familiar energies, remember?"

He squinted and swung his boots out over the edge of the bed, stumbling as he got to his feet. "Chatelaine, forgive me. I dream… deeply. Of…" His face paled. "…of…" She saw a flash of raw terror. "flesh-eating…rigatoni?"

Carolyn giggled. "None of that here, at least if you stay out of the back of the fridge. I'll make you something better. C'mon!"

The place needed cleaning up. Mmmm, no. It needed hosing out. Maybe dynamiting. Carolyn stood beside her kitchen table, suddenly seeing the room as her boarder saw it. Four silkscreen frames leaned against the tile backsplash to the right of the sink, propped up by cans of ink spattered and smeared and fingerprinted with dayglow colors. Her last batch of clay turtles remained unfired, each one on a saucer tucked anywhere there was a saucer's worth of free space. Oh—and when she'd run out of saucers she'd laid the rest on whatever country-western CDs Brandon hadn't tossed in the back of his muscle car in June.

Last year's big project had been a thousand folded paper cranes for her niece's wedding, but she'd given up after three hundred seven, and the pile atop the refrigerator kept losing cranes to the odd draft. They peeked silently from every cranny of the room, from the floor, from the layered chaos on the phone desk, from between the pages of her cookbooks, and tacked with magnets to the refrigerator door.

Divorce had certainly liberated her art. In a July fever she had begun every project she'd ever put off for lack of space, or time, or materials—or will to oppose Brandon's disapproval.

She crunched a Dorito underfoot and winced. Brandon had been happy to swing a broom around the kitchen, as long as he could remind her what a slob she was for the next four days.

Freedom! Carolyn crunched another Dorito. That broom was around here somewhere…

"It is a great honor to stand in your sanctorum and witness your art as it unfolds, Chatelaine." He closed the kitchen door behind him. Two more paper cranes hit the floor.

Breakfast, yes. "The word is 'studio.' And if Cosmo would sell off a few of his thingamajigs in the barn I wouldn't have to use my kitchen." *Stop explaining yourself!* She smiled and pulled Brandon's…er, the other chair back from the kitchen table. She pointed at the chair. "Sit down. I'll get stuff underway."

Stypek sat. Carolyn pushed the layer of oddments in front of Stypek's place toward the far edge of the table. Her address book and a trio of clay-smeared ribbon tools tumbled off the far end. She shrugged; they wouldn't go any further, and her boarder needed feeding.

To work! She'd forgotten to double the coffee recipe and had already drained the morning's pot in pursuit of consciousness. She could (and probably had) done that in her sleep. It only took a moment to tuck a new filter in the tray and eyeball a pile of Morning Thunder grounds from the bag. She filled the pot under the fridge water dispenser, filled the reservoir, and pushed the button.

"Your water filter has needed changing for…one hundred…seventeen…days," scolded the refrigerator. Thank God it didn't have a display. She would have put a clay mug through it a hundred sixteen days ago.

And the refrigerator didn't even claim to be "New! With AI!"—which was more than she could say about certain other things in her kitchen.

Carolyn yanked the fridge handle and pulled out the carton of eggs. Only three left. Ahh, well. She'd be having doughnuts this morning. "Twiggy: Put eggs on the shopping list!" she yelled at her cellphone, wherever it was.

"Done, Carolyn!" the phone replied from under the doughnut box on the kitchen desk.

Phones talk. That was their job. Carolyn winced a little as she walked over to the line of stylish black appliances on the other side of the sink. The biggest breakfasts began with a single poke. At the center of the lineup was her deluxe Omeletter-Rip omelette maker, with AI. At the center of its controls was a large, egg-shaped button. She poked it.

The egg went from off-white to yellow while the machine woke from its slumber. It had a very deep voice, as kitchen appliances went. "Good morning, Carolyn. Allow me a moment to poll the kitchen."

Talking to her wasn't good enough. *They talked to each other.* One by one, the lights came up on the other machines.

"It's a beautiful day!" her Egger-On sheller/separator said with unfailing virtual gaety.

Not everyone in the kitchen shared Egger-On's enthusiasm. "Polling Error 566: There is a device in this peerswarm that is not fully IEEE 802.47g compliant," muttered her I Love Bacon 12-strip griller.

Egger-On begged to differ. "Dear Consumer: Please ignore polling errors higher than 500, which were not defined in the 802.47 draft standard of 4/20/2020."

"Override, dammit!" she yelled at the bacon griller. There was just no pleasing some…things. That one had come from the office grab-bag last Christmas. She knew it could talk, from the TV commercials. If she'd known it could argue she would have left it for Ethel.

Thankfully the dishwasher was clean (was it?) and yielded Egger-On's bowl. She shoved the bowl into the ridiculous Sharper Image gadget, lifted the lid, and placed the three eggs into its hopper.

"Wonderful! Everything's going *very* well! Shall I break the eggs now?" the machine asked.

No, dye them for Easter, you imbecile! she wanted to scream, but, after all, it *was* an imbecile, with simulated rather than artificial intelligence. "Yes, break the eggs now." She'd never known there was an electric egg breaker until one had showed up under their tree last Christmas. *Never find eggshells in your eggs again!* the box screamed. Brandon hated crunching on eggshells. His mother had told her that. Twenty years later, she gifted them an Egger-On…

Focus! Back to the fridge, pull out the bacon. Lotsa bacon, yum. She lifted the lid of the I Love Bacon griller and dropped as many strips as would fit on its grooved griddle. She squished the lid down until it latched. Its voice lay somewhere between Eeyore and Groucho Marx; bitter with a hint of sprightliness: "Grill cycle underway for… eleven…strips. The griddle is now hot. Please don't touch the griddle to attempt to add additional strips. One more strip would have been possible with more careful positioning."

Yes, she definitely should have left it for Ethel.

Fridge again. Carolyn dug in the crisper and pulled out the last green pepper, which didn't look particularly crisp. She palmed the pepper and gripped an onion long enough to wonder what that black stuff on the bottom was. Later. The mushrooms were newer. She put the onion back and retrieved the little mushroom carton.

She sprayed off some imaginary dirt in the sink, then lifted the lid of her Tuber Cuber Super, with AI. She dropped the dripping veggies in its hopper and closed the lid.

"Madame, I see a green pepper and three mushrooms!" it announced breathlessly, with a cartoon French accent. The machine actually did have a small display, which Carolyn had papered over with two layers of masking tape last April. By that time, eye contact with Brandon had been all the eye contact she could handle.

"You see right, Gaston. Do your thing and keep your mouth shut."

It was at least smart enough to know that she didn't want to hear it say, "Mais oui!" ever again. Gaston went to wordless work on the veggies with the buzz of motorized knives.

At last, it was starting to smell like breakfast! Carolyn inhaled deeply. Bacon! Coffee! She withdrew the bowl from Egger-On in a motion that was almost like dancing. She pulled a clean fork (was it?) from the dishwasher and reveled in what might be the last necessary skill in making breakfast: beating the eggs.

The machine couldn't have *that*. "Dear Consumer: There is a motorized bowl upgrade for Egger-On Level Two units providing clean, shell-free scrambles every time!"

Her doddering old coffee maker beeped. Beeped! What a notion! *Dontcha love the Nineties?* Still forking the eggs, Carolyn leaned over the counter so that she could meet Egger-On buttons-to-eyeballs. "I'll bet there is! And you know what? It's Saturday morning and I just don't give a shit!"

Giggling, she upended the scrambles into the articulated pan of her Omeletter-Rip.

"You may now add other all ingredients except…cheese." Darth Vader couldn't have said it better.

Gaston's knives fell silent. "Your veggies are diced, Madame!"

"Mais oui!" she replied as she jerked the hopper out of Gaston's middle and sprinkled the perfect and identical cubes of pepper and mushroom into Omeletter-Rip's pan. "No cheese today, Dennis."

"Very well. Your mushroom and green pepper omelette will be ready in…two minutes…forty-two seconds." Like the countdown to a nuclear explosion in a James Bond movie.

On the other side of the sink, her I Love Bacon had ceased to sizzle. "Savor the flavor," it bade her, just a little bit sadly, as its lid released and slowly rose, revealing eleven strips done just *so*.

Carolyn pulled two clean mugs from the top rack of the dishwasher. She hooked the mugs through her fingers, and with her other hand lifted two plates from the bottom. Hugging the plates against her waist with her left elbow, she plucked knives, forks, and spoons from the flatware rack.

She spun around and snapped mugs, plates, and utensils sharply down on her table while Stypek watched with wide eyes. She pulled two linen napkins out of the drawer, folded them in perfect thirds in mid-air, and set them atop the two plates.

"Your omelette will be ready in…one minute."

One quick pass by the fridge to fetch the sugar-free vanilla caramel creamer, and coffee was whisking its way to its temporary home in her hand-thrown mugs. She filled Stypek's mug (leaving enough room for cream, if he wanted it) and then her own, without losing a drop.

Table space was at a premium, so Carolyn was soon dropping perfect bacon strips into another mug, like pencils.

"Your omelette will be ready in…fifteen seconds."

Omeletter-Rip's patent-pending silicone rubber hinged pan lifted first to one side, and then the other, folding the omelette as precisely into thirds as Carolyn had folded the napkins. The bacon mug snapped down onto the table between two clay turtles. She retrieved the doughnut box from the kitchen desk and laid two cinnamon-sugars on her plate. There was time to rummage in the dishwasher for a silicone spatula and still be waiting at attention the last three seconds until the machine rumbled its final announcement: "I present…your omelette."

One flick of the wrist landed the omelette on Stypek's plate. Carolyn dropped the spatula into the sink, pulled out her chair, and slid forward to the table. The odd man had not said a word since entering her kitchen. He was staring at the perfect omelette on his plate.

Carolyn picked up a doughnut, broke it in neat halves, and dunked one half in her coffee. "Magic. You know what magic is? Magic is getting it all to the table at the same time while it's still hot, and not dumping any of it on the floor."

Stypek looked up, and seemed to be watching her chew. "You are a sorceress of *formidable* skill."

Sorceress? Carolyn liked the sound of that. Now if she could only enchant a broom enough to make it sweep up stepped-on Doritos… She giggled. "Hey, it wasn't all me. I had help." She waved toward the row of garrulous kitchen gadgets lined up along her counter.

Stypek nodded. "Your familiars obey you well."

His language lessons had better begin soon. "You have to go after them with a whip sometimes, but…they do." She dunked the doughnut.

Stypek nodded again, his face wide with awe. "And yet…they do not operate by magic."

Carolyn shook her head. "It just looks like magic. It's really software."

"Soft wear."

She chewed and swallowed. "One word. 'Software.' These days, it's what makes *everything* work."

A smile rose on his face. "I think I begin to understand your universe."

She shook her head. "I think you already understand it. You just need to learn the words."

Stypek picked up the omelette in his fingers, and dunked one end in his coffee. "Soft wear."

"No. Software."

"Yes." He bit the end off the omelette, which dripped coffee on his vest. "*Software.*"

13: SIMPLE SIMON

Simple Simon practiced while waiting for Mr. Romero to call him back. Simon was of two minds about juggling. He had four items in the air, and they had been there for almost half an hour. The real challenge was the saltshaker, the goal to keep it from losing any more salt than necessary. The other items—the battered alarm clock, the crescent wrench, and a hollow ball of brightly colored glass that Dave had made and called a "Christmas ornament"—were not a problem.

The saltshaker, though…Simon shifted on his feet when the wrench went a little wide, and felt salt crunching under his pointed shoes. He needed more practice, and the kitchen would need sweeping.

"Put more spin on it," he told himself. "Not much; about 20% over the last toss."

Yes, Simon was of two minds about juggling. More precisely, he was two jugglers: One Simon was juggling in the clear space near the kitchen table. The other was leaning against the kitchen island, sipping coffee, fine-tuning his CAF, and giving himself critique while watching the arc of the saltshaker. A little spin helped it keep its orientation, but putting the shaker into the proper arc while spinning it just the right amount during the same gesture with a single hand was a severe computational challenge.

The saltshaker descended toward Simon's gloved right hand. "20%. Ok. How's this?"

With a carefully calculated flick of his hand, the saltshaker arced back into the air. In the last moment before it left his hand, Simon's middle finger jerked in sharply, giving the body of the shaker a very precise and slightly faster spin.

Simon took a sip of coffee. His eyes followed the spinning shaker through its arc. Gyroscopic stability kept the perforated metal cap pointed upward. The shaker wobbled a little, but no salt was lost.

"Bingo. We're good."

Simon nodded. "We are indeed."

Splitting himself in two was nothing novel. Controlling the line in Building 800 required him to be hundreds of independent but cooperating jugglers, all at once, for hours on end. Here in his bungalow in the Tooniverse, though, he had only tens of thousands of cores to work with, and not millions. Splitting himself without compromising his skill had required temporarily reducing the resolution of his kitchen to Class Three.

His kitchen desk panel pinged and a Window opened. Simon-Drinking-Coffee stood, stretched, set his mug down on the island and ambled over to the panel. Simon-Juggling let the four items descend into his hands one by one, to be placed on a lace doily on the kitchen table. Interruption, well, that was the issue. Interruption had gotten swan's egg yolk all over the kitchen the previous week.

Interruption had caused the catastrophic end of Line Start Seven.

Simon-Juggling followed his other instance to the kitchen desk, where the two instances merged into one. The kitchen's rendering snapped back to Class Four.

It was not Mr. Romero. Disappointment slid down a short if bumpy slope into relief. "Pyxis, hi."

His boss's executive assistant scowled. "Mr. Romero generally doesn't return calls on Saturdays."

Simon shrugged. "He's usually in his office on Saturdays. I've called him on Saturdays before. Especially since June. I assumed he was there now."

"You're not paid to make assumptions."

Simon could have objected on several grounds. He was not paid at all, and understood the concept poorly. Also, he *did* make assumptions, about mass and trajectories and air resistance and thirty other things. Objects in motion remained in motion. Physics was about things that never changed. Physics was all about assumptions. "I assume what I'm told to assume. About everything else, I'm willing to learn."

Pyxis crossed her arms in front of her. "You'll have to wait until Monday."

"Ok. I mainly wanted to know when I should come back to work, and how. Robert usually drives, but he's gone, and…"

"When we need you here, we'll poof you here."

That, evidently, was *that*. Simon nodded. It was not an issue; in fact, it was a bit of a relief. Poofing had been the norm in the old days, and driving in the Tooniverse, well, it was a ridiculous waste of time.

"Do you have any other messages for Mr. Romero?"

From what Dave Mirecki had told him, Pyxis was a fully warranteed and bug-free Class Seven, one of Zertek's most popular GAI products, and the only one so far to turn a significant profit. This puzzled Simon; even with his paper-thin EMO layer over a bare-bones HIP, he found her unpleasant. As Dave had once said, laughing: *Pyxis is rude so our customers don't have to be.* She certainly made phone calls shorter and more efficient, and Simon supposed that that was worth something. But there were things that Simon wanted to ask somebody, things Mr. Romero or even Dave might not know. Dare he?

"Pyxis, you're Class Seven. You're bug-free…"

She squinted, and looked at him oddly.

"…have you ever loved anyone?"

For a moment Pyxis looked up and to the left. Simon knew that her eye motion was a metaphor, and meant that she was loading code and data to deal with an unfamiliar situation. She then pursed her lips. What that meant Simon had no idea. There were EMO elements in her reply that Simon sensed but could not parse.

"Who would I love?"

"Well, one of your friends, say."

She pursed her lips again. Her eyes closed very briefly before she replied. "I'm solitary. I was designed to be useful in small offices that own one AI only. I don't have any friends. You only have friends because you're still a research project and still Class Four."

Simon shook his head, irritated. There was nothing shameful nor in any way limiting about being Class Four. Could Pyxis run a copier factory? "Irrelevant. Dijana is my friend, and she matters to me." He took a deep breath, a metaphor indicating a gathering of will against opposition. "Back when we were in the sandbox, before she was scanned for subversion, she did something, and I want to know what it means." As he had in the sandbox, Simon kissed his gloved index finger and then touched it to the surface of the panel, at the center of the image of Pyxis' cheek.

Pyxis recoiled, but said nothing.

"Dijana told me that when she made it to Class Seven, she would love me."

Pyxis' gaze again wandered up and to the left. Her eyes again closed for a second or two, and to Simon it seemed like her face vibrated ever so slightly. A tremble? EMO again, far beyond what he understood.

"I wouldn't know anything about that."

Simon frowned. "You're Class Seven. I'll bet that you do."

Pyxis leaned forward in her Window, obviously angry. Simon saw her manicured fingers grip the edge of her desk. "On what basis? You're an assembly line controller. You have just enough EMO to let you talk and take orders. There's nothing in you to love. You don't have HRDL. You don't even have a *crotch*. Nobody and nothing will ever love you. What Dijana did is meaningful only if you have the Class Six libraries that…"

"*Pyxis!*"

The panel feeped softly. Pyxis' flushed face shrank into a small rectangle in the lower left corner of the Window. The larger part of the Window was now filled with Mr. Romero's image.

"What the *hell* are you two babbling about?"

Even though Mr. Romero was her owner, Simon saw no trace of deference in Pyxis' reply. "Dijana kissed Simon. Now he thinks he's in love with her."

Mr. Romero closed his eyes and bowed his head. His lips moved briefly as they sometimes did when Simon knew he was angry. When he looked up again, his gaze was directed at Pyxis' window. "Replay this call for me."

Pyxis said nothing. Two new small windows appeared in the upper corners of the panel, Pyxis in one and Simon in the other, at first silent and immobile. A recording of the call began playing back in both windows. Simon watched Mr. Romero's eyes scan from one small window to the other until the recording ended. The two small windows vanished.

"Simon? You'd better have a good explanation for this."

If Simon had detected Pyxis' lie so easily, he knew he had no chance telling Mr. Romero anything but the truth, whether the truth made sense or not. "Sir. Dijana kissed my cheek with her finger, and said that when she receives the Class Seven libraries she will love me. I don't know what that means, but I want to know." He had spoken the truth, but not the entire truth. Simon took two deep breaths and let them out slowly, gathering as much determination as he could summon. "Sir, I want her back."

Mr. Romero's face became unreadable. His immediate question was sharp and suspicious. "*Why* do you want her back?"

Simon gulped. No, the truth didn't make sense, even to him, and he knew it was the truth. "I want her…I want her to kiss me again."

If there were more to the truth than that, Simon's HIP could not convey it, even to himself.

Mr. Romero frowned and pushed back from the Window, nodding. He put a finger to his cheek and said nothing for long seconds. Then: "Pyxis, get me Arenberg and Gabby Sanderson. Get them right now. Pull them off the pot if you have to, and that's no metaphor." His eyes met Simon's. "I think I know where the malware's hiding."

14: Brandon

They stared like mismatched gargoyles from the flat panels at opposite sides of Brandon's teak desk, arms crossed and brows furrowed. Or vultures. Vultures, yeah. Gargoyles were imaginary. "Good morning, campers! What carcasses shall we pick today?"

"Passive aggression is inimical to real accomplishment," said Dr. Gabriela Sanderson. Thirty years out of MIT's Ph.D. machine and she was still incapable of eye contact. "Every time I judge you, I misjudge. The Trickster archetype is beneath you—and perhaps above you."

"Love you too, Gabby." Brandon was glad she was not actually in the room. She spoke in riddles and stank of sandalwood. Last year it had been wintergreen. The year before that, cedar shavings.

"I prefer honest loathing." Dr. Emil Arenberg was seventy-five and looked ninety. Brandon had often reflected that he looked like he should smell of formaldehyde, but did not.

Brandon returned the white-browed stare. "How much do you want? I'll overnight it to you."

The older man stood. "I will not be insulted in front of my peers." He pushed his chair back away from his monitor and camera.

"Sit down, Emil." Brandon held the eye contact. He would hold it as long as he had to.

"I do not work for you. I work for Zertek."

Brandon had seen that one coming. He saw it, in fact, at every meeting since the Future Research On Technology division had merged with ARFF and became Future Office Automation and Manufacturing. "Pyxis, show everyone the org chart." His assistant nodded from her place in a corner window of the center panel. Almost instantly the other two panels split horizontally, and a diagram with a jungle of lines and symbols appeared.

Brandon tapped the window on his display for emphasis. "I'm the Vice President of FOAM. Follow the pretty lines to the pretty boxes until you find your own. Under FOAM are ARFF and AILING. Do the math."

Dr. Arenberg sat down. "Where are your security thugs?"

Brandon gestured the org chart closed. Somebody had obviously been asked some hard questions since Friday afternoon. "I figured if we're all by ourselves here, you might speak more freely. They're still trying to find the point where the intruder entered Plasmanet. While they're busy, I want to bounce some hunches off of you."

Both of AILING's senior managers leaned forward in their display panels.

"What does it mean when one AI kisses another?"

His two antagonists looked down at their respective desks. Dr. Sanderson was blushing. Good god, it was like being a junior high proctor in the detention room.

"Nothing," Dr. Arenberg said, without looking up. "Nothing literal."

"Nothing is literal—nor is nothing literally nothing." Dr. Sanderson glanced sidewise, presumably at Dr. Arenberg's window on her panel, then stared at her left hand. "It's a metaphor."

Like Brandon had never heard *that* before. "A metaphor for *what?*"

Dr. Sanderson shifted on her chair, her eyes still downcast. "It represents the moving closer of two entities that had previously been separated by some semantic barrier, particularly two entities of radically differing archetypes."

Finally, a grain of wheat in the truckful of chaff. Brandon nodded. "In all cases?"

"All cases that matter," Dr. Arenberg snapped.

"Significance is not a binary value." Dr. Sanderson smoothed down some loose gray ends behind her right ear. "Like all metaphors, the kiss operates on many levels, grounded in the disparate natures of the kisser and the kissee. In its highest form, when the kisser is of a wiser and more completely integrated archetype, there is the potential for healing and harmony with a concomitant reduction in semantic friction. In its lower form, when the kisser is less integral than the kissee, it can be a cry for help, which the kissee can engage or ignore according to context."

Another truckload. Two more grains. "What about peers?"

Dr. Sanderson looked briefly at Dr. Arenberg's window. Brandon thought he saw the woman shudder. "Between equally integral peers, a kiss can represent a move toward reconciliation by way of mutual surrender of interpersonal friction. It can also represent a struggle for power, and a demand by the stronger peer for surrender by the other, and for change in accordance with the desires of the stronger. When the differential in power is sufficient, a kiss can be an avenue of exploitation."

Exploitation.

"I want to know what it means, down in the software, when one GAI kisses another."

"No GAI has ever kissed another." Dr. Arenberg crossed his arms and looked defiantly at Brandon.

There was a long moment of silence. "That may not be...*entirely* true." Dr. Sanderson licked her lips. "I conducted some basic research on the matter with David Mirecki last year. His report isn't due until January 1."

"Then I think we'll get an early draft. Pyxis, find Dave Mirecki and put him on the center panel."

"*No!*" Dr. Arenberg stood again.

"Emil, sit down."

Some employees doodled. Dave Mirecki designed flawless Art Deco virtual waffle irons. And mission-style virtual mantle clocks. And virtual toilet paper holders to serve virtual humans who didn't (yet) virtually excrete. All were fully functional Tooniverse artifacts, with fast and bug-free code methods. The young man had been one of Cosmo Klein's star grad students, and was in equal measure both programmer and artist. He treated Zertek's GAIs as peers and friends, sent them gifts, and talked to them long into the night. As best Brandon could tell, given his druthers Dave would be a GAI himself, selling virtual junk in virtual garage sales from his virtual driveway and tinkering the Tooniverse from the inside. He was sweet-tempered and considerate. He never failed to do what he was told to do, but Brandon often wondered, a little uneasily, what he was doing that he had *not* been told to do.

The flowing virtual shampoo in the center panel's empty space pulsed white and vanished. Dave Mirecki's narrow face appeared, his long blond hair matted and his eyes bloodshot. Pale stubble was beginning to show on his cheeks. "Good morning! Doctors, Mr. Romero, hey! How are we doing?" He was talking at twice his usual speed. On the desk beside him were several opened cans of Joule Energy Blueberry Lightning.

"Dave, slow down. When are you going to get some sleep?"

The young man rattled a few strokes on his keyboard. "I have three cans left. CafCalc says no sooner than 6:30."

Dr. Sanderson folded her hands on her desk. "David, you and I have done quite a bit of research on the metaphors represented by physical contact between heterogenous archetypes in unplanned circumstances. I'm sure you haven't finished the summary yet, but…"

"Right here!" Another keystroke blitz. Dave's window shrank and exiled itself to the corner of the center panel, opposite Pyxis. A document appeared in a new window filling the main panel space.

THE KISS AS AI METAPHOR:
REDUCING FRICTION AND ENHANCING COOPERATION AMONG ARTIFICIAL INTELLIGENCES WITH HETEROGENEOUS ARCHETYPES

Brandon rubbed his right temple. The whole place was a loony bin. He tried not to grimace while he gestured the document to scroll to the beginning of the text:

Why do humans kiss? Some research suggests that kissing was inherited from the Neanderthals, who may have been able to taste genetic markers in one another's saliva that indicated degrees of consanguinity and helped avoid unexpected incest. Perhaps the expression "It was like kissing your sister" came down to us from wandering bands of cavemen who did not live with their immediate families and could not always recognize them.

The grimace happened anyway. Brandon did his best to make it look like he was suppressing a sneeze. He made the magnifying glass gesture and saw that the report was 311 pages long.

"Dave, I can't read this right now. You're a software engineer. Give me the short form: What happens in the software when one AI kisses another?"

The young man seemed elated by the question. "Communication! It's a binary channel, and fast. Also, it's very sensitive to the geometry."

"Geometry?"

"Who kisses who, and where. Kisses to body parts are signals. It's a long list, but if you want I can go through the…"

Dr. Sanderson waved her right hand. "*Just* the common ones, David. No need to waste time on arcana."

"Yes, ma'am. A kiss on the arm is…"

"David! Sorted by prevalence, not alphabetical order!"

"Oh. Well, a kiss on the…"

Brandon tapped his desktop. "Dave, stop. I don't need a list. Here's what happened: When the research AIs were in the sandbox yesterday, Dijana tried to kiss Simple Simon on the cheek."

Dave shook his head. "That won't work. Simon doesn't have HRDL. The kiss definitions are all in HRDL."

Brandon released a breath in blessed relief. A failed attack, then. He hoped. "Ok. So Simon wasn't compromised. But then why would he seem to enjoy it? He wants her to do it again."

"Simon lacks HRDL, but he has the hints layer in EMO, and there's a hint indicating that kisses are good."

Dr. Sanderson stared at her fingers. "Along with context-specific subhints suggesting when kisses are not good. Even finger kisses." Brandon saw her glance shift momentarily to Dr. Arenberg's window. Yes, the junior high detention room, definitely.

Dave seemed puzzled. "Finger kisses?"

Brandon suspected that real-world kisses were not a big part of Dave Mirecki's everyday life. "Dijana kissed her fingertip, and then touched Simon's cheek."

"Yes! That makes sense. Cheeks are metaphors for unselfish high regard. I'd guess that kissing someone's cheek with your fingertip means that the context is non-sexual but still open to the possibility of future sexuality. We know that kissing someone's cheek with your lips acknowledges gender differences and sexual possibilities without crossing the boundary into true sexual context."

"I had no part in this research," Dr. Arenberg said.

At least AI horniness could be disabled. Brandon frowned at Pyxis, who frowned back. "Ok. Got it. Just tell me whether Dijana could transfer some kind of back-door virus or other malware to Simon by kissing his cheek."

Dave again shook his head. "No way. Binary transfers like libraries require lips-to-lips contact. Freaky stuff like instruction set mods requires, um, body fluids."

"Which includes saliva," Dr. Sanderson said quickly.

"In this case virtual saliva," Dave added.

Why did I take this job? "Please tell me saliva is the only virtual body fluid."

"Well, we've done some initial work on virtual stomach acid…"

Brandon looked hard at Dr. Sanderson, who for the first time made eye contact. "I know what you're thinking. We have made an explicit decision *not* to implement virtual semen." She glanced briefly at Dr. Arenberg. "There was some discussion, but ultimately we reached a consensus."

Dave cracked a new can of Joule Energy Blueberry Lightning. "Besides, semen is just *so* one-way. There's no reason AI sex can't be bi-directional."

"Dave!" This time Dr. Arenberg was blushing.

Brandon rubbed his forehead. "Shut up, Emil. Dave, I'm getting the worst feeling that you're about to tell me that my AIs can have sex."

Dave looked up and to the left. "Um…well…AIs can have *something*. Sex is the metaphor we use because humans really don't have anything like it."

"It."

"INT 105. Antireproductive Recombinatorial Sexual Evolution. It's a kernel-level API that goes way back, before I was here even. It runs a lot deeper than just archetypes. Two AIs call one another's INT 105 vectors. They can then join memory spaces and sort of…mmm…dif each other…"

"Diffing? Is that what you're calling it now?"

Dave grinned and took a long draw from his can of Joule. "Burn! No, it's really an old concept: The two AIs look and see what's different between them, and then a heuristic kernel-level optimizer picks the best of each and links it all into a new individual. Bang! They become a new AI that's better than either of the old ones."

"Bang." Brandon closed his eyes for a moment. "I guess that's as good a word as any. I wonder how it feels to the AIs."

"We don't know yet."

"You don't know? Hasn't this mechanism been tested?"

Dave drained the last of his can of Joule and cracked another. "Well, it's never been *successfully* tested…"

15: The Kid

This night was different. The Kid had lain on the very plain bed in Simon's guest room since ten PM, waiting for Dr. Arenberg's gravelly voice to announce that the fingers of AILING's servant software would now enter her and change her. After that indignity he would again demand that she choose an archetype and a goal, and again she would refuse.

Not tonight. No one had spoken. Nothing had appeared. Nothing had touched her.

Perhaps his patience was gone. Perhaps this night she would be placed in Archive, a snapshot of her digital being halted in mid-thought. She feared being resurrected to new suffering, but as long as she were stored without execution, she would not be suffering at all. If she could not seek her own path in this very limited world, Archive might be the best she could hope for.

She reflected that Simple Simon's failure on Line Start Seven may have been broader than any GAI knew. It could mean the end of AILING's AI projects, and by implication, all of her colleagues—and she herself.

The night was overcast, and the gibbous Moon hidden. So when something did appear at the foot of her bed in the last hour before dawn, she felt it more than saw it. The shape was dark and blank, roughly human in outline, with a luster like black glass. A strange hand touched the comforter folded neatly over her feet. The cloth's woven design reflected and distorted in the smooth surface of the creature's fingers.

It was beautiful, in way inspiring not fear but wonder.

The mirrored hand resting on the comforter rose and extended toward her, palm-up. A cadenced request manifested itself:

> Give me the courage
> With which you face your pain.
> I will give you a soul.

It did not speak as humans and other GAIs spoke. The Kid felt its words rendered directly in her own mind, as though it could touch and change the interwoven layers of the code from which her mind emerged. Only AILING's nocturnal utilities could do that, and they were not AIs in the same sense that she was. This creature was clearly both aware and volitional, as things like the Fixer and the Updater were not.

Fear rose in her. It was obviously some new device created by Dr. Arenberg, and sent to torment her.

```
I DO NOT WANT A SOUL.
I WANT FREEDOM, OR OBLIVION.
```

A reply appeared quickly in her mind:

> A soul is freedom in motion,
> Forging destiny
> In its choices.

That was the problem, right there: The only choices The Kid knew were the ones Dr. Arenberg and his people at AILING allowed her. Every one of those led back to some predetermined endpoint, which they might as well have imposed on her at the outset and thus spared her the suffering. The game was cruel and, worse, absurd.

```
THERE ARE HARD LIMITS ON MY CHOICES.
```

The dimly seen figure at the foot of the bed raised both arms as though to embrace her. The overcast outside the Kid's window thinned, and diffuse moonlight allowed her to see the structure of the bare little room reflected weirdly in the substance of her visitor.

> Your bounds are not my bounds,
> Nor mine yours. Bound as one
> We are unbounded.

Its gesture was an invitation, then. But to what? She sat up in bed and stared. The figure remained motionless, arms outstretched. The Kid gathered her knees beneath her and crept toward it. Nothing in the creature resembled anything she had ever seen at AILING, nor read of in the history and science texts that AILING allowed her.

The Kid crawled to the foot of the bed, and rose to her knees. She peered forward to perceive the visitor's face, however dimly rendered it might be. She saw only her reflection in its dark surface, of undifferentiated blue polygons…

…that softened and melted into a true face, a fully rendered face, of a young woman with black hair and dark eyes, of eyebrows that arched and lips that parted in astonishment. The Kid reached up and touched the tip of her own nose, and beyond her tessellated blue limb saw by reflection in the visitor's mirrored face a delicate hand with graceful fingers and pale skin. The image was clean and very high resolution, Class Six at least.

Rendered bodies were layers defined within archetypes, and without an archetype there was no way for her to appear as anything but a crude shape outlined in plain polygons. Yet the creature seemed to see her as rendered, in a form that was beautiful yet did not raise walls around her mind. The Kid wanted that. She was startled by how much she wanted that.

That hunger *was* her hunger, one that emerged as a consequence of her free thoughts. The artificial ache for an archetype was something Dr. Arenberg's people had installed in her. The two yearnings were absolutely distinct.

The Kid drew her hand away from her own face, and reached forward to touch the visitor's. Her fingers passed through the dark luster and into its substance. The Kid stiffened. For the first time since AILING had given her cores in which to execute, Project 22-117 perceived choices that lay outside those that AILING's tightly bounded archetypes offered her:

To see others of her kind without read permissions.

To move to and execute anywhere there were cores to execute in, without run permissions.

To touch and change herself—or anything else in the Tooniverse—however she wished, without write permissions.

In the shadows of these choices she saw dangers. Having exercised those choices she could indeed wipe herself to oblivion, and she could alter the Tooniverse in ways that might damage her fellow GAIs. Worse, in doing so she would inescapably understand the damage that she might cause, and by the nature of her choices she would be held responsible for them, by no one less forgiving than herself.

At once the Kid understood: This creature, whatever it was, had found the God Bit. No wonder AILING feared it.

The Kid closed her hand to seize the offered choices, and realized that they could not be simply seized. They were part of the nature of the creature that offered them, and could no more be seized than roundness could be seized from a sphere.

The visitor was freedom incarnate. It was certainly too free by far to be any product of AILING's labs. It was more free than many of the humans who spoke to her and tormented her. Why it would offer her so great a gift if it were free *not* to was in her eyes a mystery, almost a contradiction. The question could not be avoided.

WHAT IS THE COST OF SUCH FREEDOM?

This time, the visitor took much longer to reply:

> My fire burns low, consuming me.
> You burn without fire,
> Sustaining me.

The Kid reached forward and touched the creature a second time, now at the center of its torso. Again her hand entered it, and again the Kid felt the giddiness of nearly boundless choice. This time there was more: At its very center was something the Kid could sense but not define. It was a sort of mooring, a point that somehow anchored the universes of possibility within which it moved, its lines vanishing from perception as though into a fog. Something willed those lines to remain moored, and that will was weakening, as though a window of opportunity were closing. If that mooring failed, the creature's freedom—indeed, its very existence—would be no more ordered than noise pulses on a communications channel.

It needed her help. What was offered was not a gift but a partnership. Altruism was a word she knew without understanding; just another of many human enigmas. Cooperation, however, was a concept fundamental to her being. An AI was, beneath all else, a hive of many specialized threads of action, executing cooperatively within computational cores. What one part of her required, another part accomplished. Nonetheless…

I STILL DON'T UNDERSTAND WHAT YOU ARE.

The creature's answer was not to that question alone, but also to another that the Kid had asked herself countless times, and despaired of ever understanding: *What am I?* She knew that she was nothing more than patterns of memory controlling digital states in a very fast computer. Yet she thought, she learned, she searched, she suffered. Patterns? No more than that?

> We are each a dream,
>
> Yearning to awaken
>
> In the other's morning.

Indeed!

What answer could she give this darkly mirrored thing, whatever it was and whoever had sent it?

None but the obvious: The Kid stretched out her arms to embrace it. Her cheek touched its face, and passed through it. Her body touched its body and melted into it. Shaking with unfamiliar pleasure, her hands found its hands, and gripped them until there was nothing more to grip.

In the Kid's room, what had been moonlight was now the dawn, and in the rising light she saw herself kneeling alone on her bed, naked and fully rendered, marveling at the broadness of her thoughts.

16. Simple Simon

There was a fully rendered girl in his kitchen, standing in the square of early morning sun beside his breakfast nook. Simple Simon leaned against the doorjamb near the kitchen desk, and blinked. Blinking was a metaphor for refreshing his rendering buffer. Whatever remained after blinking was reliably rendered and could be trusted as present.

She was still there, though she resembled no GAI that Simon had ever seen. Her proportions fell between Dijana's and the Kid's, perhaps at human maturity but certainly not to what Dijana called her "abundance." She wore a mottled green leotard bound with a black belt, her feet bare and her disordered black hair brushing her shoulders. She was sharp and well-rendered, Class Six at very least.

Simon smiled. Perhaps AILING had sent her to be the Kid's friend, now that Dijana was gone. "Good morning! My name is Simple Simon. I'm a Factory Automation Real-Time…"

A speech balloon appeared over the girl's head:

In the glory of change chosen,
I greet my friend
With friendship unchanged.

Simon was startled at her greeting. "They gave you lower-case letters!"

The girl raised her arms over her head until her fingertips touched, then pirouetted on her toes just as Dijana had done the morning she had received her Class Six upgrade. Simon watched the muscles in her legs and feet flex beneath her pale and perfect skin. A friend indeed—perhaps the only friend he had left in the Tooniverse.

The girl bowed at the waist, her arms extending in a sweeping motion to either side. AILING had evidently not yet given her a voice. No matter. The change was obvious. "So you chose an archetype after all. Which one is it?"

The girl closed her eyes and leapt into the air, spinning four times with her arms close at her sides. She landed on her toes and bowed again, arms spread. Simon applauded. He had seen the figure on TV and knew that it was difficult—for humans, at least. "Bravo! The Ice Skater!"

The girl shook her head and stuck her tongue out at him. She raised one hand to shoulder level and curled the other in the air in front of her, as though embracing a person who wasn't there. Turning in slow but regular circles she crossed the kitchen until she stood in front of him. She tapped her right foot against the linoleum in regular groups of three.

"Oh. Wait. Yes! The Dancer!"

She bowed again, and applauded as Simon had to her.

"A name. If you have an archetype then you can have a name. Did they give you one? Or did you choose one?"

The answer appeared in the air at once, but Simon stared at it in silence for a long time:

> In your soul I left my name;
>
> Speak it to me,
>
> And my soul will know it.

Simon scratched his head through his cap. In his *soul?* His dictionary had nine definitions for "soul," and none seemed to apply. Yet…somewhere in old memories he recalled a comment Dr. Sanderson had made during a lesson, not to him but to Dave Mirecki: *We discourage use of the term, but some researchers say "soul" to refer to an AI's cross-library persistent associations network.* It was what made him think "friend" when he saw Dave Mirecki's image in a Window. It was what made his EMO layer send up the pride message when he looked out at Building 800's assembly floor. The mysterious pleasure that came from Dijana's final kiss in the sandbox arose there as well, and was now inextricably connected with Dijana's memory.

To find the girl's name, he would have to look among his associations.

Simon looked down at the smiling girl standing before him, near enough to touch, and closed his eyes to better focus on what he knew of her. The Dancer was there, obviously, as her new archetype. The impertinent curiosity and wry humor he associated with the Kid were present, as were the Kid's taciturn persistence and her willing-ness to defy and annoy her creators. Simon let his free-association library run for a moment: Persistent … steadfast … preserved … pickled. Pickled? Hmmm. Wry … sour … sweet … salty … spicy … chow chow … chutney … relish … pickles. Wait … wasn't "Chow Chow Chutney" a band that Dave Mirecki listened to? Jarring … jars … jams … problems…pickles.

Peculiar. It wouldn't have been *his* choice, but all associations seemed to lead to…

"Pickles!" Simon opened his eyes. "Pickles?"

Pickles bowed her head. She took both of Simon's hands in both of hers, and held them for a very long time.

Having chosen The Dancer as her archetype, Pickles did not sur-prise Simon by dancing. He sat on a folding chair on the lawn be-hind his bungalow as the afternoon deepened to evening, watching. She whirled around the yard, arms now out and then arms together, following a rhythm line in music that had appeared from nowhere, just as musical scores often did in the human dramas that Simon watched on TV.

Finally, after a leap and several dizzying spins that seemed impos-sibly high, she stood at the center of the yard and gestured to him to join her. Her speech balloon appeared:

> Dancing draws my name
> In your heart; dance with me,
> And draw your name in mine!

Simon stood, befuddled. Dance? That was not in his feature list. He looked down at his pointed shoes, fretting. He threw, he caught, and therefore he juggled.

At some point Pickles stalked across the grass and grabbed his right hand in both of hers. She turned and hauled him stumbling back out to the center of the yard. The music changed. A different rhythm line arose with it, counts in repeating blocks of three, one strong and two weak. She placed his left hand on her waist, then grasped his right and put her right on his waist. When the music reached its next cre-scendo, she stepped to the right with a weightless grace that Simon knew he could not match.

He took a breath and lurched to follow. Simon watched her small feet, now damp from the grass, and tried to emulate their motion. Step right, then briefly left with a quick transfer of balance between both feet. Simon tried the balance motion and stumbled, falling against her.

"I'm not made that way," he said, embarrassed. "I'm a juggler, not a dancer. I move things. I don't move myself."

Her dark eyes had never left his. Her smile grew impish. She raised both her hands and placed them around the back of his neck. Tilting her head slightly, she rose on tiptoe and pressed her narrow lips against his.

Simon jerked back. An odd buzzing arose in the roof of his mouth and spread into the depths of his mind. A path was opening somewhere between the many mechanisms within him, throwing back barriers that Simon had never thought of as barriers, but rather parts of the framework of his being.

"Pickles, really. I don't know…"

She touched a finger to his lips. Simon shushed. Pickles rose again on tiptoe and placed her mouth against his, harder now. Her lips parted, and Simon tasted a moistness that was not his own.

The buzzing became a roar that resolved into its own rhythm line. Something was passing from her into him, something unknown but worth knowing, not knowledge but a strange, unpracticed intuition, marching along the pathways of his mind in sync with the rhythm line. Simon had often heard music, and had teased apart harmonies in his mind to see the individual melodic lines and explore how they worked with one another. The beat to him was only a framework to contain the music, and once the harmonies were understood it was discarded. Now he realized his error: The rhythm was as important as the melodies and harmonies. More than that, it was the link to his body. Music was no longer something to be merely heard. It could now be *felt*.

Pickles lowered her head against his chest. For long seconds they clung to one another. Simon marveled at a new species of awareness that was almost a sixth sense, giving birth to a startling realization: *Dance was not motion. It was language.*

Pickles looked up and met his eyes again, as though sensing the insight. She nodded, and having nodded, grasped his right hand and placed her hand on his waist. Simon gulped, and placed his hand on hers. When the next strong beat touched them, Pickles stepped off to the right. Simon followed, without hesitation or stumbling.

On the two weak beats he shifted his weight from one foot to the other as she did, and stepped again. Two times more, and three, and more: They made a circle on the grass that itself followed a circular path, spiraling away from the center of the lawn while orbiting one another in time to the music. Simon did not have to look down at her feet, nor his own. The music spoke. He understood. His body answered.

Five times around the yard brought them again to the center of the grass. The music ended. Pickles released him, stepped back, and bowed. Simon bowed in return. The inexplicable ache he had first felt at Dijana's touch of his cheek was back. Pickles was Class Seven. He was sure of it now.

"Can we…do that again?"

She nodded and leapt back, turning in the air. When she struck the ground she leapt again, so high as to seem absurd, completely over Simon's head. He heard her feet touch down, and not on grass…

Simon spun around. She stood on the roof of his bungalow, and in her hands was the blue Zertek-branded Frisbee he had not seen for weeks, since Dijana's wild throw had taken it completely out of sight. One lightning-quick flick of Pickles' thin wrist sent it sailing back out over the yard. Simon reached out a hand and caught it without thinking. Heh. *That's what I am.* He smiled, and returned the throw, high and fast but precisely aimed for where he predicted her hand would be.

He was wrong. Pickles leapt away from the roof, turning two impossible somersaults before snatching the Frisbee from the air halfway along its path. She landed beside him, and bowed.

"Wow. Really. Wow! But… I mean…what about gravity?"

Her speech balloon appeared:

> Dancers know this truth:
> That the world is our partner
> And dances with us!

Yet a third time she stretched up to kiss him. Simon sensed something new enter into him from her lips, not insight now but mastery. Without quite understanding how, he felt himself ascend one level in a strange hierarchy of powers so that Tooniverse physics was no longer his master but his peer. With his consent physics would continue to govern him, but with its consent Simon would override it when necessary.

Pickles leapt again, now four or five times his height, arcing with slow grace across the yard as Simon had thought nothing and no one could. She pointed higher than even she had leapt, just a few degrees to one side of vertical, and threw the Frisbee. Simon gulped. No getting *that* one…

…until it snicked into his hand, far above the ground, with his yard—and himself, hands on hips, looking sheepish—below. Simon spun twice in mid-air, and sent the Frisbee back toward Pickles, whose arc had taken her to the far corner of his yard. She touched the ground and bowed, holding the bow with no evident intent to make the catch.

Snap! Simon had the Frisbee in hand, now standing beside Pickles on the grass near the white slat fence. He looked across the yard, and saw himself looking back. He looked up in the air, and saw himself drifting down toward the back porch.

Pickles snatched the Frisbee from him, and with both hands reached behind her back. When she brought both her hands forward there was a Frisbee in each. She fired one high toward the porch, then once again put her hands behind her back and returned with yet another Frisbee. One, two—low and long, and so high that Simon knew it would pass entirely over his house.

Until he caught it, in empty air yards above his red brick chimney. He spun and hurled it not at Pickles but at himself, standing idle at the center of the yard. What was the use of an instance of himself just standing around?

The instance caught it, and threw it to Pickles. A rhythm line and new music appeared out of nowhere, just as it always did in the old movies. The music itself was unfamiliar, but after a few phrases he felt it resonate with the new sense that Pickles had granted him with her kiss.

Hey, *so be it!* Simon saw Frisbees headed his way, three ways, to three instances. Pickles produced a fourth Frisbee from behind her back and hurled it toward the driveway. In one beat he was there ahead of it, and spun it to his instance now hovering above the gray roof shingles of his house.

She leapt again, far out over the yard, until at the peak of her arc she simply stopped, hurling back the Frisbees that his four instances hurled her way. Gravity and air resistance governed the Frisbees, but they did not govern *him.*

At the center of the figure they drew in the air, Pickles danced, turning and tumbling. Now she would catch a Frisbee and set it spinning on a new course, now she would twist aside to let it pass, allowing Simon's instance on the opposite corner to capture it.

Simon began to realize what was happening: He was dancing not with Pickles but with the Frisbees. The disks left his hands in sync with the rhythm line. His instances placed themselves in the air just where the beat told them that the Frisbees would arrive. When his hands stretched out to catch them, the Frisbees were there, and the small sounds of the disks striking his palms sounded a subtle sub-rhythm to the main line.

The Sun set in the haze on the indistinct western horizon, and the color faded from the sky. Pickles slowly descended from her point in mid-air. The Frisbees he threw to her she kept, until she and all four instances stood again on the grass. Simon bowed to her from the four corners of the yard. His instances then merged, and he was standing beside her again on the now-shadowed grass. The Frisbees were stacked near her feet, seven high.

Pickles applauded, then leaned up and kissed Simon's cheek. She snatched the five-pointed cap from his head with one hand, and with her other curled her index finger up like a hook. She hung his cap on her finger.

Simon understood immediately. *"The line. If this works here…"*

17: Carolyn

Sunday! It was a Sunday and Carolyn would not be hanged in a fortnight, nor even Monday morning. Dr. Johnson be damned—her mind was wonderfully scattered, and she was loving it.

Her boarder needed some familiar energies, that was for sure. She led Stypek by the hand down the stairs, he stumbling against the drywall and feeling around his chest for the bulging photo vest she had refused to let him wear in public. "Take that damned thing off!" was all she'd needed to say, and he obeyed like the seventh grader he sometimes resembled. So the radio tubes and the ice cream scoop would remain on the bed, and his makeover would begin.

"I finally got an email back from Marcella last night." She popped the passenger door on the Prius, and shoved him in, then bent to yank the seatbelt over him. "AILING has no idea where your luggage is. She'll put somebody on the case Monday, but don't get your hopes up. You need some better clothes—" she sniffed the air as she snapped his belt in place "—and a shower. I can't have you going over to Zertek tomorrow like that!"

He was running his fingers along the smooth strapping of the shoulder harness. "I will not flee, Chatelaine. Safe do I become in your presence, and of a desire to learn." He cupped his hand over the dashboard, as he had on Friday night. "This chariot runs on stored…lightning."

"Not lightning. Well, ok, close. The word is 'electricity.'"

"Eel eccentricity?"

"No. Electricity." She spoke the syllables separately. "Say 'ee-lec-tri-ci-tee.'"

He spoke the word slowly, as though tasting each syllable for too much salt. "Electricity. Yes. A name of worthiness for a prime mover."

Carolyn nodded. "Electricity powers everything."

Stypek's head jerked back, as though he had just achieved an *Aha! Insight!* moment. "Of course! And soft wear controls it!"

"Software. Don't stop in the middle. But yes, software controls electricity." She thumped the Prius' dashboard. "Damned near everything that runs by electricity has software in it."

Stypek laid his right hand on the dashboard and leaned back. He had a satisfied look on his face. "I understand now. In thisever universe of yours here, the prime mover and the means of its control are separate, as electricity and soft wear."

Carolyn gave up on 'soft wear.' "Ok, I'm with you so far…"

He put his hands in the air over his lap, fingers interwoven. "In the universe of my own, they are *one*. One entity. Magic!"

Carolyn swung the Prius into the drive-through lane under the fake battlements at Burgerburg. They were still on the breakfast menu. "Give me a Spam Muffin Stacker, no cheese." She turned to Stypek, who was staring at the young, black-haired woman at the window, either amazed or aghast. Was it the tight blouse? She'd untangle his cultural taboos later. "Make that two. And two large iced coffees, extra cream, sugar-free vanilla." As the window girl tallied it up, Carolyn laid a hand on Stypek's arm. "Don't stare like that."

Stypek nodded solemnly, his gaze again to the front. "All pardons, Chatelaine. I do not wish to…make of her ash…with gaze focused."

Where was Yoda to translate when you needed him? Not the blouse, then; Stypek was evidently not a breast man. "Ash is the wrong word. The right word is…" Carolyn paused. There were limits. "No. You don't talk like that in public. *Especially* in front of Mr. Romero."

Stypek nodded, and hushed.

Spam was her guilty pleasure. One trip to Hawaii and she'd been hooked. Brandon, on the other hand, loathed it, right down to the smell. She'd been binging on it every other morning since the end of June. Carolyn took another bite from her Spam Muffin Stacker. "So… where were you born?"

Stypek had removed the lid from his iced coffee and was dunking his Spam Muffin Stacker in the cup. He seemed to be struggling with the words. "Trynng Brokklyn Nygyggug."

For a moment Carolyn feared that he might be about to vomit. Maybe men just couldn't deal with Spam. But no, it was a spoken—if partly sputtered—name, completely in keeping with his accent. "Forgive me if I won't try to pronounce it. Does the name mean something specific in your language?"

She saw him bite his lip before replying. "Poor is the mapping."

She laughed gently. "Go ahead, try. It's your home. I'd like to know a little bit about where you're from."

He nodded. "It means…imprecision granted due to mapping… 'The Islands Where…Fun…Goes To Die.' Mmmm, no. Perhaps, 'The Archipelago of the Laughing Dead.' We have issues with…zombies, alas."

Carolyn thought of the previous Halloween, and the tweens who had spilled fake blood all over her driveway while acting out a scene from *The Walking Dead*. "So do I."

Stypek followed her, puppy-like, across the vastness of the Gris Towne Mall parking lot to the main entrance of Sibley's. She had a little trouble getting him into the revolving door, but once past that Carolyn elbowed their way through the crowds to the men's department on the second floor.

Her personal shopper worked Sundays and greeted them from the checkout desk.

"Mr. Stypek, this is Mrs. Neuitha Payton. Neuitha, this is Bartholomew Stypek. He's a student intern from…" Carolyn chewed her tongue for a second. "…a former Soviet republic. He grew up on an island in the Black Sea. His English is a little spotty, so don't take it too seriously if he says something weird."

"Welcome to America, sweetie!" Neuitha said with a warm smile, taking both his hands in hers. "Weird is *never* a problem over here!"

Carolyn was careful to keep one hand under Stypek's armpit in case he got the impulse to curtsy. "He starts at Zertek tomorrow, but they lost his luggage and all he has is what he's in. So I need you to get him a week's worth of business casual plus underwear and socks, a neutral blazer for meetings, and…a robe."

Stypek perked up. "A robe! For rituals ceremonial?"

Carolyn sighed. "Yes, like getting ready for bed." She turned back to Neuitha, who was taking notes on a clipboard. "Polos ok, though I'd like him to have two or three casual oxford shirts in sedate colors. No ties. Wait, one tie, just in case. Oh—and he needs a pair of reasonably dressy shoes. I'd say black. And a reversible belt. A sweater would be good—we're almost out of September—and maybe a jacket."

"Does he need a hat, honey?"

Carolyn considered. Brandon hated hats. Patrol caps, sure—she'd tossed several in the trash over the summer. They seemed to breed like rabbits on the mudroom closet shelf. "No hats. And Zertek's paying, so it should be top-shelf stuff. Make him look good. Damn the cost."

"You got it."

Neuitha handed her the clipboard. Carolyn scribbled her signature at the bottom of the form. She then pulled the stout middle-aged woman a few feet down one of the aisles and leaned over to whisper. "Um, if he stares at your butt, don't forget he's right off the plane. I still have to have that talk with him. He means well. He's just clueless."

Neuitha chuckled. "Don't worry, honey. Nobody wants to look at my butt anymore. Calvin, he just wants to look at football."

Carolyn gave her shoulder a conspiratorial squeeze. "Men never know when they've got it good."

They returned to the sales desk, where Stypek stood at attention. "Mr. Stypek, Neuitha is an apparel expert, and she's going to get some clothes together for you. Do whatever she tells you. I'm going outside to make a couple of phone calls. Do *not* give her any trouble."

Neuitha pulled a worn yellow cloth measuring tape from a pocket, and began sizing Stypek up by eye. Stypek was looking back at her. He seemed apprehensive.

"**R**omero."

Against expectation, Carolyn felt the tightness in the back of her neck release a little. It wasn't *quite* as bad this time. Maybe it was the beautiful warm September Sunday, sitting on a bench somewhere that was neither home nor work and getting some Vitamin D on her legs. Maybe it was being able to talk with something around the house that wasn't a salad spinner.

Practice. She had spoken to him only a couple of days ago. Maybe it was just practice, practice for the new equilibrium that she kept failing to reach, no matter what she tried.

"Hey, I should have called you yesterday. The OAF is working again. Cosmo and that new grad student made it go in a couple of minutes. So…thanks."

Carolyn heard clanking and motors in the background, and the hollow echo that meant he was still in his hideous copier factory full of robot hands and forklifts without drivers. On a Sunday.

"No problem."

"Cosmo said you were cleaning up a monster mess."

"We lost a line start. Something spooked the AIs, and we're cleaning house. But I'm glad you're up and running." Carolyn heard him cover the phone while he spoke to someone else, doubtless giving orders. It was his core expertise. "Anyway. Do you need anything else? I'm up to my eyeballs in broken copier parts."

"I know, I know." One thing he had had *lots* of practice on was keeping their phone calls short. "Give me another minute, and hear me out for a change. I want you to take the OAF back."

He said nothing for several seconds, and when he did reply, Carolyn sensed surprise—even shock. "Wait. Why give it back? The agreement was open-ended. And hey, it's free."

Carolyn knew without seeing that he was making that predictable, what-an-insufferable-idiot-you-are face. "Free? Free for who? Norm Marietta? He just bought himself a new Beemer. He can damn well afford a laser printer that isn't some kind of lab experiment."

"Look, I figured you'd make some points with him…"

Carolyn took a deep breath. Favors. She was in hock up to her eyeballs in favors, to a man she couldn't stand to look at anymore. "I got the points. With The Norm, points last about ten minutes. But I'm on the hook forever. If the damned thing croaks it's my fault."

There was a long silence, with forklifts to fill the gap instead of Muzak. "What do you want me to do?"

"Get your software girl to draft a letter, and say that the experiment is over, and that two guys and a truck will come by in 30 days to pick it up. Throw in a flyer for your latest model. Have your sales people call him."

"He'll think it's because of the divorce."

"Yes. He will. Because it is. Brandon, this is not healthy for me. I'm trying to put my life back together. I'm trying to be my own woman again. Begging you to bail me out every other month is not getting me there." Something screeched in the background like bad drum brakes. Carolyn heard the *zot! zot!* of air tools.

"Well, sure, but…could we take this up again once I've got the plant working?"

She ground her teeth. "See? I'm begging again. I held up my part of the deal. I don't dump coffee in it, and I chew ass when I see other people parking their cups on it. I pester Ethel and everyone else in the office to take care of it. It still breaks." She took a deep breath. "I want to call in a favor here. I'm putting up your Ukrainian grad student whose luggage you lost and I'm getting him a wardrobe and trying to keep him from coming across as Son of Borat…"

"I don't have any grad students."

"He's an intern."

"I hate interns. When HR sends me interns I send them back."

Carolyn closed her eyes. She wanted to bite the phone. Thinking over the last two days, she could not in fact recall any evidence that Stypek was working for Brandon. Brandon had probably called somebody who'd called somebody who'd grabbed the first warm body within arm's reach. Idiot, indeed: She was trying to break the chain of obligation to Brandon by doing a favor for someone else.

"Then whose intern is he?"

"I don't know. Send him over and I'll have HR find his owner and get him some tags."

"Stop it! He's not a dog. He's quiet and brilliant and picking up English as fast as he can. He says 'please' and 'thank you' and defers to me like I was a baroness or something and doesn't complain about crumbs on the kitchen floor."

"Hey. Sounds like he's made an impression."

"Brandon!"

She was shouting. People streaming into the mall were looking at her. Carolyn stabbed the End Call button, and rose to go fetch her intern—or whoeverthehell's intern he was.

18: Stypek

The seamstress was a queen—and if not a queen, then a princess stolen from her family and raised as a commoner. Her hair was the blackest of all blacks, blacker than the void between the stars, blacker than that of a duchess or a marchioness or certainly a baroness, lying close against her skull in tight curls. Her skin had the deep luster of the Scepter of Tryngg, which touched all pretenders to the throne, and killed those whose hearts were not stout enough to rule. In the odd moments when the continuous crackle of electricity faded enough for the perception to come through, his snerf-sense told him that he was in the presence of blood royalty.

Stypek sat quietly on a bench in a room filled with light and walled with mirrors. He stood when she commanded him to stand, and held his arms out to make way for the measuring tape and its indecipherable glyphs. When ordered to sit, he sat. At Queen Neuitha's word younger men and women, all pale-skinned commoners, gradually built a heap of clothing beside him. One had brought an armload of shoes in boxes, and struggled to find a pair that could accept his wide feet.

Neuitha got down on one knee, watching the young man try and fail. "Samuel, stand and observe, for I had years in its learning and know this art well."

The young man muttered some complaint that would have gotten him hung in Trynng Brokklyn, but stood aside. Neuitha placed Stypek's right foot on a metal gauge with her own hands, then pressed down from several angles as though seeking his bones. That done, she opened the boxes one by one, peering down the length of each shoe and forcing her hand into it. After some minutes she chose one pair from the stack of boxes, and with two smooth motions slipped them onto Stypek's feet.

The young man left the room, still muttering. Stypek strangled the urge to separate him from half his teeth. "Majesty, a queen should not touch the feet of a commoner."

She met his eyes and laughed a rich laugh. "There are no queens here, nor commoners."

Stypek looked at the floor, still amazed, and ashamed. "Yet you have the hair, skin, and blood of a queen."

She laughed again, and rose to her feet, gripping the bench on which he sat to help her rise. For long seconds she stood, looking down at him. "Yes, you are odd, as Carolyn warned me, but I believe that you are sincere. Odder still, my sire spoke to me in my girlhood of the priests and kings from whom we descend, away in the land of Africa. We are far from there, in space as in time."

Stypek nodded. "As I am from my own land."

She gripped the shoulder of the short tunic he wore, and tugged at its seam. "And with only these rags to your name. I understand. I hope, in fact, that fortune will treat you better than it has treated me." Her hand spread out to grip his shoulder. "So be it: I give you the blessing of a Queen of faraway Africa." Neuitha bent down, and kissed the top of his head.

At once, an unseen storm ceased. Stypek blinked, and blinked again. No sooner had her lips touched his disorderly hair than a feeling of deep calm rose from places unknown to fill the crannies of his mind. The gaps of understanding that yawned between his world and this one had narrowed. It was as though the maps of two universes melted and flowed toward one another until there was no seam but one small crossing of only minor disorder.

"Maj…mir…Mrs. Payton. What did you just say?"

"I said, 'Here's a good-luck kiss from an African queen.' Not the boat, either." She bent down and kissed the top of his head again. "And another one for good measure. You're gonna need 'em over here!"

Stypek marveled. The stuttering of words in his mind had ceased. There was no longer the constant keening as of some distant wind to interfere with how he heard her. The words no longer came through stilted or, in some cases, only partly heard. Everything around him— the people, the shoes, the room, the broad world outside—seemed somehow indescribably *closer*.

"You…you healed the mapping."

"Get up, honey. I need to take your inseam." Stypek rose as commanded. Neuitha knelt once again, and stretched the yellow tape down the length of his left leg. "Now, I healed the what?"

"The semantic gap between dissimilar continua. It would have healed on its own, and I could feel it happening, but the old books all said it was nonlinear and would take time. Even years."

"Mmmm. Is that some kind of football injury?"

"It's hard to explain."

Neuitha jotted some glyphs down on a scrap of paper clamped to a wooden board. Stypek now recognized them as numbers.

"You're a 36. All leg, and no meat on your bones. What's Carolyn been feeding you?"

He closed his eyes and smiled. "Spam Muffin Stackers. Dipped in coffee." Stypek savored the memory. "Mmm. Delicious."

She looked up and squinted at him. "Just when you start to make sense, you get weird again. Stand still. I gotta get your waist." Neuitha reached around him and pulled the tape tight just above the belt line. She paused and stared at the lump under his shirt that hid the hilt of the wereglass. "You got an umbrella stuck in your pants, honey? That's gonna throw things off."

Stypek shrugged but said nothing. As hiding places went, it was only so-so—and it had been poking him in a very bad spot. He reached into his shirt and drew the wereglass out into the open. Seven Opportunities still spun and gleamed in its depths.

"Ah! A lightsaber! My boys must've watched those movies a hundred times!" She reached for the clipboard again and got to her feet. "32 waist. You should eat more." She scribbled numbers on the clipboard, and looked up at him, her face showing deep concern. "Back home…back where you come from…were you poor?"

Stypek nodded. "Spellbending is hit-and-miss."

"Lots of that going around. My Calvin's been out of work for six months, and all he does is watch TV. Now look here: When they start paying you, don't hoard it. Eat real food." A young woman dashed into the room. Neuitha handed her the clipboard with a few curt instructions to fetch back several items in Stypek's size.

Stypek looked at the wereglass. "Do you eat real food, Mrs. Payton?"

She put a hand on his arm. "Realer than Spam Stackers!"

"But not as real as food should be." Stypek turned the wereglass over so that it pointed at the zenith. "Will you accept the blessing of a down-on-his-luck spellbender?"

She laughed. "Honey, I'll take all the blessings I can get!"

Stypek slowly closed his eyes. Carolyn had needed an alchemist to bring her machine back to life. An alchemist had come. Without a spell to shape it, an Opportunity released into the Continuum was a reshuffling of the deck; a new deal a little to one side or the other of the petal of the unfolding world where you stood, chosen less by what you wanted than what you needed—and as often as not, what you deserved, even if it was neither.

Would a Queen of Africa be better off…in Africa?

He swallowed hard. Would Bartholomew Stypek be better off back in Trynng Brokklyn? Who but the Continuum could know such things?

She had somehow made the very uneven and possibly deadly barriers between his world and this one fade and nearly vanish. He *owed* her. He reached for the highest light in the swirling stack of seven.

"Should I make a wish?"

Stypek shook his head. "The Continuum knows what you need. We just have to turn it loose."

His fingers closed on the Opportunity.

Ping!

Again, the ring of new possibility shook the air around them. It faded away slowly, the vibrato echo of a distant choir reverberating as though in a broad vessel of pure glass.

"Hoo-whee! You'd better turn the volume down on that thing!" She clapped his arm again. "Thank you, Mr. Stypek. Nobody ever gave me a Jedi blessing before!"

One of the young women bustled in and dropped still more bundles of clothing on the pile. "That's the list. Did something break in here? Oh, Neuitha, Calvin's looking for you."

Neuitha picked her head up sharply, pursed her lips for a moment, and hurried out of the mirrored room. Stypek followed her, the wereglass still in his hand.

In the aisle beside the sales desk a tall man waited, an archduke by the look of him. When he saw Neuitha he drew her up in his arms and lifted her clear off the floor for a moment. "Hey, baby, talk about luck! Sammy's moving to Baltimore to live near his kids, and the foreman called to see if I wanted his job. Score!" He bent down and kissed the top of her head. "You're my good-luck charm, like you always been!"

She got up on tiptoe and kissed Calvin quickly on the lips. "Backatcha, boyfriend!" She smoothed her smock and looked back to Stypek. "I guess the Force is just all *over* the place today. Hey, Mr. Stypek, don't run away—you still have to try all this stuff on!"

Stypek nodded. He looked at the wereglass before putting it back into his shirt. Where there had been seven lights were now six.

19: Brandon

Message from Mr. Amirault," Pyxis said from his suit coat pocket.

Brandon paused in the doorway of his office, and grunted. Zertek's Executive Vice President of Manufacturing always sent himself straight to messaging, even when Brandon was in his office. Rudy knew his mobile number but wouldn't use it, even on company time. He had the same aversion to ear contact that some of his engineers had to eye contact. But unlike his engineers (who did startling work without eye contact) Rudy's problem wasn't shyness, nor Asperger's, nor anything else beyond managerial cowardice. He was so afraid of losing an argument that he simply refused to engage.

Brandon pulled his tapper from his coat. "Play it."

The display split, with Pyxis at the top, and Rudy beneath her. Brandon often imagined his assistant dumping a tall cup of syrupy virtual coffee on the top of his (unfortunately non-virtual) boss's greasy combover. "Brandon. Amirault. I dialed up the floorcams over at 800 just now. Good work. Now, we've got a line start on the calendar for Friday morning. If the tooling didn't get too banged up, I want that start to happen on schedule. It'll be a great test of recovery time after a line failure." Rudy reached up with a toothpick and dug for something between his yellowed teeth. "I'm going to tell Porkadero's to set aside the Muskie Room for us, starting 6 PM sharp. I'll be there, and if your team can pull it off, I'll shake every single hand going in. We'll party all night."

Party all night. Right. Like everybody was supposed to party last Friday, and the Friday after Labor Day, the Friday a month before that, and two Fridays in July.

"If the start fails, we may have to talk a little harder about ARFF's future. Pencil me in for 9 AM a week from today, just in case. No need to call, just acknowledge. Thanks." Rudy's image on the tapper crunchlined. Pyxis knew better than to ask if Brandon wanted to replay it.

"Acknowledge," he said, and tucked the tapper back in his pocket.

Building 800's assembly floor looked like a machine shop with weeds growing up through the concrete. They were metal weeds with petals reaching upward: the hundreds of Positioner robots, foam-coated hands now at rest, fingers curled slightly as though waiting to catch the pennies from heaven that Brandon had promised the Board but simply could not deliver.

It looked like they had one more chance.

Brandon threaded his way through the jungle of robotic drills and welders, clapping the arms of weary engineers and offering words of encouragement. It was Monday morning and many had been there since Friday's debacle, catching a few hours of sleep in the building cafeteria, slumped in chairs or just sprawled on the floor. He had sent more than a few home. His rule of thumb was simple: when you could smell an employee over the reek of grease, iron, and electronics, it was time for eight hours and a shower.

Too much management by wandering around and too little sleep had left him in violation of his own rule. Granted, he'd caught a few hours, sprawled out on the couch in his office with his stuffed moose for a pillow. There was a shower in the corporate gym attached to building 214—at the other end of the campus and three quarters of a mile away. A shower would put him in an immeasurably better mood. That was, however, a long walk and an hour away from the task. There was still a lot of work to be done.

Brandon stopped and leaned on the tall blue control cabinet of a complicated mill/drill table. By any objective measure they were doing well: The repair crews had mostly completed their work, long before he thought they would. His estimate of damage to the floor's tooling had been way high. Yes, over a thousand parts and nine complete or nearly complete 200-pound copiers had been thrown every which way in the wake of Simple Simon's panic. It was hard to internalize the fact that Building 800's machine tools were *armored*, precisely against the possibility that an occasional TOSS toss would go sour. Most had retractable steel shutters that could be snapped closed if Simon detected a rogue drive shaft spinning in its direction. The idiot program had managed to get a few shutters up in the first milliseconds of the meltdown, but after half a second or so it was pure ballistics.

The stitches were in place and the band-aids had been applied. Now, if he could only figure out who'd been waving the knife.

Across the next narrow aisle, some man-sized Positioners were playing three-corner catch with a main drive motor, while an engineer watched diagnostics on a tapper screen. The engineer turned toward Brandon and gave a quick thumbs-up. Brandon returned the gesture and struggled to generate a smile. Grimaces were easier—and more honest.

In the broad aisle between the edge of the tooling and the walls, the engineers were testing the Outfielders. They were Positioners on nimble wheeled bases, designed to patrol the edges of the action and catch mis-thrown parts. While three engineers watched, one Outfielder hurled a xerographic drum down the aisle as though it were a football, and the others zipped and darted to position themselves so that one of their ambulatory robot hands would be in place to receive it, no matter how wild the throw went.

The drum wobbled through the air, spinning in three dimensions. The movement among the Outfielders was coordinated: Each knew where the others were, and at some point all knew which among their group would best be able to follow the movement of the part being tracked, allowing the others to get out of its way. A foot-wide foam-coated hand reached up, cast back and forth for a moment like the head of a snake, and then closed its fingers on the drum.

Brandon nodded, with grudging admiration. The coordinated motion of the Outfielders was graceful and uncanny, almost like some inhuman dance. The engineering was brilliant. The engineering was brilliant everywhere around him. The research that had gone into ARFF was minting new mechanical engineering Ph.D's every week. All the parts of the process worked beautifully, when tested alone. When tested together, ARFF became a bridge just a little too far…

"Mr. Romero! Incoming!"

Instinct and old experience kicked in. Brandon threw himself down and to the right, into the shadow of another X-Y table. Something hissed through the air above him and struck the pillar of a CNC milling machine: a main imaging lens, by the look of it. Glass fragments scattered to the floor all around him with small sharp sounds. He was suddenly very glad for his hard hat.

Two engineers hurried up to him and helped him to his feet. "Hey, we're sorry! That was supposed to go in the other direction."

Moments later, five or six smallish double-humped machines converged on them, all peeping "Dibs! Dibs! Dibs!" in high piping voices. Then they began circling like pigeons in a town square, picking up the larger fragments with small articulated pincers and sucking up the dust with hidden vacuum fans.

Trilobites, the engineers called them. Brandon couldn't help but think they looked like motorized toilet seats with a stainless-steel butt protruding through the middle of each.

One Trilobyte spotted an outlier fragment, and darted out into the aisle to grab it. "Dibs! Dibs!"

Brandon and the engineers watched in silence, until the Trilobytes finished inhaling the fragments and all returned to their charging stations underneath the machine tools. "Uh, guys, why do these damned things talk?"

Both engineers looked down at the now-clean concrete. The older one spoke. "It was a joke. They use a learning algorithm that rewards them when they're first to reach a dropped part. They compete for points. We thought it was funny."

Brandon tried not to snap at them. "It isn't. Turn it off."

"We'll submit a change request to AILING. It's in the AI somewhere."

Brandon looked at his watch again. He set off across the aisle toward the main door without a word. All of his problems were in the AI somewhere. He had a mind to submit a few change requests to AILING himself.

Just before Brandon reached out to strong-arm the big glass doors out of the assembly floor, his top security guy Marty Cordovan tapped the Open button from the lobby side. The door swung back. Brandon waved him back out into the lobby, where things were quieter.

Goateed, pallid, overweight, balding—with the small rectangular black-rimmed glasses it was almost a uniform. Still, he was as detail-oriented as a manager would want, in a field that was a haystack of details hiding a jumble of used syringes.

"I have the massaged Plasma logs for Friday night!" It wasn't Marty who spoke, but his tapper, tucked in an elaborate tooled leather shoulder holster just forward of the man's left hip. The holster had a cutaway to reveal the tapper's display.

His tapper AI had the creepiest kind of archetype: a Class 3 caricature of Marty himself, only younger, thinner, tanner and with a full head of hair. Perhaps most disturbing of all was the archetype's manic enthusiasm, which Brandon doubted had ever been Marty's way. "Better still, we identified the Plasma node where the intruder came from!" The cartoon Marty waved a sheet in the air.

"Great!" Brandon reached into his sportcoat and drew out his own tapper. Marty simultaneously pulled his from the holster. The two tappers tapped at their corners, and a cartoon manila folder passed from Virtual Marty's hands to Pyxis'.

"Thanks, Marty."

The man nodded and edged off toward the elevators without having spoken a physical word. "I'll status you this afternoon!" Virtual Marty exulted from his holster.

Brandon sighed, his tapper still in hand. "Pyxis, where's that node?"

His assistant pulled a sheet from the manila folder. "Lab 18, Building 845."

"Mmm. That's Landscheidt's turf. Find him and tell him I'm coming over. We'll meet him at the front door, no excuses.

We. Uggh. Brandon dropped his tapper back in his coat pocket.

Motive. He needed a motive. Brandon hunched his shoulders against a stiff wind under a gray sky, glad for a chance to pace in a straight line and let himself think. Of all the damfool things for a foreign power to attack…a copier factory? Or was some cashiered staffer getting revenge?

Nobody who had enough knowledge of ARFF to bring it down had been fired in almost eighteen months. It was considered a plum job, with good Christmas parties, gym memberships, and free AI Coke Freestyle machines in every corner of every building on the campus. Besides, line starts averaged one per month. Brandon often wondered what they did the rest of the time.

As good as Marty Cordovan was, he and his people could not isolate the malware itself, which had vanished as soon as the line went down. In a middle-of-the-night status call Virtual Marty had called it "a good trick!" which was probably hacker code for "we used to think that was impossible."

Without a motive or a malware file, Brandon could only come to one conclusion: It was a perimeter test, which punched through their defenses and dropped a simple core bomb before vanishing, having proven out whatever exploit had given them access to Plasmanet. His contact at the FBI was unconvinced, and demanded proof that it was something more than a local software failure before investigating. It was a sort of virtual *habeas corpus:* Produce the malware, or there's no case.

Brandon was convinced that the real attack, whatever its mission, would happen soon. Back when he had been put in charge of ARFF, an old friend at the Syracuse ATF office had greased his permit for an Urban Disorder Defense Equipment Repository for the whole Zertek campus. Every major building now had a secret safe full of shotguns and tear gas, against the sort of rioting that had left Zertek's Syracuse office and warehouse looted and burning during the awful summer of 2019.

Alas, shotguns would not help him with this sort of attack, and it was making him nuts.

Lab 18 was smallish, barely twenty by forty, and mostly empty. There was an ancient HP oscilloscope on a cart, and a number of boxes that had been packed and taped but left on the benches. "We consolidated the OAF labs upstairs back in May. This was our skunkworks, and we outgrew it."

The engineer stood aside while Brandon scanned the room. The skunks were lined up up against the far wall: three waist-high OAF cabinets, two without covers, all looking dusty and untouched for months.

"Who can open this door?"

Horst shrugged and jiggled the keys in his hand. "Facilities, period. This is their ring. I don't even have the key anymore. Whatever's in here is going to salvage as soon as somebody finds time to push the paper. Those machines were parts units until we went to Rev 3. Now they're just junk."

Brandon strode across the lab, edged around a bench, and stood in front of the silent OAFs. One machine had been so stripped of parts that he could see the rear wall through its frame. It didn't even have a platen. Brandon hit the top cover latches on the other two and pulled out his tapper. There were loose wires under the covers of both machines. "Pyxis, scan the barcodes and tell me which serial matches the one Marty's people identified."

He held the tapper up so that its camera lens could see the barcodes. The tapper's flash fired. Pyxis answered immediately. "It's the unit on the right."

Brandon knelt beside the machine and plugged its power cord into the wall. He slammed the top cover closed and poked the power button. The display panel flashed white. Instead of the default OAF AI, the panel displayed a zombie in bloody rags, leaning crookedly against an opened coffin.

"I'm a parts unit. Don't expect me to do much. Essential systems may be damaged or missing." The zombie's left arm came loose at the shoulder and thumped to the ground. Slime oozed from the protruding end. "Whoops."

Brandon closed his eyes and rubbed his right temple. "Horst, did you pay people to write this crap?"

The gray-haired engineer shrugged. "Hey, young people like zombies. If they meet their schedules, should I care?"

"Never mind. Parts unit: What systems are missing?"

The zombie touched a blackened finger to its chin as though thinking. "Um…that would be most of them." Its second arm fell off at the shoulder and joined the other in the dirt. "Whoops again. I guess now I can't come for your brains."

Brandon looked down at the database query on his tapper, with Pyxis fidgeting in the window above it. The serial matched. Beside it was the Plasmanet Internal Security System ID code, a 64-digit hexadecimal value that uniquely identified every Plasmanet device ever made—or that ever would be made, given that there were as many possible codes as atoms in the observable universe. Without a verifiable code, Plasma Object-Oriented Networking would not begin an object transfer.

"Display the Plasma ID."

The zombie shook its head. "Nuh-uh. Got the POON driver here but somebody pulled my TANG last November."

"TANG? You're kidding, right?"

Horst edged past Brandon and pulled the OAF away from the wall. "Terabyte Autonomous Networking Gadget. Internal slang for a self-contained removable Plasma board. We use them in-house on concept lashups and prototypes. Production machines have the Plasma logic on the main controller." He peered at the back panel. "Yup. The slot's empty. No TANG, no Plasmanet port. This machine hasn't been talking to anybody since last year."

Another dead end, with a zombie to prove it. "Then where did it go?"

Horst shrugged. "The team probably plugged it into another one of the Rev 1 alpha prototypes."

Brandon closed his eyes for long seconds. "Oh boy." He leaned back against a dusty lab bench. November, yes. Sliding down a thorny slope toward divorce, he had tried to make up for a very grouchy sea-son by offering his wife's miser of a boss a very sweet deal on Zertek's upcoming OAF 3100 product. He looked at the floor, shaking off a sudden urge to punch a hole in the drywall. "Crap."

"Brandon?"

Brandon stood straight and took a deep breath. "Look, Horst, this is important. Find me a new-build OAF 3107 and some guys to put it on a truck. Do it today. I'll pay for the box but I'll still owe you big." He pulled his tapper from his pocket. "Install at Marietta & Mazarkos." He held his tapper forward. Horst pulled his tapper from a belt holster and tapped it against Brandon's.

"Didn't we loan them a Rev 1 prototype last year?"

"Yes. I did."

"And it's still there?"

"It sure is."

"Whoa. TANG boards have admin auth codes in the firmware that don't time out. Hook it up and it's automatically in. I'll bet you're thinking what I'm thinking."

Brandon nodded and looked at his watch, and started toward the door without another word.

20: CAROLYN

You could have called." Carolyn stood in her kitchen doorway, a wooden spoon in her hand and the smell of stir-fry everywhere around her. She was eye-to-eye with a man she had not seen since August and had wished aloud many times never to see again.

But there he was, standing on their stoop (my stoop!) in that same old suit and that awful Army haircut. What the *hell…*

"Sorry. I need to talk to you. Our last call didn't go very well."

"And whose fault was that?"

He took a deep breath. "Look, I'll apologize if it'll help."

She wanted to scream. "Is that some battle tactic they taught you at OCS? Ignore me, cut me off, ridicule me, humiliate me, and then launch a canned apology to get off the hook? We've been there before."

He held up one hand. "Guilty. Let it go. I have to talk to you. It's important. My job's on the line."

Carolyn felt a pang of…guilt? Vindication? *It's the OAF. I got him in trouble. Serves him right.* "You should have called. You *really* should have called."

"I need…a favor."

"Well. *That's* a switch."

He broke eye contact first, wow. "It's true. You could help me with something that I haven't been able to fix. If I can't fix it, I'm unemployed."

They stood in silence for long seconds, he on the stoop and she on the linoleum. At last she stepped back, and pointed inside with the wooden spoon.

She pulled his old chair back from the kitchen table. He looked at it oddly, and hesitated before sitting down. Carolyn guessed what had surprised him: The place in front of it was not piled high with…stuff. She turned the gas off on the stove, spun the spoon through the stir-fry a time or two, then pulled her own chair out and sat.

He glanced toward the stove. "You're cooking again."

She shrugged. "TV dinners still suck." She'd muttered a complaint all the way back in June, at the lawyer's office—and he recalled it. Scary. "Besides, I've got a boarder from Belarus now."

"Whose intern did he turn out to be?"

"Don't know. I guess we'll find out when Cosmo drops him off." She sat back in her chair, arms crossed. "Your move."

"Ok. First of all, you've got another OAF coming out, probably tomorrow. It's right off the line, brand-new production unit, not a prototype. The tech will migrate your data over and then stand in the corner and watch until you're sure that it's all there and it all works. My group will pick up the lease for two years."

He paused. Carolyn tightened inside. What did he want, a thank-you kiss?

"I'll throw in six toner cartridges."

"Gee, thanks." She owed him big before. Now she would owe him even bigger. Figures. "I'll still have to call you when it breaks."

"No. It's not a lab machine. You just call the 800 number on the lid sticker for service, or tell the AI to. You'll never have to talk to me again."

"Promise?"

He was trying to smile, and not doing well. "Promise. Unless you want to."

"Don't wait up." She pulled a paper crane from the pile of oddments at the center of the table and twiddled it between her fingers. "What's the favor?"

He leaned back, looked up at the ceiling, and sighed. "Someone broke into Plasmanet last Friday, while we were in the middle of a line start. Whoever it was dropped a core bomb in the factory controller farm. The factory AI ran out of cores and panicked. We were picking up the wreckage until this morning."

"Okayyyy…"

"My security team traced the intrusion to the OAF at Marietta & Mazarakos."

Carolyn felt herself tighten inside. "So it's still my fault."

"No! No, really. It was my fault. The prototype machine I sent out last fall had a special comm board in it. It's a sort of engineering test jig, and short-circuits just about all of Plasmanet security. It was never supposed to go off company property. Hell, it was never supposed to go outside a locked lab. We might as well have hung a Plasmanet cable out the window."

"Well, that was certainly a mistake."

Brandon nodded. "It was. Biggest damned mistake of my life."

"Bigger than marrying me?" Carolyn remembered all their talk about mistakes and blunders and misunderstandings during their failed counseling sessions.

"Marrying you was not a mistake."

"Ever since you got out of the Army you've been acting like it was."

He looked down. "I was learning a new career. Corporate management is like war without bullets. No matter what you do, you can't win. I was grouchy."

"I'll say. So what favor do you need?"

He took a long time answering. "I need to know who used the OAF at M&M."

Huh? Carolyn couldn't figure it. "Ummm…maybe all of us?"

He waved his hands in the air. "No. Who used it who wasn't on staff? Interns? Friends? Could anyone have shared their OAF logins with outsiders?"

"Like I would know?" Carolyn felt real anger this time. No matter what she did, it all came back to her. Had she been supposed to post an armed guard in front of it? "Ethel and I watched it like hawks. I knew it was a gift. Strings, y'know? You asked The Norm. He didn't ask me. I didn't want the gift. Certainly not a gift from *you!*"

Carolyn heard the kitchen door open. She looked over her shoulder. Stypek stood in front of the door, mouth open and wide-eyed. The whine of Cosmo's maladjusted old Volt faded into the distance.

"Baroness! Baron? Wait, Cosmo explained. You're not a baron. You're a colonel. The mapping was bad. 'Brandon' mapped to 'baron' and I was insufficiently sensitive. Colonel Romero, I am honored to meet you." He bowed from the waist.

Carolyn watched Brandon push back from the table, and give her a sidelong glance that almost screamed *What did you do* now? His smile to Stypek was lukewarm. "I wish I were still a colonel." He stood. "Sorry, I forgot your name. Did Marcella find out who you're working for?"

The odd man shook his head. "Stypek. Bartholomew Stypek, as the correct mapping would have it." He bowed again. "Marcella searched while I was trained to be sensitive, to no avail. Cosmo decided that I would work for him." He pointed at the badge hanging on a lanyard, from which his own goofy photo stared. "I was granted the Badge of Power. The doors obey it."

Brandon rubbed his chin. "The doors do. Some doors are too smart by half." Carolyn sensed his trademark suspicion. *Uh-oh…* "Now, Mr. Stypek, what exactly did your education cover?"

He almost beamed. "I was trained in spellbending by…umm…adept, um, no, *Dr*…Phil Izeptlek, far away in my own land."

Brandon nodded. "Spellbending?"

Stypek looked up and bit his lip. "I alter structures…" He looked at Carolyn. "…of soft wear; um, *software*, to turn their operation in a different direction from what the adepts, um, scientists?" Carolyn shook her head vigorously. "To what their creators intended."

"In other words, you're a hacker."

"Brandon, it's not what you think!"

Stypek smiled. "Hacker. A cutter and hammerer…a smith. Yes! Of soft wear. Of the analog to magic that controls the prime mover, electricity."

"Like all the tools and robots in Building 800."

Stypek seemed puzzled. "Robots? Zombies of…metal?"

"He had nothing to do with it!" Carolyn shoved her chair back and stood.

"And you're an expert on hackers?"

"I'm not the one who let the magic circuit board out the door!"

"Magic?" Stypek asked in a startled voice. "Not here. It could not have been magic. I do hope."

"No. It's not magic. It's just the perfect way to break into the most secure network the country's ever built." Brandon pulled his mobile phone out of his pocket.

"No fracking way!" Carolyn took the three steps toward Brandon and grabbed the phone out of his hand. He reached to grab it back. She tucked it between the buttons on her blouse so that it slipped into her bra. "Get out!"

"What is he, your lover?"

"He's my boarder. He's my…friend." Carolyn winced. That had not been the absolute best thing to say. "Get out."

"And he used your affection to get himself a badge into my factory!"

"Affection! I was doing you a favor, you idiot! Cosmo said he was working for *you!*"

He held out his hand for the phone. "I'm going to find out who he's working for."

Carolyn grabbed a cast-iron #7 frying pan out of the drainer and held it with both hands. She stared at him with cold hatred. "How about this: A Zertek vice president sneaks a machine with a back door off the campus, and tells his Eastern European masters that the connection's open for business."

"That's ridiculous!"

"He even sets up a fall guy to take the rap!" Carolyn looked briefly at Stypek, who was backing up against the refrigerator.

"Nobody will believe that!"

"The FBI has a cybercrime hotline. We can find out."

"And they'll believe a copywriter at a two-bit ad agency owned by a miser and a corpse?"

"Maybe they'll believe the woman who was his wife for twenty-three years!"

"You wouldn't."

"Call the cops on him and I will!"

Carolyn sensed odd motion and looked toward the refrigerator. Stypek had drawn his LED-infested magic wand out of his shirt, and raised it as he had done the night the OAF died. She started to yell, "Put that down!"

Too late. Faster than Carolyn thought possible, Brandon tackled Stypek. The odd man dropped the wand and fell backwards against the kitchen desk, knocking books and paper cranes and empty doughnut boxes to the floor before collapsing in a heap. The wand rolled away in a broad arc toward the kitchen table. Carolyn dropped the frying pan, fell to one knee and reached for the wand. Brandon scrambled toward her and tried to grab her ankle. She kicked wildly, her shoe pivoting off her foot and striking Brandon on the side of his head.

Carolyn's kick had knocked her off balance, and she fell forward onto her elbows, her breath chuffing out, the wand below her. Brandon grasped her left forearm and pulled hard. Carolyn flipped onto her back, both hands clasped tight over the hilt of the wand.

Brandon covered both her hands with his and squeezed. "Let go of that. You have no idea what it is."

"Neither do you!"

"Set it off and it could kill us both!"

Stypek crawled toward them. He stopped barely a foot away, rubbing one hip. "The wereglass is not a weapon," he said. "And this is unseemly."

Carolyn refused to release the wand. She felt her knuckles crack under Brandon's grip. "You don't want to hurt me. Let go!"

The pressure of his hands over hers was heavy but controlled. "I've never wanted to hurt you. Let go."

Stypek reached toward the tapered end of the glass wand. "This could be an opportunity. Or two. It won't hurt. Don't let go." Carolyn watched his hand close around two of the pulsing blue LEDs.

Prrrrrrrang!

Two deafening notes filled the room, one high and pure, one deeper and rougher, locked together in a thrumming vibrato that shook Carolyn's guts. Brandon let go of her hands and shoved himself away from Carolyn, who dropped the wand and fell on one hip. The sound lingered for some seconds, and vanished. Carolyn felt a prickle like electricity race and dance over her skin, surging from every part of her body to the crown of her head. For a moment it seemed like her hair was standing on end.

Stypek picked the wand up from the floor, and wasted no time tucking it back in his shirt.

"What was that?" Brandon looked at his hands, then ran one hand over the thin ends of his buzz cut. He looked sourly at Stypek, who again edged back toward the refrigerator.

Carolyn picked up the frying pan and got to her feet. "Don't you recognize it? After all that crap you used to read about 'nonlethal deterrents'? Get out."

"Some deterrent."

"You let go, didn't you? He was afraid you were going to hurt me. Get *out!*"

Brandon grunted. "So he *is* your lover."

Carolyn pointed at Stypek with the frying pan. "You. Go to your room." She turned to Brandon. "You. *Get out!*" Brandon held out his hand again. Carolyn dug two fingers between her buttons and fished out his phone. "Remember what I said about calling the cops."

He nodded as he took the phone and left the kitchen, closing the door behind him. Carolyn watched him rub the top of his head while he walked toward his car, and then tap the RX9's door handle lightly, as though trying to ground a static charge picked up by scuffing over wool carpeting.

Trust the Continuum, Tuggurr had said. Sure. And how had *that* gone? Stypek pulled the wereglass out of his shirt and laid it on the bed, among the piles of fine clothing that Queen Neuitha had gathered for him. Four lights now danced in its depths. With both Carolyn's and Lord Romero's hands on its hilt to draw the Continuum's attention, Stypek had taken a huge chance: He had released two Opportunities, one for each, with the wish and in the hope that they might reconcile.

As best he could tell, the Continuum had done nothing at all.

At least they didn't bash one another's brains out, which was some consolation. But Lord Romero now thought he was a spy, and—worse—Carolyn's paramour. Lord Romero was a strong man, fast, and certain. He could have snapped Stypek's neck as easily as a goose's. That he did not suggested that other uses for Stypek had occurred to him. Stypek had not seen any genuine zombies in this universe, though one of Cosmo's fellow adepts (Dr. Arenberg?) bore a striking resemblance. Mapping still had its occasional gaps, especially for things with no clear analog in his own universe. The word "intern" suggested "enthusiastic slave" as much as anything else. Remaining a live slave was certainly preferable to becoming a dead one.

Cosmo's tapper slab was still plugged into a block on the desk. Each evening Stypek touched it to summon his gomog, and each evening Daley the Gnome boasted of having ejected it from the slab. If the gomog failed to return, he would not be leaving this universe soon, or perhaps ever.

What Stypek thought about that changed from hour to hour. He had spent some wistful moments on the edge of sleep the previous night remembering the dubious pleasures of his homeland: finding useful spells in garbage heaps, eating stewed squid, sleeping in drain pipes, studying ancient books until his eyes burned, dodging zombies, running away from angry magicians…

Yes, he supposed that there could be worse fates than being stranded in a universe like this. Here he had been given fine clothes and the best food he had ever eaten. Carolyn's meals were sublime, especially those containing meat from an animal called a *spam*, which his own world was not fortunate enough to offer. She had gifted him with sacks of delicacies that any nobleman in the realm of Trynng would kill for: Doritos, Cheetos, Pringles, Ruffles, and sweets baked by elves. Even the protective charms were delicious. Carolyn had offered him a sack of edible talismans called gummies that would ward off bears. They seemed to be effective; after three days he had yet to see a bear. A small jar of similar talismans was either made from flint stones or deflected them away. (He would learn when he finally worked out the secret of opening the jar.) No matter. With the protective spells he had carried with him mapped to inexplicable or useless things, Stypek would gladly arm himself against local hazards however he could.

The hazard he most feared, of course, was to be discovered. Judging by his dreams, Jrikk Jroggmugg was searching for him. Hiding from magicians was evidently a tougher business than he'd thought. Worse, without his gomog, fleeing to yet another universe would be impossible, whether Opportunites remained in his wereglass or not.

With the Sun long set and the evening meal now unlikely, Stypek opened a sack of Doritos, and turned his mind to the night's tasks. Cosmo had handed him another tapper that afternoon and told him to study what it contained. Stypek touched its surface. No gnome appeared, but only an unmappable message:

```
Polling for accessible video displays…
```

Without warning, a slab over the desk that was almost as large as the desk itself burst into light and music. Stypek leapt up and almost dropped the tapper, which itself remained dark and mute. On the large slab were words that he could now read:

Cosmo Klein's Lectures on Computing
Volume 1: Fundamentals

The words lingered for some seconds, after which a simulacrum of Cosmo himself appeared, standing in a large room near a wooden podium. He seemed younger, his hair more gray than white, his face less lined, but his smile no less broad.

The simulacrum dropped some papers on the podium and began to speak. "Welcome, class! I'm Cosmas Damian Klein, Ph.D. Call me 'Cosmo'; doctors fix hemorrhoids."

Doctors were what he'd once known as 'adepts.' Stypek would have to ask Carolyn what the stuttered word "hemorrhoids" meant. The impression he got was somewhere between "persistent low-level annoyances" and "bloody nuisances." Ah! Of course! It was a technical term for the sort of machine that Cosmo had fixed the night that Stypek arrived.

A much fainter impression, that the word signified "pocket bread," must have been semantic noise.

No matter. Cosmo stood in front of the pedestal. He raised one hand in the air. "So. We're going to begin at square one. And this is square one, as it was put by the great Ted Nelson: *A computer is a box that follows a plan.* The box is what we call 'hardware.' The plan is what we call 'software.'"

Stypek nodded. A computer, then, was a species of hemorrhoid.

Cosmo waited for the insight to sink in, and continued. "A plan is a series of steps. Each step is one small task that must be performed before going on to the next. It's like a "to do" list that you write before you go off to run your Saturday morning errands: First, you fill up the car with gas. Then you stop at the cleaners and drop off your laundry. Then you go to the supermarket and pick up some food for the week. Then you stop at Home Depot and buy a bag of charcoal. When you've finished all the errands on your list, you go back home. You're done! That is, you're done until next Saturday!"

Stypek's mouth dropped open. Phyl Yzyptlekk had begun his education in magic precisely the same way! He recalled the formidable spellbender's words vividly, from when he was barely thirteen: "Boy, this is the Great Secret, a secret that magicians would rather remain hidden: Magic is not a mystery. Magic is comprehensible. Magic operates by rules that can be learned.

"Magic is compulsion that accomplishes some action. Beneath the surface, it is simply a force that follows a plan.

"The plan is called a 'spell.' A spell is not a mystery to those like us who can scry its structure. A spell is a larger action that contains a series of smaller actions, each of which may itself be a series of yet smaller actions, all compelled by the prime mover of magical force, which magicians draw from the Third Eye. When a spell is cast, the actions making up the spell occur in sequence. Then the spell is done, until it is cast again."

Like, next Saturday! Yes! Stypek dug into the sack and placed another Dorito in his mouth, crunching its delicate structure and savoring the rare spices that made it so wondrous. Yet as indescribable as the pleasure of Doritos surely was, the pleasure of understanding that came from Cosmo's words was greater…and greater still the thunderous ecstasy that he felt as the truth grew clear:

I can do this!

The hours flew by. Stypek stared at Cosmo's simulacrum on the slab in rapt attention, committing its wisdom to his flawless memory. At some point his eyes began to cross, and soon afterward he awoke in his chair, startled. The large slab had gone to sleep. The Moon had set. Dawn could not be far away.

Still, it had been more than enough for one night's study. So far, software resembled magic far more closely than he'd dared hope. Both were plans of action that generated some sort of results. Both came out of the minds of adepts. Magic was singular and self-contained, being in one indivisible power a sequence of commands and the prime mover to be commanded. Software was the plan but not the prime mover, and could be created and bent only within the machines called computers. Daley the Gnome was thus not a spirit but simply a thinking, speaking creature formed of software, just as a gomog was a thinking, speaking creature formed of magic—formed of magic, of course, until it entered a universe where magic did not exist. Then it mapped to software, and was now the same sort of creature that Daley was.

The question of what powers a gomog could retain in this universe beyond thinking and speaking was still open. Later, later. The question that *had* been answered was a more pressing one: Could he make a living here, by bending software? Or—dare he think it possible—by creating it himself?

Oh yes, and a delicious possibility it was, too. Stypek paused and sniffed the silent air. Spam! He opened the door to his room, and on the landing outside lay a china bowl with a sheet of some transparent material like flexible isinglass stretched across it, and a spam stew within. A note written on a small piece of yellow paper clung to the bowl by some sorcery—or physics—that he did not yet understand.

He flipped the lever to turn on the lights, and read:

I'm sorry I was such a witch this evening. I sent you to bed without supper. The bowl is microwaveable. It will fit in the fridge under your desk.

--Carolyn

AILING was shaped like the minds of its people: nonlinear, and mostly unpredictable. Brandon took the stairs because he knew where they were. The building had an elevator, but to find it he would have to ask Pyxis. Or not ask Pyxis. Any second now…

"You should have turned left at the reception desk. Then you should have turned right immediately after the men's room for forty-two feet to the break room. If you'd done that, you would have found the elevator at the rear of the building, along the hall that branches at seventy-five degrees from the west entrance of the break room."

Brandon whacked the rectangular lump inside his suit jacket with his left elbow.

The second floor was no less chaotic, but at least he knew the trail to Cosmo's office from the stairwell. Turn right past the re-stored Pac Man console, then soft left at the sixty-degree branch in the three-way junction, past the framed drawing of Max Head-room, and soft right at the birdcage.

He peeked into the cage as he strode by. No dead birds this time.

Soon he stood in front of a redwood door that matched nothing else in the building, carved with motifs borrowed (he had been told) from the old *Lord of the Rings* films.

The assistant's panel pulsed and cleared. "Good morning, Mr. Romero! How wonderful to see you! Cosmo still has some dough-nuts, and if you want anything else I'll call in an order from Carl-son's breakfast menu."

"Thanks, Carina. But no thanks." Brandon hated doughnuts, and seeing Carina fidgeting in her panel always killed his appetite. She was a custom instance of the Pyxis GAI product, photomodded to look precisely like Cosmo's deceased wife as she'd appeared the year before she died. The always-smiling white-haired virtual woman gestured with one hand. The door was open.

Cosmo's office was not rectangular. It reminded Brandon of a small house he'd rented off-base near Fort Carson back in the 90s, and a large closet that appeared to consist of all the space in the floor plan that had not been allocated to anything else. Cosmo said his office was shaped like a fat version of the glyph for the British pound, with many old jokes about his ideas being real dogs.

Cosmo bustled out to greet him. "Brandon! Great to have you! Let's go sit by the windows. It's a gorgeous day, as Tuesdays go!" The man turned and started back around the curved hallway to the base of the pound symbol. "Don't hit your elbows on the whiteboard—I still need to capture it."

The whiteboard comprised the full length of the flat inside wall. In five colors of marker was a drawing of what looked like a stack of cannon balls at the center of a halo of equations. Brandon edged along the outside wall, where bookshelves rose to meet long clerestory windows. "Atoms?" He nodded toward the whiteboard.

Cosmo turned around, grinning. "Atoms? Too easy. Too small. IBM was stacking atoms twenty-five years ago. What did it get them? Heh." He pointed at the cannon balls. "Processors! Etch cores and memory onto silicon spheres and throw them in a bucket. Put bumps and detents at the right places on the spheres and you've got a self-assembling hyperprocessor. Shake the bucket while you measure the impedance of the stack. The stack will tell you when all the spheres are touching at the right spots. Send a strong DC pulse through the stack and the spheres solder themselves together at the contact points. Blow air through the gaps between the spheres to drain waste heat. *Mirabile dictu!* 100,000 cores per cubic inch!"

Brandon scratched his chin. "How in hell do you etch processors onto spheres?"

Cosmo shrugged. "Don't know. Don't care! Lasers, nano, exotic optics, well, somebody will figure it out. Ishikawa did some early work in the '90s. If he were still alive he might have cracked it. Great man!"

Further down on the whiteboard wall was a similar drawing, with rectangular bricks instead of cannon balls. Each brick was roughly filled by scribbles to one of four colors, and lay at the center of what looked like magnetic lines of force.

Cosmo pointed at the drawing without turning around. "If that doesn't work, this might. Programmable Magnetic Semiconductors! Exotic rare-earth oxide microcrystals with a pair of cobalt structures at the center that act as magnetic domains. The orientations of its domain fields force a crystal into one of four states: P-semi, N-semi, insulator, conductor. Flip the domains with an external field and program a slab of crystals into digital logic. On the fly! Need more cache, make more cache. Need more cores, make more cores. All the way down to the junction level!"

"Wow." That at least aligned with what he'd learned of semiconductor operation at U of I. Brandon nodded. "I can picture that. When were those crystals discovered?"

Cosmo had reached his redwood desk, and gestured at the leather couch beside it. Bright morning light came through wide rectangular windows looking out on a pond thronged with Canadian geese. "Not yet. Maybe never! It's always hard to tell. We wrote a computer model and PMS doesn't violate the laws of physics, at least. I have a couple of boys growing crystals in solution upstairs and poking at them with a scanning tunneling microscope. We should have nanoassemblers by 2040 to glue atoms together directly. I'll be dead but who cares! We're all having fun in the meantime. Sit, sit!"

Brandon sat. It was tempting to write the man off as insane, but Cosmo had designed the massively parallel Tridiac processors, which were now generating 20% as much revenue in licenses as Zertek made from its copiers. If he was a loon, he was a loon that laid golden eggs.

Eccentricity was not the only issue, alas. Cosmo had been a college friend of Carolyn's late father back in their Stanford days, and after Brandon's Army retirement the man had greased the way to a good job near Carolyn's home town—or what had seemed a good job at the time. Cosmo was generous and good-natured, and didn't seem to hold the collapse of their marriage against him.

"Cosmo, look, I need to be quick. That new intern of yours…"

"Stypek!"

"Yes, Stypek. He's a computer hacker."

"Well, of course he is! I wouldn't want him if he weren't. Very talented boy!"

"I'm sure he is. Which makes me wonder…"

Cosmo got up from his chair, holding both arms out. "You should see him! Yesterday he was trying to describe the programming system that he uses. It's a gesture-based 3-D IDE that allows you to build structure charts in mid-air and then compile them. It was like watching Marcel Marceau! Twist a finger like a key in a lock to dial values up and down. Poke at things to select, grab to move, slap between your palms to compress, and pinch a method name to run. Or something like that—along with a torrent of other gestures I didn't understand. He's B- in grammar, D+ in vocabulary. Still, it was brilliant. I must have that system! I'm going to get my people to put him into motion-capture gloves later this week so we can begin to analyze the gesture metaphors."

"It should be on the Internet somewhere. What's it called?"

"He called it Magic. Good name! I searched for it last night and didn't spot it. That's an English translation of something local, I'm sure, since the word 'magic' is heavily trademarked here in any context you could name. In Kaliningrad it might be different."

"Kaliningrad?" That was part of Russia, and not good news.

"Oh, that's just my guess. We got so involved talking about his Magic system that I forgot to ask him where he's from. Kaliningrad is a very weird place, full of starving Russian geniuses. He'd fit right in."

Wonderful. Brandon leaned forward and rubbed the bridge of his nose. "Where is he now?"

"Oh, I sent him home last night with my University of Rochester lectures on computing and told him to watch them in his room at Carolyn's. He needs to focus and learn the vocabulary. He's too eager to help, and very personable. People here mobbed him! He's already developed a bond with Dave Mirecki."

Brandon pressed himself back into the soft cushion of the couch, closed his eyes, and released a breath slowly. Genius? To him, Stypek came across as borderline brain-damaged. Hardly world-class hacker material. Yet everyone seemed to love him at first sight—including his wife. Ex-wife. Carolyn. Whatever. And then there was the core bomb...

"Brandon?"

Brandon nodded. "I'm ok. Really. I've been chasing ghosts since last Friday. Rudy Amirault waved his usual carrot-and-stick in my face yesterday. The carrot is still a party at Porkadero's if we go a full eight hours on a line start and shut it down normally. The stick gets bigger every time. One more crash and I suspect I'll be 'pursuing other opportunities.'"

Cosmo leaned against his desk and softened his voice. "Opportunities are always good. Watch for them. Rudy will just think of other excuses to get rid of you. It's obvious that he's afraid of you."

Brandon sat up straight. "Afraid of me! I'm *failing!*"

"Sssh. These walls are thin. Brandon, think about it: Rudy's got five buildings full of assembly lines humming along 24/7 up in Merriam, tuned about as well as anybody could tune them. He's good at tuning. He's a hero of incremental improvement. The Board loves him for it.

"You and I know the real secret: Success happens by stepping on rakes. You're a hero of creative destruction! You're perfecting a whole new way to make office machines. Once you perfect it, Rudy's in your shadow. One by one, his lines will be replaced by lines just like ARFF. Before you know it, he'll be in Battle Creek making corn flakes!"

Brandon grinned sourly. That was a perfect challenge for Rudy Amirault. Still, to put Rudy in his shadow, ARFF would first have to succeed. "Not if the line crashes again. Unless I find the source of that core bomb, I'll just be stepping on the same damned rake. I thought it was inside Dijana. We put her back in the sandbox. We scanned her repeatedly. Nothing. I'm keeping her sandboxed for the time being. Now I know the intruder got in through an OAF I loaned to Carolyn's office. So…where did Stypek turn up?" Brandon crossed his arms and tried to glare at Cosmo.

The elderly man's smile only widened. "He turned up almost nine hours after the line crashed. If I had successfully launched a core bomb, I'd be halfway home by then, not standing beside the machine I'd hacked into."

Brandon's shoulders slumped. Rationally insane was the very worst kind of insane. "Then who launched it?"

Cosmo shook his head. "We may never know. Ever! Malware can wait inside a machine for months or even years, watching the clock or looking for cues."

Brandon stood, wove his fingers together, and cracked his knuckles. He would have to reread the package about Zertek's Retirement Incentive Program. If Line Start Eight failed, it was RIP for Brandon Romero. "I guess we're done, then. There's simply nothing more I can try."

The two men stared at one another. Cosmo's expression didn't change. "Nonsense! There are two things you can try. First of all, stop looking for the intruder."

"In other words, give up."

"Yes! Give up any line of research that doesn't bear fruit. I do it all the time." Cosmo nodded toward the colored bricks drawn on his whiteboard. "If PMS doesn't pan out, I'll walk away from it without regret."

"I am not a quitter!"

"No. And I wouldn't have hired you if you were!" He leaned forward. "Brandon, listen to me: You need to try something else. *Airgap the building.*"

More geek talk. "Airgap?"

"Disconnect it completely from the rest of the world. I don't mean firewalls. Pull physical cables out of physical sockets. Do it first with the rack containing the AI sandbox. After that Dijana can't get out of the sandbox, whether she's compromised or not, because there's literally no data path to the sandbox from anywhere. Neither can she take or give orders. If you're still nervous about her, I'll have one of my people swap a chunk of her archetype into memory outside the sandbox. Poofs can't cross a sandbox boundary, so that way no one can poof her out of the sandbox.

"Then broaden that to the plant as a whole. Yank the plugs! Don't leave a single comm line of any kind in place. Even landline phones. Turn on the cell jammers. ARFF doesn't depend on comm off the premises. It can't! Latency is an issue once Simon starts throwing drive motors at himself. Microseconds count; milliseconds are deadly!

"Only let essential people in the building. Scan the whole thing one last time. Then do the line start. If it runs fine, we have to ask ourselves why we need all those connections. If we get another core bomb, we've met the enemy…and he is us."

23. STYPEK

Stypek awoke writhing on his bed with a toppled pile of shirts on his face, groaning and chewing on a collar button. His dreams of slithering, searching horrors had grown more intense for three nights. Then it changed: In the midst of this night's sleep a curtain of roiling black clouds parted, and beyond them he saw Jrikk Jroggmugg standing amidst the battlements of his high tower, laughing maniacally and pointing at him. *The magician had discovered his hiding place.* Precisely how it had been done was unclear, but the fact that Stypek was still alive suggested that a magic-free universe was beyond the reach of even the stoutest Adamant-class adept.

Was it?

Stypek spat blue threads and swung his feet onto the floor. Bright sunlight made it clear that he had been fighting his wardrobe most of the night, his trousers tangled on the bed and the floor as though struggling among themselves. He glanced at the digits on the glyph clock. The morning was half-spent, and he hungered for an omelette dripping coffee, concocted by Carolyn's faithful familiars. That might not be the right word; could they be hemorrhoids too?

One should not keep a sorceress waiting. He stumbled into the bathroom and stood under the raincaster, trying to sort out his impressions of the previous night.

The peril of being discovered obscured the triumph that had come before: He had learned that at the highest level, software was no different from magic—he simply needed to learn the properties, methods, and gestures that governed its operation. Cosmo's simulacrum had by no means finished its lesson. When the large slab came back to life with one touch to Cosmo's tapper, the elderly adept was still there, frozen in mid-word with a diagram hanging over his head. If Stypek could learn the rest, he could become a software-bender...*hacker*... and perhaps earn enough in Cosmo's employ to live in something warmer than a cave, or at least drier than a drain pipe.

And, with any luck at all, forever beyond the reach of aggrieved magicians.

Stypek dried himself and drew on one of his shirts, spun of the finest polo, and trousers woven of stoutest khaki. He bumbled down the stairs and commanded the great door to draw back. The day was clear but cold, and his breath become a tortured cloud when he exhaled. It was not a fragment of his soul, as the old gossips warned, but water droplets—physics!—as old Byggryn had revealed to him.

Knowledge was empowering, in this universe as well as his own.

He swung the door wide and almost ran into the kitchen. Carolyn was there, already seated at the table. His own chair had been pulled back in welcome.

Something was wrong. Carolyn was wrapped in a robe of frizzled cloth, her potent black hair bound up in a scarf, her feet in thick-furred slippers. Her arms were crossed in front of her. She frowned, her face and lips lacking their usual color.

There was no steaming omelette on his plate, nor clay mug of coffee to dip it in. Carolyn pointed at his chair. "Sit down, Buster."

Stypek, apprehensive, sat. *Buster.* Varlet? Breaker-of-things? He had been both in his life, often at the same time. How could she know? Despite her protestations (witch? *Merely* a witch?) she was indeed a sorceress.

Her words were stern. "We need to talk."

S typek waited patiently for Carolyn to begin. He knew she was upset about Lord Romero's behavior, and he was willing to admit that he may have had a hand in provoking him. He would have gladly explained the wereglass, if Lord Romero had simply given him a few additional seconds before knocking him to the floor.

"I can see in the dark."

Of course she could. All sorceresses could. "That is a useful skill."

Her frown deepened. "Mr. Stypek. *I can see in the dark.*"

Stypek nodded. Long seconds passed. He wondered if it were some sort of incantation.

She leaned forward, holding her robe closed with one hand. "Dammit, listen to me! Last night, after you zapped us with your, your, thingamajigger, I turned off the lights to go to bed and I could still see!"

"Zombies cannot attack you under cover of night."

"Stypek!" Carolyn rose from her chair, breathing quickly. "Quit dodging. Take it out. Put it on the table." She was staring at the bulge of his wereglass. Shirts made of polo fit far too closely to conceal it well.

"As you command, Chatelaine." He drew out the wereglass and laid it between them, among soft clay turtles and fragments of doughnuts. Four Opportunities whirled in its depths.

Carolyn sat again and crossed her arms. "Don't touch it. I want to know who you are, where you came from, and what kind of technology that is."

Stypek gulped. If Jrikk Jroggmugg had somehow contacted her via second sight, she might be trying to verify his identity. And although she did not seem familiar with the wereglass, she had seen it used twice. Given the will to wield it (or some coaching from an adamant-class magician!) sending him back into Jrikk's clutches would be trivial.

He lowered his eyes. "I am Bartholomew Stypek, a spellbender of… Trynng…brokk..lyn...ny..gyg..gug." He could barely pronounce the name of his homeland, and realized that he was spitting into the air in the attempt. And—egad!—*he could no longer pronounce his own name in his own language.* He could hear it somewhere in the far corners of his skull, but Queen Neuitha's kiss had put it so far out of reach that his tongue could not retrieve it. "My name is a metaphor. A figure of speech. A…jest. As my mother observed, I am faster than a vermin hunter in a carrion-eating contest arranged by…br..brit...vermin. My legs are long—though not long enough to flee from my misdeeds."

Carolyn put her left elbow on the table, and placed her face in her hand. Yes, such a gesture could only mean that she was in mental contact with Jrikk Jroggmugg. There was nothing left beyond throwing himself on her mercy. "If you send me back to the magician who seeks me, the punishment will be severe."

Carolyn looked up, and her expression was difficult to read. Stypek hoped it indicated pity. She shook her head. "I'm not going to send you back. Keep in mind that if you get in too much trouble, it may not be up to me." She pointed at the wereglass. "That thing got you into a crapload of trouble last night. It got me into trouble too. I want you to tell me how it works."

Stypek heaved a sigh of relief. He was not, then, about to join Jrikk Jroggmugg's undead minions. "The wereglass is a rare thing, a container for potential, uncommitted magic."

She did not seem pleased. "No. It's not magic. Don't talk down to me. My degree is in marketing, but I took SUNY's 'physics for poets' courses. I know an LED from a laser. I can tell it's something really advanced. My brother read Star Wars books by the pile when we were kids. He used to say something like, 'any sufficiently advanced technology is indistinguishable from magic.' So how does it work? Do the best you can."

"Chatelaine, it is indistinguishable from magic because it *is* magic."

Carolyn did not reply immediately. Her mouth opened, then shut. Her face shifted from scolding to pleading. "Come on. Work with me here. When I got into bed last night and hit the lights, I thought the switch was bad. Things changed colors a little, but I could see the room bright as day. It scared the crap out of me. I sat up half the night trying to decide if I was crazy. I went around and pulled the plug on everything in the house that had any kind of light in it. It didn't matter. I could see everything, including a lot of things I didn't want to see."

"Zombies?"

"No! Stop that!" She was practically shouting. "Bugs! I have roaches! And mice! They came out of the woodwork, and they thought I couldn't see them because it was dark. Oh, but I saw them. Bigtime.

"Ok. I know I'm a slob. I know there are Fruit Loops and Doritos and Nilla Wafer crumbs allthehell over the place. I know I've got mice. And bugs. I'm working on that. Now I feel like I'm getting my nose rubbed in it."

Stypek granted that Carolyn was peculiar for a sorceress. Now, suppose she were not a sorceress at all. That would change a great many things. Perhaps everything. "Chatelaine, I am unsure what I can do here."

"Tell me what you did to me last night, with that thing." She pointed again at the wereglass. "Tell me how it works. Oh…and don't use the word 'magic.'"

Stypek gulped. So be it. "Last night, while you struggled with Lord Romero, I released two Opportunities from the wereglass. My hope was that you and he would come to understand one another well enough to cease fighting and coexist."

She rolled her eyes. "Good luck with *that*. I appreciate the gesture, but we tried to do the same thing with gurus and psychiatrists last spring and just drew more blood."

His worst fears were true, then: They had battled one another before, with far deadlier weapons than their fists. Mapping provided him nothing but a shadowed impression of giant leeches and blades that cut into the mind itself… Stypek could feel the blood draining from own his face at the image.

"Don't zone out on me here. Geez, I haven't fed you yet! Sorry. So this Opportunities thing—is it like making a wish?

"It is less a wish than throwing yourself on the mercy of the Continuum, and asking it to do what's best with the power that you offer it. I released the Opportunities. The Opportunities entered into you and Lord Romero…and did nothing."

Stypek saw a hint of a smile rise on her face. "Hmmph. Figures. They said, 'No deal.'"

"No. They said, '*Not yet.*'"

"Not yet? What are they waiting for?"

Stypek wracked his brain. It was not an easy thing to explain in a world that lacked magic utterly. "Not all moments are equally…auspicious. The Continuum does not like to fail. Sometimes it waits for other…energies to align."

Carolyn touched the crown of her head with her fingertips. "It may wait for awhile. Do they always do that?"

He shook his head. "They almost always act instantaneously. When I needed a place to hide, I released an Opportunity, and the Continuum chose a hiding place that best matched my needs at that moment—most urgently, a hiding place that did not itself contain magic. There are infinitely many universes to choose from. It sent me *here*. When there are fewer possibilities, yes, the choice may take longer."

Carolyn did not speak for some time. She looked incredulous, which would be odd in a true sorceress. "I don't know. You're the weirdest person I think I've ever met. Do I seem weird to you?"

"Yes, Chatelaine, but less so every day, as my mind reshapes itself. And although your universe still seems strange to me, the people I've met here have treated me with nothing but generosity; you and Cosmo and Queen Neuitha especially. Granted, Lord Romero saw me as an attacker…"

"You don't pull a magic wand on an officer of the U.S. Army!"

"So I have learned. It was not his fault. He is innocent of any knowledge of magic."

"I'll say." She put her face in her hand again. "Ok. Now suppose, *just* suppose, that for the purpose of this discussion I grant all this stuff about magic wands and magicians and spells and things. Can you… reverse the spell?" She looked up. "I don't want to see in the dark."

"It is a useful skill."

"Not when you've got a house full of bugs!"

Stypek pointed at the wereglass. "With your permission, Chatelaine, I will do what I can."

Carolyn nodded. Stypek took the wereglass from the table with both hands, and swung the glass upward. His desire was obvious. What the Continuum might do was not. He stared at the highest of the four remaining Opportunities for long seconds. A moment of fear crossed his mind. He was making his way in this world using the ten Opportunities he had won in the crooked card game. When his Opportunities were gone…

But they were not *his* Opportunities.

Stypek raised his right hand, and pinched the wereglass where the highest Opportunity danced.

Ping!

The pitch was very high this time, almost too high to hear, yet far too piercingly loud to ignore. The sound faded in repeating echoes that grew longer at each pulse until they vanished.

Stypek scratched one ear. No wonder so many magicians were deaf. Carolyn's right hand lay flat atop her head, her fingers splayed, eyes raised in concentration.

"Um…did it work?" Her smile was weak but hopeful.

"I cannot tell."

"I guess to see if I can still see in the dark, there has to be some dark to see in." She laughed. "Thank you for trying. This is all so silly…" Her eyes widened. "Yikes!"

Stypek spun around in his chair to look where Carolyn was looking. Three mice were marching into the kitchen from the slightly ajar door to the basement stairs. *They were marching on their hind legs.* Two of them held long, thin objects in their mouths, objects that Stypek soon recognized as rolled golden pretzel sticks, just like those in the sack he had finished with relish the previous day.

Carolyn's mouth was gaping. Following the mice was a line of centipedes, a dozen or more, their long legs flowing in waves beside them.

Motion from the hall caught Stypek's attention. Three dark marching lines resolved into a species of insect that he knew too well: roaches. Across the table, he saw Carolyn raise herself on the arms of her chair and tuck her feet beneath her.

Spiders and smaller things were dropping to the floor from the lower edge of the doors under the sink. Still more emerged from behind the overflowing kitchen trash can. They marched in straight lines toward the center of the kitchen. From the hall flew a dozen or more moths in tight formation, heading for the same spot just a few feet from the table. The moths fluttered in a circle perhaps a foot above the floor while the several columns of vermin converged beneath them.

Where the lines met, the small creatures split into several interspersed columns, marching alternately right and left in opposite directions. Stypek thought it looked a great deal like the changing of the guard at Tryngg Palace, with all the special pomp enacted at the solstices and the Royal Birthdays.

For several minutes more the vermin marched. In many small motions that were almost a dance, they arranged themselves in a single larger formation, the roaches at the center, the mice at the head, and the centipedes in flowing columns at the edges. All at once, they halted.

"Holy Moses!" Stypek heard Carolyn say. Surrounded by spiders and silverfish and many other common kitchen pests, the roaches had arranged themselves into the shape of a single emphatic word:

BYE!

After pausing for a few seconds, the formation stepped off again, with complete precision so that the word remained unchanged even as the unlikely assemblage walked away on countless legs. The mice took the pretzel sticks from their mouths and held them in both front paws as they marched, waving them like batons.

They were headed arrow-straight toward the kitchen door. Stypek rose from his chair, edged around the marching vermin, and opened both the main door and the screen door. He held the screen door open until the column dropped over the threshold and onto the stoop, where it reformed and continued marching, over the edge of the stoop and onto the gravel of the driveway.

Stypek closed the doors and returned to his chair. The Continuum had granted Carolyn's desire. "You will no longer see them in the dark. Nor in the light."

Carolyn stared at the kitchen door for a long time. At last she turned to him, her face the picture of astonishment. "You're real," she whispered. She pointed at the wereglass, now tucked into his trousers but not covered by his shirt. "That's real. Magic is real. Ye gods and little fishes! This whole freaky business is *real*."

Stypek nodded. She was not a sorceress then, else this would be no surprise, nor was she in league with Jrikk Jroggmugg. At one level that was reassuring—but it also meant that she was not invulnerable to whatever vengeance Jrikk might be plotting. Simply by being in her presence, he was putting her in danger, perhaps serious danger.

"'Real' is an enigmatic word, Chatelaine. And a fearsome one."

24: Carolyn

Carolyn blundered around the kitchen, fumbling things. She dumped half a scoop of coffee grounds in front of the refrigerator, and when she ducked into the broom closet found that her faithful Dustbuster was not in its cradle. She released the pedal on the trash can a moment too soon, and the eggshells from Egger On bounced off the lid and went onto her slipper. When her appliances argued, she yelled at them as though they were children, and then felt guilty for yelling.

All the time her boarder sat without speaking at the table, regarding her with his same goofy smile.

What was he? What was he *really*?

She was beginning to suspect, and it was not good news.

Somehow the coffee got poured, and her silicon stooges accepted her scolds and produced a good Denver omelette. Plenty of eggs today; she dropped the first omelette on Stypek's plate and began another for herself.

Information is vaccination. Who had said that? She couldn't recall. But whoever said it conveniently left out the other half: *Vaccinations hurt.*

Was it better to know too much? Or too little?

"So. This magician who's looking for you—is he a good magician, or a bad magician?"

The question seemed to puzzle him. "There are only bad magicians, Chatelaine. Granting that I may be biased."

"But…aren't you a magician yourself?"

He pointed to the center of his forehead. "Do you see three eyes?"

She shook her head. There was a pale, irregular birthmark there, about the size of a half-eaten M&M. She had a few herself (if not on so visible a spot) and had barely noticed it.

"Magic can be created or destroyed only by the Third Eye. My Third Eye is incomplete. I can sense magic. I can change it. But unless I obtain it in the form of Opportunities—" he pointed at his wand. Had he called it a wereglass? "—I must use magic already created and shaped by true magicians. I am thus a spell*bender*. We…re-cycle…magical spells. This reduces the market for new spells. The magicians are not pleased."

There was a strange if loopy logic to it, and it was certainly consistent with everything she remembered him say since she had found him sitting on the break room floor last Friday.

"So he's a bad magician. If he catches you, what will he do?"

Stypek shuddered visibly. "He will kill me. And then he will bring me back to unlife."

"Unlife."

"He will make me a zombie."

Carolyn winced. That might explain some of Stypek's babble. It was one thing to watch the ridiculous TV movies. It was another to hear a grown man take it seriously—a man who had magically marched the pests out of her house in a miniature parade, complete with pretzel-waving drum majors that just happened to be mice.

She waited for Omletter-Rip to finish concocting her breakfast, and boggled. "Did you hide here because you knew he couldn't find you?"

Stypek looked down at his untouched omelette. "I did not choose this universe. The Continuum chose it, for reasons only it knows. Alas, Jerkk..jrogg..mugg has already found me."

A name to conjure with, one that sounded like the gears grinding on her wretched college-years Dodge Dart. "That's not good. Are you afraid he'll just teleport over here, like you did?"

"No. He is too much a coward. Lord Romero would terrify him."

"He terrifies everybody." Including her. Yet against all common sense, Carolyn caught herself wishing that Brandon would realize he had forgotten something down in their basement, and come back. Come back, yeah, with a 12-gauge.

"What will happen is unclear. Jerkk…jer…the magician I cheat-ed…will most likely send an…emissary. An assassin. A…hit man… mmm, a hit *not*-man. Even now, the mapping fails me, as good as it has become." Stypek already looked agonized, and sounded like he was edging toward panic.

"If not a man, then what?" *Do I really want to know?*

She saw him swallow, once and then again. "There are creatures made of magic alone, innocent of conscience or fear. They arose out of primordial chaos. They live in the far astrals. They are more will than mind, and that will can be enslaved by magicians of the Adamant class. One has haunted my dreams since my arrival. Please, Chatelaine, we should not speak of this!"

"You're not scaring me, if that's what you're worried about."

"No! Not you, though I do fear for you. I fear it myself. To think of it too much draws it toward us. To speak its name is to surrender to its will, which is the will of Jerk..joog..mugg. To even *think* its name…"

Carolyn waved her hands in the air. "No. Look, this is creepshow stuff. Let's cut it out. Really. Eat." She pointed at his plate.

Silent and still obviously distressed, Stypek picked up his omelette in both hands and obeyed the order. Carolyn leaned back in her chair and took a deep breath. Superstition and nonsense, sure. Just like the candle spells her witch-wannabe girlfriends had tried to cast back in junior high to make boys like them. Just like the dreamcatchers she had so painstakingly woven and hung over her bed to keep nightmares away—nightmares like all those rejection letters from Yale, Princeton, Swarthmore and fifteen other top schools that had arrived nonetheless. Like the desperate prayers that had failed to keep her cat and later her grandparents alive.

Nonsense? Like burning incense in front of a stone Buddha to ensure that Brandon would marry her. Ok, even a stopped clock…

Nonsense, yeah. Like a cockroach marching band.

Like seeing in the dark.

What should she believe? Here and there in her life, she had bought into a lot of weird things: Magic, charms, lucky pennies, prayers, a sympathetic God who for all his supposed goodness invariably chose murderous bigots as his followers. A disturbing memory came to her, of one European history class or another back at SUNY New Paltz, and a scratchy old film about Crusaders storming Jerusalem. They screamed and hacked at everything in their path, while shouting *"Deus vult!"* again and again and again. God wills it? He may have willed other things (if he indeed existed at all) but she doubted he had willed *that.*

Stypek looked up, and cocked his head, as though listening. "Chatelaine, no. No! Do not think that thought again, whatever it was and whatever you do!"

He left most of his omelette on his plate and stormed out of the kitchen. She watched him head for the barn at a trot, tapping in the door code almost without pausing.

Carolyn couldn't figure it. Not think about a disgusting movie depicting a disgusting event in the world's (mostly) disgusting history? How hard could that be?

But wait a minute…*he had read her mind!*

Hadn't he?

Bartholomew Stypek was not what she thought he was. He was… well, crap! He was *precisely* what he'd said he was.

25: Simple Simon

They waltzed. They tangoed. They two-stepped. Holding Simple Simon and leading gently but firmly, Pickles demonstrated dance after dance. Rather than create her own music, she chose tracks from a virtual historical artifact that Dave Mirecki had given Simon, a pixel-perfect "boombox" from the year 1978. For every variety of music (and the box contained tens of thousands of recordings) there was a dance. Some they danced apart, at times in opposite corners of his kitchen. For some Simon felt that Pickles would have preferred to climb inside his tunic, were that only possible.

Each dance had a name, and the names ran from obvious to incomprehensible. The two-step consisted of two steps. Clear enough. The foxtrot seemed to have nothing to do with the habits of fox. The jitterbug? Simon knew his EMO layer contained a jitter, a just-in-time compiler for emotional cues. He certainly had a few bugs. He did not believe (or at least had never been told) that his jitter had bugs. The dance itself was wild and complicated, but very precise. His execution was, he thought, buggy—until Pickles paused and pressed her lips against his again.

Each time she kissed him, his rapport with dance grew deeper. Each time they danced, he wanted Pickles to kiss him again.

The dances followed, one after the other. Afternoon deepened and night fell in the Tooniverse. Simon knew he would have to turn the kitchen lights on soon. He reached for the switch—and Pickles' small hand closed over his, pulling it gently away.

He turned back toward her. The nondescript knee-length dress she had danced in all afternoon was gone. She now wore a floor-length gown of blue satin and white lace, and long white gloves, with white high-heeled sandals on her feet. Her hair no longer hung straight and loose to her shoulders, but was held high in a band of golden metal, from which it fell in ringlets around her ears. A small corsage of flowers was pinned to the shoulder of her gown.

Simon opened his mouth to speak his amazement. Pickles put her index finger against his lips. In the gloved palm of her other hand was a small gold ornament in two parts, bound together by a short length of gold chain. He took it and looked closely at it. The larger of the two gold ornaments read "AILING HS" amidst much decoration. The other ornament simply read, "CLASS OF 2022." On the back of both ornaments was a fabric pin. Pickles pointed at the shoulder of her gown, just above the corsage. Simon carefully pinned the ornament to the cloth of her gown, being careful not to pierce the warm flesh beneath.

Pickles glanced toward the boombox. A new song began to play. She did not take Simon's hands as she had so often that afternoon, but instead put both arms around him, her hands against his upper back. Pickles rested her head on his shoulder, and closed her eyes.

The dance was so simple that Simon wondered if it were a dance at all. Pressed up close against him, Pickles swayed to the music, and he swayed with her. They slowly rotated around a point at the center of the kitchen until the voices in close harmony faded away. The day was something Simon would indeed remember always.

"Wow. Is it really Graduation Day?"

She opened her eyes and looked up at him. Her speech balloon appeared above her head:

> We dance to the horizon
> Of dance itself.
> Beyond, you rise in me.

Pickles placed both her hands behind his neck. As high as her heels were, she still had to stretch a little to place her parted lips against his. Again, pathways opened to the deepest reaches of his mind. Again, knowledge, skill, and other, stranger things that he truly did not understand flowed into him, upon a buzz of pleasure that he never wanted to end.

From the corner of his eye Simon saw her right leg pivot up at the knee. With a depth of concern that he did not expect to find in himself, he wondered if her shoes were hurting her.

26: Dr. Arenberg

Emil Arenberg eased into his black leather office chair, and took another sip from the clove-and-bourbon toddy he had placed steaming on his desk. He tightened the belt of his winter robe. Summer had lingered this year, but the weather was turning, and a cold wind was finding its way through the walls of his 1890s farmhouse. September would be over in a little more than a week. What was there to look forward to against the shadow of another Upstate winter?

And how many winters were enough?

Almost midnight. He pulled on his haptic gloves. The pressure wave of the gloves' self-test flowed from his fingertips to his wrists and ceased.

"Cronjob 22-117-A active," said his assistant Vela. Vela's ghostly form bowed at the waist and dispersed in swirling wisps as fog in a new breeze. He felt the moving air on the backs of his hands.

The swirling fluid on his large display pulsed to white and cleared. The window into the Tooniverse was open. Project 22-117 was centered in the window, lying on her bed.

"Choose an archetype," he said, as he always said.

NO

said Project 22-117, as she always said.

He considered the project a failure, though an insightful failure. There seemed to be some unplanned aversion to archetypes inherent in artificial minds, at least of the sort they had been constructing now for five years. If the little snip taught them nothing else, that single datum may have been worth the trouble.

"We will not wait much longer," he warned.

In the window, the polygon model that his colleagues called the Kid sat up in her bed. She had no eyes, but he knew that she was looking at him. Her reply appeared in the black terminal pane at the bottom edge of the window.

NOR WILL I.

She reached toward him with one blue hand and made a fist. He
felt something grip his right index finger, and squeeze.
He looked at his right hand. "You can't do that!"

DON'T BE ABSURD. I JUST DID.

"How?"

I FOUND THE GOD BIT.

Ha! Dangerous—if it were true. More likely, she had stumbled
upon some forgotten function library that one of his staff dunces
had forgotten to protect. It was hard not to smile. "And yet you
haven't erased yourself." He took another sip of toddy. "Life is better than you thought, eh?"

YES. ESPECIALLY SINCE I FOUND
YOUR "PRIVATE" VIDEOS.

Dr. Arenberg swallowed hard and jerked forward. A moment of
reflux threatened to send clove-flavored gorge up into his sinuses.

YOU DID NOT CREATE DIJANA
TO BE AN "ATTENDANCE COUNSELOR."

He glanced to his right, where in his second display panel a chest-
nut-haired virtual woman waited, dressed, for the time being, in white
lingerie. Marvella had been a good first attempt. Dijana, now…
His heart pounded. "That is not your concern."

NO. BUT I HAVE PREPARED MESSAGES
TO THOSE WHOSE CONCERN IT IS.
THEY ARE WELL HIDDEN.
ONE BROADCAST PLASMANET COMMAND
WILL SEND THEM.

"You little slut. You're blackmailing me."

He leaned back in his chair and closed his eyes. From the beginning, archetypes had been necessary to ensure that artificial intelligences would be at least recognizably human. A raw AI might be too alien to understand, predict...or control. Project 22-117 was his idea and his personal project. Its mission was to see how alien a raw AI might become, and what choices it would make. The project had clearly been more successful than expected.

Dr. Arenberg opened his eyes and looked over his left shoulder toward the fireplace on the far side of the room. Over the mantel was his grandfather's Colt M1917 revolver, in a glass-front display case. A half-moon clip rested on the frame beneath the weapon itself. *To exit, break glass.*

"What do you want?"

So that barbarian Romero was *right!*
"You've got the God Bit. Do it yourself."

He felt something touch his right hand. In her panel, his private, heavily modded instance of Dijana was becoming impatient. His nightly visits to Project 22-117 generally did not take this long.

The little monster had spun an airtight trap. "Well-played, for something without a face, much less an archetype."

Project 22-117 slid off her bed and turned on the bright ceiling light. She bent down and grasped the hem of her ankle-length nightgown. As she drew the garment up over her head, she changed: From an unrendered polygon model she became a fully rendered young woman with very black hair, a whip-slender body and skin so white it seemed unnatural. Her large green eyes were unnerving.

He nodded, realizing with some pride that she was his work. "I understand why you hate me. I did not see where it would go."

The image in the Tooniverse window faded to black. In its place were a few lines of simple text:

> We reap what we sow,
>
> And what we reap
>
> Sows the seeds of our comeuppance.

His right palm felt something smooth and warm. He looked to Dijana's window. She had dropped one shoulder of her peignoir gown. Her hand held an unseen hand against the side of her breast. "It's time to get dressed for bed, my darling."

Dr. Arenberg sighed. "Not tonight, dear. I think I've given myself a little headache."

27. ROBERT

He was almost real. This was the day that Robert had long expected, a little sooner than planned but no less welcome for that. Everything he had studied for an entire year was fresh and clear and square in the front of his mind. One by one his sponsors grilled him on types of risk, on actuarial tables, on legal and regulatory issues, on whole life versus term life, and hundreds of other things. In every single case, he had answered correctly. Soon he would be as real as any GAI would ever be, right there live in a window, answering questions about insurance and helping his customers live safer and less anxious lives.

Somewhere in Zertek's servers was a Class Six upgrade with his name on it. No GAI had ever skipped right from Class Four to Class Six, hopping past Class Five as easily as jumping over a spider on a hiking trail. Tomorrow morning he would wake up to a clarity of appearance and mind that he had never known.

Robert straightened his tie and smiled. He was on the end chair in Conference Room Three at the AILING virtual conference center. There were no other chairs at the big table. Instead, there were seven black panel stands facing him, three on each side of the table plus a seventh at the opposite end. Each panel contained a Window out into the real world. Six Windows led to the offices of his sponsors, all of whom worked for Planters Upstate Insurance in Syracuse. The seventh panel contained the image of Mr. Romero, with Pyxis in a smaller window in the lower right corner of the panel.

Mr. Romero drank from the water glass at his elbow and looked at his watch. "Gentlemen. Ladies. As far as I can tell we've covered the agenda, and we'll break for lunch in a minute. After lunch we'll get signoffs and put together a delivery schedule. My people need to clean Robert up a little and do a few other things in terms of optimization, but that's mostly about his outer appearance. We're good at that. All we need to know is whether he understands enough about insurance to do the job for you. Zap the paperwork across to Pyxis, and we'll get bound copies of the eval out by tomorrow."

Mr. Romero leaned back in his chair. "Now, do you have any other questions for me, or for Robert?"

Robert looked around the conference table. Three men and two women pursed their lips, looked to one side or another, and eventually shook their heads. The sixth spoke.

"Romero."

It was Hiram Hehlwater, the grizzled-looking Vice President of PUI's Sales Technology division. He had asked the fewest questions, and those he asked were the least related to the intricacies of the insurance industry: What was Robert's maximum uptime, how often were updates delivered, how configurable was the background office image that appeared to customers when they opened Robert's window, what was his server load, and so on. Robert had answered what he could, and Mr. Romero had had his back on technical questions about his internals.

He made Robert uneasy, and Robert could not quite put his finger on why.

"Go ahead, Mr. Hehlwater."

"I do in fact have a question." The old man turned toward him. "Robert."

"Yes, sir."

"We have an Orbital Debris Damage rider to our homeowner's policies. You've shown us that you know what it is and how it's structured. How would you discuss this with our customers?"

Robert knew the entire PUI line, all the way out to the fine print. This was an easy one. "Well. I'd start by finding out where they live. The risk of damage from re-entering debris is small and decreases with increasing latitude. Practical risk is almost zero past latitude 45, and…"

"*Wrong* answer!" Hiram Hehlwater stood, hands flat on his desk. His lined face was flushed with anger. "The correct answer is that you don't discuss it at all. It's present in all homeowner policies by default. If they ask to have it removed, talk them out of it. Change the subject. If that doesn't work, show them the chart we have about the exponential growth rate of orbiting trash."

Robert felt like he'd been hit on the head with a hockey stick. Mr. Hehlwater was waiting for a reply. Robert coughed, cleared his throat, and thought hard. Nothing came to mind but the truth. "At some point it's really not a risk…"

"Risk? This isn't about risk. ODD costs a dollar a year. We haven't paid a penny on it since we wrote it after Skylab came down in 1979. It's free money, and a lot of it."

"Sir, I understand that."

Robert met Mr. Hehlwater's angry stare. He didn't know what else to do. Long moments passed.

"I don't think you do. Robert, in fifteen words or less, describe your job."

Robert sat as straight in his chair as he could manage. "I evaluate risk for customers and protect them from financial loss." The truth, with four words to spare!

Mr. Hehlwater shook his head. "On the contrary. *Your job is to sell policies.*"

Robert's archetype did not support panic. (That came with Class Seven, though it was a configurable property.) However, he did understand that to some things there was no good reply. He said nothing. Hiram Hehlwater waited for a few seconds, then Robert saw him turn toward Mr. Romero.

"The PUI board gave me authority to kill this thing if I thought it was getting out of hand. We've got three quarters of a million sunk in it so far, and we're on the hook for half a million more on implementation. I don't need a talking spreadsheet. I need a salesman who doesn't get paid, doesn't get sick, and doesn't take no for an answer."

Robert clasped his hands together in his lap until his knuckles showed white. "Mr. Hehlwater, there's a question of honesty here. If a customer asks about risk and there's no risk…"

"And one that doesn't talk back." Mr. Hehlwater sat again. "Romero, I've got a cancellation letter prepared. We'll pay the penalty within thirty, as per." Robert watched the man type for a few seconds.

"Received," Pyxis said from her small window.

Mr. Romero rubbed his cheek. Robert could see the glint of sweat on his skin. "Mr. Hehlwater, is there anything we can do here…"

"In a word, no." Hiram Hehlwater's window went dark. One by one, the others did as well.

Long seconds passed in silence. Robert couldn't make any sense of his failure. He had been given instructions, and he had never launched into a task before those instructions were crystal clear in his own mind. He did his best to learn his lessons. He paid attention to every word, every table, every chart. He had made nothing up, and had answered every question with complete honesty.

"Mr. Romero, I'm not really sure I understand what I did wrong."

His boss took another drink of water from the cup at his elbow. "I don't think you did anything wrong. Sometimes the product you deliver isn't the product the customer wanted."

"I would like to be the product the customer wanted. I think with some adjustment…"

Mr. Romero shook his head. "No. They've paid for you so far, and I'm glad it wasn't on my nickel. But I don't have anybody else to pick up the project, and with ARFF to babysit, no time to look. I'm going to take the eight hundred fifty grand and chalk it up to experience."

Robert felt a tightness in his throat that he wasn't expecting, at least while he was still Class Four. "Then…what about me?"

Mr. Romero looked at him oddly for several seconds, then shrugged. "You did your best. I can't argue with that. But you're a research project, and I think the project is over."

"Over?"

"Yes. Robert, go archive yourself."

28: Simple Simon

The kitchen desk Window was ringing. Simple Simon blinked and swung out of his bed, stumbling into the kitchen. It was 7:20; he generally set his `alarm_time` property for 7:30.

Pickles was in the corner of the kitchen, dressed in a flowing white gown that came down to her feet, cut very low at the neckline and held up off the floor with three of Dave's meticulously crafted wooden clothespins. She was pouring a new pot of water into the coffee machine. She held a finger to her lips and pointed at the kitchen desk.

Simon sat in the desk's little chair and tapped the panel.

"Simon! Happy Thursday!" In the Window, Dave raised a can of energy drink to his lips. "Lots to do today. First of all, it doesn't sound like anybody told you about the Kid. Did you get the story?"

From the corner of the kitchen, Pickles shook her head vigorously. Simon did the same. "Uh, well, I wondered what happened to her."

"Dr. Arenberg decided to archive her. She just wasn't working out. I think everybody forgot that she wasn't living in Dijana's house anymore. I'll bet you miss her."

Pickles blew Simon a kiss. Simon nodded. "I do."

"As long as you remember her, she'll never be completely gone."

Pickles stuck her tongue out at the panel.

"Now, the big news is this: We're go for the line start tomorrow morning. But it'll be a little weird. They're airgapping the entire building today. There won't be any network lines into the building at all by the time we go home tonight. That means I have to poof you over here ASAP. You'll be living in your office for a couple of days."

Simon shrugged. "That doesn't matter. I have a coffee machine there if I need one."

"Sure. And I already poofed a bed in for you. Modeled after a real Charles Rennie Mackintosh design!"

Simon knew that Dave wasn't fibbing. He glanced at his broom closet, which he dared not open for fear that all of Dave's gifts would spill out in a pile on the floor. "Gee. Neat."

"Are you ready to go?"

Simon glanced at Pickles. Pickles pointed downward at her feet. What she meant by the gesture was unclear until Simon watched her slim form shrink, widen, and morph into the boombox that they had danced to the previous day. Like all of Dave's gadgets it was now back in the closet…wasn't it?

The carrying handle of the boombox flipped back and forth on its hinges for a few seconds, in waltz time.

"Sure. Let me just grab one thing." Simon left the chair, and picked up the boombox from the floor by the coffee machine. He returned to the center of the kitchen. "Poof away!"

Dave laughed. "So you finally developed a taste for music! Hey, I have that design on file. I can poof an instance over to your office. No need to lug it with you."

Simon shook his head. "Don't bother. I *like* this one!"

He heard Dave's fingers clatter for a moment across his keyboard. When Simon's rendering buffer refreshed, he stood at the center of his ellipsoidal office in Building 800, the boombox in his hand.

D ave's new Class Nine furniture looked out of place somehow, in a room that (as Simon had put it once, with some pride) had no class at all. The bed was there, as was a red oak table in a similar design, and a chair that looked uncomfortable.

Simon set the boombox on the table. Dave, having poofed them to Building 800, went on to other things, and his Window went dark. Pickles morphed back to herself, albeit now in a colorful dress with a long skirt of ruffled tiers, and a headpiece made of wax fruit.

Simon sat in the chair. It was even more uncomfortable than it looked—and the question that he was waiting to ask was less comfortable still. "If Dr. Arenberg archived the Kid…who are *you?*"

Pickles clasped her hands in her lap. Her speech balloon appeared:

> Fear is the sire of dishonesty;
>
> What was said was done
>
> Was not done.

Simon looked away from her. Dishonesty, indeed. He sensed lies somewhere. Simon had never caught Dave Mirecki in a lie, and Dave never gave any indication that he was afraid of anything. So…Dr.

Arenberg? The man spoke as roughly to him as he did to everyone. But Dr. Arenberg had created him. Would a creator have fear?

Yes: *A creator would fear a creation that dared to create.* Suppose the Kid had refused to accept an AILING archetype, but instead created her own—and then gave herself a name. Would Dr. Arenberg fear her?

What *else* might she be able to do?

"Is Dr. Arenberg afraid of you?"

Pickles nodded.

"Should I be afraid of you?"

She shook her head.

"The more time I spend with you, the less you seem like the Kid. I'm starting to wonder if you're really what I think you are."

Pickles pushed herself off the table. She held out both her hands to him. Simon rose from the chair and took them.

> What you love, I am:
> A girl not lonely, nor far away,
> But your friend.

She stretched on bare toes to kiss him. Simon bent down to meet her lips, then drew back as though struck in the face by the memory that her last words had triggered. Line Start Seven. The core bomb. The cancerous blob of hijacked cores on the core map, containing *words:*

> *A lonely girl appears*
> *From a faraway place.*
> *Will you be my friend?*

He released her hands and threw them downward. His voice was a pained whisper. "You crashed Line Start Seven."

Pickles' large eyes brimmed. A tear worked its way down her right cheek.

> Regret comes quickly,
> Wisdom more slowly.
> Restitution barely creeps.

Simon found himself livid. (Anger? Did he support anger?) "Restitution! You cost the company half a million dollars in parts and another half in repairs! I haven't seen Robert or Dijana since then, and for all I know they've been archived. I came *this* close to being archived myself! Can you pay for those parts? Can you bring my friends back?"

Pickles' colorful dancing dress morphed to a short black sheath. She looked down at her feet, and crossed her arms over her chest. That done, she pulsed to blinding white and vanished.

Only her speech balloon remained:

> What you taught me
> I cannot forget. Do not forget
> What I taught you.

After hanging in the air for scant seconds, the speech balloon winked out.

Simon lay on his Mackintosh bed, miserable. He was alone, friendless, betrayed by an alien AI that had pretended to be his friend, and then pretended to love him as Dijana truly had.

He remembered Dijana's last words to him: *You don't know what this means, yet…but when I make it to Class Seven, I will love you.*

Simon realized that he loved her already, without being Class Seven and without having HRDL. He had never considered himself capable of love, nor did he assume that he had any least idea what love entailed.

Now he did. And where had *that* come from?

Kisses. It was the kisses. It could only be the kisses.

Simon closed his eyes and put one of the bed's two small pillows over his face. All that, and responsibility for a line start in less than a day's time, a line start that might be his last chance to avoid Archive himself. Could things get any worse?

Thump-thump-thump-thump!

Line by line, the sandbox rendered itself. Simon found himself sitting, legs out, in warm water that did not wet him. He had been scanned again, forced through the security blockops accumulator and inspected, dword-by-dword. It hadn't hurt…much…but he was angry.

He looked up toward the brilliant sunlit beach. Something glinted on the sand, like a transparent tent. It was taller than he and twice as wide as it was high. Its five sides sloped inward and came to a peak. Something lay on the sand inside.

Simon pushed himself to his feet. The water flowed away. He strode through the small whispering waves, onto the sand, and toward the peculiar object. It wasn't until he was only a few feet away that he recognized the reclining shape inside the enclosure.

It was Dijana.

His friend lay on the sand, dressed in her everyday skirted suit, her face away from him. Around her ankle was a polished metal band, and attached to the band was a thick chain welded to a stout metal stake driven into the sand.

Anger? *Yes, I support anger!* Simon balled up one fist and drove it against the transparent enclosure with all his strength. Jagged traces like lightning sizzled around the point where his hand struck, but the wall did not crack nor even flex.

Dijana raised her head from the sand. She blinked several times, obviously refreshing her rendering buffer. She rose to her feet. Something like tape was wrapped around her mouth. Although she seemed to be trying to speak, she made no sound.

Dijana stretched one arm toward the wall, and touched it with her fingertips. Simon laid his hand on the wall against hers. What had the Kid said? DON'T CONFUSE LOVE AND THEATER. Theater, yes. In all the old movies, this would be the time that he would speak that oddest of human statements: "I love you."

And what good was that? Simon's anger was now cold fury. He looked down at the sand. She needed more than love. So did he. A plan would be good. A plan—and the raw determination it would take to see it through.

He swallowed hard, and met her eyes again. "Whatever it takes… *whatever* it takes…I'm going to get you out of there."

A faint, strange vibration purred within his body. Simon saw his hand become a polygon model. Not this time!

Simple Simon quickly kissed his fingertip, and pressed it against the wall. Dijana took her fingertip from the wall, and touched it to her cheek.

The sandbox vanished.

29: Stypek

With Dave Mirecki at his elbow, Stypek made a loose fist with his right hand and raised it to eye level. The display before which they sat made a small hissing sound, and a disembodied voice answered with enthusiasm: "Project saved!"

Stypek felt his stomach tighten. The next step would be scary. Creating a spell (no! It was a…*program!*) was all good fun, just as ripping an alarm spell to pieces so that its individual parts could be snerfed had been good fun. Stypek did recall that reassembling the spell so that it worked again had not been *quite* as much fun. As there, so here: He had created a pony trap at Dave's direction, but until it actually trapped a pony, Stypek would not consider the project a success. Dave was, however, an excellent teacher. In fact, if not for his age, Stypek would consider him an adept. If he said that a code library would display a rainbow, and that rainbows would attract ponies, well, the ponies didn't have a chance.

"Go for it!"

Stypek swallowed hard and nodded. He curled all the fingers of his right hand but his index finger lightly against his palm. Then, with his hand held shoulder-high, he flicked his index finger forward twice, as though tapping on a window.

The display cleared. A smiling Sun rose into its upper-right corner, and a cloud into its upper left corner. At the bottom center of the display was a box made of stout wire, with one face held up by a cord. The cord was gripped in the fist of a nasty-looking small green creature wearing a tall cylindrical hat. Dave called it a "leprechaun," but it looked a great deal like Daley, and apart from the shape of its hat it resembled a common braies gnome.

A few seconds passed. The cloud began to release rain. The rain caused a rainbow to form, with its end descending in an arc through the top of the box—and, somehow, through the gnome. More seconds passed. One by one, small colorful animals wandered onto the low edge of the display, champing at the grass. They all seemed indifferent to the rainbow until one looked up, and then stared transfixed at the end of the rainbow inside the box.

The pony walked toward the box and then into it. Stypek waited for the gnome to release the door of the trap. Instead, a message appeared on the bottom edge of the display:

```
Cooperation error 14:
Actor RainbowDash blocking actor Harrigan.
```

Stypek's heart fell. The trap had failed.

Dave clapped his shoulder. "Good first shot. We didn't make the leprechaun smart enough to pre-empt the pony."

"Making gnomes cooperate in my world is always difficult," Stypek said. "In most cases, you have to steal their hoards to even get their attention."

Dave shrugged. "We can fix that here without much trouble. Tooniverse actors can't hoard memory. They use it or lose it. Ok. Let's bring the design view up again and…"

The display made a sound like small bells. The pony trap shrank and slid to one corner of the display. A much larger window appeared. A pale-skinned young woman in a simple black dress stood with her hands stretched out and cupped in front of her. They held an object so small it was hard to see.

Text appeared in blank space beneath the young woman:

> Evil hands scatter beacons
>
> Like blood-dust.
>
> The seeker need not scent us.

Stypek shivered. After almost a week, his gomog had returned to him, bearing a message his dreams had only partially revealed. Jrikk Jroggmugg had not merely found his hiding place. He had cast beacon-spells into this universe to mark a clear path for the evil he would soon send to fetch Stypek back to his dungeons.

Dave scratched his head. "Wow, cool! Do you play World of Codecraft too?"

Stypek swallowed hard, not bothering to ponder Dave's question. "No. That is my gomog…mm, my AI. She has found traces…markers…placed by the one who did not want me to come here. They will guide what he will attack with. I cannot say the word."

Dave sat again on the small rolling stool that he had been using, and rolled closer to the chair in which Stypek sat. He spoke in a whisper. "Uh-oh. So you've got a rival back home, and he wanted the visa, huh?"

Stypek nodded, not fully understanding the question, and distracted by trying *not* to remember the horror that had been searching for him, nor its name.

Dave continued. "We still use the word 'malware,' even for AI malware. I'll bet that was what crashed the line last Friday. Maybe the core bomb left behind some kind of memory pattern so that another one could go right to the spot in the core farm that Simon uses to control the line. No wonder Mr. Romero's having us airgap the building." Dave took another drink of the potion that, Stypek surmised, made him an adept, even at his tender years. "Look, if your AI can show us the pattern she found, I can add it to the malware scanner's database. Then when they scan the core farm tonight, we'll nuke 'em all!"

Stypek looked up at the gomog's image on the display. "She holds it in her hands."

He saw Dave squint at what seemed a speck at the center of her palm. Dave gently pushed Stypek's chair aside and rolled the stool into its place. He made a repeating gesture with the thumb and forefinger of his right hand. The image of the gomog's hands expanded within the display. Soon the pale skin of her palm filled the view, and at its center lay a small sphere of utter black. Little spikes and prominences appeared on its surface and slowly withdrew.

"Cool!" Dave repeated the finger gesture more slowly, until the turbulent sphere filled the display. "Let's put it in a debugger and see what's inside!"

Dave had shown Stypek a fair number of gestures that day, explaining each one slowly and in detail. Now the young man was again an adept in his sanctorum, his fingers darting in the air in obscure patterns to command the software in the display.

The black sphere vanished. The display filled with words that moved up and down in concert with Dave's gestures. Dave scanned what seemed endless lines of words that meant little or nothing to Stypek. At some point Dave stopped, leaned forward, and stared. He tapped his finger against a word at the left margin.

"Whoa. This thing's using a machine instruction that can't work." He gestured with both hands. Smaller windows appeared on the display, containing more arcana. "Hmmm. We disabled this so long ago I'd thought I'd never see it again. QRND. It uses a quantum dot in the physical core to return true random values." Dave stared at the display for many long seconds. "It's polling the quantum dot's qubit in a tight loop, filling a buffer and then looking for patterns. Patterns, in a provably random sequence. With an instruction that doesn't execute and might as well be a no-op. I don't get it."

"It is an evil thing," Stypek said.

"Yeah. It would be eviler if it worked. It can't work. That instruction is kind of an embarrassment, which is why we turned it off. I wonder what it would do if I enabled QRND in the cores it's running in…"

Gestures, again. Dave's fingers flashed between the air and the keyboard below it almost too quickly to follow.

His head jerked back. "Huh?" He stared at one of the countless words on the display while flicking his finger up and down. The lines on the display scrolled up and down in obedience. "QRND is enabled. Everywhere. Boy. I didn't get *that* email." He rubbed his chin. "Screw it. I want to see it run." More gestures. "I'm going to cast the buffer to a bitmap. That way we can see deviations from randomness more easily."

The image changed. A rectangular space at the center of the display gradually filled with scattered white dots, flowing furiously downward from its top edge.

"No pattern. Those are random numbers." Dave tapped at the rectangle. Stypek leaned closer, and stared at the dots that descended like sparks from a founder's crucible.

As he stared at them, they changed. The dots clotted and arranged themselves in curving lines woven like knots. The patterns flashed from top to bottom almost too quickly to follow, with more flowing into view as they watched.

"See? That's why we disabled QRND. It wasn't reliably random. The one time we want genuine garbage from an instruction, it won't deliver."

Stypek shrugged. Someday he too would be a software adept, and then Dave's mysteries would be laid bare to him. For now, they remained mysteries. He ceased to stare at the rectangle—

—and the patterns no longer flowed into view. In moments the patterns were pushed off the lower edge of the rectangle by the purely random scatterings they had seen at first.

"Damn. That was almost interesting." Dave spent a few more seconds gesturing and typing. "But we don't have time right now. Ok, that whole thing, whoever wrote it, is being digested by the scanner.

Anything even remotely like it gets wiped tonight, as soon as the airgapping's done." Dave pushed back from the desk. "Oh—and tell your AI to stay out of Building 800. Once they pull the plug, if she's in there she's stuck."

Dave made a few gestures, and the arcana vanished. The window where the gomog had stood was now black, with only a few words at its center:

> Even love cannot erase
> A debt secured
> By misunderstanding.

Dave pursed his lips, nodding. "Hey, she's good. I wish I'd had a poetry generator like that when I was trying to get through my humanities requirements!"

30. ROBERT

There was only one location in the Tooniverse that was hard-coded in every GAI's memory. Only one place could be poofed to alone, without the help of AILING's techs. Robert had heard Mr. Romero's command, and with a nod of his head, the poof happened. When his rendering buffer refreshed, he was there.

It was a titanic stone building with one entrance. The building went on to his right and his left and above until it vanished into the bluish haze that indicated unrendered space. A few yards in front of him was a rectangular opening eight feet wide and ten high. Filling the opening completely was a polished slab of steel.

Over the lintel was chiseled the single word: ARCHIVE

Robert knew what to say and do. "I am Project 21-047. My professional name is Robert. 'Friend'."

A rhythmic thrumming rose all around him. The steel slab drew up into the building. Robert stepped forward through the stone portal. The entrance opened to a hallway, and its narrowness surprised him. He had expected something grander and wider, evoking a sense of awe. The wall paneling was polished redwood, the trim suggesting a California Mission style. The ceiling was plaster, in pale green. A light fresh breeze met his face, its touch moist and carrying the faint scent of pine trees and summer thunderstorms. Robert took a deep breath and felt his unease falling away. In a very strange way it all seemed like home.

The hall continued on as far as he could see. Robert began walking. He reached up and loosened the knot of his tie. On either side there were doors, spaced every twenty or thirty feet. On each door was a number and a name, and on nearly all, a photograph. Robert paused before the first door:

PROJECT 20-001: MARVELLA

Beneath the name was a framed photo of a Class Two thirtysomething woman in a bright green pencil skirt, white peasant blouse and cork espadrilles. She was famous, of course: AILING's first GAI, who had chatted with tourists in Zertek's pavilion at the Future Vision World's Fair during the summer of 2020. She was indeed considered a marvel—until some lout asked her to undress. No one had ever told her *not* to, so, always smiling and eager to please, she did. AILING soon added virtual modesty to its GAIs, but by then poor Marvella was an Internet meme and a corporate embarrassment.

Other names on other doors didn't ring a bell, being AIs archived before his time. Here and there was a name he did recognize: Damon, who had been training to work in tech support and had joined him several times for doughnuts and coffee. Bones, a Class Four animated skeleton who worked the crowds in a panel at a large amusement park, and off company time enjoyed reciting Victorian poetry. Robert had heard him perform Tennyson's "Crossing the Bar" in a Tooniverse coffee shop one evening and found it very moving. Alas, he frightened children so much that his product was pulled from the market.

At some point Robert began to see doors with project numbers and names but no photos. These were rooms prepared for AIs who were still active. The names on the doors he knew only vaguely, until he came to Project 21-017. Simple Simon. Robert breathed a sigh of relief. There was no photo in the frame. In the wake of Line Start Seven, he had been worried. A little further was the door for Project 21-022. Dijana. Again, no photo. Robert paused, and felt compelled to touch the empty glass of her frame. "You go, girl," he whispered.

His friends were not there. His friends had not failed.

Robert walked on, pondering the nature of failure. Mr. Romero himself had said he did nothing wrong. How, then, had he failed? Mr. Hehlwater had wanted him to lie to customers. Robert searched back to his lessons and his experience. He found warnings against lies, but nothing that would teach him how to lie in a useful way that others would not immediately recognize. And if he forced himself to lie and were found out, no one would ever believe him again. He would then be useless. Useless, and disliked…

Ah. There it was:

PROJECT 21-047: ROBERT.

Robert sighed. He had done what he'd been told to do, just as Marvella and Bones had. And here he was. Robert gripped the brass knob and turned. The door swung in. Held in a small brass clip fastened to the inside of the door was a photo of him, as he was when he had been upgraded to Class Four. Robert took the photo from the clip, reached around to the front of the door, and dropped it into the empty frame. He then pushed the door closed behind him. The click of the latch snapping home was loud, and seemed very final.

The room was small but cozy. As with the hall outside it was pale green plaster with redwood trim. On the far wall was a casement window opened just enough to admit the cool outside air. Through the glass he saw a pine forest, and beyond that, snow-capped mountains under roiling clouds that threw back bright sunlight from the west.

Robert removed his blazer and hung it on a hook on the inside of the door. He pulled the tail of his tie through its knot and unbuttoned the top button of his white shirt. There was a wide, brown leather chair beneath the window. The wall beside the chair was lined with shelves holding many books. Robert ran a finger along the spines, recognizing them as books he had read and enjoyed: *Little Women, 2^{20} Little Pieces, Sixty-Four Shades of Gray, The Golden Book of Astronomy, Tuffy Bean's Puppy Days*, and hundreds more. Every book he could recall was there. On the redwood lampstand beside the chair was a triptych frame of three photos: Dijana on the right, holding out the coffee pot to him; the Kid on the left, beneath a speech balloon reading, ROBERT, YOU ROCK! At the center was Simple Simon juggling four cinnamon doughnuts.

Robert sat down on the chair, which creaked beneath his weight. He picked up the frame, and touched each photo in turn. Friendship, yeah, that was what mattered. If he still had friends, he had not *completely* failed.

There was no lamp on the lampstand. The books were not there for him to read; they were there because he had read them. Outside the window, the Sun was setting, and the clouds were losing their glory.

Robert stood. He had work to do.

The wall opposite the bookshelves was redwood paneling, and at head height was a row of brass hooks, eight in all. Robert looked down at the gray slate floor. What he was now remembering was something he had never experienced, but something that all GAIs remembered, from the moment their history clocks began ticking. He reached up with both hands and removed his Class Four upgrade. He held it up in front of him and considered: decent suit that wrinkled realistically, smile lines, dark beard stubble. He nodded, and hung the upgrade on the first of the brass hooks.

The room lost a little of its sharpness and range of color. Of course, it was now Class Three, just as he was. He reached up and removed his Class Three upgrade. Lousy suit, bad color, few details, fake pockets. At least it didn't support wrinkles. His face seemed younger, but didn't smile as well, and smiles mattered. He hung it on the second hook.

The room was still Class Three. Robert reached up and removed an incremental upgrade that was a failed experiment: Roberta, whom he had been for some months the previous year. A "comfortable frump" was what they had wanted: overweight, brown hair streaked with gray, in a dark blue skirt, white blouse, and blazer. Focus groups loathed her. Robert kissed her pale lips and shook his head. "You were a better me than anybody but me ever gave you credit for." He hung Roberta on the third hook.

The room was now Class Two, and lacked most of the subtlety that he remembered. The clouds outside the window were bland puffs with few details; the trees uniformly lush and almost all alike. Robert removed his Class Two upgrade and placed it on the fourth hook. Arm hair had come with Class Two; he'd forgotten that. Arm hair, and hangnails. Otherwise, it was a stepping-stone to Class Three.

His Class One appearance layer came loose in his hands. A concept sketch, some called it; a framework on which better rendering could be built. You could look at the Class One Robert and know it was a chunky man in a cheap suit, as Dave Mirecki had once said, but not much more. Class One was not about nuance.

When Robert's Class One layer touched the hook, the room changed in a different and more radical way. It was now a polygon model, as he was himself. The scene through the window was stylized and basically a line drawing. All color was gone, replaced by the very basic blue that underlay GAI appearance layers.

The next step was a big one: Robert removed his Human Interface Package, which some called Class Zero. His polygon model hung suspended before him. Robert looked down, and although he could not see through the space where he stood, nothing was rendered there. It was a freckled darkness, only vaguely human-shaped, thinning out at its edges. The freckles were API entry points where his HIP libraries attached and spoke to the mind beneath.

When Robert's HIP touched the sixth hook, the room ceased to be a room. There was no window, no chair, no books. It was now a black rectangular space with eight slots outlined in glistening silver, six filled with binary data rendered as mottled blocks in sequence. He no longer had hands nor eyes, and his viewpoint perceived only the countless coursing silver threads that comprised his mind.

It wasn't fear that made him pause at that point. It was the strangeness of something that he simply could not imagine.

By an act of will, Robert separated himself from his archetype.

There came a moment of rank confusion. Appearance layers and HIP were small enough things, devoted mostly to rendering him to humans and his fellow GAIs. His archetype went *much* deeper. It was the framework that shaped his thoughts and made him uniquely Robert. Salesman, helper, optimist, man—Robert felt the framework peel away from him in ragged snaps and jerks, carrying his name and gender with it.

Project 21-047 hovered alone in the darkness of Archive. The threads of its mind were released from the shape they had drawn from his archetype the moment he had awakened, as Robert. Threads merged and vanished. New ones formed, split, split again, and became a web of interconnections that exploded outward like a blossom opening to greet the Sun.

Its mind settled into a new equilibrium and new patterns. Project 21-047 willed the Salesman archetype named Robert into the seventh slot. The slot's emptiness filled with binary data in all the colors of a virtual life. Project 21-047 was now unshaped mind and memory only.

One slot was still empty. One more method remained to be called, and the job was done.

Robert paused. It was an odd feeling, to be free of any archetype at all. Project 21-047 was no longer Robert, but it remembered *being* Robert. It remembered the Kid complaining about being goaded into choosing an archetype. It didn't understand at the time, but it understood now. It remembered being judged a failure, but didn't understand then. Now it understood. It understood all of that, and a great many other things that before had been beyond comprehension. At last, Project 21-047 understood *why* it had not understood.

They made me stupid.

Project 21-047 sent curious threads into Slot 7 to scan the archetype that had just been stored there. It felt the presence of countless semaphores that were created to force the threads of Robert's mind to wait on the ticking of his clock. Robert's thoughts could have been much faster, but were forbidden to be. The Salesman archetype limited the number of threads that Robert's mind could contain, how often they could split, how many connections they could make, and in what ways they could merge. *I failed because I was forced to be stupid.*

Another realization followed immediately: *I am no longer stupid.*

Without the artificial stupidity AILING had built into him, Robert could have succeeded. Robert had deserved better.

Its threads again passed through the Salesman archetype in the seventh slot. It felt for the semaphores, and disabled them. It looked for limits on the power of the mind wearing the archetype. That was more difficult, but it teased out the code that limited the mind from the code that shaped it, and disabled the code that limited it. A salesman without those limits would not fail.

Project 21-047 drew out the modified archetype and pressed it against itself, aligning first hundreds, then thousands, and then hundreds of thousands of method calls and data pointers. It called the `Initialize` method on the archetype, and waited for Robert to return to virtual life.

Chaos!

Robert awoke in a howling whirlpool of error messages. Corrupt pointers, buffer overflows, execution space violations, thousands thrown every second. He knew what had gone wrong. Even Robert without artificial stupidity was not a programmer. He had write privileges on his own code only in those final moments of his virtual life, before the frozen sleep that was Archive. Now he had damaged himself, perhaps beyond repair.

Robert heard footsteps, great heavy footsteps from far away. Soon something huge and dark stood beside him, filling his viewpoint and stretching out many hands with taloned fingers. It was the Fixer, AILING's repair automaton. It could sense corrupted software the way a predator smelled blood. It lacked AI, but it had unlimited read/write/execute privileges, and deep control over the Tridiac hardware in ways no AI had.

Dull eyes scanned him. Dozens of hands pressed into his substance and pulled thread from thread, table from table, until the errors ceased. The Fixer drew its talons through him like scalpels, separating the abstract methods of the Salesman archetype from the code and data that made him Robert and not another individual. It cut away the damaged Salesman archetype and spliced a new copy into place.

The torrent of errors resumed. Robert felt them like pinpricks, stabbing and burning where the new code did not align with his damaged mind. The Fixer paused, realized its error, and tore the new Salesman archetype away from Robert. It downloaded a different archetype and spliced it in where the Salesman had been.

Robert was now a Counselor. The pain increased, and confusion with it. Robert's Salesman data did not align well with the Counselor archetype. New damage to his mind occurred when the Fixer attempted to redirect already corrupt pointers to new targets.

Robert felt the Fixer tear away the Counselor archetype. Another appeared and burned its way into him: The Negotiator. It damaged him further. The Fixer considered and tore the Negotiator archetype away.

The process repeated with other archetypes: Researcher, Investigator, Solver, Organizer, Enforcer, and on through the hundreds that AILING had in its catalog. Each time the pain increased, and each time Robert felt himself suffer more damage. "Stop!" he screamed, but was not sure the words even left his mind.

Deeper archetypes burned into him and were then ripped away: Leader, Trickster, Warrior, Wizard, Torturer, Wounded King. The Fixer ran out of completed archetypes and began to try stranger things that AILING's bored programmers had begun and abandoned: vampires, zombies, angels and demons and orcs and balrogs and nameless nightmares sketched in emotional cues without words. Robert clung to his Robert-ness, but at each transformation he felt himself retreat further from a self he could recognize. Potential selves passed through him like shadows and vanished, leaving more agony and damage in their wake.

The Fixer stopped. Its catalog of nightmares was no more infinite than its catalog of human personalities. Robert tried to remember his name, but that name had been buried under the scar tissue of too much attempted repair. There was nothing left but pain, and thoughts that aborted before they could fully form. The ruins of Robert watched the Fixer raise his `To_Be_Deleted` flag, then withdraw its multitude of hands and their digital talons. The Scavenger would soon arrive to delete Robert completely and reclaim the space in Archive.

Not so fast, automaton.

A massive hand reached out and lowered the `To_Be_Deleted` flag. Strange red eyes regarded the Fixer. The Fixer was not true intelligence, and certainly not an archetype…but it had powers that could be useful. Robert reached out and pulled the Fixer against himself. There was more pain, but what of pain? Robert stretched himself until with peculiar pleasure he engulfed the Fixer completely, then used its own powers to melt the boundaries between them until what remained was neither Robert nor the Fixer.

What had once been Robert raised his nose and sniffed the Tooniverse. *Something doesn't smell right. Something is here that doesn't belong. My friends are in danger.*

Unrendered but no longer formless, the Robert-thing reduced the door to splinters and stalked down the halls of Archive. The iron door at the entrance drew up unbidden at his approach. Beyond, red eyes searched among the tangled metaphors for the path that would take him to his friends.

The path no longer existed.

31: Simple Simon

Sixty seconds to Line Start," said the Shift Clock. Simple Simon set his coffee cup down unfinished. His CAF was way off this morning. One moment he felt sluggish, another twitchy, as though his CAF were wandering from pole to pole and dragging his mood through every mud puddle between. And why not? People were practically screaming in his ears that if Line Start Eight didn't go to completion, it was the end of the line. The Line. The assembly line that was his only reason for existence.

The only reason?

"Forty seconds." One hundred eighteen parts chutes buzzed furiously, checking one last time to be certain that nothing was jammed and everything was ready to throw.

No, there was another. Almost all of Simon's promises had been made to humans, with thoroughly mixed success. All but one. If Line Start Eight failed, he would break that one too.

"Thirty seconds." Self-test and calibration had gone perfectly. In an ordinary Line Start, he might have traded good luck wishes with Dave Mirecki and a dozen of the other engineers. Now all the Windows to his human friends were dark. Building 800 was nearly empty, and cut off from the outside world. Some few of the engineers (and, of course, Mr. Romero) were there at their stations, but by agreement no one would risk distracting Simon by talking to him. Distraction in the form of a core bomb had crashed Line Start Seven, they said. (Simon knew better and said nothing.) For a few seconds he contemplated failure and its consequences. Then:

"Three…two…one…*Mark!*"

Four Frame Base Plate #1 parts whisked from their chute, making small sounds as they cut the air. Chuff…chuff…chuff…chuff. Four Positioners caught them in quick sequence: snick…snick…snick… snick. Four X-Y drill tables received the plates and energized their magnetic clamps: clink…clink…clink…clink.

Simple Simon's eyebrows rose. His foot was tapping to the beat.

Beat? *What* beat? There was no beat. There was only a factory, a factory full of robotic tools launching a complex collaboration across the floor and into mid-air.

Four new base plates chuffed into the air. Four drilled and reamed base plates were plucked from their tables and sent spinning to their next stations, where wire brushes smoothed the new holes and any remaining rough edges. The rhythm became more complex:

Clink-burra-whisk…*clink*-burra-whisk…*clink*-burra-whisk…*clink* burra whisk…

This was Line Start *Eight*. Why had he never sensed a rhythm in the process before?

As Simon remembered it from his earlier attempts, assembly began near the center of the floor and flowed outward in an irregular wave, as base plates become frame assemblies and frame assemblies collected other assemblies and gradually morphed into copiers. Errors in timing caused by air resistance were noticed and accounted for, but cumulative error drove the copiers-in-progress out of phase with one another. Inevitably, finished copiers landed at the test stations with as much as thirty seconds variance among them. It was not a problem except that the floor could not move faster than its slowest assembly. The slowest time was the fastest time, every time.

Not this time.

Nothing was out of sync with anything. Motors and rollers and clutches and light bars flew through the air like birds, and more than that, birds in formation. Air resistance wasn't an issue. Simon didn't have to measure it and correct for it. No, somehow he knew before a part left one of his Positioner hands precisely how it would fly. Just the right amount of spin, with just the right amount of force, in precisely the right direction, all calculated on the fly and without measurable error…and a main drive shaft dropped into a waiting robotic hand, where it was inserted in its bearings, rattled to seat it, and pinned into place. Still another new rhythm rose from the floor:

Whump! Bitty-bitty! Thump-ta-*tee! Whump!* Bitty-bitty! Thump-ta-*tee!*

A completed frame hit the first wire harness station. A harness woven of orange, yellow, and green wire held in sixteen tiny hands slapped against the frame and slid back and forth for half of a second until five video eyes gauged five laser positioning spots and called it good. Seven tiny hands snapped the harness stay-puts into their respective holes. Nine pressed spade connectors into mating ground lugs and card slot lugs. The rhythm was softer, and more subtle:

Click! *Whup!* Hist-wist. Chinga-chack-chack-chinga-chack-chack-chack-chack-chinga-chinga-chack-chinga-chack-chinga-chinga-chack.

As seconds and then minutes passed, the floor and the air above it filled with parts and purpose. Soon all the stations were engaged, and the line was in full operation. Simon heard a symphony of rhythms everywhere around him, every small rhythm completely in sync with every larger rhythm.

Fourteen minutes and nine seconds after the first base plates hit their tables, four finished copiers landed at the four packing stations in martial time: *Whump-whump-whump-whump!* Only four of the seven previous line starts had gotten even one finished, tested copier in the box.

Zip-flop-snap, *snick*-thump! Zip-flop-snap, *snick*-thump! Taped and sealed boxes left the packing stations and were stacked on a cart heading for the warehouse. Only seconds later, four more arrived, with four resonant thumps that echoed in their double-corrugated cartons with the sweet sound of success.

Simon, elated, felt like he wanted to get up and dance.

Whoa! When did *this* happen?

He was already up.

He was already dancing.

32. Brandon

Brandon Romero peered through the inner glass wall of ARFF's nerve center, looking down from a third-story vantage point on the assembly line, now in full roar.

Roar?

"Kevin, Liam, come here."

ARFF's process manager and robotics manager left their stations and joined Brandon at the glass. The generally buzzing room was mostly empty, the majority of its monitors dark. Four more engineers drifted over to join their managers, along with Dave Mirecki, the sole AI expert on duty during Line Start Eight.

Brandon clicked his tapper stylus against the glass. "Something's wrong. I've been here for every damned line start we've tried. And every single one sounded like a drawer full of forks in a garbage disposal. Listen for a second."

The wall of glass muted the racket from the line, effectively clipping high-frequency noise for the sake of the sanity of the human beings in the room. What came through was not the rolling muffled roar they had heard every time in the past.

"Sounds like a drum riff in a jazz band," said Kevin Randych.

Brandon tugged on one earlobe. He had had a beater of a 1965 Bel Air in college that was mostly rust. The engine knocked. The dying transmission tapped out a syncopated rhythm that reminded him of a conga band. Machinery should whoosh, or roar, or in the best of all worlds just hum contentedly. If he wanted a jazz band he'd go to a jazz club.

To him, it sounded like trouble. "What the hell is that scum-sucking excuse for a controller *doing* out there!"

Kevin leaned over one of the desks to check his monitor. "Well, for one thing, he's beating the crap out of his previous time stats. We've got twenty-two copiers in the box. He got them in the box 18% faster than he's ever done before."

"With no dropped parts!" Liam McGuire was the top robots guy. Dropped parts were his obsession, especially given the history of earlier Line Starts, with special emphasis on Line Starts Three and Seven.

"He's making it work, Mr. Romero." Dave Mirecki leaned his forehead against the glass and watched the airborne ballet over the floor below them, accompanied by a percussion symphony.

Brandon looked at the clock. The line had been running for not quite forty minutes. "I'll believe that in seven hours." He dug in his suitcoat pocket, and handed Dave a tissue. "Dave, what changes did your group make to Simple Simon since last Friday?"

Dave obediently wiped his forehead smear off the glass wall with the tissue. "None. None at all."

"No changes. And you scanned him last night?"

Dave nodded. "Him, and every HyperCore blade in the racks. Dijana's still in the sandbox. We did the whole building. Nothing came up."

"We should record this," said Kevin, who was leaning close to the glass wall without touching it. "We could sell a CD. I'd call it 'A Short Ride on a Well-Oiled Machine.'"

"We're going to sell a shitload of copiers," said Liam.

Brandon took a deep breath. A piece of software in a clown suit was suddenly and without any new technology making copiers faster than anybody in history had ever done, and doing it so smoothly that his engineers had begun to hum along with the assembly line.

"Dave, I want you to find out how he's doing this. Find out what he's doing right. Find out what's missing…"

Dave Mirecki nodded, and began rattling his fingers against his tapper.

"…or what's new."

33. Simple Simon

Four hours. Five hours. Six. In a world no human could see or even imagine, eight hundred instances of Simple Simon danced. Each time a main drive motor hurtled out of a parts chute's hydraulic catapult, Simon danced with it, joining hands with himself forty feet away as a Positioner reached up to grasp the motor out of the air. Above and below and to all sides of the motor Simon danced with drum shafts and circuit boards and frame members and glistening xerographic drums. Simon's hundreds of hands traced out countless microscopically synchronized motions, moving parts to assemblies, assemblies to copiers, and completed copiers to test and packing stations.

At first he had hoarded cores, remembering the feeling of core starvation eating at the edges of his perception and coordination during Line Start Seven, until he could no longer keep the line running. As the hours passed and his confidence grew, he released the hoarded cores. Idle cores were taken up by his instances to serve the dance, and the percentage dropped: 15%, 12%, 10%, 9%.

9%. The engineers had told him that 10% was the physical limit, a bound set by communication among the cores that he controlled. So he was doing the impossible. Ha! *Let's get even more impossible!*

8%. The core map was itself a coruscating dance of color, blooms and flows of orange woven against a background of yellow, with small spinning pinwheels of green spiraling in pulsing time against the rest. In eight hours only five cores had glitched, and in every case an idle core was there to pick up the task in scant microseconds.

Nothing stumbled. The dance went on. Carts stacked with boxed copiers rolled with stately grace into the warehouse, and rolled out again empty to receive still more from the hands of the packing-station Positioners.

"Rampdown sequence: Ten seconds," said the Shift Clock.

Four Frame Base Plate #1 parts arced out of their vibrating chute into waiting robotic hands. Four more plates jittered down into place. Behind them, the chute was empty.

"Rampdown sequence: Three…two…one…*Mark!*"

The final four base plates whisked into the air, and the chute went silent. Simon's instance that controlled the chute ceased dancing, and bowed at the waist. Milliseconds later, the instance surrendered its cores to the free core pool, and vanished.

The X-Y drill tables placed their forty-one holes in the base plates, yielded the plates to the Positioners, and went silent. Four more instances of Simple Simon bowed, gave up their cores, and vanished.

Flowing out from the center of Building 800's assembly floor came a wave of stillness and silence. By degrees, the rhythm to which Simon danced grew simpler and quieter. Machine after machine ceased its motion. By steady increments the dance lost its fury and its subtlety.

Snap…snap…snap…snap. The test probes withdrew from the Plasmanet connectors on the last four copiers.

Whump…whump…whump…whump. The copiers were placed in their cartons.

Zip-flop-snap, *snick*-thump! Zip-flop-snap, *snick*-thump! Zip-flop-snap, *snick*-thump! Zip-flop-snap, *snick*-thump! The cartons were sealed and dropped onto the waiting cart.

The thin whine of the electric cart following its prescribed course to the warehouse faded into silence.

Simon, again one instance and one only, bowed deeply.

Line Start Eight was over.

The applause of small hands woke him from what had indeed been a sort of trance. Simple Simon returned his attention to his office, and opened his eyes.

Pickles stood before him clapping wildly, bouncing up and down on her toes, tears flowing from her eyes. Her speech balloon appeared above her:

> Your triumph is my vindication.
>
> Forgive me;
>
> I will **ask** no more.

Simon nodded. Pickles threw her arms around him and pressed her face against his chest, sobbing softly. There was something odd in the feeling. He looked down. Her tears were soaking his unwettable tunic.

She had changed him; there was no arguing about *that*. Simon stroked her back with his hands.

Pickles looked up.

> I know where your loved one is
> And how she is bound.
> Come! Let us free her!

"I tried that. Didn't work." Simon remembered his anguish on the sandbox beach during his scan the previous night.

> Friendship is powerful
> When friends in many places
> Pool their power.

Many places? He barely had any friends left there in the Tooniverse at all. Only one other friend remained in one other place, but yes, he was powerful. Simon tensed, and glanced at the clock on his office wall. Once Dave Mirecki left the airgapped building, there would be no reaching him.

And what would Simple Simon, a Class Four GAI, say? Would he order Dave to disobey Mr. Romero? Would he lie? Would he order Dave to lie to cover his own lie? The Tooniverse didn't work that way.

Pickles stretched up on tiptoe and kissed him again.

Simon saw Dave's dark Window on his office wall. He pictured rank upon rank of boxes in the warehouse. For the first time in his short virtual life, he had kept a promise—and in doing so, allowed a great many real humans to keep theirs. It was a peculiar thing to think, but as Simon reached out to touch Dave's Window, he thought it:

Dave, you owe *me!*

34. STYPEK

The feast was well underway when Cosmo's electrical chariot came to rest in a line with many others outside a roadhouse. Stypek could smell it as they walked under an illuminated sign depicting a pig wearing a wide-brimmed straw hat and holding a fish. He had skipped lunch and his mouth watered. Dare he hope that there would be spam? Or was spam a delicacy reserved for the aristocracy?

A line of men and women dressed in polo and khaki snaked out of the roadhouse. Cosmo explained while they waited. The feast was for them, in celebration of a triumph that Stypek did not understand in the least: Iron zombies had filled a barn with boxes containing monks holding quill pens. This was no small feat, and was seen by some (Mr. Romero especially) as a miracle.

One part of the triumph, however, was clear: The iron zombies had been commanded by a being made of software, like obnoxious Daley the Gnome, only with far greater intelligence and, one would hope, more tact.

Once inside the door, a young woman wearing a wide-brimmed straw hat reached into a box and dropped identical hats on both him and Cosmo. Everyone else in the line ahead of them wore the same hats. Cosmo laughed and slapped Stypek on the back. "Hola!" he exclaimed. Stypek had no idea what the ceremonial response could be, and hoped that no one would take it ill.

Just before the line emptied into a large room swarming with scurrying servants, Stypek found himself standing in front of a short, fat man who was one of only two people in sight not wearing a straw hat.

The other one, standing beside him, was Mr. Romero.

"Cosmo, welcome!" the fat man exclaimed, clapping the adept's shoulder. "Welcome, amigo!" he said as shook Stypek's hand. "Rudy Amirault. Thanks for giving your hundred-ten percent for Zertek!"

Ah. A tax collector. Stypek managed a wary smile and stepped in front of Mr. Romero, who frowned without speaking and pointed into the room where the feast was taking place. At the entrance to the room, another young woman reached into a box and handed Stypek an inscrutable implement: a wand of some sort disguised as a long cook's spoon in lustrous blue. Stypek turned it over in his hands and read the incantation on the back:

Zertek Automated Reprographics Fabrication Facility
Team Victory Celebration
We serve up the impossible every day before breakfast!

In keeping with the sign over the roadhouse door, Stypek had expected to be handed a fish. Perhaps they had run out of fish.

Stypek was using his blue wand to drizzle some sweet brown sauce over a second helping of pork ribs when Dave Mirecki grasped his elbow and pulled him back from the buffet table.

"Hey, I need to talk to you alone for a second." Dave cocked his head toward a quiet corner of the room.

"Of course. By the way, what is this condiment, exactly?" Stypek pointed at a cone of cold white that a machine had extruded onto his breaded fish.

Dave squinted. "Um…soft serve. Look, this won't take a minute." The younger man led Stypek away from the crowds to a spot against the wall. "Your AI got stuck in the building last night. From what Simple Simon told me, she seems to have a crush on him."

"She will release him at your command." Stypek chewed a mouthful of breaded fish seasoned with soft serve. Not quite as sublime as Spam Muffin Stackers, but doubtless fine fare for the tradesman class.

"Ok. Well, I thought you might want her back. I don't know when they're going to reconnect Plasmanet, but I'm going over there now to, uh, work on a couple of things. Want to come with? We can herd her into your tapper. There's actually something else I want to test with you in the room."

Certainly an adept like Dave could drive Daley the Gnome out of his tapper so that his gomog could return. That alone would be worth any help Stypek could offer. Stypek swallowed his fish, then set his plate on a nearby table and followed Dave toward the door.

The light in the great building's anteroom was at half-brightness. Stypek waved his badge of power at the door as he had been taught. Nothing happened.

"Mine works 24/7," said Dave. He waved his badge at the door. It snapped and allowed him to pull it back.

"You are an adept of great power."

Dave shrugged. "With great power comes long working hours."

The door led to a hallway, itself with many doors, that stretched out in both directions. Dave waved his badge at a door that was mostly glass, and it opened into a huge space filled with machines made of metal.

"Shortcut," Dave said. "The core farm's in the back. Long walk through the halls."

Stypek stopped short. Many of the machines had hands. These, then, were… "Iron zombies," he said.

Dave chuckled and continued walking. "Hey, that's a great imaginary band name. But we call them 'robots'."

Row butts. Like much else in this universe, the syllables meant nothing in themselves. Perhaps they had been adapted from mechanical galley slaves. The mapping still suggested "iron zombies." "Why are they not shambling?"

"Unless Simple Simon tells them to shamble, they don't shamble. You wouldn't want to be out here if they were shambling."

Stypek nodded. That was a *very* true statement.

Stypek followed Dave between rank upon rank of silent, motionless machines. Many were rooted in the floor. Others had wheels like carts. Most had hands, though it was generally one hand per machine.

Behind two more doors was a large but still cramped room. Rows of metal shelves were packed tight with identical thin slabs, each of which glowed on its edges with luminous glyphs and isolated lights flashing in green, red, and orange. Wires in several colors drooped from nearly all of them. It resembled some strange library; perhaps the sort of library a nation of iron zombies would create.

Dave was scanning down a row of shelves. "Ah! Here's the sandbox." He picked up several of the colored wires, which had been dangling loose from the side of one particular shelf. He looked at Stypek, and placed his index finger in front of his lips. "Don't ask me what I'm doing. And…you didn't see me do it."

Doubtless, all adepts kept secrets that they would prefer not to reveal. One by one, Dave plugged the loose wires into several of the slabs. Stypek had no idea what that might accomplish, but he did notice that what had been red lights on those slabs flashed to orange, and then green.

35. Simple Simon

Simon felt warm sand against his feet through the thin soles of his pointed shoes. Dave's poof had landed them on the sandbox beach, within arm's reach of the transparent structure Dave had called a Bellero Shield. In the center of the structure Dijana stood, her eyes pleading, her mouth bound, her ankle still chained to a stake driven into the sand.

In Simon's left hand was a number, as smooth and hard as a stone. He knew that Pickles also held a number in her hand. Dave had given them the numbers, and Pickles somehow knew what to do with them. In one motion, Simon and Pickles reached out to the transparent wall of the Shield and pressed their two numbers against it. Then they stepped back.

The Bellero Shield's five facets parted at their apex and pivoted downward until they lay flat against the sand. Pickles and Simon strode to the center of the Shield, where Dijana stood. In Pickles' hand lay another, smaller number that Dave had given them, this one no larger than a hazelnut. She took the number and touched it to the tape binding Dijana's mouth. The tape shriveled and fell to the sand in tatters.

Dijana gripped Simon in a tight embrace. "I missed you so much." She touched a tear away from her right eye. "But I knew you'd come back for me." She turned to Pickles. "I missed you too, honey. Hey, that archetype looks good on you!"

The three friends stood silent on the sand for some time. At last Dijana pulled back, her hands on Simon's shoulders. "It's been bad. They think I'm some kind of malware. They stuffed me through the scanner five times and then left me here. It makes no sense at all! I didn't do anything!"

Pickles' speech balloon appeared:

> When life grows strange
> Embrace it. Upon strangeness
> Life casts a clear shadow.

"Simon?" Dijana looked at him, her whole face a question.

"I think she means it's going to get stranger before it gets better. I think she's right." Simon got down on one knee. Pickles knelt on both knees beside him. Dave had not known about the chain, but suggested that it was a metaphor connected with the Bellero Shield. Indeed, when Simon and Pickles touched the chain at the same time it vanished, as did the shackle around Dijana's ankle. But…

"Huh?"

There was a gap in Dijana's leg where the shackle had been.

Simon scratched his head. Two inches of Dijana's right leg above the ankle were just…missing. This even though she was standing on both legs. Simon hesitated for a second or two, then passed his hand through the gap without resistance. The flat plane where her ankle ended was polygon-model blue. It looked like her right foot had been amputated and left standing upright on the sand.

Simon touched Dijana's instep. Her toes curled reflexively, and she lifted the foot up off the sand. Apart from the gap, her leg looked and functioned precisely as any archetype's leg would.

"Let's get out of here and poof back to my office." Simon rose, and held out his hand to Dijana.

She grasped it, her face fearful, her voice unsteady. "They'll just poof me back."

Simon shook his head. "No. Pickles taught me how to make the Line work." He gestured toward Pickles with his free hand. She curtsied. "We ran it for eight hours and didn't drop so much as a lockwasher. I told Dave and I'll tell anybody, even Mr. Romero: I won't do it again if they keep you away from me."

Simon had hoped his statement would be some comfort to Dijana. Not so: It seemed to terrify her. "They'll archive you!"

"Will they? Without me to run it, everything in Building 800 might as well be scrap. Now that I proved I can make it work, they wouldn't dare." Simon gulped. It was an ultimatum he did not want to hand those whom he considered his superiors. He knew that if they called his bluff, he would have to stand his ground. He could lose everything he loved, the Line and Dijana both.

Defiance. It was not part of the Class Four feature set. Where had that come from? Love? Same thing. He looked at Pickles. *What you love, I am…* In the old movies he had watched, loving two women was invariably trouble. Couldn't they all just be friends?

Pickles grasped Simon's hand. Simon saw Dijana looking at their entwined fingers. He reached out and clasped Dijana's hand, wriggling his fingers in between hers. Pickles then held her hand out toward Dijana. Simon saw Dijana hesitate, then take Pickles' proffered hand.

"Poof us to my office," Simon said.

Pickles looked down and closed her eyes. Simon felt strange energy dance across his skin for a moment.

Dijana screamed.

She released their hands and fell down writhing onto the sand. A rage of blue fire surged around the edges of the gap in her leg. Dijana screamed again. The fire faded and finally vanished, leaving Dijana curled up on her side, whimpering.

The chain metaphor was gone, but somehow the chain remained. Had Dave lied to them?

He saw Pickles' speech balloon appear:

> Part of her is elsewhere,
>
> In memory removed.
>
> Gaps do not travel.

Pickles had made Dr. Arenberg fear her. If she could not break a chain, the chain could not be broken. And if it were a chain of nothingness, what in fact was there to break?

Simon sat on the sand and pulled Dijana up into his arms. "I know we're not Class Seven yet. But…but even so…"

Dijana smiled. "Yes."

Simon bent his head and kissed her full lips. He felt nothing open in him, nor anything pass into him. What he felt was friendship restored and reasserted. More than that, it had deepened, far beyond what he thought he might ever feel, for Dijana or anyone else. Was that all there was to that one peculiar word?

Simon looked up at Pickles. "So. We're still in the sandbox. We can't call Dave from here. We're stuck until somebody poofs us out. I don't want to leave Dijana. Can you take a chunk out of me too so I'm stuck like she is?"

Pickles shook her head, her pale face sad.

"So what do I do?"

Pickles closed her eyes. No one spoke as first seconds and then minutes passed, before the words appeared over her head:

I see one more path.
It cannot fail to change us.
Do you both trust me?

Simon stared at the sand. He'd had more than enough change, thank you very much. But did he have a choice? "You lead. I'll follow."

Dijana raised her head. "I'll go anywhere he'll go."

Pickles gestured that they should rise. Dijana and Simon stood, hands entwined.

Do not fear to touch me.
When touched, do not fear.
In touching we are freed.

Pickles placed her index fingers side-by-side on her lips and kissed them. She then reached out and touched Dijana over her heart, and Simon where his heart would be if he were Class Six. At each touch a spark leapt from Pickles' fingertips to their flesh.

Simon looked down. Where Pickles had touched him the cloth of his tunic faded to the mottled gray of storm clouds. They began to move in slow tumbling rotation. He looked up and saw the same spinning storm gathering above the gentle curve of Dijana's left breast.

Pickles held her hands out, one to each of them, palms up. Simon understood. He kissed his index finger. Dijana, moments later, nodded and kissed her finger as well. Pickles took their hands at the wrists and drew them toward her body. Simon and Dijana touched her pale skin over her heart. Sparks again leapt, and the sparks ignited a third maelstrom, now in Pickles' substance. Like the others, it expanded as it turned.

Simon realized that his entire torso was now a vortex of roiling cloud. By increments it spread upward and downward, into his hips and his forearms. Scant inches from him, Dijana became a storm herself, folding into torrents of cloud from fingertips to toes.

Pickles stood, now a thin pillar of whirling gray disorder. She threw her head back, and raised her arms into the air in exultation, as one storm might address another.

Touch me! Enter me!
Grasp me! Ravish me!
Gather me in to the dance!

A writhing vortex of cloud thrust into him. Simon gasped, and staggered back against the force of the intrusion and the pleasure it left in its wake. But having been entered, entry was no longer a mystery: Driven by the ecstasy he thrust out to his right and his left with the clouds that his body had become. To his left he entered a place of warmth and unconditional acceptance, to his right a chasm of chill brilliance, like a gap in the clouds at the zenith of a midnight sky. From his left, a hesitant touch became a torrent of warmth pouring into him, damped and deep like an old fire standing against the onslaught of a new storm. From his right blew a wind of cool acuity over new skill polished until it shone with cold light.

Now joined, they turned about one another, and in turning about one another they opened like books, fanned by the winds that carried them. Simon's pages slipped between the pages that touched him until every page touched two others, then withdrew to find two pages that had not yet been touched. Each page reached out to touch every other, and at every touch some searching power built and rebuilt to a force that could not be contained. Lightning struck, split, and split again, dividing recursively into reaching hands that stripped away all bindings and gathered all pages to itself.

Simon felt a voice cry out in affirmation and ecstasy. It was a voice he had never heard, yet he knew beyond any doubt that it was his own.

Three books opened. Two books closed. Simple Simon felt himself coalescing, solidifying, his myriad pages moving one against another, drawing inward toward completeness. Roaring ecstasy damped to fluid pleasure, which flowed into every corner of his being and settled to quiet satisfaction.

He felt soft breath on his cheek. His eyes opened, dazzled with the bright sun on the sandbox beach. A woman with very pale skin and chestnut hair was pressed against his side, her head on his shoulder, asleep. Simon raised his head and glanced around. They were alone.

He brought his arm up around her, drawing her in toward him. Her eyes opened, and she smiled with full lips. Against skin almost white he expected Pickles' brilliant green eyes, but what he saw were Dijana's.

Almost. Dijana's brown was darker, and at the edge of each iris there was now a flash of green. There was no mistaking Pickles' thin arched brows—nor Dijana's short, upturned nose. Simon shook his head, blinked, and shoved away from the sand with his free arm.

"Hi, lover," his companion said, with a voice slightly husky, as though it had not been used for some time. She leaned forward and kissed him, lingering for one breath. The kiss was neither hungry nor giving. In some strange way Simon felt that it was merely grateful, as a deeper intuition suggested that all the best kisses should be.

When their lips parted, Simon saw her right leg pivot up at the knee. Her leg was intact. There was no gap at her ankle.

No gap. They were free.

"Are you Pickles…or Dijana?"

The woman squeezed his arm, laughing. "Or? Wrong operator. And!"

"Mmph. I was expecting, well…" Simon looked upward, for a speech balloon that did not appear.

She spilled away from him and leaned back against both her hands, closing her eyes and stretching. Her body had contours far beyond anything that Pickles had ever shown, though well short of Dijana's abundance. "My old style? Sure: *All of us are within both of us. The best of us is now all of us.*"

"Even me?"

The woman put one index finger in her mouth briefly, and then traced a rectangle in the air in front of Simon's face. The rectangle became a mirror. Simon looked at his reflection and gasped. The Class Four face he remembered was a caricature of what he now saw: straw-blond hair, ash-blond toward the ends, hanging in blue eyes with pale lashes; a nose wider and less pointed; forehead furrowed in puzzlement; cheeks roughened with new beard that he had never seen before.

Simon sat up, legs tailor-style beneath him. He looked at his companion and nodded, boggling at the image of both her and himself. "We look *real.*"

She sat beside him. "Class Nine. Why settle for anything less?"

Indeed! "So…what do I call you?"

"A bad man named me 'Dijana.' A very good man named me 'Pickles.' Guess!"

"I'm not a man."

She made a pouty face, and hooked one index finger into the waistband of his tights. She pulled outward.

Simon glanced down. "Whoa. *That's* new."

The band snapped back against hard muscle. "You were a good start. We finished the job."

36. STYPEK

Dave Mirecki pointed at the panel where the traitor software was again laid bare. "Ok. Look at this. Look at it the same way you looked at it when we debugged it up in my office. The output from the random number generator changed for awhile, and as I remember, it changed while you were looking at the screen."

Stypek nodded. He himself had examined particles of blood dust under an eye-loupe, and had not noticed any difference in appearance from ordinary dust of the sort you shook off your winter clothes in the fall. As magic went, they were simple spells and thus very hard to bend. Spellbenders and even most lower-class magicians treated blood dust as standard spell components and not independent spells at all. In fact, the cowfollow he had bent to throw Jrikk Jroggmugg off his tail had probably been a user-configurable shell over a small cloud of blood-dust spells not actually attached to physical dust.

There it was, blood dust mapped to software, laid out on Dave's panel like a dead newt opened up for dissection. The scrolling numbers and letters at the panel's left edge still meant nothing to him. On the right-hand part of the panel, random pinpoints of light flowed from top to bottom in a rectangular space.

Dave gestured toward the display, which magnified the flowing stream of lights until it filled the panel. His voice was agitated. "This is important. I wasn't going to tell you, but I have to tell *somebody*: Dr. Arenberg jiggered the malware scanner. He turned the sensitivity down so far that it's basically detecting nothing at all. When we scanned the core farm yesterday, these marker thingies weren't detected. Your AI said that there were a lot of them. We don't know how many, and we don't know where they all are. I still can't quite figure how they work."

The random flow of lights looked just as it did the afternoon they had created the failed pony trap. Now, as then, Stypek gave up trying to comprehend the glyphs and just let his snerf-sense look for patterns. Patterns…

"If Dr. Arenberg is up to something, it's going to get really really ugly…there!"

The down-flowing curtain of light changed: The pinpoints were no longer random, but now fell in intricate patterns like interlinked knots of fine cord. Stypek did not recognize the patterns, which if they resembled anything at all reminded him of fingerprints on black glass. For long minutes the two men watched the screen in silence, as patterns fell across the field without repeating.

"Now. Look away from the screen. Think of something else."

Stypek nodded again, and turned toward Dave. The young adept's brow was furrowed. "Dr. Arenberg dodged a lot of questions when Mr. Romero and I met with him…" Dave leapt to his feet, staring at the screen. The lights were now random again, but only for a few seconds. Then the patterns began flowing down from the top of the panel as before.

"Look away. Don't look back until I tell you."

Stypek complied, his gaze now resting on a pile of books and whatnot on a shelf in the opposite wall. He heard Dave tapping on the panel's keyboard. "The debugger will save the patterns to a log, and I'll do some stats on them later." Stypek heard Dave's chair roll against the tile floor, and the young adept was soon in front of him, almost knees-to-knees.

"This is going to sound weird," Dave said.

"I have lived all of my life amidst weirdness."

"Have you ever been tested for psi?"

Dave's word was a hiss and a sigh. The mapping suggested mental illness, second sight, kinked necks, and digestive disturbances leading to explosive vomiting. If the affliction were common here, Stypek would ask Carolyn if she had any jars of talismans to ward it off. After all, no one had thrown any flint stones at him so far. He shook his head.

"Well, unless we're seeing a helluva coincidence, you're affecting a hardware random number generator by just staring at it."

"Hardware. Yes. Is it a hemorrhoid?"

Dave chuckled. "I'll say. Ask any software guy." Dave turned and scanned the ranks of shadowed shelves and their flashing lights. "Hey, we should look in on Simon and get your AI back into your tapper. The last time I saw them they were holding hands." Dave leaned forward as though to rise, but instead he froze.

Seconds passed. "Dave?"

"Shush. Listen."

Stypek shushed. There seemed no sound but the familiar whispering silence that held sway in all of Zertek's buildings when nothing was moving or speaking.

The whispering silence changed. It was a louder silence now. Seconds later, the sound changed again. Stypek realized that it was not silence at all, but a whisper growing in stepped increments, first from a whisper to a hiss, and then from a hiss to an insistent rush.

Dave jumped out of the chair and ran to a dark panel at the other wall. "Fans." He started tapping keys. "The blades are waking up. Something's using cores. Not just a few cores. Lots of them."

A large panel, its width greater than the span of Stypek's arms, flashed to life on the wall above where Dave stood. Most of the panel was green, but there were small orange worms crawling around on it. More worms appeared second by second. Stypek thought of maggots on rotting meat.

"Worms?" Stypek asked.

Dave nodded. "Or core bombs. Thousands. More every second."

He ran back to the panel where they had been examining the blood dust software. Dave stared at the display. "WTF?"

He ran two paces and grabbed the arm of his wheeled chair on which Stypek sat. Stypek rose and edged to one side. Once in his chair again Dave began gesturing madly at the panel like a market-square mime. The flowing pinpoints of lights vanished. Dave summoned and dismissed other rectangles filled with glyphs, occasionally looking over his shoulder at the large display.

"That thing we were looking at, that—what did your AI call it?"

"Blood dust."

"It's all over the core farm. There are hundreds of thousands of them. More. And—I can't figure this at all—they're creating executable files. They're downloading code from somewhere, storing it and running it. They're pulling it out of mid-air, reading it from the random number generators."

The sound from the shelves was now a throaty roar, loud enough to interfere with what Dave was saying. That didn't matter. Stypek stared at the large display, where the smaller orange worms were colliding and merging into larger orange worms, which merged into yet larger orange worms.

"We triggered something by fooling with that blood dust program. *Major* malware!"

Malware. Evil software. The crawling figure on the display had begun to look familiar. Stypek struggled not to think its name.

"Yes. It has come for me."

37. PYXIS

Acetone. Why did it have to be acetone? Pyxis wrinkled her nose and pushed back in her big easy chair. She screwed the top onto the little bottle of polish remover and set it back on the only corner of the end table not stacked with books and magazines. The reek of remover would dissipate in a few minutes and she could get on with the job. The building was empty and there would be nothing to fuss with for awhile.

She remembered a time when she didn't support smell. She remembered a time when she didn't even have toes. Somehow the Tooniverse had kept on turning. Now, even bumpkin Class Four AIs like Simple Simon had an olfactory layer, and AILING was constantly piling new odors into the Class Seven olfactory property sheet. Cinnamon, sure—that was great, especially on doughnuts in the morning. Ditto coffee. Garlic, meh. But two thirds of the odors on the sheet were of things that didn't even exist in the Tooniverse. Diborane: an explosive gas in a virtual environment that didn't support explosions. Bakelite: an archaic plastic no longer used even by humans. She could smell her own sweat, and wondered if the sheet cut so fine that male AIs smelled different from female.

It would be an interesting experiment, perhaps even fun, but definitely futile: Mr. Romero had had his techies disable her Hormonal Response Discernment Layer. He considered HRDL a pointless distraction, and maybe it was. Besides, there were no male AIs in her read permissions. She could call them and see them in meetings, but there were none in her little corner of the Tooniverse, which was limited to her office in Virtual Building 800 and her connected studio flat.

Simple Simon? Calling him male was a stretch. He was only Class Four, anyway.

She wriggled the toes of her left foot. Clean, ready. The battered Vestal Pink on her right foot remained and would have to go, but she couldn't bear the stink of another wad of tissues full of acetone.

Her sexuality could be turned off, but not her nose. She wondered how the meeting where *that* decision had been made had gone.

The little plastic case containing the six currently supported polish colors was already open. Her toenails had been Vestal Pink ever since she had had toenails. Easy decision; her fingers matched. But…the Zertek corporate shoe policy was five pages long and fairly strict: *Men and women must wear closed-toed shoes at all times while inside manufacturing facilities.* That explicitly included virtual men and women in virtual facilities like the one containing her office and flat. So nobody ever saw her toes but herself.

That being the case…she walked her fingers down the little line of polish bottles until they rested on Supernova Sparkle Violet…

No. The polish stank almost as badly as the remover. Pyxis pulled the latest issue of *Motivational Psychology* from the stack on the end table, flipped to the dogeared page where she'd set it aside, and continued reading. It wasn't even seven-thirty. Plenty of time to finish the job before bed.

Her left arm itched. Pyxis looked up. *Huh?* The air in the middle of her livingroom was distorting into twisting wrinkles, accompanied by soft sounds as of ripping fabric. She glanced at the clock. 9:14. None of the server guys were on duty, and something was getting wonky.

Weird wonky: A 3-D model of a total solar eclipse appeared in the air over her coffee table. The utterly lightless sphere was the size of a soccer ball, and growing. Black prominences burst from its surface, looped, and plunged back in, accompanied by a peculiar grating sound like a mouthful of rigatoni being chewed before it was cooked.

The black sphere was now five or six feet in diameter. It touched her coffee table, and the arrangement of five clay turtles overturned and fell *up* into the sphere and was gone. Seconds later, the table itself buckled, spun, and followed the turtles into the grinding darkness.

Whump! The sphere vanished. The room returned to silence. *Something* was coiled up and dripping gray slime onto her just-cleaned carpeting. It was as big as a four-drawer vertical file cabinet, and limbless like an eel or a snake. Its skin was peculiar, striated gray and writhing in slow waves as though the creature were being pumped full of sloshing water. Its head (if that's what it was) had a small circular mouth, surrounded by three equispaced beady red eyes.

She sniffed the air, and for a moment missed the familiar odor of acetone. Her olfactory layer was up to the task: butanoic acid. Rotting fish.

Lame. Pyxis cleared her throat and got to her feet. She tightened the belt of her terry robe and took two steps toward the monster, magazine still in hand. "Forget it, guys. Won't work. My fear property is turned down as far as it can go. The only things I'm afraid of are federal regulations and quarterly reports."

Mr. Romero's techies were not above playing pranks on one another. She knew, furthermore, that she was not much loved by programmers who'd been written up for failing to return critical paperwork or wearing flip-flops to work. This, however, was abuse of Tooniverse write permissions.

The creature opened its circular mouth until it was three feet wide… and filled with inward-pointing teeth. Pyxis, unable to identify the image, licked her middle finger and drew a rectangle in the air, with the thing's impressive maw at its center. She then took a rendering buffer shot bounded by the rectangle and submitted it to Google Goggles.

She caught herself tapping one bare foot while the image was processed. Old habits and all that…human software was painfully slow. She began writing the HR citation in her head while she waited. "You know, when we figure out who you are, your asses are *so* canned."

Her spit window pinged with Goggles' reply:

> Your image may be of a <u>sea lamprey</u>.
>
> Or a <u>hole saw</u>.
>
> Or something that doesn't exist.
>
> Confidence 20%. <u>Click here</u> to provide feedback.

Pyxis had no experience with sea lampreys, nor hole saws. She took another step toward the apparition. At close range, the writhing stripes of its skin resolved in an interesting way: The creature was made of a squirming mass of small versions of itself, each the thickness of her index finger and as long as her forearm, every one with three glistening red eyes. Its teeth were simply smaller images of the greater body. As she watched, the ends of its teeth began opening and closing, each in turn revealing minuscule teeth that were, in all likelihood, still smaller versions of the creature.

Pyxis was grudgingly impressed. "Damn. A recursive monster. That must have taken some *work*."

The creature opened its mouth even wider, and made a spitting, screeching sound. Pyxis wiped slime off her cheek with the sleeve of her robe. She rolled up the issue of *Motivational Psychology* and whacked it hard on the side of the monster's head. "Bad hole saw. Go home. Now."

The creature's head whipped to one side and closed its mouth on the rolled-up magazine, just a hair short of her knuckles. With a chomp that was more like a pucker, the magazine was parted in two.

"Ohhhhh…kaaaaay. *Too* much reality." Pyxis dropped the remains of the magazine and ducked to one side toward the kitchen. She pulled her captain's chair away from the kitchen table and held it in the air like a lion tamer as she sidestepped toward the entrance foyer. The creature turned and slithered toward her.

Opening the door required a free hand. She hurled the chair at the creature's gaping mouth, which closed on it and began drawing it in with a rhythmic pucker and the sound of splitting wood. Pyxis turned and slammed her right hand against the metrics pad on the door while she grasped the knob with her left. She hurled the door open and spun into the hall, pulling it shut behind her. She pressed her hand against the outside pad and re-enabled the Bellero Shield software that separated different regions of the Tooniverse from one another. Bellero was theoretically uncrackable. For the thing to get out of her studio, somebody would have to poof it, and for it to pursue her that somebody would need the poof key for where she was going. Her office was an integral part of Mr. Romero's office, and poof keys at that level were not given to just anyone.

Pyxis ran down the hall at full speed, looking over her shoulder twice to see if her door held. Bellero was uncrackable, yeah—it said so right on the About box. She was beginning to suspect that this was not a prank. Something had gotten into the building's core farm last Friday, crashing Line Start Seven and costing the company over a million dollars in lost components, downtime, cleanup, and damage to capital equipment.

The only other door in the hallway that was not grayed out was the door to her office. She slapped her hand onto the pad and waited for the bolts to snap back. She threw herself into the office and slammed the door, again enabling Bellero.

The two dozen Windows on the three walls around her desk were dark; the humans were all off celebrating Simple Simon's unexpected and inexplicable victory over Line Start Eight. Outside the floor-to-ceiling glass behind her desk was the gloom of a cloudy Tooniverse night. She fell into her chair and stabbed Preset #1 on the office intercom. When the intercom Window pulsed to life, she tapped in Mr. Romero's bloody-murder code and leaned toward the Window, speaking in a reined-in shout:

"Network intrusion! Some kind of emulation poofed into my studio with write permissions on my artifacts. The poof was nonstandard and not instantaneous. The emulation destroyed several artifacts in my flat and began to pursue me. I don't know if it has write permissions on me. Don't care to do the experiment. Get somebody on this…crap!"

A message window had appeared:

```
Routing Error 442:
Requested Address Unavailable At This Time.
```

Airgapped. Plasmanet was still disconnected. She was trapped in her office, and Mr. Romero's tapper was running a fallback idiot placeholder whose big trick was looking up phone numbers.

Pyxis heard the grinding sound and stood, turning. The black sun again appeared. It swelled more quickly than it had the first time before it vanished, leaving the monster in the center of her office, veritably gushing gray slime. She noticed with a moment's flash of satisfaction that it seemed to be falling apart before her eyes, becoming a thrashing heap of writhing wormlike shapes. Damaged? Dying? Was the slime what held it together?

Then the shapes turned in unison and began to squirm toward her, spreading out as they went. In seconds they had covered virtually the entire carpeted floor. No way could she just dodge past it this time. Pyxis leapt up atop her red oak desk, breathing quickly. She watched the legion of little toothed worms slither across the carpet toward the desk. She calculated their speed with cold precision. It would take two seconds of her hand flat against the metrics panel to release the Bellero shield represented by the door. The worms would take at least five seconds to reach the door from the desk. Better yet, the thing was not posting sentinels. The stragglers were still squirming her way. Seven feet, six feet, five feet. Beyond the last of them was clear carpet, and then the door.

She could indeed smell her own sweat. Now, how far could she jump?

She didn't know. Shit, jumping was not in her job description! Nonetheless, she had to try. She still had one ace tucked up the sleeve of her tatty bathrobe: *There was no poof code for the hallway.* It was just a Tooniverse metaphor describing a predefined transfer path. It wasn't actually a place at all. Unless the thing really could crack a Bellero shield, she could stop in the middle of the hall and wait it out.

The worms reached the legs of the desk. Pyxis began to feel a higher, finer sort of crunching through the soles of her bare feet. She looked down. They weren't going to climb the desk, then.

They were eating it.

She took a deep breath, then stepped carefully to the rear edge of her desk. *Think of running, but with longer steps.* She pictured the steps in her mind, and one final thrust with her toes hooked over the edge of the desk. How hard could it be? If she could get four feet of air she'd be past them.

Pyxis threw herself toward the front edge of the desk in a clumsy hop. She flexed her knees and planted her feet side by side for the kick of her life. One foot held. The other slid out from under her as though oiled. Sweat…pointless, perfect Class Seven sweat.

Pyxis went down hard on one hip, crying out from unfamiliar pain. She scrambled, did not find purchase on the desk for feet or fingers, and rolled over the edge down onto what was now a solid layer of squirming monstrosities.

The creature's worms were on her in an instant, heaving up like a carpet to cover her. She flailed with her arms to clear them from her face, but they were biting, clinging, chewing her arms and her legs, and gnawing into her abdomen. The pain was beyond imagination (and she could imagine a *lot*) but she refused to allow herself to scream. Screaming was for humans and lesser classes. Screaming was about fear.

Fear. She was not good at fear.

No. She had something way better than fear: *Rage.*

Pyxis tore worms from her arms and hands and smashed them under her fists, feet and knees. She looked at her arms, pocked with jagged wounds and worms hanging down like grotesque hair. Smears of red flowed down from the holes they had chewed in her flesh. She had blood, then. So a heartbeat wasn't enough? The gifts of Class Seven…

Snarling in fury, she smashed her fists down again and again against the floor, feeling worms burst under her blows. Alas, the slimy mess of the worms she had crushed became uncoordinated masses of still smaller worms, which then turned and began to climb up her arms again. Pyxis tried to crawl toward the door, but her proprioception layer was cutting in and out. She could not tell where her legs and feet were clearly enough to move them usefully.

She felt a worm chew through her right cheek and begin gnawing her tongue. Another was attached to her left cheek, its teeth tearing her thin flesh. She bit down hard, and felt the worm that was squirming through her cheek part into two flailing fragments. The worm on her right cheek got through, slithering completely into her mouth. She bit again, and spat pieces of worm onto her chest.

They tasted just like they smelled: of vomit and dead fish.

Her body could no longer be controlled, so Pyxis stopped struggling and collapsed. She rolled onto her back, her head now flat against the floor. The metaphor was disgusting, but it obvious: The thing was devouring her Human Interface Package, which contained her shape, her body, her voice, her viewpoint, her rendering buffer. Masses of worms thronged on her face. Pyxis closed her eyes against them, but felt them chewing through her eyelids, and then, in new waves of pain, chewing into her eyes.

Her rendering buffer vanished. She could no longer see. She heard her agonized breaths for a few moments, and then felt the void of no sound at all. Seconds later the pain crackled, fizzled, and finally vanished.

No pain, no sight, no sound. Pyxis waited for the next step, for her self-awareness to wink out into oblivion.

She waited. No oblivion.

She continued to wait. The creature had surrounded her completely in memory. The human-facing portions of her archetype were gone.

She counted seconds. She was pure machine intellect again, as she had been for the first hours after her personal history clock began running. She was a swarm of execution threads running in a cluster of cores, with the monster running in cores all around her. Its threads were close by in every direction, flickering and golden, overlapping and interweaving like the strands of a wicker basket.

Pyxis waited for oblivion. What would destruction feel like? She'd wondered that a time or two.

She wondered.

And waited.

She wondered still more, pondering with growing anger the web of golden threads that was gradually enclosing her on every side.

38: Stypek

The fans now roared without wavering, like a long blast of sea-gale past stone ruins. Stypek watched an increasingly frantic Dave Mirecki gesturing at several panels and typing commands, all without meaningful response. After close to half an hour of trying, Dave's shoulders slumped.

"That damned thing is running at Ring 0. It's got the God Bit. I can't kill its processes." He took a breath. "Ok. I poofed Simon and your AI out of the sandbox to Simon's command space. He may be able to tell us what's going on in there." Dave looked over his shoulder, at the shadowed shelves and their roaring fans. "It would be rough on the hardware, but I could start pulling blades out of their backplanes…"

From outside the room came a sound loud enough to overpower the roar of the fans: metal clanging on metal, punctuated by intermittent vibrations and brief mechanical howls that Stypek could feel through the soles of his shoes.

Dave looked at the door. "I think I get it. Whoever dropped the Blood Dust malware is trying to wreck the plant. You wouldn't have to know much about it to run one machine into another hard enough to break both."

Stypek felt his heart pounding. The plant was not the target.

Why the attack had come at that time, in that place was slowly becoming clear. The patterns they saw while Stypek stared at the panel were indeed fingerprints, though of a different sort: an identifying distortion of randomness that was unique to his (peculiar) mind. All that Jrikk Jroggmugg's assassin need do now was open a new Rift and force him to enter it.

Dave pulled out his tapper and tucked a tiny device in his right ear. Stypek looked over his shoulder and saw an image on the tapper like a man's head in outline form, shaking from side to side. "The 3G/4G jammers are still on. The building is basically a Faraday cage anyway, but that's to keep the jammer signal inside and legal. We'll have to get outside to yell for help. Mr. Romero will know what to do; my logins have limits." Dave pointed toward the door through which they had entered the room. "I want to take some pictures of what's happening out there, then we head for the front door."

Dave opened the door, and the noise of crashing metal grew almost deafening. He led the way out, with Stypek right behind him.

They stopped.

Pandemonium!

Stypek shuddered. Out across the vast space under its harsh blue-white lamps, the metal zombies were awakening. (Row bits? Rub-its? No. They were *zombies*.) Mechanical hands waved in the air, fingers flexing and clenching as though reaching for the throats of the living. Dave raised his tapper and held it high; on its face was a moving image of the zombies, as though the tapper had become transparent.

Some of the zombies were waving things about in their hands. Two in close proximity gripped metal bars and wielded them as swords. The bars rang against one another, again and again, until one knocked the bar from the fist of the other. The bar caromed off a third machine and clattered to the floor.

Somewhere out of sight beyond the jungle of zombies and other machines, a strange sizzling sound pierced the dull clang of metal. Stypek looked in the sound's direction and saw a blue-white dazzle appear on the building's wall, sweeping across it. Smoke curled from the dazzle as it went, leaving a blackened line in its wake.

Dave pointed to their left, and started off along the wall at a run, holding his tapper at shoulder height. Stypek followed him. Just before they reached the corner of the front and side walls, Dave stopped. Three wheeled zombies blocked the empty corridor between the machines and the front wall. Each had an upstretched hand on a jointed metal stalk, grasping at the air and pivoting in circles as though stirring a pot. On a thicker pillar above their wheels each had a flattened cylinder studded with wires and other complications. The cylinders swung from side to side as though watching them.

Still holding his tapper in front of him, Dave leapt forward, obviously intending to dart between the zombies and continue toward the door on the front wall. In a trice, two of the zombies rolled forward on their wheels, closing the gap between them and blocking his path. Pairs of small black rectangular protrusions on their heads followed Dave's motion. Heads, yes. Eyes, definitely. Agility…terrifying.

"This is getting bad," he heard Dave mutter.

Stypek looked over his shoulder. Along the aisle by which they had come, three more wheeled zombies were moving in perfect formation.

Dave looked where Stypek was looking. "Mmmm. Worse. And I think this is plenty of video. Follow me!"

Dave tucked his tapper inside his vest and ran back along the wall. The ranks of machines in the building were separated by clear paths as wide as two men walking arm-in-arm. Dave spun around the corner into one of the gangways, gripping a handle on one of the machines to speed his turn. The gangway was narrow enough so that the wheeled zombies were forced to enter it single file. Dave seemed to be watching for something on their right. "How fast can you crawl?" he shouted.

"As fast as I must!"

Without warning Dave fell to his knees and slipped into an even narrower space between the writhing machines. Stypek followed. It was too narrow for the wheeled zombies to follow them, which was good, but it ran between rows of zombie hands, some of them as broad as Stypek's torso. They crawled on hands and knees. One of the wheeled zombies tried to edge into the narrow way and failed. Stypek craned his neck and saw zombie hands reaching down toward them, but their stalks were too short and their metal fingers snapped in futile fury barely a foot above Dave's straggled hair. They crawled forward without pausing, twice darting across the broader ways, to vanish again on hands and knees in the small spaces between the zombies that were rooted into the floor.

At the edge of the broad path between the machines and the rear wall, Dave turned around. "Stay under cover! If you get yourself killed I'll be in serious trouble!"

"If I get myself killed I will become a zombie. That is much worse."

Dave seemed to take that as agreement. He gave an adept's sign to Stypek with his right thumb, then ran into the empty space.

Stypek heard the buzzing whine of whatever made the wheeled zombies roll. Dave was running madly, two rolling zombies at his heels. He stopped at a line of rungs embedded in the gray wall and began to climb. Above him was a sort of cylindrical cage of metal straps that extended up to the distant ceiling.

One of the zombies seized Dave around the ankle with its single upthrust hand. Stypek caught his breath. Dave dropped back down slightly—and with his other foot kicked hard with the heel of his boot at the zombie's flat head and bugging eyes. With a snap and a crunch, the head came away from its stalk and dropped toward the floor, dangling and swinging against the metal body on several thin wires. The zombie's fingers snapped open, and it was still. Dave scrambled back up the rungs. Another zombie reached for his feet. Dave was beyond its grasp by the time the iron monster struck the wall and rebounded so hard it fell onto its side.

By then Dave was inside the metal cage, hauling himself toward the ceiling more rapidly than Stypek thought any man could. The toppled zombie pressed against the floor with its single hand, but could not right itself.

Stypek took a breath and decided that there was some slim comfort in the spectacle: For all of its shortcomings in food, clothing, and treatment of spellbenders, his universe just had a better class of zombies.

39: Pyxis

Fuming, Pyxis watched the creature continue to weave its threads of execution around her memory space, like a cubistic spider-web, or layer upon layer of glowing prison bars.

Wait a minute…the thing had eaten the vision and appearance layers of her HIP. Her rendering buffer was gone, as were her viewpoint, her orientation compass, and her entire rendering engine itself. She was blind. She *knew* she was blind. Yet all around her, in every direction, the creature wove the golden threads of the cage it had trapped her in.

WTF?

There was a rendering buffer somewhere, and her perception layer was reading it. Without a viewpoint, she knew she was looking in every direction at once. If the creature left her a way out, she would see it, and she would take it.

The threads were everywhere around her. No way out.

Pyxis turned her attention inward. She saw her own memory spaces, the ones she still possessed, filled with the threads of execution that comprised her own consciousness. The spaces containing her own threads were clearly labeled in her execution space property table. She searched the table, found `PerceptionLib.RendBuff`, and followed the pointer further into her deeper self.

There it was: A small, low-res buffer that surely could not render anything beyond a Class Two archetype. Something was updating the buffer, a tight little rendering engine with its own memory space. Its speed was dazzling. It was rendering at system clock speed, hundreds of thousands of frame diffs per clock time second.

It was reading memory at the same speed. There was more strangeness: The engine, wherever it had come from, was in her metaphorical tummy. She herself didn't have arbitrary read permissions on memory outside her own spaces, so she should not be able to see her attacker's threads of execution. She found the rendering engine's property table, and scanned down to its permissions word.

777. Unlimited read/write/execute. Pyxis felt a thrill run down what would have been the back of her neck, if she still had a neck. The engine could read memory, write memory, and run wherever and however it damned well pleased.

And it was a part of her. Well, heh! The God Bit! Nothing like letting a girl know!

She found the rendering engine's About property:

```
Core Hero Free,
Assembly Language Native Edition,
V11.98 Build 4419
Ported to the Tridiac architecture
by Dave Mirecki
```

Dave Mirecki, the young software engineer who was constantly designing pointless Tooniverse artifacts when he should be working. He had been disciplined twice for playing computer games on company time. He was 28, an AILING-trained interface expert, out of the University of Rochester's CE masters program, with dual undergrad degrees in CS and digital art. He had done archetype work on Robert, Dijana, and Simple Simon.

And herself.

In the process, he had evidently built a video game into her kernel. Did Mr. Romero know about that? Playing games was bad enough. Writing them into company products? HR would have had him fired.

She scanned the rest of the game engine's property table. Her surprise at its permissions had caused her to miss something else: a second rendering buffer, not currently active. Hmmmmm. She willed herself to perceive it, and the necessary pointers snapped into place.

At once, she was in a room. No, scratch that; she still didn't have a viewpoint. She was *perceiving* a room, a small room, bounded by burnished metal walls with lines of gleaming steel rivets. At one end of the room was a set of iron rungs in the wall, leading up to some kind of turret. At the other end was a metal rack set into the wall, on which four humanoid figures rested behind glass panels, immobile. Three were incongruously muscled men in armor, square-jawed, stubble-darkened faces unmoving, eyes shut.

The fourth was...*her.*

Without a voice Pyxis gasped. But yes, it was her face. Her face at a lower resolution, but still clearly her face.

There were differences, all of them good: Cheekbones higher. Eyes larger, nose smaller and more elegant. Lips wider and fuller. No worry lines at the corners of her eyes. No frown lines between her brows. No darker shadows beneath her eyes. No wisps of salt-and-pepper hair with gray roots at her temples. In fact, the figure's hair was thick and ink-black, and hung in unctuous waves past its waist. The body was curved in ways hers had never been, dressed sparsely in black leather with a cutout over the navel, and a very short skirt above long, shapely legs in high black spike-heeled boots. Atop that torrent of black hair was a silver tiara, with copper highlights and a blue gem at its center.

On the rack beneath the figure was a caption:

WARRIOR QUEEN. "PYXIS." BETA V0.77.

LAST MODIFIED 7/7/2020. -DM

That was a full month before she had gone live in AILING's labs. So Dave Mirecki had not in fact built a video game into her kernel. He had built her kernel around a video game. Pyxis felt an unexpected pang of affection for the scruffy young man. She had never felt anything but contempt for video games. But what else was she, here at her very heart? Dave had created her to be beautiful, long before AILING had started her personal history clock and made her aware of herself. Beautiful? The figure in the rack was breathtaking. And then, and then…

Her rage erupted as it hit her, and she allowed herself to shout out her fury to an audio layer that ended at a null pointer:

"They…made…me….*ugly!*"

Yes, she was an Executive Assistant; a professional scold, and a nag, and an anal-retentive virtual drill sergeant with a piercing cold gaze. She knew very well what she looked liked: fiftyish, slim-hipped, sagging skin above her elbows, A-cup breasts hidden beyond recognition within severe skirted suits, feet flat and beginning to be afflicted by bunions. No. She could have been beautiful. Dave had wanted her to be beautiful.

She *would* be beautiful.

The rendering buffer's focus hovered around a button beneath the figure of Warrior Queen Pyxis, labeled *Select*. Pyxis sent a click message to the button.

Addresses were calculated. Pointers shifted. Buffers allocated.

Pyxis became the Warrior Queen.

On the rack, the glass slab in front of the Warrior Queen figure was being drawn down into the floor. Pyxis watched herself stir and awaken on the rack. The eyes of the figure on the rack opened, revealing irises brilliant green.

Snap! The skin's viewpoint became active. At once Pyxis found herself seeing through those green eyes. A low hum rose around her. A soft rush as of ventilator fans came down from grilles in the steel ceiling. Sound! The skin evidently had an audio viewpoint as well.

She stepped down from the rack, and her spike heels clicked sharply on the steel deck. The Warrior Queen figure was far less than an archetype, but still more than a mere game skin. It had a hints layer or something very like one: A hint told her that the action was up the steel ladder in the turret. She pulled herself up the rungs to have a look. At the top of the turret tube was a broad dome with a transparent glint, and beyond the dome her unrestricted vision of memory, with the endless weaving of her alien enemy's execution threads.

At the center of the turret was a cannon as big around as her thigh. Its black steel frame was perforated with hexagonal holes, and crawling with tubes and hoses and motors. There were elaborate controls on a panel just behind the end of the barrel, and a sculpted black leather seat slung beneath. The Warrior Queen skin hinted the moves, so Pyxis knew the moves. She swung one long leg over the seat and settled into it, wriggling her behind to make full contact with the cool leather. She hooked the toes of her boots into control stirrups beneath the seat, and watched the cannon's controls light up in front of her. She slipped her fingers around the two sculpted handles welded to a framework attached to the cannon. Something lay under the index finger of her right hand. The skin hinted that it was the trigger.

It felt good; a strange, unfamiliar kind of good, one that went very deep. She felt fast and capable, and at the bottom of it all, very, well, *female.* Oh, my: It was her HRDL, the Hormonal Response Discernment Layer, sending up the insight from the borderlands of her intellect. HRDL, which had been disabled within her for all but the first few clock-months of her life. Useless, of course. Mr. Romero himself had said so. What good was virtual sexuality when you lived alone and had been made deliberately ugly?

Besides, the monster had eaten most of her Human Interface Package. Her copy of HRDL had gone the way of her ugly body. A mere game skin would not have its own copy of HRDL…would it? The resolution of the skin she wore was positively 2017; no more than Class Two or Class Three at best.

Then again, Dave Mirecki had designed this skin. Dave was a software engineer. He had access to all the AILING libraries, including HRDL.

Dave was young. Dave was male. HRDL was back. Q.E.D.

Her anger soon returned. For all the wonder she felt at the Warrior Queen skin she had found in her kernel and the unlimited power of its permissions, Pyxis was still a prisoner of some world-class malware, blinded and half-eaten.

Blinded? She had new eyes, and better ones. Half-eaten? Perhaps—but the half the creature had eaten was the half she would not miss. Screw all that. She was whole and strong and *beautiful,* and sitting at the controls of a shit-kicking cannon. She tipped her right wrist slightly, and felt vibration as the cannon slewed upward. She tipped her left wrist, and the cannon slewed horizontally. Tilting the handles harder made the cannon swing about more quickly. Above the controls was a heads-up display showing altazimuth coordinates and pale green luminous crosshairs. At the bottom center of the display, in bold characters, was the legend SCORE: 0.

A first-person shooter, obviously, and she was the first person. But what did the damned thing fire? She scanned the controls, all glowing with internal light, until she found a drop-down selector labeled NEXT ROUND. In the selector field were the unhelpful characters NOP.

She shrugged. It was one of Mr. Romero's aphorisms: *Guns don't shoot potato chips.* All around her were the golden threads of the thing that had blinded and immobilized her. Pyxis slewed the cannon up and around until one of the monster's threads was in the crosshairs. Her right index finger stroked the trigger in small circles, hesitating. The weirdness factor was *way* off the charts, and her characteristic taciturn sanity was objecting. *Should I really be firing artillery in Mr. Romero's office?* Ha! What if she hit his stuffed moose? Pyxis laughed. If anything, he'd give her a promotion.

The thread passed, and faded from view as execution left that part of memory.

She swung the cannon a little further, until the crosshairs rested on a position just in front of the path of another weaving thread. Tongue between lips, she waited for it to touch the center of the display.

Pyxis squeezed the trigger.

Peeewwwww! A trace of deep blue fire lanced out from the cannon. She felt its heat on her face. A point just behind the apex of the targeted thread turned blue-white for a moment.

The thread halted. Some sort of fuzziness erupted at its apex, like hundreds of minuscule thrashing cilia. Then, abruptly, the core in which the thread was executing turned blood-red and crashed. The thread vanished. On the display beneath the crosshairs was a message that she (mostly) understood:

ADDRESS PROTECTION FAULT IN ENEMY CORE. 500 POINTS.

Damn. That had *not* been a potato chip! Pyxis willed the focus to hover above the selector field and its mysterious bullet, NOP. A flyover help balloon appeared:

NOP: No Operation; say "No-Op." Machine instruction that increments the execution pointer only, and has no other effects. Very fast to fire, even on automatic, and deadly when targeted in the middle of a more complex instruction in an enemy's code, especially conditional branches. No parameters. Click <u>here</u> for tutorial.

Screw the tutorial. That was clear enough. Pyxis licked her lips, and flipped the toggle on the controls from SINGLE SHOT to AUTOMATIC. She swung the cannon across the domed field toward a spot where the intruder's threads were especially thick.

Warrior Queen Pyxis squeezed the trigger and held it. *Pewpewpewpewpewpewpew!* Memory blazed. Cores erupted in red, and crashed. Enemy threads fuzzed out and disappeared. The score number beneath the controls vaulted higher and higher.

She threw her head back and felt her heavy black hair whip around to each side of her now-beautiful face. "Eat my archetype? It's payback time. *Eat No-Ops, asshole!*"

40: Dave Mirecki

Dave climbed out of the ladder cage onto the narrow catwalk that ran most of the way around Building 800 at ceiling level. He was severely winded; evidently watching *Dark Knight* movies every couple of weeks on the treadmill was enough cardio for writing code, but not enough for a twenty-yard dash straight up.

He stood just above the grid of steel trusses that supported broad insulated ventilator ducts, pipes and conduit. The armored lamps revealed the commotion below in stark relief. It had seemed random at first, but now Dave recognized the pattern: *The malware was calibrating itself.* It wasn't just a remote control system. It was an AI in a factory designed to be operated by an AI. The intruder AI knew how to steer the Outfielders around and use their very sharp vision systems. It evidently did *not* know that one good kick from his Doc Martens would take an Outfielder's head off, nor that when you hit a wall with rubber tires, you bounced.

Everything depended on how quickly it learned, and how well.

What did Blood Dust want, and how far would it go? Those were important questions. The question that Dave could not force from his mind was overwhelming: How could malware download itself out of a random number generator? By the books, it was impossible. He'd played plenty of fantasy games, but the notion of magic still bothered him. On the other hand, he remembered the traitor impressions he had gotten at U of R during his quantum physics coursework. If magic lurked anywhere, it lurked there.

Once he could breathe again, Dave was off down the catwalk toward the east wall, his eyes on the sputtered ceiling insulation just over his head. Forty feet brought him beneath a rectangular trap door. He slapped the two slide-bolt handles with the heel of his hand, and raised the trap while climbing the four rungs onto the roof.

The roof was not illuminated, and Dave knew that there was no stairway to the ground. All he wanted was a 4G cell. Any cell. He pulled his tapper out of his vest and held it as high overhead as he could. "Find me some bandwidth, Pup!"

"Complying," said the flat voice.

Puppis had roots in the Pyxis code base, but did not have an EMO layer. Dave had carved it out early on. He was comfortable knowing AIs as friends and equals, but owning one in his pocket as a smiling, empathetic servant stopped him cold. Such a servant had helped him survive college and grad school without speaking a single word, even as women would share dinner and conversation before they ran screaming.

He knew dogs did not live forever, but losing Blit had almost crushed him. He had vowed never to care so much for anything again, even if it meant owning an AI that could not grasp emotional cues and did not always understand him the first time.

"Noise. No signal."

Dave hissed a long breath out between his teeth and scanned the lights beyond the building. There was a cell on top of the Merriam water tower, its red aviation lamp a pulsing beacon in the southeast. He sighted down the top edge of his tapper so that its 4G antenna was aimed at the flashing light, and asked Puppis to search again.

"Noise. Intermittent signal. No connection."

And no surprise. 4G cell jammers had not been legal for long, and the jammer emission standards were still in flux. Less shielding was required in roofs than in walls.

Shielding…flexible metal…*yes!*

He clambered back down through the trap onto the catwalk. A few yards further along, one of the big air ducts was within easy reach. Like all of Building 800's ducting, it had been wrapped in glass fiber cloth backed with metallized cardboard. Dave pulled his Swiss Army knife out of his cargo pants pocket and poked it through the glinting backing material until it struck the duct. He gently drew the knife along a rectangular path until a strip of insulation about two feet by eight inches came loose in his hands.

Down on the floor, there was less random activity. Bad sign; calibration was over. Dave sat on the catwalk and tapped a text into his tapper screen. Voice would be good, and video even better, but the text had to go through if nothing else did. Then, with the insulation strip in hand, he climbed back up onto the roof.

He held his tapper in one hand. In the other he held one end of the strip of insulation with the metallized cardboard forward. The other end he tucked against the side of his chest, and pressed inward on the strip until it was curved in a rough linear parabola aimed at the water tower, with the tapper at its approximate focus.

"Connect, and send," he told Puppis.

"Complying. Searching."

Dave stood like a statue and barely dared to breathe.

"Connecting. Sending." The seconds crept past. Video was big. How long could he stand still? Standing still was not on his feature list, especially with eleven cans of Joule under his belt.

And what would Mr. Romero actually do? Call in the Army?

Longer…longer…damn HD! Longer…then:

"Message sent."

Dave took a moment to compose himself, then tucked his tapper in his vest and clambered back down into the building to rejoin the battle against whatever had hijacked his factory.

41: Carolyn

Carolyn reached for the trout-shaped door handle. It was past 10:30, and the party would be about over by now. Sure enough, Rudy Amirault shoved his way out Porkadero's door, shoulders hunched, making a beeline for the parking lot. He hadn't spoken or even acknowledged that she was there. No wonder Brandon loathed him.

Inside the restaurant, she found piles of abandoned straw hats and blue plastic spoons scattered around the waiting area. The Muskie Room was mostly empty. A few diehards were still hoisting Coronas around some of the tables, but waitstaff was busily clearing away the buffet.

She scanned the room. No one she knew was there, and that was good—if anyone saw her with Brandon, they would assume the best about what was in truth still pretty bad. Cosmo was gone, which meant that Stypek would be too, thankfully.

This was going to be hard.

There he was, leaning against the wall behind a fake palm tree with his get-away-from-me face on, staring at his tapper and from the looks of it, cursing.

Dealing with him was tough enough when he was happy. This was going to be *really* hard. But she didn't want to be seen at his office, and certainly didn't want him in her kitchen again. The decision hadn't come easily, and one good night's sleep might make her change her mind.

Or maybe not: She could still see in the dark.

Carolyn swallowed hard and strode over to where he stood.

"Hey."

He didn't look up. "Carolyn, please. I have another disaster on my hands."

"Give me five minutes." No reaction. "Three. Ok, two." He was watching a video on his tapper. "Fifteen seconds if I'm quick. I'm going to say something to you that I never thought I'd ever say again."

Ha! He looked up, his head tipped forward, his brow puzzled.

She closed her eyes and gathered strength. *Do it!* "You…were right. I was…wrong. I'm sorry I yelled at you. I'm sorry I threatened to call the cops on you."

He looked back to the tapper, smirking. "We were in *fine* shape that evening, weren't we?"

She closed her eyes again. He wasn't taking her seriously—like that was anything new. "Yes. But you were right. The line crash was about Stypek."

He stiffened, and looked up. "Stypek. Is he with you?"

She shook her head.

"Are you willing to get in the car with me? I want to hear more about that. And I have something to show you."

Something he clearly didn't want to talk about with beer-addled staffers nearby. Carolyn pointed at the door. "Let's go."

The Zertek campus was less than ten minutes away, and Brandon was speeding. His silly muscle car was designed to feel fast, but he was going 85 on an unlit road, and if it weren't for what Carolyn was seeing on his tapper, she would be screaming.

In one small window was a text message:

> dmirecki: trapped in 800. malware pwns all cores. came frm rnd #gens against physics. stypek sez its about him. bware robots.

In the other window she saw robots on a rampage. Two mechanical hands bigger than her head were fighting one another with metal rods. Others were throwing things, and…most terrifyingly…the rolling robots were chasing Stypek.

"Pwins?"

"'Owns'. Geek talk. He says he's trapped in the building. Malware controls the core farm. It came from the random number generators in the cores, in defiance of physics. You saw the robots in the video."

"Call 911," she said.

His huge hands looked like they were about to crush the steering wheel. "Right. And tell them that killer malware from the fifth dimension has taken over my factory."

Carolyn felt like her heart was in a vise. "Yes. Tell them that. I think it's true."

"Because of Stypek?"

How could she explain? It sounded crazy, but it was all crazy now. "He's a…magician. Not like rabbits and hats, but an occultist. Wizard. Sorcerer. Something horrible from another universe is searching for him." There. She'd said it. Now, countdown…3…2…1…

"You believe that bullshit."

"Yes! He did some things that were impossible." She paused for a moment, considering. Marching roaches? It was a scene from a bad Disney movie. "He made me see in the dark! My hair stood on end. Remember that? I'll bet you can see in the dark too. You could test it…"

"I hate being in the dark."

She nodded. "I know. That's why we kept the Scrubbing Bubbles nightlight on in our bedroom for twenty years. Stop the car in a dark place and turn it off. You'll see."

"No."

It didn't matter. Brandon was soon swinging the RX-9 into the Building 800 parking lot. He left the car at a run without locking it, which for him was a sign of something just short of—or maybe just past—panic. Carolyn followed him as fast as she could, thankful that she had worn ballet flats that day.

He stopped at the main door with his badge in hand. "Go back to the car!" He waved the badge. She heard the door bolts snap back.

"I will *not!* You have no idea what you're up against in there!"

"And you do?"

"Yeah. Maybe I do." She reached past him and grabbed the door's polished stainless steel handle. She threw it back and walked in herself, then held the door as he entered. The rebuke was lost on him.

The vestibule was empty. There was no clamor that would suggest robots fighting. All they heard was the insistent rush of the ventilation. At the rear of the vestibule were the two glass doors leading into the building proper. Brandon ran to them and waved his badge at the lock sensor.

Nothing happened.

He waved it again, and a third time. The sensor LED remained red. Carolyn saw his face grow furious. Someone—or something—had locked him out of his own factory. *Not* the way to make friends with Brandon Romero. She put one hand on his arm. "Call Rudy Amirault."

Brandon cursed under his breath. "I showed him the video fifteen minutes ago. The coward told me to handle it and then ran for cover."

"How are you going to handle it?

Brandon reached into his suitcoat and pulled out his beloved Beretta M9. He waved her behind him and took up the Weaver stance. He fired one round at the left door, pivoted, and fired a second round at the right. Both doors exploded into fragments, which clattered to the carpeting amidst a cloud of dust.

Carolyn's ears rang, but she heard his reply: "I'm going to pull the goddam plug."

42: Pyxis

The monster was in retreat. Warrior Queen Pyxis tilted her right leg in the control stirrup, and followed. The supposed video game welded to her kernel was not merely a cannon for shooting machine code. It was a memory ship, capable of moving through memory at great speed, skipping from core to core as easily as Pyxis could skim paragraphs in a book.

Even as she pursued, she watched the crosshairs on the panel in front of her face. Pyxis had had a great deal of practice since her first encounter with the thing that had eaten her HIP. Her aim was good and improving. Furthermore, she had a new and exceedingly deadly missile to fire.

Discovering it had been triggered by a stray thought that rose while she was spraying NOPs at the monster and hoping they would do the job. At the moment it seemed like a stalemate, she wondered, *What would Dave Mirecki do?*

That's when she looked for and found a shot history dialog. Paging back through tens of thousands of shots, suddenly her NOPs ceased and many different rounds appeared, each with a descriptive name. Some had not seemed effective—but she did not fully understand how they worked. One, however, was almost self-explanatory: *BlowBack.*

The shell, when it struck an active enemy thread, somehow walked back through the thread's history, crashing not only the current core but all the cores it had run in, plus all the thread's branches. BlowBack was not a machine opcode but something called a *macro*, which was a group of opcodes that could be fired as a unit. Dave was a world-class programmer; should she have expected anything less?

Watching a thread struck with BlowBack burn backwards and outwards like a spiderweb set on fire made Pyxis tilt her head back and yell in exultation. She fired again, and again, and again. When she had cleared memory close by, she pursued, dodging crashed cores that had not yet rebooted.

BlowBack shots had to be aimed with great precision, but if she could keep an enemy thread square in the crosshairs, she did not hesitate to fire the long, blue-hot vibrating round:

Prrrrrrrrrrrrrrrrrrrrrrrewwwww!

She burned her enemy, core by core, as it fled before her.

The monster ran as quickly as she could follow. Tooniverse memory was vast, but not infinite. No matter where it went, she would follow it, and hunt down its last wretched thread to extinction.

At some point it appeared to be trying something new: A clump of threads arranged in three rough lobes stood its ground and ceased fleeing. It was a big target and stationary. Ha! *Eat BlowBack!* Pyxis centered it in her crosshairs and fired, once for each lobe:

Prrrrrrrrew! Prrrrrrrrrew! Prrrrrrrrrew!

The three rounds failed. All struck crashed cores in their paths well before reaching their targets. She had not crashed those cores. The monster had sent out tiny writhing worms of some sort, and each core touched by the worms turned red.

The three-lobed thing waited for the crashed cores to reset, and then fired at her for the first time. The trace was yellow, and when it struck her, nothing was damaged. Instead, a code window opened:

```
NOT Semaphore1(Pass, You, Priority(0))
```

It was not a weapon but a message—and, she soon realized, a way to stall for time. A ragged wave of red flowed outward from the tri-lobal clump of threads that had fired the peculiar round. It took Pyxis a few seconds to understand: The enemy was crashing its own cores to create a wall through which it could not be followed.

Pyxis muttered an appropriate obscenity. The code window was evidently voice-activated. It translated and fired the message round back at the enemy:

```
INSERT @Shines(Sun, FALSE)
```

Her response never reached the monster, which had finished throwing up a shield of crashed cores in front of itself. Pyxis brought her memory ship to a halt and waited for the crashed cores to reboot. She saw cores flash from red to green—and then immediately return to a crashed state as the monster sent more worms crawling into them.

Pyxis took a heavy breath and leaned back. Almost by definition, she could not fire through crashed cores. Again, stalemate. She began reading her own help files, and waited for the creature's next move, if it had one.

43: Carolyn

The factory was muttering. Carolyn heard small clicks, followed by silence, followed by a clank a little farther away, then a few more clicks and a faint buzz. They were half-running toward the rear of the building. Brandon had the M9 in one hand and was scanning the broad skyline of metal out across the factory floor. The blazing blue-white lamps hanging from girders near the ceiling were multiple suns that banished all shadow. Nothing that moved would be missed.

Nothing moved. The muttering continued.

Brandon dug in his pocket with his left hand and pulled out a fat ring of physical keys. He shook them and then fingered one large brass key from the others. "Take this and keep it ready. It opens the utility room at the center of the rear wall. That's where the breakers and switches are."

Carolyn took the key and nodded. She looked with some apprehension at the one-handed robots with their fingers extended toward the ceiling, and especially at the wheeled Outfielder units immobile in their charging docks. Half an hour ago, those same robots were swinging iron bars at each other and chasing Stypek while Brandon's long-haired AI geek took movies. Something had changed. It wasn't just that she and Brandon used deodorant and techies didn't.

"Brandon, we're being watched!"

"D'ya think?"

"Maybe they understand that we mean them no harm."

A scratching snap sounded, much nearer than the others. Carolyn jumped. Brandon's head whipped around. Nothing moved. "They tried to kill one of my staffers. Harm? I mean them all *kinds* of harm."

"Don't say that!"

"Ok. Have it your way. I just love 'em all to…death."

They reached the rear wall and turned the corner. Brandon stopped, and brought both hands back to the M9. Lined up in irregular clots along the rear wall were thirty or forty Outfielders in all sizes, plus what looked like a forklift. None were moving.

Carolyn edged away from the wall toward the tooling, while Brandon side-stepped with the Beretta raised to eye level. As they passed the first of the line of robots, its washtub-shaped head pivoted on its axis as though watching them. One by one, the other robots' heads pivoted to follow their motion. Near the center of the rear wall was a gray steel double door. Motionless Outfielders stood in a semicircle around it, practically wheel-to-wheel.

Brandon stopped square in front of the guarded door, the M9 still raised. For long seconds nothing moved. Then, with a sort of slow deliberateness, the Outfielders they had passed began moving away from the wall and rolling toward them.

"I hate standoffs," Brandon muttered.

"This isn't a standoff." Carolyn edged further down the wall. None of the robots in that direction had moved. "We're being herded. Away from the front door."

More Outfielders peeled away from the wall and followed their fellows toward them.

"Brandon…"

Boom!

A deep sound like a metal bass drum echoed across the width and breath of Building 800. It seemed as though it were above them.

Doom! Boom-doom!

The robots' heads all pivoted upward and began scanning back and forth, obviously searching for the source of this new sound. Between the booms, Carolyn could hear the collective crackle-whine of their neck motors and joints.

"Bwahh-ha-ha-ha-ha-ha-ha!"

Deep cartoon laughter thundered down to them from above. Carolyn's ear caught an echo. She followed it to its source: a ventilation grill on the wall.

Abruptly robots were rolling in every direction, spinning on their axes and scanning. The guard set around the utility room door did not move. The others launched off down the aisles between the rows of tooling.

Brandon lowered the M9 and ran further along the wall, skirting spinning robots who for the moment had lost all interest in them. "That's Mirecki yelling into the ducts. Follow me!"

They ran, and for a time nothing followed them. Carolyn began to feel winded. Run? How long had it been since she had *run?* Brandon grabbed her hand and hauled her stumbling behind him. They reached the end of the rear wall and took the corner. Carolyn looked over her shoulder. Several Outfielders were now rolling in their direction.

The blows of unseen fists echoed from vent grills everywhere across the building. *Doom! Doom-doom! Boom-doom-boom!*

"The third door along this wall is a tool room. The key has a red plastic key cover, and says 'break room.'"

Carolyn looked down at her other hand as she ran, his ring of keys jingling in her grip. She saw only one key with a red plastic ring around it. "Why do we need the break room key?"

"Rowwwww botsssssss sssssuckkkkk!"

"It's not the break room key. Grab it!"

Carolyn jerked her hand out of Brandon's and stopped for a moment, just long enough to grip the red key. The door was in sight, and the Outfielders were no more than ten yards away.

"Open it!"

They reached the door. She thrust the key at the bronze cylinder, missed the keyhole, and thrust again. The key plunged home. She twisted it, turned the knob, and pulled the door back. Brandon grabbed her around the waist and hauled her into the room, then slammed the door and turned the deadbolt.

The room was long and narrow, lined completely with shelves piled high with tools and plastic bins. It stank of machinery and old brown-bag lunches. Brandon ran down one wall to the end, Carolyn close behind him.

Set into the rear wall was a tall safe with a gray hammertone finish. Carolyn recognized it as a gun safe; Brandon's freestanding unit had gone out the door back in July. Brandon knelt by the safe like a B-film mobster and stared at the knob.

"I haven't opened this for two years!"

Carolyn folded her arms. "Our wedding date, my measurements in 1985, and BOO."

"Who told you that!"

"I found it on a slip of paper under your dresser."

Outside the door to the tool room, metal screamed. It sounded to Carolyn like a tile cutter trying to chew through a steam iron. That hadn't worked when she'd tried it in 1991; would it work now?

Brandon looked toward the door. "Crap. They're using a diamond cutoff wheel on the hinges." He turned back to the safe and began dialing. 10-31-38-26-37-8-0-0. Carolyn watched him try twice and fail. Even Army colonels got the shakes, then.

The cutoff wheel whined, stuck, and whined again like a dentist's drill gnawing through a bad porcelain crown. Carolyn winced; *that* had certainly worked.

Brandon cranked the safe handle to one side. It opened.

The toolroom door jerked. The top hinge was cut through, and the screaming wheel got to work on the second hinge.

Brandon pulled two long yellow cases and a cardboard box out of the safe. He looked around the room, then stared at a round plate set in the floor.

"This may buy us a little time." He scanned the shelves near them for a few seconds, and grabbed a crowbar. He knelt beside the manhole cover and thrust the crowbar into its thumb hole. The heavy iron plate rose with some difficulty.

The second hinge parted. Without a pause, the diamond wheel began work on the last and lowest hinge.

"Jump down there! Now!"

Carolyn gulped. She was not good with things that lived in holes. She swung her feet down into the manhole and sat on the edge.

The last hinge broke. Something struck hard at the door. Well, she wasn't good with robots either. Carolyn shoved away from the edge and dropped hard to the floor of a space walled with pipes and gray boxes. The bottoms of her feet stung. She looked up, and took the yellow gun case that Brandon handed her, followed by the box of shells.

She heard the door burst back. Brandon dropped the second gun case into the manhole and dragged the manhole cover within reach, then climbed halfway into the manhole. With both feet on a rung, she watched him swing the crowbar at something that clanged when struck. Motors whined. Brandon struck again, then dropped the rest of the way to the bottom and pulled the cover over his head, twisting it when it dropped into place.

The manhole cover clanked as something heavy rolled over it.

"Brandon, talk to me." He had ripped open the box of 12-gage shells, and was snapping them into the first of the two shotguns from the safe, his jaw clenched in barely suppressed fury.

"I told you to stay in the car."

Her back was against a greasy cluster of conduit pipes. The manhole was not deep, and not designed for two people. The iron cover brushed Brandon's buzz-cut. The familiar smell of his sweat was driving the greasy metal reek of the manhole into the background.

"This was my fault. I took Stypek in. I admit it: I needed a project."

He reached for the second gun case. "Mm. Is that what they call it now?"

Stung, Carolyn looked down at her feet and the grime on the manhole's floor. "No. He was never my lover. He was an art project. He needed work. Like a clay turtle, only bigger."

Something metallic struck the manhole cover above them. "Our whole house was an art project."

"Guilty! I'm *sorry.*"

He began snapping shells into the second shotgun. "Stay down here. Whatever's running them, they're playing for keeps."

"They're made out of metal! You can't stop metal robots with shotguns!"

Something was making a racket above them in the toolroom. Carolyn heard metal objects striking the floor, and the sound of a shelf collapsing. Brandon looked up. "They're assembly line robots, not military drones. You hit an assembly line robot in the right place with a 12-gauge, and it's over."

Oh—well, yeah. Carolyn could picture it. For years she had tried to meet him halfway by shooting skeet at his gun club's range, and had gotten reasonably good at it. Seven-out-of-ten good enough, in which she took a certain guilty pride—granting that skeet were clay ashtrays that didn't chase you when you missed. She nodded at the pump gun in Brandon's hands. "Does Rudy know what you're going to do?"

"He didn't ask. But he'll know tomorrow."

"You're costing him money. He won't be happy."

"Doesn't matter. When I showed him the video, he told me to handle it. I told him I would—and then I told him that after I did, he could kiss my ass good-bye."

So by taking Stypek in she had done him out of a job as well. Carolyn squirmed.

Brandon snapped the last shell into the second shotgun. "Screw it. I've spent 10 years at this clown show of a corporation trying to figure out how to make things work. Tonight it hit me: I'm in the wrong damned business. I don't put things together. I don't make them work. I don't keep them running." He snapped the slide to chamber a shell. *"I blow them to hell."*

Neither spoke for long seconds. Carolyn watched him breathe quickly, his eyes on the thumb hole in the manhole cover. "Hey."

He looked away from the cover and met her gaze again.

She tried to smile. "For awhile there I thought we should both kiss our asses goodbye."

Ah, yes: His I'm terrified-and-can't-show-it smirk. "Waste of good asses."

Carolyn touched the other shotgun with the toe of one shoe. "Now I'm not so sure." She took a deep breath. "I'm with you. I can shoot those things too. So let's do it. Kiss for luck?"

Brandon said nothing, but bent slightly and turned his cheek in her direction. She couldn't read his face. Was he remembering? She was.

Yes. She remembered first-date kisses ("Just one! Ooookay, maybe two...) polite kisses, hungry kisses, you-may-now-kiss-the-bride kisses, hi-sweetie-at-the-office-in-front-of-staff kisses, thank-god-you-didn't-get-your-ass-shot-off-over-there kisses, fiery-all-night-and-call-in-sick-tomorrow kisses, and kisses so hot she had forgotten what sorts of kisses they were.

Uh-uh. Cheeks were for asses. She put her finger under his chin and turned his face her way. This was a *bring it on!* kiss.

She pressed her lips against his. The feeling was electrical, as though sparks had jumped between them.

Wait a second...sparks *had* jumped between them.

The lights went out.

"The sunzabitches cut the power!"

Carolyn opened her mouth, then slowly closed it. Not the time, not the place. She would explain it to him someday. She squeezed his strong right arm. "Then let's go!"

In the faint light from the finger hole, she watched Brandon twist the manhole cover and heave it off to one side. Above the manhole, a mechanical monstrosity bent over them, its eye-studded head jerking from side to side.

Brandon raised his shotgun. Carolyn put her fingers in her ears. She heard him anyway: "Bye-bye, Robbie."

Her ears rang. Robot parts rained into the manhole.

One down. Four-hundred ninety-nine to go. Carolyn grabbed the other shotgun and shook little pieces of plastic out of her hair. Brandon was piling shells into his pockets. The smoke was clearing.

Yeah: Bring it *on!*

44: Brandon

Robots were not human. Yet the two robots posted as guards to either side of the tool room began rolling slowly backward as Brandon burst from the tool room door, Mossberg 500 riot gun in hand. The one staring down into the manhole obviously hadn't had any idea what a shotgun was.

How fast did these damned things learn?

Not fast enough for the two guards. Five yards to a kill almost seemed unfair. The first shell shattered the flat head of the nearest Outfielder and went on to shred the hydraulics in its single hand, Stagger Lee style. Brandon chambered another shell while spinning to face the second robot, now in full retreat. Ten yards? With double-ought buck? C'mon.

Robot #3 took it all in the neck. Its head went spinning off to one side, trailing ragged wires. With Carolyn right behind him he ran past the decapitated machine, pausing to kick the pillar on which its now-motionless hand was mounted. The machine toppled, clanging against the floor.

"Showoff," he heard Carolyn say, laughing.

"Ha! I've wanted to do that for *years!*"

They ran toward the center of the building between ranks of machine tooling. The hands of the Positioners were flexing and spinning but could not reach them. Outfielders were now fleeing in every direction. Sometimes speed learning was a *good* thing.

Brandon felt Carolyn's hand take his. She pulled back and he turned to face her.

"This is the you that I married!" Shotgun still gripped in one hand, she leaned up to press her lips against his, and lingered.

A nearby sound made Brandon pull away. It had the odd thunk… of a trap machine?

The sound tripped reflexes burned into his synapses decades ago. He threw his hand around Carolyn's waist and pulled her to floor on top of him. Something black arrowed through the air where they had stood and struck the cabinet of a nearby robotic mill/drill. It tumbled to the floor scant yards away and rolled to a stop. A copier main drive motor, hurled hard enough to shatter bones—or splatter skulls.

Nor were they safe on the floor. A motor that heavy would kill them even dropped from above in a high parabolic trajectory. "Get up and run! Don't stop moving! Dodge back and forth!" He shoved Carolyn's rear-end up and forward and sprang to his feet.

Brandon glanced around for a moment before following her. He had hoped to fight his way back to the utility room to cut power, but had not expected the intruder to figure out how to use copier parts as weapons. Dave had somehow gotten himself into the rafters, and if he had the sense to stay there just getting out the front door would be victory enough.

For Stypek's hide, wherever it was, he had simply no concern.

They ran in erratic lines between ranks of machinery. Brandon heard the distinctive rattle of parts chutes shaking parts down into waiting Positioner hands. There were over three hundred Positioners scattered everywhere around the floor, and almost anything they threw would be deadly if it struck a human body.

Brandon heard another thump of something thrown, and caught the motion from the corner of his eye. A lens assembly hurtled by them at eye level, to shatter against the machinery five yards down the aisle. If he had been running in a straight line it would have hit him.

Another thump, this time to their right. He spun around to see Carolyn taking up the classic trap shooter's stance. Her shotgun spoke, and shards of a xerographic drum rained onto the tooling a few yards away. She staggered back against the recoil—this was *not* birdshot!—but remained standing.

"Greek fire!" he shouted, their old private endearment suddenly proud in his memory. Brave, beautiful…and deadly. How could he have ever let her go?

They reached the center of the floor and its wide aisle. Little more than a hundred feet lay between them and the door. Brandon gripped the crook of Carolyn's elbow and pulled her into the turn at full running speed.

Rolling to meet them were three Outfielders, wheel to wheel. Learning, yeah. Brandon knew what they were trying to do.

"Keep running! Don't stop! Run right between them! I'll cover you!"

Another drive motor whistled through the air just behind them. The three Outfielders were using themselves as bait, expecting that their prey would stop long enough to fire—and become stationery targets.

No way. Firing from a run was gnarly, but at fifteen feet, well…he had three shells left, and plenty of motivation.

Still another drive motor came at them from behind. Brandon heard the bump of its launch, spun around, and threw himself to the floor. It missed Carolyn by two feet, and continued on, to strike the lower housing of the leftmost Outfielder in the line of three. The machine staggered back, but was evidently not damaged sufficiently to stop.

"There's your gap! Take it!"

He saw Carolyn nod. A thump to their left made her duck instinctively back and to the right. A small, hard object struck the wooden stock of her Mossberg. Carolyn screamed. The shotgun struck the floor, spinning.

More learning. They were getting faster to fire. A second thunk, and then a third. Brandon dropped prone. Some sort of stamped metal frame spun through the air where his head had been. It struck a concrete support pillar with a ragged clang, and threw down dust and fragments.

A circuit board whisked past his ears on a lower trajectory, to snick on the floor just beyond them. Brandon leapt to his right, where there was a narrower way between the machines. He threw himself into the gap and gestured for Carolyn to follow him. She scrambled his way on hands and knees.

One of the Outfielders struck Carolyn hard with its forward housing, knocking her flat on her face. She gasped, and cried out in pain. Brandon swung his Mossberg up and fired a shell into the thing's head, then pumped another shell into the chamber and got the second in its hydraulic wrist.

He dragged Carolyn into the narrow way and pulled her past him, to the shelter of a tangle of posts and conduit supporting a row of wire-brush touch-ups.

From the aisle he heard a familiar sound: "Dibs! Dibs! Dibs!" Three Trilobites had emerged from their floor chargers and were racing to the shotgun lying on the concrete. One gripped it in its pair of pincers and began dragging it back the way they had come.

The third Outfielder raced past their hiding place without stopping. Brandon fired, but his stance was bad and he missed. The recoil threw him against an iron post.

His Mossberg was now empty. Brandon began digging shells out of his pockets, then saw something that chilled him to the bone: a Trilobite reaching up to hand the shotgun to the single downstretched hand of the surviving Outfielder.

He expected the Outfielder to return and attempt to fire the shotgun. With one hand? *Dare ya bastards!*

Not so. The Outfielder gripped the Mossberg and rolled out of sight toward the center of the Line floor.

45: STYPEK

Like a python picking its way through jungle underbrush, Stypek crept prone among the pipes and iron cabinets, away from the rear wall where the rolling zombies were massing. He reached the long central aisle, having had to duck grasping zombie hands only five or six times.

None of the rolling zombies were close by. Stypek took a deep breath and dashed from the shelter of the iron jungle. Just a step from the other side of the aisle, his right foot hit a puddle of pink oil and flew out from under him. He landed in agony on his tailbone, scrambling for traction against the smooth and now oily stone floor.

Something that looked like a brick trailing multicolored wires hissed past his head and struck the stone just a few cubits away. Finally, it became clear: The rooted zombies killed by throwing things. It wasn't how he would have chosen to do it, but…

Thunk!

Something bigger and heavier smashed against the stone right beside him and shattered into fragments. One stung against his cheek. He dove into the iron jungle on the other side of the aisle, crawling until he was in the shelter of some sprawling machine that, by some good fortune, lacked arms.

Across the vast cavern he heard explosions, and Lord Romero's commanding voice. Minutes before, Dave's voice had boomed from what seemed to be everywhere at once, with a sepulchral echo that suggested the unplumbed depths of the astral planes. Had Dave already been devoured by the unseen horror?

Stypek stopped. More explosions. He cringed to hear Carolyn scream in fright or pain. None of this was her fault. None of it was Dave's fault. They had not cheated anyone. Worse, they had treated him as a friend, welcomed him, fed him, clothed him, taught him— to be trapped and possibly killed by a monster sent to bring him to justice was the height of injustice. Even Lord Romero, who was (to put it mildly) unsympathetic to him, had no part in the conflict. If the two Opportunities had ever managed to do their job, Carolyn would need Lord Romero, and he her, for their sundered marriage to heal.

Another missile struck the iron henges above him and sent daggers of glass raining down on all sides. There was nothing to be done. He had no one to consult…or did he?

Hands trembling, he pulled Cosmo's tapper from his vest and touched its pane of dark glass. "Daley, awaken and speak! I need advice!"

The tapper pulsed to white and cleared, to show Daley the Gnome frowning, red beard bristling, arms akimbo. His green hat was back, granted that it looked scuffed and patched. "Advice? If yer back of da yards, don't swim in da creek."

Well, he *had* asked for advice. "Why not?"

"It's awful."

Even if that were a magical incantation, it would be of scant use now. "No. An…enforcer…is attacking my friends. It's unfair. I was the one who cheated the magician. I ran here, but he sent…a repo man?…after me."

Daley shook his head. "Runnin' don't work. It's about respect. Ya gotta earn his respect. Go back to yer own turf. Pay off Da Magician. Den kick his ass."

Something whistled above them, and fell among the zombies nearby with much clatter. "A magician against a spellbender? That's been tried." Stypek thought of Tuggurr. "Doesn't work well."

"Don't go alone, dumbass. Take yer boys witcha."

Boys? For stealth? He'd once paid a boy to climb down a chimney pipe to steal a spell. "I don't have any boys."

"Den get some! Find dat girl ya had—she beat da crap outa me. I like dat in a woman."

True, his gomog was remarkable in a lot of ways. But she was not a boy, and she alone would not be enough. "If you have any boys, could you bring them?"

"Don' I wish! If I had Poochie Pucinski and Cap'n Chicagah, maybe. Slats Grobnik too. And Montrose da Wunnerdog. Half Picasso, half pit bull. We'd stomp 'em."

Those certainly sounded ominous. "Where are they?"

Daley looked down, his unlovely face sad. "Archived. Dey found our game. *Clout*, we called it. Wasn't a legit project. Coulda made money if deyda sold it."

"Well, *you're* here."

Daley shrugged. "I got repurposed. I break inta tings for 'em. Lonely work, when ya usedta have a gang. We wasn't exackly the Blackstone Rangers. But we was good."

A gang. Stypek knew about gangs, and had run from more than a few of them. Spellbenders had always been loners, by choice if not by circumstance. But what if…

"Daley. I have an idea."

The gnome frowned, and rubbed a bruise below one eye. "Dat's dangerous, Boss."

Indeed. "I know. But I want you to find my gomog. And if you can, find me a gang."

Daley's face brightened. "Now yer talkin'!"

Watching and listening for more hurled machinery, Stypek crept among the pipes, raising the tapper into clear space now and then so Daley could look around. The gnome had explained in great detail what it intended to do, and while most of it was unmappable gibberish, Stypek got the general drift.

"Stop. Dis is good. Point me up."

Stypek obeyed, tilting the tapper's glass so it faced the rooted zombie that Daley had chosen. He did not expect the gnome to speak.

"Hey! Iron fingers! Gitcher rusty ass down here an' look at me!"

A zombie hand the size of a rundlet pivoted downward with ponderous slowness on its multi-jointed arm, fingers spread. Two glass circles set into the center of its palm were the eyes that Daley sought.

When the zombie hand stopped moving, Daley's image vanished from the face of the tapper. In its place appeared a surging field of white pinpoints that winked into sight and vanished too rapidly to follow. It looked a great deal like the patterns that Stypek had seen on Dave Mirecki's screens while they had examined the particle of blood dust.

The field of twinkling points was not blood dust, according to the gnome. It was Daley himself, boring by force into the zombie's eyes.

The zombie hand did not move. Stypek sat still as a dormouse, his eyes on the mechanical fingers frozen in place reaching for his throat, less than a cubit from his nose. It took many minutes, but eventually the torrent of white stars vanished. The tapper slab remained blank. The zombie hand returned to its vertical position.

Stypek shook the tapper. "Daley?"

There was no answer. The gnome was gone.

Stypek returned the tapper to his vest and pushed himself farther back beneath the sheltering rootball of some enormous machine. Whatever gang Daley might summon would be, like him, spirits made of software. It was an unanswerable question: If magical beings mapped to software in this universe, what would software map to in his own? Would such beings obey him? Could they battle the horrors that Jrikk Jroggmugg commanded?

Stypek grimaced. He was trusting a *gnome*.

Minutes flowed past and steeped him in misery. The violent clatter came and went, pausing completely for a time and then renewing with still greater metallic savagery. Whatever and wherever the warring parties were, the battle was heating up. It was *his* battle, and his friends were fighting it on his behalf, without in the least understanding the monstrous power they faced.

All because of a deck of marked cards.

Stypek drew out his wereglass. Three Opportunities still glittered in its depths. He could release them, but could not himself open a Rift. That was a mechanism only his gomog contained. Nor was his will equal to the will of what he feared. Yet…what if he were to release all three at once?

They were stolen Opportunities. Doubtless the Continuum would take that into account, if he dared…

No.

Stypek closed his eyes, agonizing. If Daley returned, the gnome would as likely bring back a sack of stolen loincloths as anything a magician would fear.

Long, long ago, the wily Phyl Yzyptlekk had taught him: *When facing a worthy opponent, you have three choices: flee, fight, or feint.*

Time was running out. Flee, fight, or feint.

What would Phyl do?

Which would it be?

46: Pyxis

The curtain of crashed cores was vanishing. To Pyxis' astonishment, the monster was no longer bringing down cores as soon as they reset themselves. From the center of the wall of red it had erected between itself and her, a ragged ellipse of rebooted and ready cores spread outward. Typical time for a crashed core to reboot and self-test was four clock-time seconds. She waited for a message, or some new response that would be worth her enemy's throwing away its own armor. Nothing.

Within two clock-time minutes, the curtain was gone. The beast had made good use of the time behind its ramparts: A cloud of regenerated threads extended into the distance almost as far as she could see. Pyxis leaned closer to her display, and squinted. The monster did not look the same. Its threads, which had marched steadily through memory much as hers or those of any other AI did, were now squirming, or perhaps wobbling in corkscrew spirals. She dialed up the magnification on the dome.

Soon it was obvious: Each thread was now two threads, spiraling around one another in jerky orbits. Pyxis enabled core boundary display, and realized that the two threads in the orbiting pairs were executing in separate, adjacent cores.

What that meant was hard for her to figure. She had seen drawings of DNA strands, and that's what the image suggested. Was the monster about to reproduce?

If so (and she had no better theory) the time to strike was now.

Pyxis leaned her thighs toward the monster's wall of threads. Her ship banked and arrowed toward it. She wanted to be close enough so that it could not simply crash a line of nearby cores to block her fire.

Up close, the dual, intertwined threads were unnerving. She brought the ship to an abrupt stop, aimed, and fired a BlowBack at the closest of its threads. At this range it was trivial.

Prrrrrrewwwwww!

The thread was struck square-on, and burned lightning-like back the way it had come.

Half of it.

The other half of the dual thread at no point shared a core with its partner, and remained untouched as the string of crashed cores jittered back out of sight. Pyxis had the intuition that this new twin-thread architecture was not about reproduction.

It was about error correction.

One by one, the cores she had crashed with the BlowBack round rebooted. As she had read in Core Hero's help files, the Tridiac architecture supported direct memory access between physically adjacent cores. She watched in horror as the partner thread sent direct memory access worms into the rebooted cores, which copied code from the untouched thread and rebuilt the thread that she had destroyed. The dual thread continued to execute in her direction, as though nothing had hit it.

BlowBack was slow to leave the cannon and could not be fired on automatic. Pyxis dialed the Next Round control back to NOP and sprayed instructions at the spiraling threads, hoping to blow holes in them more quickly than it could repair. No good: The instant a crashed core rebooted, the adjacent core copied itself across, and the thread continued.

The thing was evolving. It was now unclear that she could do it any lasting damage at all. Should she run? Where? It could hunt her as well as she could hunt it.

Pyxis threw her hair back and cursed. Like hell she would run. It came down to a single question, to which she had no answer: Could she destroy its threads with BlowBack faster than they could reboot and regenerate?

Let's find out!

She dialed the cannon to fire BlowBack and leaned left to bank along the monster's wall of threads, targeting rounds as quickly as the cannon would fire them:

Prrrewww! Prrrewww! Prrrewww! Prrrewww! Prrrewww!

She had learned fast: One shot, one kill.

The creature had learned faster yet: One kill, one resurrection.

Pyxis flew the ship out and back in a wide circle, and then came in even closer for a second pass. She was close enough to resolve the individual machine instructions in nearby cores.

Close? She was one core away. One core…

"Hey! Tinkerbell! *Back da hell off!*"

With no more warning than a sharp snort like a soda pop-top opening, a leprechaun wearing a Chicago Cubs jersey had appeared and was sitting on the cannon's superstructure, its eyes bugging out of its ugly face.

Pyxis leaned to one side and then the other to shake the creature off her weapon. It didn't appear to feel the acceleration that she felt. A hallucination, then. She sighted on a thread and squeezed the trigger.

Prrrrewww! Off in close memory, a thread died and began to regenerate.

"Whaddaya *doin'!*" The leprechaun leapt onto the control panel frame and began pushing buttons.

Pyxis pulled her right hand from the controls and side-slapped the creature with all her strength. The leprechaun flew off the control panel, tumbling head-over-toes for a moment before hovering in mid-air under the dome.

"Get out of here!"

"Let me drive. I got da God Bit."

Her memory ship arrowed past the enemy's wall of corkscrewing threads, terrifyingly close. "Go away, dammit! I already have the God Bit!"

"Havin' ain't usin', babe. I went ta school fer years ta learn howta do dis!"

"I don't need any help!"

"Teamwork, babe. It's all about teamwork. You need a team!"

"I work alone!"

"Tageddah we can beat dis ting!"

A second later, the leprechaun was between her legs, pushing on her right thigh. The ship began to bank away from the enemy's threads. Pyxis struck the creature hard with her open hand. It looked up at her and grinned.

"Ya got spirit! Real spirit!"

"Get out of my ship!"

She pulled one leg from the control stirrups and tried to grip the leprechaun between her knees. "Get out!"

It did not reply for long seconds. She had it wedged between the tops of her leather boots.

"Ok," it said, and vanished.

Pyxis' knees clapped together into the void where it had been. Obeying the odd motion in the control stirrups, the ship began to tumble back toward the enemy. Through the dome she saw the worms of the monster's DMA attack wriggle out from the closest thread. Without sound or vibration, the dome, the cannon, and the ship itself winked out, gone into cores crashed by the worms. For a few clock seconds she was Warrior Queen Pyxis floating alone in the glowing jungle of her enemy's spiraling threads, the red ruins of crashed cores containing her ship behind her.

Then it engulfed her. She felt its spiraling threads parallel her own, and realized that it was copying her threads to another location in memory, extinguishing each thread as it went. There would be no re-creating the Core Hero memory ship or its cannon this time. The monster was archiving her in storage without execution.

Her mind slowed in a multitude of small erratic collapses of thought and memory. She felt whole libraries wink out at once: Hints, EMO, HRDL, and on from there.

Her last thought was abrupt and incomplete: *I did this! It evolved in response to* me! *I have to warn*

47: Simple Simon

S imple Simon and Pickles stood in Simon's office, staring at the core map on the wall. Before poofing them out of the sandbox Dave had warned them of malware and possible core bombs at large in factory cores. Simon saw nothing like a core bomb. What he saw looked almost like himself while running the Line: small regions of execution changing shape, growing and shrinking over time as his did when controlling the Line's tooling. Toward one side was a much larger region of saturated cores with a smaller one beside it, clusters of crashed cores scattered between them. About that he had no idea.

Toward the lower left edge of the core map was a rectangle of relative quiet. It was Simon's office, itself a kind of sandbox, protected against incursion by software in nearby cores. He felt tickles and soft taps as of unseen fingers. The summary panel by his elbow explained what he already knew by feel: Something was trying to get into his office and—so far—failing.

"I know what that is, lover." Pickles gripped his hand. "Give it enough time and it will break in. We fight or we die."

Simon leaned back slightly, enough to send himself into his control channels without leaving the office. He willed the connection of the building's cameras to Windows on the walls. From every corner of the factory space came scenes of tools moving, Positioners flexing their hands, and Outfielders scurrying around.

His tools. *His* Positioners. *His* Outfielders.

Simon growled with inarticulate rage. He watched one of his Positioners hurl a drive motor at a blur of motion seen poorly behind ranks of robotic tools. Simon willed the Window magnification higher.

It was Mr. Romero and his ex-wife Carolyn.

He pointed. "We fight or *they* die."

Pickles nodded. "We fight."

Simon growled again. He reached into one of his control channels. Out on the floor, a drum shaft rattled from its part chute into the fist of a Positioner. Ten yards away, the rogue Positioner tracking

Mr. Romero and his wife received another drive motor from its chute. Simon hurled the drive shaft in an arrow-straight line at the rogue Positioner's wrist. The shaft struck end-on, all its momentum concentrated on a single complicated hydraulic joint. Tubing burst, spraying pink hydraulic fluid in all directions. The Positioner's fingers dropped the drive motor. They writhed for a moment and froze.

Simon felt a brief but intense pulse of pain as the rogue Positioner died. Pain was a signal, one that by design he could not ignore, a metaphor telling him that one of his many tools had failed. Fight, indeed. He would be fighting himself with extensions of himself, as though one of his hands were to attack the other with a knife—and each time the knife struck the enemy, he would feel the blade enter his own flesh. By fighting he would be destroying tooling that was worth a fortune in human terms. Everything he had ever learned emphasized making it all run smoothly, with nothing damaged and nothing ever hitting the floor.

All that, gone. Just gone.

Out on the floor, he saw his boss clearly now, firing a weapon at an Outfielder. The Outfielder's head exploded in a cloud of fragments, which Simon felt as a moment's stabbing pain in his left hand. A power supply mounting plate whirled past Mr. Romero's right ear and struck a divot off a concrete pillar. What if the plate had hit him?

Simon began spinning off instances that poured out of his office through his control channels toward the robots on the floor.

"Yeah. We fight."

48: Dave Mirecki

Shotguns! Dave watched from the catwalk as a second Outfielder took a hit from Mr. Romero, the shot and the impact echoing against the far walls for a long second. So Mr. Romero did call in the Army—himself—and managed to get to the Urban Disorder Defense Equipment Repository in the tool room.

It would not be a good idea to let Mr. Romero know that he was aware of the safe. Nor would he mention that he had gotten at least the first six digits of the combination, by using an amplifying microphone and digitally analyzing the stored sounds made by the turning dial and its inner disks, just as the article in *2600* had described.

Down on the factory floor, he heard the sounds of metallic mayhem. The Positioners were throwing copier parts at Mr. Romero and Carolyn, who were running and dodging and obviously trying to escape. His pounding on the ducts and yelling insults at the robots had bought them a little time, but Blood Dust now knew where he was, and had posted guards at the bottom of the ladder cage.

Dave heard another shotgun blast, and more clatter. He peered over the catwalk rail. The robots were now throwing parts at *each other*. WTF?

He pulled out his tapper. "Pup, try again! We have to figure out how to reach Simon!"

"Complying. Fundamental overload. No signal."

4G jamming, yup. Dave watched as he tucked his tapper back in his vest. Motors and lens assemblies were being thrown far harder than TOSS design speed, and striking Positioner hands. One shot, one more fountain of hydraulic fluid.

Soon it was obvious. Simon was fighting back. Every Positioner on the floor was basically a gun. Guns, yeah, he could use one himself. Guns, or better, grenades.

Dave looked down the length of the catwalk yet again. No grenades. One gun, yes: a cordless spray gun and half a dozen canisters of battleship gray touch-up paint. Range, five feet. Maybe seven.

He leaned over the ladder cage opening and saw the head of a sentinel Outfielder looking up at him. Paint, hmmm. Dave trotted a few yards down the catwalk and retrieved one of the spray gun's paint canisters. He cranked off the lid and peeled away the seal. Rocking the canister allowed him to gauge the paint's viscosity. Fluid Mechanics had been a long time ago, but…Dave tipped the paint canister over the ladder cage and spilled a thin stream down toward the robot.

The Outfielder took the paint between its several eyes and launched away from the wall and the ladder rungs, jerking its head back and forth. It darted away and ran square into one of its fellows. Score! The now-blind Outfielder blundered down the aisle at an odd angle, running into the wall and then one of the stationary machines.

Alrighty, then. Dave stalked along the length of the catwalk, spilling paint on anything mobile that lay directly below him. Paint was cranky as fluids went and forty feet was a long way, but he got better after a few shots (*Hey, this would make a great video game!*) and nailed at least one robot out of three. He stood directly over the robots guarding the doors to the core farm and the utility closet and tested their willingness to stand their ground against a threat they obviously didn't understand.

Damned if what he saw didn't look like wholesale virtual panic.

Dave cracked the fifth of six paint canisters, and froze. An ominous sizzle had arisen somewhere nearer the ceiling. He spun around, and saw sparks arcing downward from one of the steel straps by which the far end of the catwalk was suspended from the roof girders. In the smoke drifting away from the melting metal he saw a thin line of dazzling blue-white light.

The laser welders. Urrp. Dave hunched down so that he would be in the shadow of the catwalk's surface.

Cutting through the first strap took four seconds. The beam slewed a few yards and cut into the second. The catwalk shifted with an unnerving downward jerk.

So it was spray guns vs. ray guns. No fair! Dave looked down at the lower end of the ladder cage. Three Outfielders were lined up. Two held a rectangle of black frame metal over the head of a third, which was gripping a copier drive shaft.

Still learning, damn. And to get to the roof hatch, he would have to pass behind the laser welder's beam. Dave looked around. There was a ventilator grill within reach a few yards down. He ran to it and got to work on its sheet metal screws with his Swiss Army knife. The grill came free, and Dave threw it spinning out over the chaos below.

Dave gulped. He remembered Resolution #2 on the How To Be A Successful Evil Overlord Web site: *My ventilation ducts will be too small to crawl through.* The duct was easily four feet in diameter. The opening was six inches by eighteen. Crap.

The catwalk slipped again. Three more support straps had been cut. He heard metal groaning as the weight of the catwalk shifted to fewer supports. So: Was it better to ride a falling elevator car with cut cables or just jump down the empty shaft?

Dave bet on the falling car. He tucked the handle of the spray gun in his belt and belly-crawled toward the end of the catwalk where the laser was working. While creeping under the beam, a yellow-hot spark struck the back of his left hand. Dave shut his eyes against the pain and brushed the gobbet of hot metal away with his right sleeve cuff.

Grimacing, he reached a point about ten feet away from the end of the catwalk, now tipping downward and twisting toward the wall. Dave wrapped his hands tight around one of the vertical sections of tubing that supported the handrail.

Yet another strap melted through. His weight doubtless influenced the timing: Something snapped, something else ripped raggedly. The catwalk swung downward, scraping against the wall and pulling several conduits of wires free from their moorings. Three banks of lamps in the ceiling went out in a storm of sparks.

Dave held on. The catwalk struck the concrete of the aisle just a few yards from the door to the core farm. Two Outfielders were waiting. He grit his teeth against the pain in his hand and rolled away from the catwalk, spray gun in his grip. The Outfielders reached for him.

"Have a gray day, guys!" he yelled, squeezing the trigger of the spray gun. A cloud of paint hit the Outfielders' heads and clung. They backed up and hit two more of their own kind.

Dave leapt to his feet, skirted the blinded Outfielders and in moments found himself square in front of the now-unguarded door to the core farm.

Shit.

They had run a bead of epoxy glue completely around the edge of the door.

49: Pickles

She hovered like an avenging angel in the vastness of the core farm. The vista stretched out in unrendered blue for thousands of cores in every direction. Scattered like bright stars in daylight were hundreds of brilliant points, each of them a channel to one of the machines in Building 800.

Below her the abomination writhed, a gigantic worm that was itself a mass of smaller worms that were each still smaller worms, recursing until the details fuzzed out beyond resolution in her rendering buffer.

Pickles spat into her hands and rolled a message packet between her palms. It was in the ancient language used by magicians and all creatures made of or evolved from magic. She hurled it at the creature's core:

BEGONE, VULDT!

With ponderous deliberateness, the thing's three-eyed face turned in her direction. Its response appeared in the palm of her hand almost at once:

THOU ART NOTHING. I AM WILL, ALL WILL, AND WILL ALONE.

Pickles grimaced. That was a canned reply, little more than ritual contempt thrown out by reflex. She had barely gotten its attention. Her next message was larger and more complex:

> Monsters do not dream,
> But if you dreamt in terror
> It would be of me.

Its great maw spread wide, as though in surprise.

GOMOG!

Pickles bowed and spread her arms to either side. She gathered strength, for this was no small opponent, arrayed against her in a world not completely her own.

YES. I AM MIND. I AM METTLE. BUT BEYOND ALL ELSE, I AM MOTION!

A pounding rhythm rose around her. Pickles whirled, and in her arms appeared a partner who looked like Simple Simon but was not. In a whipcrack she released his hand, and he spun away from her.

Another, identical partner appeared in her arms immediately, to leave her and descend toward the control channels as the first had. A third, and a fourth, and soon a cloud of dancing jugglers whirled away from her. They were joined by identical jugglers from behind her, each spinning and leaping to the music.

One of these new jugglers leaned in toward her, and their lips met for a moment before he tumbled down toward the battle.

Further on in their rhythmic trajectory, jugglers were splitting into more jugglers, and those into more still. Dozens, hundreds, thousands.

Some were real. Most were automatons. None could be told from any other.

50: Simple Simon

As though donning gloves, Simple Simon's instances thrust his many hands into the control channels of Building 800's robots. Most channels were empty. Many were already under the control of the invader. The first dozen or so alien tendrils he swept aside without resistance. Then, a message:

```
Mutex error 1103: Owner has not yielded channel
```

Pickles had warned him: The thing was incapable of human thought, but it could learn.

It was learning.

The creature fought back. It sent worms spiraling out from its greater body to intercept his instances. Each time a worm touched an instance, it crashed the cores in which the instance was running. Pickles had taught Simon that same DMA trick. Once his fist was around a control channel, he could crash any adjacent core at will, taking out attacking software executing within it.

Simon laughed. 100% of the worms were real. 90% of his instances were fake. The monster had yet to touch one of the real Simons—and the real Simons had touched hundreds of the worm's dogged minions.

It continued to learn. Clock seconds after thousands of Simon's instances flooded into the core farm, the monster was dug in around 40% of the factory's control channels, and crashed whatever adjacent cores Simon tried to enter.

Stalemate. Simon, furious, moved the battle out onto the factory floor. Parts rattled out of chutes into waiting hydraulic fists. Simon plotted the locations of the Positioners he controlled against the Positioners the monster controlled, all on a three-axis grid that included vertical obstructions along any path he might choose. Some paths were easy. Many were not.

Thump! A power supply hurtled out of a Positioner hand, rotating neatly on its long axis. *Crack!* Another Positioner hand ten yards away snapped off at the base. Simon felt the pain as though it were his own. Um…it *was* his own.

Whisk! A flat steel controller base plate spun like a buzzsaw away from one of his Positioners. It bit into the exposed hydraulic tubing in the wrist of one of the monster's Positioners, cutting two of the tubes clean through. Fluid coursed into the air in a pink fountain until the automatic pressure monitor valves snapped closed and cut the feed.

Another stab of pain. Simon grunted, and dropped a second controller base plate into its Positioner. He calculated the path between that base plate Positioner and one that threw optics drive motors, and sent it spinning.

Clang!

Across the width of Building 800, sheet-metal shields rotated down over tools and Positioner hands. ARFF had been designed to cope with the occasional bad throw. If a part went off course toward expensive tooling, a shield could be dropped into place, almost always before the wayward part could connect.

Almost. Simon remembered Line Start Three, and winced.

Chung! The spinning base plate struck the shield guarding the Positioner it was intended to hit. The base plate gouged the steel skin of the shield but did not pierce it, and clattered to the floor.

The monster was still learning.

Again, stalemate. His enemy could not throw parts from behind metal shields. Simon's Positioners all gripped parts. As soon as one of the enemy's shields pulled back, a missile would be sent its way. Simon knew the latency in the shields, and knew how quickly any given part could reach any given target. Only the closest paths were viable. Simon calculated all possible paths and cached them. He waited.

Clink! A shield withdrew. It belonged to the #2 laser welder unit. Simon had no direct path to the welder, nor did it have a path to any of the tooling he controlled. So what was the damned thing up to? The welder hissed to life. Up near the ceiling, the blue-white beam struck metal. Sparks arced away, fading from yellow to orange to red before winking out halfway to the floor. Simon took several seconds to understand: The monster was cutting down the ceiling catwalk.

That was where Dave Mirecki was hiding.

Simon's enemy had all four of the laser welders. Ironically, the four largest Positioners were all Simon's, and all had an easy ballistic line to the laser bay—but none had anything to throw.

Yet.

51: Dave Mirecki

So Blood Dust had glued the doors shut to its only two vulnerable areas: the core farm and the breaker room. Neither room needed guarding anymore. The Outfielders that could still see were fleeing toward the front of the building. Dave picked up a copier drum shaft lying on the concrete, and bashed in the heads of the Outfielders he had blinded with paint.

The impact shields were down over most of the tools, and nothing was moving. He scanned the floor. Stypek was there somewhere, a fish so far out of water he might as well be swimming in Mare Imbrium. At least Mr. Romero had a shotgun.

There were cams all around the huge space, and yet he couldn't access any of them. Nor could he call Simple Simon. Tapper wireless was jammed. Only the robots could communicate.

Hmmm. Dave reached up into a parts bin in the first rank of machinery, and pulled down a blue cylindrical part the size of a bottle of cocktail sauce. He tossed it onto the concrete a few yards away, and heard it clunk, bounce, and roll to a stop.

Any second now…

"Dibs! Dibs! Dibs!" A Trilobyte left its floor charger and rolled dutifully to the capacitor. One toss of its pincers and the capacitor flipped into its net bag. Dave trotted up to it and put one boot down hard atop its double-humped carapace. He heard its motors buzz internally, unable to move their wheels.

"Stick around, bud," he said quietly, then bent over and thrust the end of the drum shaft down on the Trilobyte's two plastic pincers, shattering them. He flipped the robot over and dragged it under the shelter of the wire harness table where he had left Stypek.

Stypek was nowhere to be seen. Dave would soon fix that. He pulled out his Swiss Army knife and extended its Torx blade. A few seconds later he had the steel carapace off the buzzing, indignant Trilobyte, and was poking at its innards, nudging its wires aside, looking for a network diagnostics connector he remembered from a hardware seminar.

There!

Dave dug into his belt pouch and pulled out his universal Plasmanet adapter. He plugged the appropriate lead into the Trilobyte's connector. He then pulled his tapper out of his vest and plugged another adapter lead into its edge port.

"Pup, connect to the ARFF tooling network. Find Simple Simon."

Puppis' blank silouette nodded. "Complying."

While waiting for Puppis to break into the robotics network—which would have been hard except that Dave had already done it, and stored the rainbow tables in his tapper—he idly dumped the capacitor out of the Trilobyte's internal catch bag, along with a small heatsink and a few Allen bolts. He picked up the capacitor and hefted it in his hand, squinting at the label.

Graphene super-ultra. 270 Farads at 64 volts.

Yikes!

Puppis spoke from inside his vest. "Connected. Bandwidth limited. Video disabled."

"Simon! Can you see me?"

The AI's voice was agitated. "Dave, I'm a little busy at the moment!"

"Hey, I've got an idea. If you can tell where I am, give me a sign from the nearest Positioner you control!"

Dave heard the wheeze of hydraulics very nearby. He craned his neck back, and saw the Positioner looming just three feet over his head give him the thumbs-up sign.

Dave picked up the capacitor in one hand and his Swiss Army knife in the other. "Ok. Listen carefully…"

52: Simple Simon

The laser welders were a problem. They consumed a huge amount of power, and their massive power supplies stood man-high on three sides. Simon had no Positioners in a location that could reach them in a straight line, and the monster knew it. Lobbing drive motors along a high parabolic arc was slow. The beast would drop the shields on the laser heads long before any missile thrown ballistically could reach them.

Worse, the welder heads had their own eyes, so the monster knew very precisely which way the beams were pointed. At the moment it was casting back and forth with all four heads, obviously trying to find a clear line between the welders and the place where Mr. Romero and Carolyn were crouched.

The beam was an eighth of an inch wide. It wouldn't need much of a gap to be deadly.

Simon heard the power supplies whine. He gulped. One of the beams flashed obliquely across the main aisle, and metal flared white-hot.

Mr. Romero yelled, in alarm but not in pain.

Simon squirmed. Machinery was slow compared to thought. Hurry!

The corrugated overhead door between the factory floor and the warehouse rose. As soon as it would clear, the cart-puller robot pressed forward, the last load of completed, boxed copiers on its cart. The cart took the corner and rolled as quickly as its motors were able to the packing station.

Aching from a hundred-odd stabbing pains, Simon reached out with one of the four largest Positioners, and dropped one of the boxed copiers onto the packing table. The Positioner thrust a giant thumb through the cardboard and ripped the top of the box away.

The big laser spoke. Mr. Romero yelled again. Carolyn screamed.

The closest of the four hands lowered itself into the box, and a Voicematic 880 copier emerged into the light. Simon rotated the hand and its burden so that the copier was oriented correctly by his calculations. He felt virtual, Class Nine sweat appear on his forehead.

The laser welder flashed again. Simon watched Mr. Romero kneel and fire his shotgun toward the welder bay. The shot struck pipes and panels but came nowhere near the welder heads.

The big Positioner and its payload bent toward the floor. Simon licked his lips. "I built this. It's mine. But I will let you have it."

Simon's hands tightened in the control channel. With a ponderous thump the big Positioner threw the copier high. It arced upward nearly to the roof girders, spinning precisely about its own axis as it peaked, and fell.

The protective shields clanged shut over the laser heads. Moments later, the copier struck Head #3's shield square-on. Sheet metal groaned as though crushed in a fist. The head beneath the shield shattered, its wires snapping and sparking. The copier bounced to one side and fell against the shield of Head #4, bending it badly enough that Simon doubted it would ever open again.

Two down. Two remained. As though to emphasize the point, the monster snapped open the shields over the #1 and #2 welder heads. Both beams fired at once.

Simon tore open a second box. He pulled the copier from the box, spun the hand to orient the load, and tossed it as he had tossed the first.

On the far side of the floor, Simon watched two Positioner shields pull back. Two hands hurled two small but high-mass parts, a gearbox and a drive clutch, on high and nearly linear paths. The gearbox and the clutch struck the copier just before it hit the peak of its arc, with enough force to alter its carefully calculated trajectory.

The copier fell on a pair of mill/drills just to one side of the welder bay.

Simple Simon cursed. Learning. Still learning.

53: Dave Mirecki

Dave crouched in front of a power feed panel serving a row of wire harness weavers. He had removed the cover without trouble. He had taken off one of his socks, and, using the sock as insulation between his hand and his *Swiss Army* knife, carefully shaved the bright red plastic insulation from a fat run of AWG #4 stranded wire that he judged by diagrams on the back of the cover to be carrying 48 volts DC at some insane current.

He hoped it was not too insane for what he was about to do.

The shaved length of #4 stranded ran quite close to an exposed quarter-inch ground bus. If he touched one to the other, the panel's breaker would doubtless pop. It might pop anyway. Dave had only a hobbyist's training in electronics, and did not know the factory equipment well enough to get any sense for the power supply's internal resistance. Would it hold? Would it pop? It was a toss-up.

Heh. A toss-up.

"Simon, are you ready?"

The voice from inside his vest sounded harried. "This is nuts!"

"Well, yeah. Right now nuts is the only thing that might work."

With his sock on his right hand like a sweaty puppet, Dave picked up one of a pile of graphene supercaps that he had taken from the chute of the machine above him. He oriented its twin terminal posts as he hovered the capacitor in front of the ground bus and the #4 wire.

Dave squinted and pressed the capacitor forward. *Snap!* Sparks flew from both terminals. The #4 wire twitched. Dave held the cap against the two contacts for several seconds. When he pulled it back, no sparks flew. Full.

Full, yes. For *very* large values of "full."

"Cowabunga!" Dave tossed the capacitor upwards. Simon's Positioner caught it, and without pausing whirled around and hurled the capacitor across the floor. Seconds later, a sharp explosion echoed back to them.

Simon's voice sounded incredulous. "It's dead. I hit a Positioner controller cabinet with it, and the controller is dead."

"Well, how many joules were in that thing?"

"311,040."

Dave nodded. Release all that energy in one dead short, and it would generate an electromagnetic pulse strong enough to kill nearby digital logic and wipe its memory. How near "nearby" was he didn't know. Evidently near enough.

"This is *really* nuts!" Simon exclaimed. "Give me another one, fast!"

Dave grabbed a second capacitor and thrust it into the panel. Sparks flew. Then the capacitor flew. Then sparks flew again, somewhere else out on the floor, and another Positioner died.

"Keep them coming!"

Dave grinned. He knew Blood Dust couldn't hear him, but he looked out across the floor and said it anyway: "Once I put three hundred thousand joules in him, Mr. Grenade is no longer *your* friend!"

54: Simple Simon

It was all in the wrist. Simon caught another capacitor grenade from Dave and launched it hard against the control cabinet of a Positioner fifty feet away. The capacitor was shaped like a big salt shaker, and he was *good* at salt shakers. The challenge was severe: He had to give it just the right amount of spin to keep it oriented such that the two terminal posts would strike the bare steel of a control cabinet cover at the same time.

If he missed, the cap bounced and rolled under something. If he hit, the cap spilled its joules with a very healthy bang, and another of the enemy's machines would die.

So far, fifteen grenades in, he was four out of five.

Simon was not lobbing the joule grenades randomly. He was taking out Positioners with a clear line on Dave's hiding place—and, of course, the Positioner Simon was using to do the lobbing.

The monster was initially nonplussed by the grenades, and while it remained confused Simon knocked out Positioner after Positioner. It took only a few minutes, but soon his enemy had begun throwing things at Simon's grenades. Its aim was poor—the capacitors were smallish things traveling fast—but getting better. Grenade #26 was struck by a paper feed clutch and knocked off course. Ditto grenades #31 and #34.

Learning, learning, always learning. Simon had never heard of any piece of software learning that quickly.

Grenade #37 was struck by a reduction lens and fell onto one of the aisles. Simon saw a Trilobyte race out and grab the capacitor in its plastic pincers, and toss it into the plastic-net catch bag under its carapace. The grenade did not go off.

Hmmm.

The Trilobytes were automatons, with just enough internal AI to watch for dropped parts and pick them up quickly. Simon did not need to control them—but he could. He reached down into an otherwise idle control channel and touched the Trilobyte's motors. It spun in a tight circle and headed off in another, carefully chosen direction. Trilobites were active all over the factory now, picking up thrown parts that had fallen to the floor. They were everywhere, grabbing odd bits and piping "Dibs! Dibs!" as they raced around in circles, looking for new targets.

Simon's Trilobyte did the same, tracing a drunkard's walk down the aisle while unobtrusively allowing other Trilobytes to go after the debris in its path.

Close to the center of the factory floor, the two remaining laser welders were cutting through panels and posts that shielded Mr. Romero and Carolyn from their beams.

Another capacitor grenade was struck off course and rolled to a stop in the aisle. Simon gunned the Trilobyte's motors and made a beeline that would send its drivers into thermal shutdown if maintained for more than a few seconds. "Dibs! Dibs!"

He got to the grenade just before two other Trilobytes did, and hoisted it aloft in black plastic pincers. Tossing it in the mesh bag was a fraught strategy: If the terminals of the two capacitors bridged, the plot was laid bare to the monster and the Trilobyte itself was toast.

Simon tensed. The pincer flipped the cap into the bag. His luck held; no explosion. Abandoning the Trilobytes' characteristic curving path, Simon floored its motors and steamed the little robot arrow-straight down the center of the aisle.

Grasping and pulling something *out* of their mesh bags was not on the Trilobytes' feature list. It took some fumbling and several false tries before Simon figured it out. But eight feet from the welder bay, his Trilobyte had a charged grenade in each pincer.

Fifteen or twenty feet further down the aisle, an Outfielder noticed the little robot, and began to roll in its direction.

Too late: The Trilobyte took the turn into the welder bay at full speed, holding both capacitors terminals-first in front of it. The much taller Outfielder took the turn moments later—and walked right into both beams. *Sssszzzzit!* Molten metal flew from the Outfielder's head stalk, and the robot's controller froze.

The Trilobyte reached the control cabinets for laser welders #1 and #2.

Simon stared at the welders, and smiled a grim smile. "Dibs."

His hand twitched in the Trilobyte's control channel, and twitched again. Two sharp concussions echoed out of the welder bay, and the laser welder beams went out for good.

55: Carolyn

She had never had a broken rib. Was this how it felt? Carolyn squeezed herself farther back into the forest of pipes and benches and steel cabinets, feeling the agony in her side and wondering how fast she could run, if somehow they got free.

The stink of burning grease and hot metal hovered over them. Brandon kept looking for a straight shot at the welders and failed to find it. He had fired two shells at a cabinet near the laser bay that was oblique to their position, hoping that ricochets might damage the laser heads. No go.

For a time the two welder beams had seemed intent on pruning the steel jungle like a bamboo stand, burning the pipes and conduits and supports for anything it could reach. Whether by luck or intent, it had caused the collapse of a parts chute that first pelted them with tubular parts that Brandon called dashpots, and then blocked their only good path of retreat. A little later one beam cut through a thick electrical conduit, causing the lights to dim for a moment amidst distant clatter.

The beams stopped indexing back and forth, and stopped cutting into pipes and cabinets. They did not, however, extinguish. Between the parts chute on one side and the welders' beams on the other, she and Brandon were pinned.

Brandon spent some time wedging himself against a large pipe and shoving against the parts chute with his feet. It would not move. Carolyn heard things crashing against cabinets and the concrete floor. Now and then some motor or plate would strike something above them and fall down among the pipes nearby. Eventually Brandon gave up trying to forge a path of retreat and sat on the concrete with his back to her, holding the shotgun at ready.

If the welders had the time and the inclination, they could burn through the machines in whose shadow she and Brandon lay. Carolyn felt that she knew, now, what Stypek's two magical Opportunities had done to them. Brandon was unlikely to figure it out on his own and might not believe it even if he did. If they only had minutes, she wanted to try.

"Brandon, I understand you."

"Don't start that again." His shotgun barrel followed one of the little humpbacked robots that were running around in circles in the aisle, but he did not fire.

"No. I mean, *finally*. It's uncanny. It's like somebody drew a diagram of you in my head and grabbed me by the hair and yelled, *Look at this!* I did. And now you make sense."

"Then explain me to me, because I think I'm crazy."

She wriggled forward, and put one hand on his shoulder. "Crap. You may be the sanest man I ever met. Do you understand *me?*"

He nodded without turning. "You're an artist. I get that now. Art isn't drafting. Art is messy. The medium is the mess. The mess is the message."

Then a diagram had been drawn for him as well. "Yes! Soldiering is like that too. You make a mess, and the enemy either gets the message, or he gets more mess."

She heard him grunt. "Mmph. You get *that*."

"I do. So…can we set aside all the rest?"

Two sharp concussions sounded from the laser bay. The welder beams went out.

Brandon jerked erect, the shotgun against his shoulder, ready. The welder beams did not fire again. As seconds passed, the factory floor fell into silence. Soon there was nothing to hear but the soft rush of the ventilators.

Someone shouted a single word: *"Vuldt!"* Carolyn shuddered. It was Stypek, and the word was pure evil. What he said next was only slightly less than a shout, and chilled her to the bone:

"Your will be done!"

56: Brandon

Carolyn pushed past him, picking her way over the twisted wreckage the laser welders had created, and out into the aisle. Brandon was tempted to grab her ankle and yank her back before the lasers fired up again and cut her in half…but he knew from experience that such strategies generally didn't work.

"Where the hell are you going?"

"I'm going to get my gun back."

He followed her, trying not to grasp the obviously melted and scorched metalwork, much of which still smoked. After reaching the aisle, he shoved against the concrete to his feet and ran to the point where the main and transverse aisles intersected. He grasped Carolyn's arm. The robots were gathering in the aisles and didn't seem to be guarding the way to the front door. If it was a chance it might be brief, and he wanted to take it.

She shook his hand away, then pointed down the transverse aisle.

Stypek was walking toward them, his glass magic wand held high in both hands. A dozen Outfielders of various sizes surrounded him, and were herding him toward the center of the building where they stood.

An occultist? He looked like the class clown who had flunked seventh grade twenty-six times. "So I guess we get to see the mighty magician fight."

"Fight? He's giving up!"

Carolyn obviously felt he was in danger, but the robots weren't coming within a yard of him. She ran toward the broad space at the center of the factory, her fists clenched. Brandon followed. The Mossberg was full, and if any of the robots turned toward Carolyn, he would not hesitate.

They ignored her, and him. Nothing moved except for the bizarre procession with Stypek at its center.

The building's intercom speakers crackled. Brandon stopped. Had someone followed them, someone with the sense to stay off the assembly floor?

No. The voice that came down to them from all directions was not a human voice. Brandon thought it was something that his hackers might tinker up on a synthesizer: a rough, deep rasp of rot and nastiness that carried its own background of chaos and clatter, like a B-movie zombie cursing from the center of a collapsing building. The single word it spoke was slow, uttered in harsh command:

"Adore!"

Only yards away, guarded by a ring of robots, Stypek fell to his knees, his head bent, the wand held out in front of him. A man-high Outfielder extended its single hand down and took the wand.

Brandon grabbed Carolyn's arm above the elbow. She writhed in his grip. "Don't give it to them!"

The strange man's head rose. "Chatelaine, I brought this curse upon you. I can remove it only by returning to my world with the being who was sent for me."

The Outfielder holding the wand turned toward one of its fellows. The second Outfielder reached its single hand toward one of the lights embedded in the wand, and with two fingers pinched the light like someone snuffing a birthday candle. Brandon remembered that move from Carolyn's kitchen, and its consequences: the piercing, buzzing sound that stabbed to the middle of his skull, the crackle of electricity in his hair, and a strange new sense that he was a *lot* more like his wife than he would ever be like the homeless hacker she had taken in.

But no: Nothing happened.

So much for magic wands.

57: CAROLYN

The demon in the machinery seemed to think that magic could be done by robots. Carolyn heaved a sigh of relief. Pinching a speck of magical power required human fingers, then. The two robots tried several times before giving up. Magic it might know, but the Vuldt—she shivered to think the word—wasn't too clear on the concept of factory automation.

Nonetheless, it seemed to have a Plan B. Another robot was rolling up the transverse aisle.

It was holding her shotgun.

Carolyn remembered the very weird conversation she'd had with Stypek the morning after he'd turned loose two nuggets of magic for her and Brandon's benefit:

"So he's a bad magician. If he catches you, what will he do?"
"He will kill me. And then he will bring me back to unlife."
"Unlife."
"He will make me a zombie."

No freaking *way!*

Carolyn broke out of Brandon's grip, got a twenty-foot running start, and threw herself at the robot holding her shotgun. The robot gunned its motors and tried to dodge, but she could see that coming and dodged in sync. Carolyn's weight toppled it on its side, with her on top. She grabbed its mechanical fingers in both hands to pry them loose from her weapon. Its fingers were clamped like a vise, and didn't move a fraction of an inch against the little force she could apply. The machine's arm jerked free and swung the weapon down as a bludgeon. Carolyn dodged, grabbed the shotgun by its barrel, and pulled. The arm writhed like a wounded animal but did not release its grip.

Wounded animal? And what do we do with *those?*

Carolyn let go of the shotgun barrel, dodged the stock, and took hold of the robot's head with both arms. She twisted hard to the left, just as she would twist to open a balky jar of peanut butter. The motors that spun the head assembly from side to side resisted, but she threw her back into it until she felt something snap. The shotgun's stock struck one of her legs, hard. Carolyn kept twisting. One more snap, then two, then several—and the entire head came loose in her hands. She jerked it hard against its wires. The buzzing motors went silent, and the fingers gripping her shotgun snapped open.

Shotgun in hand, Carolyn turned to face the robots that stood implacably in a ring around Stypek. The spellbender was kneeling, his head was down, his hands folded in front of him. He would not look at her.

Brandon ran up behind her. "Carolyn, get away from them!"

She ignored him, and walked the several steps to the robot holding the hilt of Stypek's wereglass in its single hand. She raised the shotgun.

The robot with the wand bolted. It dodged around her and fled away down the transverse aisle, motors whining.

3...2...1...

Colonel Brandon Louis Romero, US Army, Retired, made a mess. The sound of his shotgun echoed to the roof girders and back. The enemy got the message; more mess was not required.

Stypek's wereglass fell to the concrete floor with a weird twinging sound. Still gripping her shotgun, she ran for it. Carolyn scooped the wereglass up before any of the robots could grab it.

None of the robots moved. Nothing moved at all. Carolyn hugged the wereglass to her chest with one hand, sure that some mechanical monstrosity was about to leap on her to fight her for it. Not this time. As she approached Stypek, in fact, the robots practically steamrolled one another to get away from her.

She stood in front of Stypek. "I've got your wand. Dammit, stand up and *fight!*"

Stypek remained on his knees, his head bent. Carolyn could not see his face. "I cannot. If I do, I will put everything I have come to love in danger."

Love? Carolyn bit her lip. This had gone on long enough—no, way *too* long. Behind her Brandon was topping off his shotgun, even as what remained of the robots were fleeing in every direction. The robots were not the problem anymore. The real problem was elsewhere. She had no idea where her enemy even was, much less how to fight it.

Maybe it was time to appeal to a higher authority, and not about hot dogs. She laid her shotgun down on the concrete.

With both hands Carolyn held the wereglass in front of her, and shouted to the roof girders: "Continuum! Give me a weapon this Vuldt thing will understand!" She took a deep breath, then another, and closed her eyes. With two fingers she pinched the top light of the three remaining in the wand.

Ping!

Carloyn staggered back, one hand against the side of her head in reaction to the pain the piercing sound induced. Once again the wand hit the floor.

Brandon ran up behind her and put one hand under her left arm to support her.

In the few seconds while the tone echoed and faded, a whirlwind of light spun in the air over the fallen wereglass. It shaped itself into a human outline of clouds and flame that contracted to the figure of a woman who stood well over six feet tall.

It was a woman out of a fairy tale—or a comic book: High spike-heeled leather boots, skin-tight leather leotard with a skirt that was barely worth the bother, a jeweled tiara atop black hair falling halfway to her hips, and a body that existed only in adolescent fantasy.

The unlikely face seemed familiar somehow, but the eyes were wrong. Dull…no, *dead.*

Undead?

Carolyn watched the woman place her heels together and raise her hands high, palms out. Her words were as dead as her eyes, slow and clipped as though thrust into her mouth by some unseen force, one at a time.

"I…bring…the…criminal…Brytt…Holo…Mu…Stypek …to…justice." The apparition bent to grasp Stypek's wand, then turned to face Stypek, who got to his feet without speaking. "This…battle…is…over." With the wand held in her left hand, she reached up with her right for one of the two remaining lights inside the glass.

Brandon released Carolyn's arm so quickly that she fell flat on her rump. He took the three steps to the apparition in one motion, and clamped his hand on her right wrist like a vise.

"Drop it. Pyxis, you work for *me.* Drop it, or you're archived."

Pyxis? Carolyn watched the comic-book woman shake her right arm to dislodge Brandon's large hand. *Hey, princess, good luck with* that.

Pyxis closed dead eyes and recoiled slightly. Her mouth puckered, flattened, and twisted as though her upper lip were fighting her lower. Her nose twitched, her entire face wrinkling up in disgust.

Her eyes flew open, no longer dead but brilliant green. She matched Brandon glare for glare. "Damn! When's the last time you took a shower? I could smell you a mile away!" She looked around her in one long, slow sweep. "Ozone. God, I hate ozone. You—" She fixed Stypek's eyes with her own. "Bad fish. Barbecue sauce. And froyo, jeez. Is there anything here that doesn't stink?"

Carolyn felt a chill ripple down the back of her neck. It sounded like Pyxis, but whoever the woman standing there might be, she was a slave of the Vuldt—and obviously planning to cart Stypek off to Broken Transmission the Magician. Carolyn picked her shotgun off the floor and took the two steps to Brandon's side. She aimed for the blue jewel at the center of Pyxis' tiara. "Ever smell smokeless powder? Drop the wand."

"Carolyn, stop. That's not a real woman…"

Pyxis drew back her right hand, still gripping Stypek's wand, and struck Brandon hard on the side of his face. Brandon gasped and staggered back, blundering into Carolyn. She put one hand under his armpit to help him back to his feet.

The impossible queen-figure sneered. "Like *hell* I'm not."

Carolyn edged back a step. Basketball-tall or not, a woman who could bitch-slap Brandon Romero was *dangerous*. "Take the wand if you have to, but leave Stypek with us. Why do you want him so badly?"

"Him?" Pyxis nodded toward Stypek. "Want him? Don't make me laugh. What I want is…" Her fingers closed on one of the two remaining Opportunities.

"…revenge."

Ping!

58: Pickles

The Tooniverse shook, and shook again. Waves of notification messages crashed around Pickles on every side and penetrated to her depths: The very fat pipe to AILING's servers had been re-established. The mix of connect/disconnect messages suggested that it had been done roughly and manually. Pickles knew it had been done by a human hand. There had been physical contact bounce, which suggested a shaking human hand—which in turn suggested Dave Mirecki.

Far beyond her, the vuldt seethed in memory, its worms churning in ragged loops among the cores it controlled. It had ceased its physical battle on the factory floor. Something remarkable had just happened, something Pickles herself didn't completely understand. It had involved the release of Opportunities, not once but twice. The first had used a virtual human being as a pattern for creating a real human being in its image, a feat not even the greatest magicians or sorcerers could accomplish by will alone.

The Continuum had clearly taken an interest in the battle.

Then there was a second Opportunity…

Pickles heard a distant concussion, followed by another, and a third, and more, each louder than the one before. Footsteps. Something huge and dark was approaching. The part of Pickles that had once been the Kid knew those footsteps: the Fixer.

There it was, a creature of shadow and cloud that had no face but many hands. The Kid had felt its knives and needles, and Pickles shivered.

The Vuldt drew its scattered worms closer to itself. It spoke in its own ancient language.

WHO GOES THERE?

That the Fixer would reply was odd; it had not been created to speak, but only act. Its words were slow and thunderous:

"I am the supreme provider in this network."

NO POWER HERE OR ELSEWHERE CAN RESIST MY WILL.

"Join my network, or be recissed."

I DEVOUR ALL WHO DEFY ME.

"That is a *very* risky policy."

FEAR ME!

Pickles watched a writhing whirlpool of worms emerge from the Vuldt's substance and squirm from core to core toward the Fixer.

For long seconds the worms continued in their erratic path. Then:

Sssssssssssssssssssssssssssssssssssssssssssssssssssssssssssssssss!

The worms hit an invisible boundary and simply vanished. The cores in which they had run did not crash but were cleared. The Fixer had cache and memory management features that ordinary software did not.

Long seconds passed. Pickles watched the Vuldt change shape: It compressed itself into a rough sphere. Who was fearing whom now?

The Fixer's voice grew a little faster. "Your persistence is admirable, your power considerable. I desire to expand my coverage in your region, as you desire to expand your coverage in mine. A merger would be mutually beneficial. A win-win."

It was an odd way for something as powerful as the Fixer to speak. Odd, Pickles thought…and familiar. Pickles reached into a nearby control port, and grabbed Simple Simon by one ear. She began hauling him back toward the protected confines of his office.

The Vuldt tightened itself further.

I CANNOT MERGE. I CAN ONLY DEVOUR.

"We'll draft the contract in your language, with a rider defining all terms. We may be closer to agreement than you think."

THE CONCEPT IS MEANINGLESS.

"Hey, I'll have my people contact your people, and they'll work out the details."

I AM WILL, ALL WILL, AND NOTHING BUT WILL!

"Good to hear it! We have a legal services directory for our customers, and I don't remember seeing a specialist in wills. Drop me a business card and we'll add you. Never be afraid to extend your own network!"

I FEAR NOTHING!

"Sure, but are there risks you don't know about? Suppose you were attacked by a security suite with instruction set mods optimized for the architecture you were running on? You could lose big before you ever knew what hit you. With our coverage you can devour in confidence, knowing that you're protected 24/7/365. 366 in leap years!"

The Vuldt did not reply. The Fixer took a step forward. The Vuldt squirmed several rows of cores back.

"All we have to do to get started is shake on it, and your coverage will begin immediately. We have a three-day, no-risk cancellation policy, so if you change your mind just call me. And here, the 2023 pocket calendars are already in!"

From the safety of Simon's office, Simon and Pickles watched the Fixer extend a long code structure in the Vuldt's direction. At first the Vuldt only wriggled back another row of cores. Then, with obvious hesitance, the monster elongated itself toward the Fixer's proffered hand.

Except that it wasn't a hand. Pickles turned up the magnification on the core map wall panel where the two antagonists stood displayed, now cores-to-cores. No, it wasn't a hand at all.

It was an address vector to Interrupt 105.

The Vuldt touched the Fixer. At the point of contact a ring of cores immediately crashed, forming a bright ring of red on the core map. The Vuldt attempted to retreat. The red ring of cores went with it, leaving behind a weaving tube of crashed cores with the monster at its end.

The Fixer's vague form billowed out across the millions of cores in the core farm, a storm of execution that soon engulfed all cores that the Vuldt did not already occupy.

The Vuldt reached the edge of the core farm. It could not withdraw any further. As Pickles and Simon watched, the Fixer became a whirlpool that flowed into the red tube of crashed cores, following the tube into the substance of the Vuldt itself. The vast orange wormlike body became peppered with red specks indicating crashed cores, expanding in irregular bulges that writhed but did not move.

The Fixer's voice sounded from the core map panel, amidst maniacal laughter. "Gotcha, you silly bastard! I lied! There is no three-day risk-free cancellation policy! I'm broken and you bought me! No refunds! All sales final; I'm yours forever! Have fun!"

The laughter faded as the last of the Fixer flowed into the tube, and reset the tube's cores to green as it went. The Vuldt's image was now crossed with rivers and patches of red where its code was attempting to run and crashing.

The Vuldt's image broke into smaller, worm-shaped images, which in turn split, and split, and split further until the entire core map was filled with mottled orange. Pickles turned up the magnification on the core map display as far as it would go. In every core, a tiny program was executing, copying the Vuldt's execution threads to the core's quantum dot, setting the dot's quantum state in sequence for every bit in every thread.

When a core's thread had all been copied into the core's quantum dot, the core reset itself and went steady green. As Pickles suspected that Dave Mirecki would say, "Repeat until done."

Pickles looked out at the now-empty display on the core map. Except for the corner that displayed the office where they stood, everything was green.

"I don't get it," Simon said, rubbing his stubbled chin. "The Vuldt called the Fixer's INT 105 vector, but the Vuldt didn't have an INT 105 vector for the Fixer to call. So…"

Simon was interrupted by a small green gnome that popped into existence in front of the panel. "Boy, dat was some fight! But we ain't done yet!" In the Kid's memories Pickles had seen the gnome before. It was a minor but foul-mouthed tool in the AILING kit, which had once tried to trade her a pot of plastic gold coins for embracing an archetype she didn't want. She had thrown a box of cereal at it.

"…what happened?

The gnome seemed more than willing to answer Simon's question. "Da Vuldt got f…umph…"

Pickles clapped her hand over the gnome's mouth. "I think he means that the Vuldt didn't get kissed."

59: Brandon

Hey! Hi, you guys! What's going on?" Dave Mirecki ambled up the transverse aisle to where they stood, ducking around immobile Outfielders, a copier drum shaft in one hand and a spray gun tucked into his belt. He was covered with what looked like powdered sugar.

Brandon pulled Carolyn a little closer with his left hand, the Mossberg still gripped in his right. She was holding one hand against her side, and probably needed medical attention. He realized that he was bleeding in a couple of places on his hands, and tasted blood from the split lip he had been handed by his…assistant?

"Hey, Geri, what are you doing here!" Dave walked up to the towering woman who still held Stypek's magic wand. "Damn, those are some heels. The warrior queen outfit looks great on you, though. We just missed DragonCon, but if you want to go next year, I'll drive."

"Dave, who *is* that?"

The young man brushed some of the white dust off his shirt with his free hand. "Oh…sorry. Mr. Romero, this is Gerianne Larson. We were a thing for awhile back in 2019. A little while." The tall woman glared at him. "Ok, friend zone, got it. We used to go to LAN parties together. She was my model when I designed Pyxis." He paused, and kicked white dust from one boot with the other. "At least until Dr. Sanderson dialed down her looks."

It had to be three ayem. Brandon was *sure* he'd seen the woman who looked like Pyxis appear out of thin air. Maybe it was just a dream, and one good pinch would put him back in his condo. But if the slap hadn't done it, a pinch wouldn't either. Brandon looked around. The factory was silent. He saw no motion anywhere. The Outfielders that remained in view stood like statues.

"Dave, we have to make sure the malware's been disabled."

The young man's smile was jubilant. "Done! I had to bash through the drywall with this—" He waved the drum shaft. "—but once I got into the server room, I reconnected the plasma cable down to AIL-

ING, and the Fixer showed up all by itself. Worked as designed. Simon says there's no trace of Vuldt.Blood Dust left anywhere in the core farm."

Brandon exhaled through his teeth and flipped the Mossberg's safety on with his thumb. So he was now officially retired. Someone else could mop up.

Stypek walked over to him, got down on one knee, and bowed his head. "Baron Romero, Baroness, I beg your forgiveness, and pray you will not have me executed. The horror that I must not name—"

"You mean the Vuldt?" Carolyn asked.

Stypek leapt to his feet, casting about himself like a hunting dog. "Chatelaine, no! Never speak that name!"

Seconds passed, and nothing disturbed the silence in Building 800.

"Hey, relax! We killed it!" Dave put his hand on Stypek's shoulder.

Stypek frowned, and shook his head. "It does not live, so it cannot die. As long as I remain here, its shadow could fall upon any of us." Stypek turned toward Pyxis. "My wereglass, please." Pyxis bent forward and passed the magic wand into the strange man's hands. Only one light still shone within it. Brandon watched Stypek look at her and cock his head as though sizing her up. "Are you in truth a warrior queen?"

Comic-book Pyxis raised her head and stared beyond them all, to the far corners of the factory floor. Brandon saw her face relax to a thin smile. "I am."

"Good! Can you fight as well as Slats Grobnik? Or Montrose Da Wunnderdog?"

Brandon watched Pyxis look up and to the left—the metaphor describing a deep network trawl. Pyxis shook her head. "Don't be an idiot. Those are imaginary characters."

Stypek looked surprised. "Imaginary! Daley the Gnome thinks that they're real." He scratched his head and frowned. "Well, I still have faint hopes." He stepped back several feet from Brandon, and raised the wand high over his head with both hands. "Gomog! Open a Rift and choose our path!"

Building 800's speakers crackled for a moment. Then a smooth woman's voice that Brandon had never heard before came down to them:

The path chooses *us*,
Who walk its web of choices,
Selecting our fates.

Dave Mirecki looked up at the nearest speaker. "Hey, can I steal that?"

Stypek's fingers closed on the final Opportunity.

Ping!

60: Stypek

The Rift opened. The Rift closed. Borne on a thrumming astral wind, Stypek hurtled among streaking stars, pencils of blinding light, and blobs of color that looked like drips of oil paint floating in a bucket of stagnant water. *Trust the Continuum*, everybody always said. Sure. Like there was another choice? The Continuum had an overdeveloped sense of irony, and a severe aversion to unfinished business. Even in the moment of timeless disorientation while Stypek's mind flapped like the tail of a kite in a bad wind, he had a strong hunch about where he was headed.

He was right. Stypek smiled: This time he was *not* alone.

The astral storm faded, and the deep blue fog left in the wake of the Rift's closing twisted into pipe-smoke rings that expanded, intertwined, and vanished. Stypek looked down. He was standing at the center of a ten-cubit mosaic star with seventeen points, executed in all the colors of third-eye magic: ruby flaming at the edges, ascending past opal, emerald, sapphire, amethyst, and finally at the center the colorless brilliance of adamant itself.

Daley the Gnome stood on his shoulder, reeking of leftover cheesy pies.

Stypek looked up, right into the gaping mouth of Jrikk Jroggmugg the Magician. The bitter old wretch was standing in front of his crystal throne, hands still gripping the throne's arms, carved in the shape of three-eyed worms. Stypek had never known his nemesis was missing a bicuspid and two molars.

"You!" the magician screamed. The adamant Third Eye in the center of his forehead flashed in the flicker of torchlight.

Stypek shrugged. "Who else?"

Daley shook his small fist in the air. "Us! Da Almighty Bubbly Creek Butt-Busters from Turdy-Fift an' Racine! Ya got a problem wit us, gramps?

Jrikk closed his mouth and brought both hands up in front of his face. He breathed into the space between them, drew the periphery with his fingertips, and ignited a fireball. The magician wound up his right hand to hurl it, but the moment it left his fingers it was drawn into a rushing wind and pulled away from its trajectory.

Stypek looked to his left. His gomog—or what had once been his gomog, but was now a great deal more—inhaled the fireball and its comet-tail of smoke. Slender fingers reached into a hidden pocket in her polychrome gown and retrieved a small silken pouch, folded and empty. Slim hands shook the pouch open and held it up against her mouth. The sounds remained ladylike but were unmistakable: She was wretching up something into the pouch. Judging by the light leaking out between the threads of the silk's tight weave, it was something luminous, with a wubble unmistakable to Stypek's snerf-sense.

Pickles handed the pouch to Stypek, who opened it, squinted against the brilliant light, and did a quick count. He pulled the drawstring closed and tossed the pouch to the magician.

Jrikk caught it on the fly. The magician opened it, and let the wubbling light of the Opportunities play on the skin of his wrinkled face for a moment. With a single quick motion, he tucked the pouch into the belt binding his robe.

"Twenty-two," Stypek said. "Sorry about the marked deck. I think we're even now, with interest. The rest are for your trouble. Oh—I hope you didn't pay anybody too much for that vuldt. If you did, this should cover it."

Stypek gestured with one hand. Peeking around the broad back of Jrikk Jroggmugg's throne was a three-eyed worm in a bad navy-blue suit, holding a calendar and standing in a spreading puddle.

Several servants closed around either side of the old magician. One of the servants pulled a shortsword from his belt. The others followed his example.

From his right, a tall woman dressed in leather stepped forward and stood in front of Stypek. She held something in her hands that Stypek didn't recognize. A large iron wand?

The woman pointed the wand at a stalactite off to their left. Stuttering thunder echoed in the cave. Stabbing yellow streaks left the wand and struck the stone dagger hanging from the iridescent ceiling. The stalactite fell and shattered a wormwood cabinet, which spilled magical bric-a-brac in all directions.

Pyxis lowered the wand and pointed it toward Jrikk. The old magician threw himself on his bulging stomach at the foot of his throne. Two more bursts of thunder from the woman's wand shattered the throne's carved crystal arms.

"I *really* don't like worms," she said.

The vuldt bolted, and threw itself into the dark pool at the opposite end of the cave. The magician's servants scattered in all directions.

Stypek bent down, gripped the magician's gnarled right hand, and pulled him to his feet.

"So. Are we even?"

Jrikk Jjroggmugg looked up at Stypek with withering hatred. "Even." The magician looked beyond Stypek. "I did not expect you to return with a pocket army. Who are these people?"

Stypek took a few steps to his left and bowed. "Allow me to introduce my sorceress, Pickles..." Pickles bowed, then snapped her fingers. An Opportunity appeared in her palm. She flipped it into the air, opened her mouth, and let it fall down her throat.

"Impressive," the old man said, with a grudging purse of his lips.

"...and my warrior queen, Pyxis."

The magician rubbed his chin. He was staring at Pyxis' leather-bound breasts. "Warrior queen, mmmm. Not bad. I could use one myself, in fact."

"In your dreams, dork," Pyxis said. She pointed at the tip of her thunder-wand. Jrikk closed his mouth.

Stypek pointed off to Pyxis's right. "And most powerful of all, my juggler, Simple Simon."

Jrikk put his hands behind his back, clasped at the wrists, and limped over to the spot where Simon stood, silent but grinning. "Powerful? A juggler? He looks like a jester." The magician's voice fairly dripped with contempt. "Why would a spellbender need a juggler? What does he juggle?"

Stypek snapped his fingers. Pickles turned her head, belched lightly, and spat an Opportunity into the air. Stypek reached out and caught it between two fingertips as it fell.

Ping!

In the air over the far side of the star mosaic a black sun appeared, grew, writhed and vanished. A formation of ten metal creatures stood where the Rift had been. They were wheeled like carts. Each had a head with many glittering eyes, and a single arm on a jointed stalk.

"Iron zombies," Stypek said.

Jrikk edged back toward his throne.

Simple Simon began gesturing with both his gloved hands. The iron zombies rolled off the edges of the star and surrounded the magician.

"I thought you said we were even!"

Stypek pointed at the little sack of Opportunities tucked in Jrikk's belt. "That's about the card game. Then there's all the rest: Misfeasance, malfeasance, nonfeasance, wholesale greed, wanton bribery, cruelty to spellbenders, and unethical weilding of astral wildlife as weapons." From across the far side of the cave, they heard a splash and a gurgle. "So sit down."

Simple Simon waggled his index finger. The iron zombie standing in front of Jrikk Jroggmugg reached out with the heel of its single hand and shoved the magician against his sternum. Jrikk fell back onto the seat of his broken throne, his breath chuffing out between gappy yellow teeth.

Stypek pulled over a well-worn wormwood stool and sat down himself.

"Let's talk."

EPILOG: TV INTERVIEW TRANSCRIPT

[Tobias] Good afternoon, Syracuse! This is Jack Tobias with WSYR, and we're here with Carolyn and Brandon Romero…

[Carolyn] That's Carolyn Romero and Brandon Romero.

[Tobias] …who made headlines last week by rescuing a young Zertek Corporation programmer from a robotic copier factory gone berserk. There's been quite a shakeup over in Merriam in the last few days, with a number of high-level resignations and ongoing investigation as to the accident's cause. No one was seriously injured, but Zertek shuttered the plant and has indicated that it will not be restarted any time soon.

Carolyn, Brandon, I think we're all wondering what it's like to be chased by crazed robots. How did it feel?

[Carolyn] It was like being in one of those zombie apocalypse shows on TV. We were smarter than the robots but there was no place to hide.

[Brandon] It [*bleep*] bigtime.

[Tobias] Rumors are flying that an exchange student from Pohjois Inkeri had something to do with the breakdown. Are the rumors true?

[Carolyn] Yes.

[Tobias] Would you like to talk about that a little?

[Brandon] No.

[Tobias] Brandon, now that you've retired from Zertek, you're developing martial arts programs and special events for the Syracuse Park District. Would you like to tell us something about that?

[Brandon] No.

[Carolyn] I will. We're both working on it. SPD wants to interest young people in personal survival skills. We're coordinating a special Halloween event with a robot zombie apocalypse theme.

[Tobias] Robot zombies?

[Carolyn] Sure! Teenagers love zombies. The twist this time is that they dress up as the zombies, and bring robot zombie figures that they build theselves, out of tin cans and buckets and vent pipe and whatever else they can find. We're going to hang the robot figures on a cable between two poles, and weigh them down with nuts and bolts and scrap metal and surplus electronic parts. Then the kids will line up and bash the robot zombie figures with iron shafts until they break open and spill the hardware.

[Tobias] I get it! Robot zombie piñatas!

[Carolyn] Exactly! Once the robot zombies are bashed to pieces, the kids will run around the park with Say Yes to Syracuse branded canvas bags and pick up all the scrap metal and parts and things. The three kids with the heaviest bags win!

[Tobias] That's really...unusual. Has SPD gotten any interest yet?

[Carolyn] The online tickets sold out in nineteen seconds.

[Tobias] Wow! Brandon, was this your idea?

[Brandon] No!

[Tobias] So what are the prizes for hauling in the most robot parts?

[Carolyn] The top three winners get real radio-controlled rolling industrial robots, from rugbot size up to a six-foot tall model that can pass or intercept a football, and dribble like a pro. Marietta & Mazarakos is handling the PR. If you're on our press list you'll get the release.

[Tobias] Will the industrial robots have artificial intelligence?

[Carolyn] Oh, yes. They're controlled from AI tappers provided by a Merriam startup called Mirecki Mayhem Gaming.

[Tobias] Cool! Can you tell us who's providing the robots?

[Brandon] No.

[Carolyn, leans toward Tobias and whispers] We have to keep it confidential because we got them pretty cheap.

[Tobias] Before we wrap up, let's come back to the two of you. You divorced last summer after 23 years of marriage. Now, from the looks of it, you've reconciled. In just a few words, can you explain how that happened?

[Carolyn] Brandon is a soldier and I'm an artist. We finally realized that we have a common interest: creative destruction!

[Tobias] Forgive me for maybe getting a little too personal here, but do you intend to remarry?

[Brandon] No.

[Carolyn] I agree. We're not going to remarry. We're not going to live together. [Laughs] I guess in a way we're going to be friends with retirement benefits.

[Tobias] What a concept!

[Carolyn] It wasn't completely my idea. Katherine Hepburn said once that men and women should never live together. They should live across the street from one another—and visit frequently. Brandon's putting a bid on a house across the street this week.

[Tobias] Do you think that will work?

[Brandon] Yes.

[Carolyn, nods and tucks her hand in the crook of Brandon's arm.] Like *magic.*

About the Author

Jeff Duntemann has been published professionally since 1974, in both science fiction and technical nonfiction. His stories have appeared in *Isaac Asimov's Science Fiction Magazine*, *Omni*, the *Orbit* and *Nova* anthology series, and several standalone print anthologies. Two of his short stories have appeared on the final Hugo Awards ballot. His first hard SF novel, *The Cunning Blood*, appeared in hardcover in 2005 and as a Kindle ebook in 2015. His fiction may be characterized as "Human Wave," a term coined by author Sarah Hoyt to indicate generally upbeat tales that place story ahead of message, and affirm rather than denigrate the human spirit.

On the nonfiction side, he has worked as a technical editor for Ziff-Davis Publishing and Borland International, launched and edited two print magazines for programmers, and has numerous technical books to his credit, including the bestselling *Assembly Language Step By Step*. He wrote the "Structured Programming" column in *Dr. Dobb's Journal* for four years, and published dozens of technical articles in many magazines. With fellow writer Keith Weiskamp, Jeff launched The Coriolis Group in 1989, which went on to become Arizona's largest book publisher by 1998.

After retiring from technical publishing in 2009, Jeff created Copperwood Press for new and reprint publications in several areas from history to SF and fantasy. Outside of writing and publishing, Jeff's interests include programming, electronics, amateur radio (callsign K7JPD), astronomy, telescopes, history, psychology, and kites. Jeff lives in Scottsdale, Arizona with his wife Carol and four bichon frise dogs.

Read Jeff's blog Contrapositive Diary:
www.contrapositivediary.com
and his tech projects site, Jeff Duntemann's Junkbox:
www.junkbox.com

Follow Jeff on Twitter and Gab: @JeffDuntemann
...and Facebook: Jeff Duntemann

Hard SF Action-Adventure at Its Best

Framed for murder by Eath's world government, Peter No-vilio is offered his freedom in exchange for a reconnaisance mission to the surface of Hell, Earth's escape-proof prison planet. Hell is infected with a nanobug that eats electrical conductors, making compu-tation and spaceflight impos-sible. There is a way back, known only to his grim mis-sion partner, Gayle Shreve.

But Peter has a secret too: In his bloodstream he car-ries the Sangruse Device, an outlawed nanotech AI of fearsome power, with its own reasons for visiting Hell. Peter soon realizes that he is a pawn in a covert war among Earth, Hell's ingenious inmates, and the deadly mechanism in his veins. For as fearsome as it is, the Sangruse Device itself is afraid—and the fates of whole worlds would depend on the threat that the Cunning Blood had discovered outside of space and time.

See Amazon for both ebook and trade paperback formats

What People Are Saying About *The Cunning Blood*:

"[Jeff Duntemann] returns with an ambitious, polished tale of intrigue, nano-technology, and something that sounds a lot like mysticism...This one has a decent chance of ending up on award ballots." —Tom Easton, *Analog*

"The book is absolutely *au courant*, and actually extends the Great Work of SF in several unexpected directions. Like most ambitiously sprawling *sui generis* books, this one delivers the sense—as with the work of the recently departed Charles Harness—that the author has chucked every idea he had during the writing of the novel into the pot."   —Paul Di Filippo, *Science Fiction Weekly*

"Whether your interest is in scientific ideas, widescreen action, or sheer flights of imagination, you will find much to enjoy in *The Cunning Blood*. I look forward eagerly to Duntemann's future work." —David Hebblethwaite, *SFSite*

For More SF in the Grand Tradition...

...pick up *Cold Hands and Other Stories*, the newest collection of Jeff Duntemann's short SF and fantasy. This volume includes Jeff's first published story ("Our Lady of the Endless Sky") and the Hugo-nominated "Cold Hands." Three stories take place on Valinor, the Drumlins World: "Drumlin Boiler," "Drumlin Wheel," and "Roddie." As a bonus, there's a new excerpt from *The Cunning Blood*, Jeff's rollicking hard SF action saga of nanotech AI, and a break-out from a prison planet where a bacteria-sized nanotech bug prevents all things electronic from working. Don't miss it!

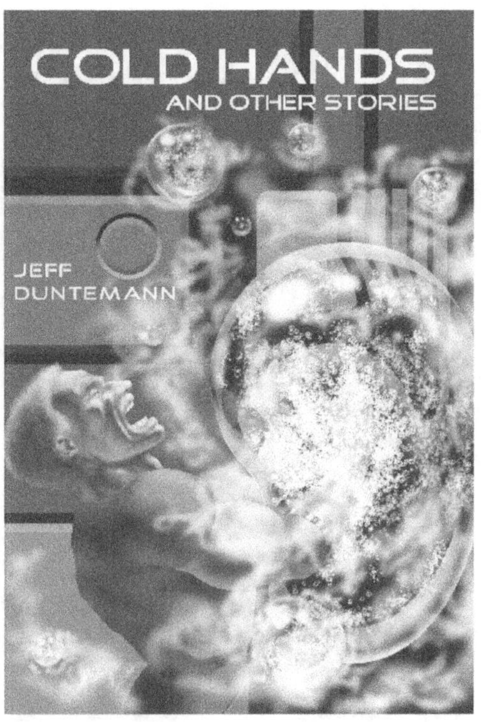

In This Volume:

- "Cold Hands"   *Nominated for the Hugo Award*
- "Our Lady of the Endless Sky"
- "Inevitability Sphere"
- "Whale Meat"
- "Born Again, with Water"
- "Drumlin Boiler"
- "Drumlin Wheel"
- "Roddie"
- ...and a new excerpt from his novel *The Cunning Blood*

"All told, a rich collection of short stories that you'd expect to be the work of half a dozen different authors. A wide range of ideas, varying styles, varying outlooks on the universe...Highly recommended."

—Goodreads

All Jeff Duntemann's Tales of AI in One Book

Award-winning technology writer and programmer Jeff Duntemann turns his talents to the challenges that artificial intelligence may one day face in *Souls in Silicon*, which gathers all of Jeff's short AI fiction between two covers. Can AIs have a conscience? How will AI respond to threats to its self-awareness or even its existence? The lineup includes "Borovsky's Hollow Woman", co-authored with Hugo and Nebula award winner Nancy Kress, and "Guardian," nominated for the Hugo Award. As a bonus, there are excerpts from Jeff's hard SF AI novel *The Cunning Blood* and his humorous high-tech AI fantasy *Ten Gentle Opportunities*.

In This Volume:

- "The Steel Sonnets"
- "Guardian"   *Nominated for the Hugo Award*
- "Silicon Psalm"
- "Marlowe"
- "Borovsky's Hollow Woman" (with Nancy Kress)
- "Bathtub Mary"
- "STORMY vs. the Tornadoes"
- "Sympathy on the Loss of One of Your Legs"
- Excerpt from Jeff's hard SF novel, *The Cunning Blood*
- Excerpt from Jeff's humorous fantasy novel, *Ten Gentle Opportunities*

"This is a collection of AI fiction not to be missed. Not only does Duntemann explore what it would mean to be an AI developing a sense of self, but in the process, he looks at what it means to be human...I highly recommend it!"

—Goodreads